"Perry, . . . leaving
the sto . . . is pro-
pelled . . . s. And
just w . . . ing on,
Perry . . . *Sentinel*

"Totally . . . ng sus-
pense . . . *Journal*

"[Pe . . . rs in
the . . . will
gra . . .
. . . *Post*

"T . . . *im* is
th . . . -be-
ki . . . *tinel*

"F . . . . . .
N . . .
. . . *iews*

"P . . . able
ta . . . *eekly*

DEAD AIM

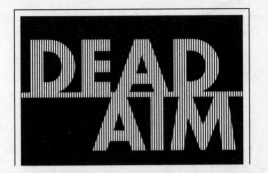

DEAD AIM

THOMAS PERRY

A NOVEL

RANDOM HOUSE TRADE PAPERBACKS / NEW YORK

2006 Random House Trade Paperback Edition

Copyright © 2002 by Thomas Perry

Published in the United States by Random House Trade Paperbacks,
an imprint of The Random House Publishing Group,
a division of Random House, Inc., New York.

RANDOM HOUSE TRADE PAPERBACKS and colophon are trademarks
of Random House, Inc.

Library of Congress Cataloging-in-Publication Data

Originally published in hardcover in the United States by Random House,
an imprint of The Random House Publishing Group,
a division of Random House, Inc., in 2002.

Perry, Thomas
Dead aim : a novel / Thomas Perry.
p.   cm.
ISBN 0-8129-6983-9
1. Santa Barbara (Calif.)—Fiction.   I. Title.
PS3566.E718 D425   2002 813'.54—dc21   2002068100

Printed in the United States of America
www.atrandom.com
2 4 6 8 9 7 5 3 1

Book design by Derek Walls

To my father,

RICHARD PERRY

ACKNOWLEDGMENTS

Thanks to my agent Robert Lescher

and my editor Kate Medina.

DEAD AIM

DEAD AIM

||||||||||||||||||||||||||||||||||||||||||||||||||

The shot was an explosion that spewed a shower of bright sparks from the pistol's muzzle into the darkness and kicked the barrel upward, but the arm of the shooter quickly straightened to level it again. The shooter fired the second and third shots into the lighted interior of the car, and the late-night silence returned. After a few seconds, crickets began to chirp tentatively again from nearby yards.

There were three holes punched through the rear window of the car, and even from his vantage across the alley behind the shooter, Parish could see that Mark Romano's head had been pounded forward, and the windshield had been sprayed nearly opaque with his bright red blood.

Parish watched as one of the women gently but firmly placed her arm around the shooter's left shoulder and took the gun from the right hand. The waiting escape car rolled up and within a few heartbeats the shooter had been hustled into the back seat. Parish leaned in to speak softly to the driver. "Go ahead. We'll finish up here."

The car moved off down the alley with its lights still out. Parish walked into the garage, stopped by the side of Romano's car, and bent to stare into the still-lighted interior at the bloody face to be sure there was no possibility of life. He reached across the body to the dashboard and took the remote control unit. He closed the car door, stepped out of the garage, and pushed the remote control button to bring the door down to cover the scene.

As he turned, Spangler emerged from the darkness at his side and pointed at the back of a house down the alley. "There was a face in that window for a second."

"Better take care of it before we go," whispered Parish. "They haven't had enough time to get the shooter out of the area."

The two men walked quickly and silently up the alley. They were both tall, but they moved toward the house with a surprising ability to blend into their surroundings, passing through each shadowy space beside the garages, moving along rows of garbage cans to make their shapes get lost to the eye among the many others in the dark alley.

The house was two lots down from Mark Romano's—they had waited for a night when the nearest neighbors were away—so the face could not have seen much from that window, beyond the six-foot cinder-block wall that separated the alley from the yard. Parish and Spangler moved to the wall, barely glancing at each other, as though they had done this so many times that each knew the steps, neither needing to check where the other was.

In seconds Parish was up and over the wall into the yard behind the house, and Spangler had made his way along the fence beside it. As Spangler went over the fence and dashed up the low steps toward the kitchen door, he could hear Parish breaking the glass in the window at the back of the house, and he hit the door with his shoulder before the musical sound of glass hitting the floor inside the house had stopped.

The door flew inward, cracked into the wall, bounced, and swung back, but Spangler was already across the small kitchen, his gun drawn, slipping up the hallway toward the back bedroom at a run. He went low, held his pistol ahead of him, and stepped into the doorway.

He saw a man in boxer shorts standing inside the room leaning against the wall, both hands on an aluminum baseball bat, waiting for

Parish to try to climb in through the broken window beside him. Spangler fired once into the man's chest as Parish fired twice through the window into the room.

Spangler's head spun so he could see what Parish had shot. It seemed at first that it was just a lump in the blanket, but then Spangler saw the telephone cord leading from the nightstand under the covers. He tore the blanket and sheet aside to reveal the body of the woman, the telephone receiver still clutched in her hand.

He moved to the window, pulled the sash up, and stepped back to let Parish climb in. Parish glanced at the man on the floor as he hurried to the bed where the woman lay. He snatched the telephone from her fingers, put it to his ear, and smiled as he set it in its cradle. "Dial tone. She hadn't gotten the call off yet."

"Close, though," said Spangler. He turned to go.

"Not yet." He nodded at the dead man below the window. "That bat isn't the right size for him, is it?"

Spangler whispered, "Kids?"

"Better check."

Spangler followed Parish into the hallway, mirroring his rapid, efficient movements. Parish stopped at each doorway on the left, put his head inside, turned to look both ways, then moved on. Spangler took the doorways on the right. Parish stopped at the end of the hall, where the door was closed. He tried the handle, found that it would not turn, and nodded to Spangler. Then he stepped back and kicked.

As the door flew open, Spangler stepped in after it. He decided that the boy crouching on the floor at the far end of the bunk bed must be nine or ten, and the little sister he had pushed behind him would be around five. Parish and Spangler seemed to have the same thought, which was that they must make use of the children's shock and immobility before they tried to run or crawl under something, as children often did. Both men centered their shots in the children's foreheads.

Parish and Spangler left the room and continued up the hallway. It did not make sense to go out the way they had come. The only car in the alley had been the one that had been used to spirit the shooter away, and there was nothing left near Romano's body that they needed to think about any further. They walked across the small, drab living room, carefully avoided a skateboard that had been left near the front door, slipped the latch, and stepped outside. They made their way around the corner to the car they had parked there, and Spangler drove them up the street toward the freeway entrance.

Forty-five minutes later, when they were driving north beside the ocean, Parish opened his window and tossed the remote control for Mark Romano's garage door opener out onto the pavement. The little plastic case broke apart with the impact and the pieces bounced a few times, cartwheeling and then sliding to a stop a few feet apart in the right lane, where they would be crushed to bits by the next car, or the next, or the one after that.

CHAPTER 2

The sun was already high, but a thin, misty layer of cloud veiled it and gave it a rainbow aureole. Mallon was glad it was not fierce and glaring, the way it could be along this beach in midsummer when the sea reflected it in painful flashes and the high pressure set in to kill the breeze. He sat on a rock beneath the cliffs and watched a squadron of pelicans flying just above the water two hundred yards out, where the big kelp beds began. He watched one of them swoop up, then plummet downward in the graceless, folded jumble that pelicans made of themselves, crash into the water, and emerge with a silvery, flapping fish. The other pelicans wheeled and spread out, working the school as the first had.

Mallon was always pleased to see them. When he had first visited Santa Barbara twenty years ago, they had been rare. On that trip, if he was out in a boat he would be lucky to see a few at sunset flying back to nesting grounds on the islands. Now they were everywhere. Three or four waddled around every day on Stearns Wharf, rolling from side to side with their wings stuck out and their long beaks agape, staring with beady prehistoric eyes at the tourists. Mallon was old enough now to have noticed that the human program of transforming the world into a poisoned desert sometimes suffered setbacks and delays.

His back and haunches were beginning to feel stiff from sitting, so he reached for his backpack. The movement brought his eyes along the beach so that he noticed the girl standing on the sand staring out at the ocean, gazing just past the next curve of the shore. He knew he should stand up and resume his walk past her, up the beach toward home, but the way she stood, it seemed to him that she could not see him. He supposed that a suntanned, barefoot man wearing khaki shorts and gray T-shirt could easily be lost to the eye among the rocks beneath the cliff. She was clearly not expecting to see anyone here; she might have walked a mile along this stretch of beach without meeting anyone at midmorning on a weekday. There was no nearby place where a person could park a car and easily climb down here.

He savored the feeling of invisibility: it gave him a chance to take an unhurried look at her. She was young. He judged her to be about twenty-five, and then detected an unexpected sense of loss. He was forty-eight, and the estimate placed her in a different generation, on the other side of a wall that made a certain kind of adventure not impossible but unlikely and maybe a bit ridiculous. He considered standing up, but he didn't want to startle her now—certainly not frighten her—so he watched and waited for her to move on.

She was pretty, with long brown hair, and that added to his discomfort because it made him feel like a voyeur. She was wearing a pair of khaki shorts not so very different from his, and a top of the sort with thin straps like strings to hold it up. She took a step. That made him feel better: this would be over soon. She paused, then leaned her body forward. Her left foot moved ahead just in time to keep her from toppling, then her right took a step to compensate, and she was walking. She kept her head down and her legs moving in a determined stride until she reached the firm margin of tightly packed sand just above the tide line, and then kept going into the water.

The first five steps were easy, the waves foaming around her ankles, then her shins. He watched her walking in, an act so familiar that he felt her steps in his own body: the first wave hit her thighs and made her progress stop, then pulled her on with its backwash. The next one hit her at the top of her legs, and made her take an involuntary hop because the cold was reaching the tender spots. She leaned a little to the side when the next wave hit her, then straightened, hugged her arms around her chest, and kept walking. She did not dive under and begin to swim as the next wave approached, although that was what he had been sure she was going to do. She simply let it go over her.

Santa Barbara had always been full of triathletes, marathon runners, and long-distance swimmers, and he decided she must be another sample of one these varieties. She would come up in a moment like a dolphin, swim straight out until she was past the breakers and the long Pacific swells rolled under her. Then she would turn north to swim along the coast for a mile or two, slosh back onto the beach, and run. He was perfectly contented with her. He liked the kind that wore plain khaki or something instead of those unappealing spandex outfits. Then he realized he was getting uncomfortable—short of breath—and he stood up quickly.

When she had gone under, he had unconsciously taken a breath and held it. But this was too long. "Pah!" He pushed it out and inhaled deeply, already running across the sand toward the water. He kept his eye on the spot where she had disappeared, leaping over the first two incoming breakers, then diving over the third and crouching to let the fourth surge over him before he pushed off and began to swim. He swam a hard freestyle, his feet kicking up a wake and his arms stabbing furiously into the water and pulling, his head turning to breathe every sixth stroke.

His mind had begun to enumerate the possibilities: maybe she had gotten tangled in a big clump of kelp, panicked, and gulped water. Maybe she'd had some kind of seizure. He reached the spot where he was almost sure she had gone down. He stroked to raise his body high, pointed his toes, and went under, feet first.

His foot hit something, and in a reflex he pulled it back, unbelieving. He realized that he had been sure he was going to find nothing, touch nothing. The odds that he could find an unconscious person out here were minuscule. He came up for air, dived, and swam straight down. The water was dim and cloudy, yet he saw her, not below but beside him. She was hanging about ten feet down, her limbs glowing white in the murk, her hair swirling in the current, radiating out on all sides. He put his left arm around her torso, stroked with his right, and kicked toward the light.

When he broke the surface, she did not move or twitch or join him in the gasp for air. As he shifted his left arm across her chest and began to tug her toward shore, for the first time he let himself think that she might be dead. He struggled to bring her to shallow water, trying to keep her head up but several times finding that he had failed, had taken a stroke with her head under. Each time it made him swim harder, desperate to get them to the beach, where he could do something.

Then his foot hit sand, and he hauled her in more quickly, finding that he moved faster if he held both her arms and dragged her through the shallow water. When he reached the tide line he beached her on the firm, wet sand, her lower legs still in the water but her head, torso, and thighs out. She still had a pair of sneakers on her feet.

Mallon rapidly went through the preparations for cardiopulmonary resuscitation, reassuring himself with a memory of his first instructor in the Air Force: "If he ain't breathing and his heart ain't beating, he's dead. Anything you do is better for him than that." He bent her head back, opened her mouth, made sure her tongue was visible. He carefully placed the heel of his hand below her sternum and gave the required ten pushes, then pinched her nostrils shut, leaned forward, placed his lips over her mouth and gave her a breath, then sat up and pushed her chest again.

She gasped, a sound like a whistle, coughed, vomited. He rolled her onto her side so she could keep coughing up water without blocking her airway. "You're going to be okay," he said quietly. "That's right. Cough it up so you can breathe." He patted her back as he remembered people doing to him when he was choking on something as a child, but a very strong message from the attitude of her body told him that it was not what she wanted.

He said, "Good. You're going to be just fine." Then he saw that her eyes were open, and that she was trying to get a look at him, but the sun was in her eyes because he was above her. He forced himself to say something about himself, just to reassure her that he was real, and ordinary, and friendly. "I saw you go under, and I was so afraid I wouldn't be able to find you."

She sat up with great effort and stared at him in absolute disbelief, then lay on her stomach, her face pressed into the sand in sorrow.

He stood up, not knowing where to look. Of course. She had not wanted to be saved. She had been trying to die.

||||||||||||||||||||||||||||||||||||||||||||||||||||||||||

CHAPTER 3

No, Mallon thought. *Not this. Not again.* He raised his head to look up at the ragged crest line of the cliffs above the beach, then turned his whole body to stare anxiously up and down the shoreline, searching for the shape of another human being. There was nobody. He looked down again at the girl lying on the sand, and forced himself to think. They were a half mile from any spot where he could climb the cliffs and get to a telephone. Even if there had been a nearby spot, he could not imagine leaving her here long enough to make a call. She might very well wait until he was out of sight and simply walk back into the water. He had to make his heart stop fluttering and concentrate. His chance to save her wasn't when he had dragged her out: his chance was beginning now.

He waited for several minutes, until she sat up and looked around again. They were both cold, and she was shivering. He got his backpack, opened it, and wrapped his towel around her shoulders. He said, "Are you feeling well enough to walk yet?"

She nodded. "I'm okay now. Thanks for helping me. But you shouldn't—"

"Good," he interrupted. "Come on." He put on his pack, gripped both her arms firmly, and tugged her to her feet. He kept his tone even and businesslike, trying to hold on to the quickly evaporating authority he had assumed in saving her, the emergency voice. "There's a set of steps that lead to the road about a half mile this way."

"I know. That's the way I came."

"Is your car up there?" he asked.

"No," she said. "I walked from town."

He clenched his jaw. He had never before seen any sense in driving somewhere to go for a walk. Now he did, and he could also see that never bringing a telephone with him had been stupid. He didn't tell her he had no car with him, because he was afraid to upset the fragile hold he still had on her.

He kept walking, moving steadily to get to the stairway. He had a very strong intuition that if he got her off the beach, she would be out of immediate danger and his responsibility would end.

At last they reached the wider stretch of beach, where the cliffs were lower and the steps zigzagged upward to street level. He stood by the first of the wooden railroad ties that had been set into the cliff. Trying to keep his hands from shaking, he took his walking shoes out of his pack, slipped them on, and waited for her to go ahead of him. He knew he had to get her up and away from the ocean, but he also sensed that if he rushed her, she would resist. Finally, she stepped on the first railroad tie, and he quickly moved in behind her. When she stepped to the second, he followed. She climbed slowly, not as though she was physically tired but as though she was reluctant to leave the ocean. She would climb a dozen steps, then turn and look over her shoulder at it with a silent resignation.

When they were at the top, he set off across the grass to the road without hesitating to give her a chance to resist or even think about where he was leading her. They walked silently until they were at the long, curving road that led between two dry hills toward the part of town he wanted to reach.

She said, "You don't have a car?"

He smiled. "Sure I do. It's just not where I'd like it to be at the moment. I always walk here."

"What for?"

"I'm an old guy. I need the exercise."

"You didn't have any trouble swimming out there and dragging me out of the ocean," she said. "You must be okay."

"You're not very heavy," he said, but he allowed himself to feel good about the faint compliment. She was right. He had saved a drowning person's life. That was not a minor thing. He judged its value by looking at the girl, her small, appealing face wreathed in stringy wet hair, her trim, small body: yes, he noted, even now, in this circumstance, he couldn't help it. He imagined how he would have felt to see her dead, and made the comparison. No, saving her had not been a negligible accomplishment. If she used her life well, saving her might be the most important thing he had ever done. Certainly this extra chance was the best thing he had ever given anyone.

He had to preserve it by never letting his attention flag, had to be sure that everything he did now was exactly right, because he could feel that it was like a puzzle solved in the dark, with answers that would help her live, and others that would kill her. He knew he needed to keep the means of suicide away from her. He constructed a mental image of the area ahead and designed a course, so they could walk the two miles to town on streets that never came within sight of the ocean. He sensed in himself the human compulsion to say things, but he resisted. There were too many chances to make a mistake, trigger a painful memory, or offend her. He also had an exact destination in mind, and as it drew nearer, he wanted to avoid the charge that he had spoken just to keep her occupied, to hide the most important information from her.

He approached the county hospital with a feigned casualness, feeling grateful that they had built it at the end of a long, curving driveway that made it look small and unthreatening. When she saw that he was turning to go up the driveway, she said, "What are you doing?"

"You almost drowned." He tried to make his throat relax, so she would not detect his tension. "You need to be checked over."

"No." She said it over her shoulder as she walked away. "I'm not going in there."

He walked quickly to catch up with her. "You're making a mistake." He meant that he had no other place in mind. He had to find somebody to share this responsibility with him, some figure of authority who would know how to keep her alive. He had to keep her alive.

She walked more quickly. "Then I'm making a mistake." She was not going to let him get her in there. Maybe she had been locked up before for trying to kill herself. Maybe she had only heard of it, but she knew.

He said, "If you'd rather go to your own doctor, we can stop at my place and I'll drive you there. But you really should get an exam." A desperate hope that he had simply missed an obstacle that was easy to overcome flashed across his consciousness: maybe she couldn't afford a doctor. "I'll be happy to pay for it."

She only moved her head enough to turn a half-lidded eye on him. His own voice had sounded false to him.

He said, "Where would you like to go? Does your family live in town?"

"No. You're the only one I know here. I drove in this morning."

"From where?"

"New York."

"Is there anybody you can call?"

She turned to him with a frown of annoyance. "Of course. Millions of them. I don't want to call anyone."

"I'll do anything I can to help you. What can I do?"

"Nothing."

"I think you need help."

"I don't."

She walked along for a few paces, and the defiant, angry posture of her body had a kind of liveliness that made him less careful.

"You tried to kill yourself."

"I did kill myself. You came after me and dragged me back. I don't have the energy right now to hate you. I think I need to sleep."

"Right." He brightened. "Things will look different to you when you wake up."

"Sure."

"My house is right up ahead. I'll get my car and drive you to a good hotel. And don't worry about the cost. I'll take care of it."

"I'll walk."

"Are you afraid?"

"Of you? No."

"Of anyone. Are you running from something?"

"I have nothing to run from." She walked ahead quickly and then across the street. After a few more steps on the sidewalk, she turned to see him behind her.

"I don't think being alone will make you feel better right now," he explained. "Want to get something to eat?"

"Why are you doing this?"

"Because you look like a very nice young woman who shouldn't kill herself. Are you dying of cancer or something—in a lot of pain?"

She shook her head. "Nope. No sickness. I had my reasons for what I did, and it's nothing you can talk me out of with your kindness and wisdom. Thanks for your concern and everything."

"Then you'll get through this. Someday you'll be really glad you didn't die. Something wonderful will be happening and you'll look back and be amazed that you might have died and missed out on it."

She kept walking. He began to follow as usual, but she stopped. "Don't. I'm fine now and I'm over it. I don't want you to be with me. I can make a fuss and make you look like a creep. I don't want to re-ward your kindness like that, but I will if you make me. So go."

He stopped and took a step backward. "If you decide you need help, I live in that house right up there." He pointed. "My name is Robert Mallon." He saw her look at the house. It was a two-story brick colonial with white shutters and a green, well-tended lawn. He hoped it looked respectable to her, and that the front windows he had enlarged for light made it seem open enough to be safe. "Come inside," he said. It was irrational, desperate.

"All right." She followed him up his driveway, while he marveled at the exchange: why he had dared to say it, why she had acquiesced.

He unlocked the door and let her in first. She moved slowly around the living room while he slipped off his backpack and carried it to the laundry room off the kitchen. He knew she was examining his things and drawing conclusions about him. "Would you like tea or coffee or a soft drink, or . . . whatever?"

"I'd like a glass of water, and then I would like to sleep for an hour."

He opened the refrigerator and took out one of the cold bottles of water he kept there for his walks. Then he climbed the stairs and showed her to the spare bedroom. "This is it. Make yourself comfortable. There's a bathroom attached, with clean towels and everything, so you can take a hot shower. There's a robe hanging on a hook behind the door. In the dresser there are T-shirts, sweatshirts, some shorts. None of them will fit you, but you can tighten a belt around the shorts to keep them up until yours dry. Anything else you need, holler."

She stepped into the room and closed the door. As he reached the stairway, he heard the lock click into place. He didn't blame her. Who the hell was he, anyway? And he supposed his behavior had struck her as at least mildly peculiar. She could not know why he wasn't able to give up and leave her alone. She didn't know that this was not his first try. He had been the last one in the family to talk to Nancy. It had been more than thirty years ago, but today the desperate, panicky feeling of regret that always came when he thought about Nancy had come back, almost as though he were getting a second chance but still didn't know what to do.

Mallon sat in the living room, waiting. He stared at the empty staircase for minutes at a stretch, listening for the young woman to do something unexpected that he would need to oppose very quickly and flawlessly. When his eyes had stayed there for a very long time without anything happening, he turned and stared out the front window, still listening for sounds from above. He was not sure what he expected to see out there, but he knew what he wished he could see. He longed for the nonexistent, the impossible: an ambulance would pull up that was unmarked, and out would come a municipal team of specially trained psychiatrists—female psychiatrists at that, strong-minded but soft-voiced—who had been dispatched because somebody on the bluff above the beach had seen what had happened and reported it. They would gently bundle the girl in a blanket and rush her off to some discreet, ultramodern clinic for the suicidal. By bedtime there would be so many antidepressants in her bloodstream that she would be incapable of imagining herself dead.

He heard the faint sound of water running in the pipes below the room, then a distant hiss of spray from above. She was in the shower. He glanced at his watch and half-smiled, then realized that the knotted muscles between his shoulders had just relaxed a bit. She had slept for two hours, and now she was in the shower, feeling the hot water pelting her skin, warming her and soothing her. She was recovering.

The thought slowly curdled. He always left supplies in the guest bathroom, still in their packages from the store: soap, shampoo, toothbrushes, combs and hairbrushes, shaving cream, razors. Could she hurt herself with a disposable razor? If she broke off the plastic and sawed away at an artery, she could probably cut her way through. Maybe the hot water was to keep the blood flowing.

He told himself that it was foolish to think of such a thing, and retorted that it was foolish to think of anything else after seeing her try to kill herself. Bright blood could be spurting rhythmically from her neck and washing down his drain right now. How could he leave her alone up there to do it? But he could hardly burst into the shower.

The sound of the water stopped. He took a couple of deep breaths to calm himself while he tried to interpret it. A few minutes went by, but he still had no conclusion. Then the sound of running water began again. It sounded slightly different to him, but he was not sure why, until it occurred to him that this time it was the bath. The sound suddenly grew louder. The door up there must have opened. He revised the impression: it must have been both doors, not just the one to the hallway, but the bathroom door too. He stood and looked in the direction of the stairs.

The girl appeared on the upstairs landing, his bathrobe cinched tightly at the waist and coming to her ankles. She said, "I'm running your bath for you. Come on up." Then she disappeared into the upstairs hallway.

Mallon hesitated for a moment. Running a bath for him wasn't a normal thing for a suicidal girl to do, or even a thing that he could have anticipated as possible under the circumstances. But it had the curious effect of imposing normalcy on the proceedings in the house. They had both been in the ocean and walked home in wet clothes. She'd had her chance to wash the sand and salt off, and now in the natural order of events, he could have his turn. He sensed that to reject her restoration of simple civility, to insist on treating her as a mental patient, someone whose acts needed to be scrutinized and mistrusted, would be a bad tactic. As long as she had a desire to behave well, he must let her. As he walked to the staircase, it occurred to him that a strange reversal had taken place. Now he was the one who was behaving irrationally, acting as though nothing had happened.

He climbed the stairs. The door to the guest room was closed. He could tell that the bath he heard running now was the one down the hall, in his master suite. It was a little presumptuous of her to go into rooms he had not invited her to enter, but he chided himself for that thought. Was she supposed to have him use the smaller guest bathroom that he had set aside to be hers? That would have felt even more awkward, because it would imply a kind of forced proximity, even intimacy. He was going to accept her gesture exactly as it had been made. What other sign of sanity could he demand of her, than her acting sane?

He entered his bedroom and stepped through it into his bathroom. The water was high in the oversized bath, and the air jets had been turned on and left bubbling. He tested the temperature of the bath water, turned it off, then closed the bathroom door. He took off his walking shoes and his shorts, pulled the T-shirt off, then stepped into the tiled shower stall. He had decided that the bath would feel better after he washed off the sand and salt, as she had done. He washed his hair, soaped himself and rinsed, then turned the shower off. He opened the glass door, stepped onto the mat, and caught a shape at the edge of his vision. He had not heard the door open, and the impression of an intruder made his muscles stiffen and his chest draw in air in preparation for a struggle. His head whirled to see.

She smiled at him pleasantly and said, "I hope I didn't startle you. Didn't the shower feel great?" She ran a hand through her long, wet hair.

Mallon took a step backward to place his body back out of her line of vision in the shower stall. "Yes, it did," he said calmly.

"You don't need to hide in there now," she said. "I already got an eyeful." She stepped close to the big bathtub, then turned away from him and let the bathrobe fall to the floor. She bent at the hips to place her hand on the rim of the tub to steady herself, then put a foot in the water. His eyes were drawn down her smooth back to her buttocks and the glimpse between her thighs.

She laughed, a sudden giggle, and his eyes shot to the mirrored wall and met hers. She had been watching his reaction. She straightened and slowly turned to face him, stood still for a moment with her arms held out from her sides. "It's just me." She sat down, and the water rose nearly to her breasts. "Come on in. I left you plenty of room."

He stepped onto the shower mat, took a towel from the rack, and wrapped it around his waist. "What are you doing?" he asked disapprovingly.

"Trying to get you into the bathtub with me," she replied. "What does it take?"

"You know what I mean," said Mallon. "Do you think you have to do this out of gratitude, or something?"

She smiled disparagingly and said, "I don't believe in that. If you were drowning, I think I would have to try to save you. I don't think I'm obligated to fuck you. It's just something I feel like doing."

He said carefully, "You're very pretty, but—"

"Thank you," she interjected. Her body gave a slight bow, and the movement dipped her breasts into the water for an instant, then out again.

"But," he continued, "I'm twice your age."

She rolled her eyes. "That's always been a great deterrent to men in the past."

"It has to me."

"Don't be a hypocrite. There are female items in one of the master bedroom drawers, and they're not your size. Women visit you and pretend to forget their underwear so you'll remember them."

He bristled. "They're a lot older than you are, and they know what they're doing. What were you searching my room for?"

"The condoms. I found them, too. A couple of big boxes, Bobby, and half are missing. All the evidence shows you're a naughty man, so don't get all huffy and waste a perfectly good naked woman." She raised an eyebrow and pointed at the water in front of her belly. "You've been down there before. A lot. Haven't you?"

He caught himself in the beginning of a smile, but smothered it and raised his eyes to stare into hers, willing himself to ignore her nakedness. "Look, I would feel as though I were taking advantage of you. Whether you feel some misguided sense of reciprocity or have a morbid impulse to see what it's like to sleep with a man who's way too old for you doesn't much matter. You've just been through a difficult experience, and you're not thinking clearly right now."

"Of course I'm thinking clearly," she insisted. "I knew this was going to strike you as oddly timed, but I didn't expect to beg and plead. We're both single, and having sex is a perfectly normal thing to do if we want."

"I don't think I should have sex with you."

"Why? Because I'm not a happy enough person to meet your standard? Then make me happier."

"I don't even know your name," he said. "What is it?"

She pursed her lips and stared at the ceiling for a second, then said, "I don't think I want to say, at least right now. But there are just two of us here, so if you speak, I'll know I'm the one you mean. We don't need names for sex, anyway. Come on. I watched you staring at my bare behind, and even now you can't keep from checking out my breasts every few seconds. The reason you're leaning on the counter that way is that you think it hides your erection. Let me tell you, it doesn't, and looking at it is making me crazy. I solemnly swear, the reason I'm doing this is because I feel like it and there's no reason not to." She paused. "Besides, I read someplace that old guys are a good experience because they can hold out longer, and they know more about women. So drop the towel and get in."

She had a sense of humor, he silently conceded. She seemed perfectly calm and in control of herself. What she was saying was not insane.

While he was considering, she sighed and shook her head at him in amusement. She stood up and stepped out of the tub at his end, and embraced him, her wet body pressed against his. "I'm not crazy, and I'm not rewarding you or punishing myself, and I'm not going to be turned down." She unexpectedly snatched away his towel, took his hand, laughing, and stepped into the tub. She tugged on his hand, to draw him in after her. He stepped over the side into the water so she wouldn't keep tugging. "What's wrong now?" she asked.

He said, "I'm trying to be sure I'm not rationalizing this, telling myself that it's all right for you to do this, just because I want to."

She sank into the water, still holding his hand so he would go down with her. "Amazing," she said. "He finally admits he wants to."

Mallon sat down and she moved to meet him, pulling his legs around her and placing her legs over his. They kissed softly, their lips barely touching at first. The tentative brush of the lips became firmer, more sustained. Mallon became aware of the silence, the only sounds the rippling drips of water from their arms as they embraced, but the silence was pleasant, part of the gentleness of the moment. Then the touches changed, and there were sounds that grew in time. After a few minutes they left the water and dried each other with thick, soft towels on the way into Mallon's bedroom.

Mallon concentrated on being very attentive, very gentle and patient, but she seemed rapidly to lose all inhibition, all shyness. When Mallon turned or moved his hand, she would be there waiting to meet him, opening to him. If he lingered for a long time in one position, she would wriggle or writhe to move them into another. The positions were clearly experiments for her, and with each new one she would whisper, "Interesting, but not my favorite," and change immediately, or "Ooh, that's nice," and stay at it for a longer time before trying something different. Mallon could sense that she had given herself permission to do anything that entered her mind, to be unfettered, even reckless. For a time, he worried that her attitude might have ominous implications, but then he decided that it could as easily be a promising sign. A few hours ago she had been trying to kill herself, but now what she was doing was grasping for life, gripping it, taking in as much as she could. Maybe she was acting out some magical oscillation between the poles, bounding away from death, leaping from one extreme to the other with the intention of ending somewhere in the middle so she could go on with her existence.

Her urge to have sex now seemed, if not perfectly rational, at least positive, but his selection as partner continued to worry him. She could not have decided to bestow her favors on Robert Mallon because of some sudden crush. He was simply the nearest unattached male, and he was unthreatening to her. He had been the lone witness to the lowest point in her life, so the big barriers that always stood between two strangers had already come down. But he could not quite surmount the feeling that she must have decided to give him a reward for helping her. For a time he grappled with the thought, feeling injured pride at being given such an offer and guilt for having accepted it. But then he saw it differently. She wanted to forget practicality and self-absorption for one night, and he was allowing her to do that without risk. And if she was trying to get her own sense of value back by doing him the biggest favor she had in her power, he would have been wrong to refuse it. He reminded himself that the decision had been made a half hour ago. The question was not whether he would do it, but how.

Her mood induced in him a strong need to make the experience singular for her. He did his best to sense the direction of each of her whims, then use his knowledge and experience to push her impulse into reality and make it a source of pleasant sensations she had not felt before. He would coax her to excitement, then nurture and feed the excitement like a fire, consciously bringing her to a higher pitch moment by moment. Each time he succeeded she would go limp in his arms for a few seconds, catching her breath and trembling. He would hold her there, giving her the illusion of relaxing the tension, but not enough time to calm down. Then he would slowly begin again, awakening her feelings once more, finding a different way to arouse her. He knew that her sensations were cumulative, so that each time he began, she was still reverberating from the last time, and from the time before that, all the way to the first. It was like climbing to a height, step by step.

Finally, he knew that she was reaching her limit. This time, it took only a touch, a signal to her that he was beginning once more. She gasped, then gave a high, ascending moan. "You can't," she whispered, then said aloud, half-pleading, half in wonder, "You can't keep doing this to me." The sound, her own voice unfamiliar to her, and the words—the admission of her complete surrender to his touch—pushed her over the edge once more. "No," she said, and then more urgently, "Please don't stop." He began to bring it to a very consciously gauged end. He knew that the best way to let her know how much he had been enjoying her, how much he liked her, and how glad he was that she was alive was simply to show her—to sincerely abandon himself at last to the sexual excitement.

When it was over, they lay quietly side by side on the bed for a few minutes, then she rolled over onto his chest. "Thank you," she whispered. "Thank you so much."

"The pleasure was all—or mostly all—mine," he said. They lay in silence for another few seconds before he added, "I hope it was the right thing to do."

She raised her head so she could look into his eyes. "It was absolutely right. I did it with the wrong man for the wrong reasons, and it was the very best ever." She rolled over onto her back. "Another bit of hard evidence that most of what they say is nonsense. As if anybody needed more evidence."

"You know what I meant," he said. "Long-term."

"Yes," she said. "I do. What you're forgetting is that long-term and short-term are the same. There were any number of ways we could have spent the time, and I picked the right one for us: the winning choice. Most of the time, people pick wrong." She sat up abruptly. "You know, I'm starting to get hungry."

"Now that you mention it, so am I," said Mallon. "Let's go to a restaurant. I know just the place."

She shook her head. "I can't. Nothing to wear."

"I can drive you to your hotel and you can change."

She lay back down. "No. I didn't bring any good clothes. Just a change and a makeup bag."

"Nobody left anything in my guest room that will do?"

"I'm not going anywhere in a thong and a sunshade."

"All right," he said. "I'll get us something and bring it back. Do you like Italian food? If you don't like Italian, there's also—"

"I do. I like Italian," she interrupted. "Thanks."

As Mallon drove to La Cucina, he reflected on the sheer peculiarity of the universe. The day had begun without even the subtlest sign that a change was about to take place. Now it was seven in the evening, and he had lived through a series of cataclysms, a succession of vivid sights and sounds and emotions that seemed to him enough to fill years. He began to allow himself to hear other thoughts waiting in the back of his mind. It was still true that he was probably twenty, maybe even twenty-five years older than she was. But she had said . . . what had she said? "That's always been a great deterrent to men in the past." What she had been saying was that an age difference had never kept women from getting into relationships, either. It wasn't a quirk of male behavior; it was a quirk of human behavior.

It bothered him that she still had not told him her name. After the first refusal, he had determined to let her bring it up again, but she had not. He consoled himself with the thought that not telling him her name could only be a way of protecting herself from future embarrassment. At least she was planning for a future. The important issue was not her relations with a forty-eight-year-old stranger, but her determination to go on at all. That was all he asked: that she not end it, the way Nancy had. He had been what? Fifteen when she had died, and Nancy had been twenty-one. She would have been in her fifties now, probably a mother with kids as old as this girl.

He saw an empty space on the street less than a block from La Cucina, so he decided he had better take it. He pulled in and walked. They certainly weren't sexually incompatible, he thought. That had been another possible obstacle that she had not given time to develop. But he had to admit that he was congratulating himself on nothing: the one thing that even the most monstrously mismatched pairs seemed perfectly capable of doing was having sex. It was only after they'd had enough time to talk and get to know each other that they wondered what they were doing together. Then he was at the deceptively plain front entrance, just a varnished wooden door with *La Cucina* over the lintel and a few windows with white curtains. He pushed his cogitations about the girl's intentions out of his mind so he could concentrate on feeding her.

Mallon stepped inside, sat at the bar, and picked out five different dinners. He knew nothing about the girl's tastes. He did know that all women ate salads and were more likely to want seafood than meat, and the fresh, clear memory of this one's body told him she watched her weight. Some people were allergic to shellfish, so he got some fish and chicken too, but then decided she might even be a strict vegetarian, so he got some pastas, stuffed and unstuffed. He stopped at a liquor store on Carrillo Street to buy both red wine and white. He reflected that it would have been best to take her to La Cucina, where there were happy people and a pretty garden, lights and music. But he knew that it would have been impossible to win the struggle about her clothes.

Mallon came to the front of the house, carrying two of the big white bags full of boxes and the brown paper bag with the wine bottles, and knew instantly that he had been wrong to go to the restaurant. The door had been opened and then pushed shut carelessly, so the latch had not caught. He pushed the door open with his foot, walked into the kitchen, and set the bags down. He called, "Are you here?" He saw the empty water bottle on the counter. He listened, but there was no sound. He walked up the stairs and looked past the open bedroom door. She had hastily and clumsily straightened the bed before she had left.

He hurried outside, got back into the car, and drove around the neighborhood in ever-widening rectangles. After twenty minutes, he drove back to the house to see if she had returned. He went upstairs, then back down to the kitchen to put the food into the refrigerator, moved to the living room, sat on the stairway, and looked out the front window, waiting for her. After a few minutes, he felt the panicky worry coming back, so he left the door unlocked, went out, and drove along the ocean. He went out to the cliffs where he had found her, surveyed the beach until it was too dark to see, then drove home the way they had walked together.

When he got home, he turned on the porch light and the desk lamp, climbed the stairs again, went to his bedroom, lay on his bed, and closed his eyes. The physical strain of saving her and the mental stress of negotiating with her afterward, then making love to her and being abandoned so quickly had left him feeling drained of energy. He had not been this tired in years. If she had just gone out for a walk and wanted to return, he would hear her come in. The door was unlocked.

He slept for three hours, awoke, turned on all of the lights, and examined the house and yard, but saw no sign that she had tried to come back. He went to the kitchen, but decided he had no desire to heat up the food he had bought. He ate a peanut butter sandwich, then stayed up until two o'clock waiting for her.

The next day he studied the newspaper, and was relieved to see that there was no mention of trouble coming to a young girl from out of town. The *Santa Barbara News-Press* had never been a paper that spent much space on troubles brought here from out in the world, but it would have mentioned a body. But on the day after that, he did see something, a brief article he had almost missed on the fourth page. "Apparent Suicide Found in Field," it said. The description was too close to be anybody else.

CHAPTER 4

||||||||||||||||||||||||||||||||||||||||||||||||||||||

Mallon drove to the police station on Figueroa Street, climbed the steps into the small foyer, and waited at the front counter for a few minutes before he got a chance to tell the woman behind it what he had come for. She asked him to sit on a bench of blond wood that matched the counter, then made a telephone call. After a few more minutes, a tall policeman with a muscular frame and curly black hair who was wearing a tan summer-weight sport coat and blue jeans came out of a door at the side of the counter. He looked around, saw that Mallon was the only one waiting, then stepped up and shook his hand. "I'm Detective Fowler," he said. "I can take your report."

He led Mallon around the counter and through another door, then into a large office with several desks in it. He set a straight-backed chair in front of one of the desks, then sat down behind the desk and placed a pen and a yellow pad in front of him. "Now, Mr. Mallon. Can you tell me how you knew the deceased?"

"I didn't," said Mallon. "I don't even know her name. I pulled her out of the ocean the other afternoon. She had tried to drown herself."

Detective Fowler squinted at him as though he were having diffi-culty hearing what Mallon had said. Mallon went on. "I thought I should let you know about it." He paused. "I'm not sure what good it does now, but it didn't seem as though I could not tell you."

Fowler nodded. "How did it happen?"

Mallon told him the story. He did not leave out the way it had felt to try to maneuver the young woman away from the ocean, to manipulate her into letting him take her to the hospital, and then to fail.

Fowler listened patiently, staring into his face as he talked, and interrupting only to ask, "What time was this?" or "Why did she change her mind?" His questions seemed intended to be polite, to make it easier for Mallon to talk, but Mallon knew they were more than that.

When he told Fowler about returning from the restaurant and finding an empty house, Mallon said, "I thought about calling the police that night, but I didn't. It seemed to me that she had gotten through it, and now she would be somewhere getting a good night's sleep. Maybe after that she would feel up to facing things. I thought that having the police show up to question her would make things seem worse to her." Mallon sighed. "I guess I was just trying to think up reasons why it was best to do nothing. I should have reported it."

Fowler shrugged. "Absolutely. Then I'd be the one who feels bad today." He added, "I mean that. Getting somebody hospitalized without her consent on a 5150 isn't that easy. All she'd have had to do was say the suicide attempt had never happened. You're not a relative, or even an acquaintance. If she was acting composed enough to convince you that she'd be okay, she could have convinced everybody else, too."

"I suppose," said Mallon. "Well." He leaned forward and began to stand, but Fowler held up his hand. He did it without urgency, but it was deliberate and authoritative.

"Do you mind?" asked Fowler. "I just need to take care of a few details, and then we'll be through."

"Okay," said Mallon. He sat back down and waited.

"Just some questions I have to ask. After you saved her life, did she seem grateful, affectionate?"

Mallon shook his head. "No. Not really. She understood that I was trying to help her—she thanked me—but at first it took just about all her patience to be polite about it." He decided he had to move closer to the parts of the evening that were more difficult to discuss. "After her nap, when she was feeling better, she was affectionate."

"She seemed to like and trust you. She walked all the way to your house and went to bed. Did you have sexual intercourse?"

Mallon was shocked, appalled at the suddenness. "No," he said firmly, then caught himself. He couldn't lie to the police. "Not right away. It was after her nap. We each had a shower, and we ended up in the bath together. It wasn't anything I intended. It was her idea, and she was very insistent." The intensity of his own reaction suddenly struck him as suspicious. He began to identify the reasons aloud, so he wouldn't sound defensive. "She was attractive, but she seemed to me to be around twenty-five, and I'm forty-eight. I thought I must have struck her as ancient. Besides, I assumed she must be emotionally . . ." He searched for a word, and came up with "unhealthy. Weak." He added, "But at the time, when we were talking about it, she seemed to be sane and in control of herself."

Fowler nodded. "I understand. I just have to ask all these things, because somebody has to, and I'm the one it fell to. If something we're supposed to get on the record came out later, and we hadn't already covered it, that might make us both look bad. Let's see. You said that at first she wasn't affectionate or friendly. Did she resent you for saving her?"

Mallon reflected. "I'm not sure. Maybe a little."

"Did you have to struggle with her, maybe to get her out of the drink, or make her go with you after?"

"No."

Fowler looked at him with a furrowed brow, as though asking him for a favor. "Sometimes drowning people get a panic grip on you— climb right up on you and hold you under. You might have to hit them to keep them from dragging you under with them."

"No," said Mallon. "She was unconscious."

"Even then," said Fowler. "An unconscious girl is just a hundred and twenty pounds of dead weight. Sometimes you have to grab them any way you can."

"I used a cross-chest pull, my arm over her left shoulder and under her right arm. She didn't fight, and I didn't have to do anything but swim. When I got her to the shallows, I took both her wrists and dragged her up on the sand. It didn't hurt her, and all I was worried about was keeping her face above the surface. When I got her to the shore I gave her CPR, and she coughed up some water. She never said anything about pain, so I assume there was none."

Fowler said, "Okay. Thanks very much for coming in and telling us about this, Mr. Mallon. It will help us clear this up. When a young woman like that dies, it's just . . . mysterious."

"You're welcome," said Mallon. He stood up to leave, but Fowler made a quiet *uh* sound, and Mallon turned his head and waited.

Fowler was looking at his notes, then at Mallon, then at his notes. "I'm sorry," he said. "We'll need to have you give the evidence guys your prints and a blood sample."

"Why? The most my DNA would tell you was that we had sex, and I already told you that."

"Standard procedure. We do it in any case like this. It's mainly to eliminate you if something should come up later. If there's a second set of prints on the weapon, you'll want us to know right away they're not yours. Likewise, blood and so on."

Mallon was sure now that the detective had been lying to him from the beginning. He had been prodding Mallon with these questions because he suspected him of something: killing the girl, or maybe rape. "It doesn't sound like standard procedure. Should I call my lawyer?"

Fowler's jaw tightened, and he let out a breath in a speculative hiss. "That's up to you. I'm certainly not going to go on record telling any citizen that he's wasting his money to get an attorney. I will say that you just spent over an hour telling me a long story voluntarily, and that I wasn't planning to ask you any more questions."

Fowler looked innocent, even mildly disappointed and insulted. But Mallon was aware that a cop conducting an interrogation had no legal responsibility to tell a suspect the truth. Mallon reminded himself that he had nothing to protect. If they wanted his fingerprints or his blood, they would get them eventually, and how could they incriminate him? He said, "Okay. I guess there's no need to wait around for my lawyer."

He followed Fowler into the hallway, and then through a door near the end of the hall. There was clearly something about the death of the girl that had not been in the papers. He chided himself for rediscovering the obvious. How could he have imagined that there would not be?

━━━

When Mallon left the police department he drove home, then admitted to himself that the only sensible thing he could do was to see his lawyer, Diane Fleming, to tell her what had happened. He turned on his front steps to go back toward his car, but then changed his mind, left it in the driveway, and instead walked down Anacapa Street toward her office. He had been sitting in the police station for hours, and he told himself he needed to walk and arrange his thoughts before he spoke with her. But after a block, he found that there was an unexpected aftereffect of failing to persuade the girl not to kill herself: it was forcing him to revisit parts of his own life.

Mallon knew much more about what might happen to him than he had told Fowler. The slow, methodical procedures of the police and the courts were very familiar to him. When he was eighteen, he had disappointed his parents and gone into the Air Force instead of going to college. After he had gotten out, he had returned to the still half-rural area outside San Jose where his family had lived since the gold rush, and disappointed his parents again by going to the police academy to become a parole officer. He had worked in the San Jose department for four years before he'd reluctantly conceded to himself that his optimistic longing to take people who had made mistakes and repair their lives had not made him good at it. All his sincerity and hard work had accomplished was to make him feel like a failure, case by case. He'd felt that he was smothering himself in problems that he could not hope to solve. He'd handed in his badge and a short letter of resignation and had gone to work as a carpenter on a construction crew.

After a year of construction work and some intensive study, he had gotten a contractor's license and hired his own crews and begun to build houses. On his father's advice, since he had joined the Air Force he had been putting all of his savings into buying pieces of farmland. He had simply held it, paying the bank and the taxes by renting it to neighboring farmers who wanted more land to cultivate.

After his construction business had begun to prosper, he met a girl named Andrea at a party, took her out a few times, fell in love, and persuaded her to marry him. It was only two years later that his parents both died—first his father, and then a few months after that, his mother. He was terribly sad, but not particularly surprised. In a way, he had been expecting it, and when it came, it seemed almost overdue. It seemed to him that they had begun to die on the day when the call from Boston had come about his older sister, Nancy.

Nancy had been the smart one, the only one who'd ever played the piano that sat in the parlor of the family farmhouse, a beautiful, tall, strong girl with an open-mouthed, loud laugh and long, light brown hair that the sun always bleached a bit in the summer. She had gone off to college in Boston when he was twelve and, according to his parents, had done beautifully for the first three years. She was still doing just as well on the day when she had made her telephone call.

The day became such a part of his history that he had never seen another month of March arrive since then without remembering. He had answered the telephone and been surprised, because long-distance calls were expensive, and scholarships didn't pay for them. He remembered being a bit confused, because she seldom called, and this conversation didn't seem to be about anything much. She had seemed disappointed when he'd told her that both of their parents were out, but she had filled the time by asking him what he'd been doing, how his grades were, and had even teased him a bit about girls. She had seemed reluctant to hang up, as though she were hoping their parents would arrive. He had offered to have them call her back later, but she had said, "No, never mind. I don't think I'll be around then. Just tell them I love them. I love you all." Then they'd hung up. The next call from Boston had been from the head of the campus police. It had fallen to him to tell the family that she'd killed herself.

It had been the most important day in the life of Mallon's family, the day when everything had changed. His parents had been different after that, in a slow decline that lasted until he was a married, self-employed, and successful contractor. And when that had been accomplished, they'd died.

Mallon went on, remodeled the old family house and moved his wife into it, and kept building his business. In time, the monetary value of the land he had bought became so compelling that he needed to devote some attention to finding something to do with it. His wife, Andrea, had always been ashamed that he was essentially a tradesman who worked with his crew and came home in blue jeans soaked in sweat and covered with sawdust. She had, since their wedding day, referred to her husband as a "developer," but had lately refined her story to promote him to a man who "owned land," and so she welcomed any sign that he was actually interested in the property, and not in getting his hands dirty.

He began to build houses on the farmland. He was one of the many beneficiaries of the steady population growth of northern California, and soon he began to act very much like the man Andrea had been saying he was. Then, ten years ago, as their growing prosperity was becoming noticeable, she had decided that it was time to leave.

Mallon's divorce from Andrea had been an ugly, drawn-out campaign with charges and counterattacks that had been painful but meant nothing, since it made no legal difference in the state of California if he was taciturn and distant or if she'd had affairs. Once they were no longer living together, the battles finally had nothing to focus on but the sums that could be produced by the sale of things that had once been treasures. Their meeting on the day of the final decree had ended the marriage in a last conflagration and a division of spoils.

The property division had required that they sell their house. It had been in his family for four generations, and had originally been a working farm. Even when he had been a boy, it still had been far enough out in the country so that he and his father used to take target practice with their rifles at the edge of their backyard. In that direction there had been nothing to hit for miles. Since then, the city of San Jose had simply grown to engulf the farm and make the hundred acres worth more than all the crops ever grown there. He had felt a deep guilt for not contriving a way to prevent the sale of the house. He had not, in any emotional sense, owned it. He had not been one of the people who had built it, or fought the droughts and the politicians to hold it. He had merely covered over a few more of the fields with grass to enlarge the yard, turned his grandmother's kitchen garden into a tennis court, torn out his father's swimming pool and put in a better one to please Andrea. He had, by default, been this generation's caretaker, holding the house for the next. When it went, he had mourned it like a death, but the house had not been a surprise. She had not liked the place.

The sale of the construction business Mallon owned had been a surprise, because he had never before seen Andrea make a decision that seemed contrary to her own best interests. He had offered her a monthly income that would have consisted of half his profits. But she had insisted on having the company appraised—trucks, tools, trailers, telephones—and getting half of the total in cash immediately.

Andrea's demand came just at a time when northern California was gripped in its most frantic growth spurt. Mallon had run out of land that he had already paid for or inherited, and had begun borrowing to buy more empty land and build developments on it. He had needed to use all his credit, so when her demand came, all Mallon had been able to do was agree to sell out and give her what she had asked for. But her timing was perfect. A much larger company made a preemptive offer just so they could keep the buildings going up without a pause. None of his crews even got a day off when the exchange was made. Mallon had told his lawyers to handle the sale, pay off the debts, give Andrea's attorneys a check for her half of what was left, and send his share to Wells Fargo bank.

A week later, Mallon had been given an appointment with two women in the private banking office in Palo Alto who were specialists in managing people's investments. He had explained that he needed to have them invest his money conservatively so he would not be left short before he found a job. The two had looked at the printout that contained his balance, and looked at each other. The older one, who had silver eyeglasses on a silver chain, wrote something on a piece of paper before she spoke. "Mr. Mallon. This is what your investments will throw off in an average year." She had spun the paper around to face him so he could read the number she had written.

Mallon had thanked the women, signed the various forms they handed him, and then walked out of their building. He'd looked up and down the sidewalk, then up at the sky. As he'd stepped along, the implications of the numbers had begun to demand his attention. The figure the woman had shown him was five or six times what he had spent even when Andrea had lived with him.

He could not stand to live in San Jose anymore, to take circuitous routes just to avoid passing by his family's farm or his old construction business or Andrea's new house. He stopped at the office one last time to say good-bye to his former employees, then drove two hundred and eighty miles south to an apartment in Santa Barbara because he had visited the city a few times and had no unpleasant memories of it. After a month he had invested in an old brick colonial house above Mission Street near State. He spent nearly a year remodeling it, doing most of the work himself, and trying to think about his future but failing. He knew nothing about the future, but the past was full of problems he had not solved. During that year, the investments he had left with the private banking people up north had begun their steady growth. At the end of the year, instead of selling the house, he moved into it. There had never again been any practical reason for Robert Mallon to do anything in exchange for money.

In his new life in Santa Barbara he walked everywhere he went, driving only when he needed to carry something bulky or fragile. He acquired a great many acquaintances, because he had plenty of leisure time, spent much of it in public, and spoke to anyone who spoke to him. He made sure he spent two hours a day getting some form of outdoor exercise and two hours reading. But at the end of ten years in the city, Mallon knew that if he disappeared, there would be little notice. He was not a person who was living a life here. He was just very, very slowly passing through.

Diane Fleming's office was in one of several low Spanish-style buildings on De la Guerra Street painted blinding white with big brass plaques beside their doors. She kept him waiting for five minutes, then rushed into the outer office and shook his hand, and held on to it. "Robert!" she said. "Come on in!" She was in her mid-thirties, and had the distinctive broad-faced blond look that half the women in Santa Barbara had. They had big legs and strong hands like small men, and their appeal was not femininity but a kind of frank robustness. "I'm so sorry to keep you waiting, but I was on a call. Sylvia should have told me sooner." She kept his hand in hers as she led him into her office and sat beside him on a leather couch, then released it.

"It's okay. I should have called for an appointment," he said. "But I need your help with something."

"What kind of something, and what kind of help?"

"I'll let you decide. Have you read about the young woman they found dead in a field two days ago?"

She nodded, her face allowing an acknowledgment that was cautious, tentative. "I did see that in the paper."

"I had pulled her out of the ocean a few hours earlier. I guess she tried again and succeeded. I went to the police and told them. They listened, then asked for a blood sample and fingerprints."

"They think *you* killed her?"

"That's not what the detective said, but I don't think he would tell me if he did. It's possible."

She rolled her blue eyes. "Robert, I'm basically a tax attorney. You're going to need a criminal lawyer right away. I'll make some calls and see who we can get. Now go home, and I'll call you later."

He had somehow expected a longer conversation, and he had especially expected that she would spend some time reassuring him and telling him there was nothing to worry about before she called in a criminal lawyer. But obviously she agreed that there was something to worry about. He saw no reason to delay her telephone calls. He stood and walked to the door. "Thanks, Diane," he said, and left. As he was walking through the reception area, he saw Sylvia pick up her phone. She said, "Sure, Diane, right away."

He went for a long walk down State Street to pick a place to have lunch, but the idea was a failure. He had no appetite, just a restlessness that kept him walking. Mallon barely saw the streets as he walked, because the memory of the girl flooded his mind. He knew that the smooth, beautiful skin he had touched was now cold and lifeless, the voice silenced, but he could still see and hear her, and the knowledge that even that vestige would fade made him want to weep.

He tried to decide whether he had fallen in love with her. He had not been naïve enough to allow himself to let go, to place his fate in her hands that way. He had been fairly certain that their day together had been as much of an aberration as what had caused it, a violent diversion from the normal trajectories of their lives. He had, at every moment, been prepared to relinquish her, to send her back to the world, where she would make a life with people her own age. But he had loved her. He had listened to her and watched her and touched her. She was a creature he had been glad he had preserved, somebody he was delighted with and wanted to live on and on, even if he never saw her again. Now that was over, beyond reach. Nobody else seemed to know what a precious thing had been wasted.

When he reached his house, Diane had already called and left a message on his answering machine. When he called her back, she said, "They're not treating you as a suspect."

"How do you know?" he asked.

"It's a long story. They also don't really know who the girl was. The name she used in the motel didn't match the name she gave when she rented the car she parked there. She left no other identification in the room, no purse, no keys. There were none in the field where she was found, either. You didn't happen to see any on her, did you?"

"No," he said. "And I didn't see any purse, either. There was nothing but what she had on."

"Which was—?"

"Shorts, sneakers, a little top with thin straps." He paused. "I remember seeing her standing there by the rocks. Then she just started walking toward the water and didn't stop. It was kind of odd. She didn't dive or swim or anything, just kept walking until the water was over her head and disappeared. I didn't even notice about the shoes at first."

"What about them?"

"She left them on," he said. "I guess she had no reason to preserve her running shoes."

"I suppose."

He opened the refrigerator and looked inside. "So I guess I don't need a criminal lawyer after all. But thanks for taking care of this. I was really beginning to wonder."

"Oh, no. You do need one, and I got the one I wanted. His name is Brian Logan, and he's a very big defense attorney, based in L.A. He's already on your case."

"If there is no case, what's he doing?"

"He's making inquiries, showing the flag. He's the one who got the police to tell him you're not a suspect. He's very expensive, by the way."

"Oh?"

"It's part of the strategy. I'm sorry to tell you this, but you don't look like a multimillionaire, even by Santa Barbara standards. You buy a pair of shorts from some store on lower State and then wear them practically until your ass shows through. You look like maybe an unemployed construction worker."

"That's pretty much what I am."

"I suppose it is, but that's not what you want to be when the police are looking for a suspect. So I hired you a lawyer that only a rich guy can afford, with a name they know."

"That gets me off the hook?"

"No, it prevents you from getting on. If they discover in the next day or two that she had help shooting herself, or find that she's been raped, you're the only one who admits having seen her. If they know who you are, they keep looking. And it's not as unfair as it sounds. You wouldn't believe how few middle-aged multimillionaires are out there murdering total strangers and then telling the police about it. So we not only make them aware that you're not going to be easy, but also that you're highly unlikely to be anything but innocent. He's on his way here, and we're meeting with him in my office at four."

At a quarter to four, Mallon was sitting in Diane's office, waiting.

Brian Logan did not arrive alone. When the door opened he was preceded by a small woman in a business suit and a white shirt that was cut a bit like a man's but was soft silk. Her eyes were sharp and her movements quick and birdlike. Once she had entered, the next one in was a young man whose function seemed to be to carry a couple of huge leather cases and lean his body against doors so they would stay open for Brian Logan.

Logan entered last. When he stepped through the threshold, Mallon felt as though he had seen him before. After that instant, Mallon wasn't sure whether he had seen him on television talking into a microphone outside some courthouse, or had seen him as one of the legal experts on some talk show about a big murder, or if he simply looked like the kind of lawyer who was on television. He seemed to be slightly younger than Mallon, and that gave Mallon a few seconds of discomfort, but he reminded himself that a forty-year-old was not a beginner, and the man's appearance was probably calculated to please juries. He had dark brown hair that was short, but thick and shiny as a dog's coat, and he wore a charcoal gray suit that looked like the outfits that major politicians wore on international visits, only with a better, more subdued tie. His shave was fresh, his nails were manicured, and the impression he gave was of a cleanliness like some clerics had, which gave him an aura of sanctity. He smiled at Diane, said "Thanks," and she realized he meant he wanted her to leave. She nodded to Mallon and retreated.

He glanced in the direction of Robert Mallon for only a heartbeat, and then seemed not to need to look more closely. His attention was directed to some papers his female assistant had snatched out of one of the leather cases and handed to him. "Good afternoon," he said in Mallon's direction, his eyes still on the papers.

"Pleased to meet you," Mallon said, and stepped forward to shake Logan's hand.

Logan endured the ceremony, then said, "Sit down," and indicated the chair Mallon had just vacated. "You went to the police voluntarily and made this statement?"

"Yes, I went voluntarily." He craned his neck to see the paper. "I assume that's the statement I made."

Logan suddenly focused on him. "Why did you do it?"

"It occurred to me that I was probably the only one in Santa Barbara who knew anything about what had happened, maybe the only one who had even spoken to her."

"So far, you are," said Logan, but his statement seemed inattentive, absentminded. He was staring at the paper again. Mallon wasn't sure whether he was comparing the statement to what Diane had told him or was just reading it for the first time.

"Right," Logan muttered to himself. It was clear that he had already finished reading the statement. "Is there anything else that you forgot to mention to the police?"

"I don't think so," said Mallon. "I was there for quite a while, and I tried to bring back every detail."

"Good," Logan said. He had a very warm smile when he used it, but to Mallon the effect was startling, like a bright light being switched on. "Now. The only other thing that might come up is anything from your past that we don't know."

He said it so carefully and cautiously that Mallon needed to reassure him. "I understand," said Mallon. "There's nothing that I can think of."

Logan ignored his reassurance. "Ever been arrested?"

"No."

"Not even a traffic ticket?" He was openly preparing to be triumphant, as though he had surprised clients with this many times.

"I've had parking tickets—I think three in my life—but no moving violations."

"Ever seen a psychiatrist for any reason?"

"No."

"You've been divorced." Logan said it as though he were vindicated now that his probing had hit something undeniable.

"Yes," said Mallon. "It was about ten years ago. Her name is Andrea, and she still lives up in San Jose."

"If the police went to her and asked her about you, would she say good things or bad things?"

Mallon frowned. "As far as I know, nobody gets divorced because they're brimming with delight about the other person. I assume she wouldn't be very complimentary, but she wouldn't say I was a criminal or something."

"Did you ever hit her?"

"Of course not."

"Push her or threaten her?"

"No," said Mallon.

"Is there any chance she might say you had?"

Mallon was overcome with frustration. "It wasn't that kind of thing at all. We had arguments, but they weren't physical. They were pretty dull stuff. I worked too much, and she was always lonely and bored, so she spent too much. It was that kind of thing. And we didn't argue very much—maybe if we had talked more, it would have saved the marriage. As it was, we both wanted the divorce. The biggest arguments were about that. She wanted everything we owned, had built, or inherited converted to cash instantly and split half and half. I knew that was what was ultimately going to happen, but I wanted to do it a lot more gradually: keep my business going and buy her out over time. She got her way, and we haven't had any contact since the final decree."

Logan said, "All right. How about other women?"

"You mean now?"

"During the marriage."

"No."

"Did she cheat on you?"

"I don't really know. If she did, I never caught her at it. I think that she wasn't involved with anyone until after the divorce was final. By then I had left town, and it was none of my business."

"Were you in the military?"

"Air Force. In the seventies."

"Honorable discharge?"

"Sure."

"Were you ever formally disciplined or charged with anything?"

"Never."

Logan scrutinized Mallon as though he were a particularly difficult witness. "Is there anyone you know of who might come forward or be turned up by the police and might say anything negative about you?"

"How can I possibly answer that?"

"I'm thinking of women, particularly. That you came on too strong, or you made them uneasy, for instance."

Mallon held up both hands and shrugged his shoulders. "Over the years I've dated some women who liked me a lot, and others who didn't especially warm up to me. I can't imagine any of them saying I was dangerous."

"I'm thinking especially of the time since you've resided in Santa Barbara," said Logan. "After all, you are a heterosexual male who— you are exclusively heterosexual?" He watched Mallon nod. "Who has lived here all this time without forming a permanent relationship with a woman. It isn't illegal, but it might raise questions in people's minds."

"I suppose," said Mallon.

"Then there is no point at all that you've been keeping in the back of your mind, hoping it wouldn't come up because you don't want to talk about it?"

Mallon sighed. "I don't like talking about my personal life, if that's what you mean, but there are no guilty secrets. I went to school, then the Air Force, then worked as a parole officer in San Jose, then a contractor. I haven't found a woman I wanted to marry yet, but—"

"Wait," interrupted Logan. "You were a police officer in San Jose?"

"Well, parole officers work for the state Department of Corrections, but I worked out of the office in San Jose. It was only four years, and it was a long time ago, in the seventies." He noticed the expression on Logan's face, so he short-circuited the question. "No disciplinary actions, nothing on or off the record. I just decided to quit because four years was enough."

"Have you told the police that you'd been a sworn peace officer?"

"No. Do you think it would have helped?"

"Probably not. At least not on a homicide. Ex-cops are all trained to shoot people, and once in a while, one of them does. They also have guns. Do you still have yours?"

"No. I turned mine in when I quit, over twenty years ago."

"No others?"

"No."

"All right, Mr. Mallon," said Logan. "I'll try to find out what the police and the district attorney have in mind. Don't go anyplace where we can't reach you quickly. I may want to talk some more."

Mallon went home to wait. Four hours later his telephone rang. It was Diane Fleming again. "Robert?"

"Hi, Diane."

"The coroner's office is going to announce their finding tomorrow morning. They're going to rule it a suicide." She paused for a moment, apparently waiting for some expression of relief. "It's a preliminary finding, but there's really no doubt. There's nothing about it that's out of place or unexplained. Brian Logan and his people have already gone home." She waited. "Okay?"

"Okay," he sighed.

"You still sound unsatisfied."

"I am."

"What's wrong?" she asked.

"I still don't know anything about the girl. I want to know about her."

"What do you want to know?"

"Everything."

Diane sounded tired, as though she were determined to humor him but dreading what he might demand. "There are people who do that sort of thing for a living. Do you want me to hire a private detective?"

"No, thanks," he said. "I know the one I want."

CHAPTER 5

Mallon punched the numbers on the telephone, listened to the ringing, then heard the connection. A voice came on that he had not heard in years.

"Lightning Quick Bail Bonds, Harry here." Harry was now probably about sixty, but the voice was still the same. It was hard, even a little challenging. For Mallon it brought back a clear picture of the short, broad-shouldered frame and the prizefighter's face with the smeared right eyebrow where the hair never grew in right over the scar. Mallon could feel his facial muscles contracting into a smile.

"Harry," he said. "This is Bob Mallon."

"Bobby!" came the voice. "How are you doing? I heard you were in Paris. You calling from Paris? You sound like you're right here."

"I'm in Santa Barbara."

"You went all the way from Paris to Santa Barbara and didn't even stop in to say hello? What the hell's the matter with you? I practically raised you from a pup."

"No, you didn't. I didn't meet you until I was a full-grown dog. And I've never been to Paris, Harry. Santa Barbara is where I live."

"Good," said Harry. "Paris is too good for you. What are you calling for? Don't tell me you need bail? What the hell did you do?"

"I called because I wanted to talk to Lydia. Is she around today?"

"You're in luck. She just came in," said Harry. He yelled, "Lydia!" A few seconds later, he said, "She's going to take it in her office. Nice to talk to you, Bobby."

"Take care, Harry."

Lydia Marks came onto the line, her voice still carrying a very faint trace of a southern accent that Mallon had always assumed wasn't real, the husky smoker's rasp in her throat maybe a bit deeper than last time. "Hello, Bobby."

"Hello, Lydia. How's business?"

"The same," she said. "You'd think there'd be less competition to lend large sums of money to people accused of stealing."

"You would. But if you're complaining, you're probably doing okay."

"Nobody in jail wants to stay," she admitted. "I'm just getting too old to keep tracking the bastards down afterward to keep them from ruining us. You have to remember I've been doing this since the days when you and I were parole officers, and I'm still doing it."

"I suppose most of them get away from you now that I'm gone."

"None of them do," she huffed. "I don't know what I ever needed the likes of you for."

"It was me that needed you," he said. "When you quit, I had to leave too."

"Are we nearly getting around to why you called?" she asked wearily.

"Yes," he said. "I want to hire you."

"To do what?" Her voice was suspicious.

"Something like what we used to do together in the old days."

"Not a chance," she snapped.

"Whatever you're remembering wasn't me," he said. "I was married at the time, and I know I wasn't cheating on her."

"Your mistake. Why do you need a detective?"

"I need to find out what I can about somebody."

"Gee, I'd love to help you," she said without enthusiasm, "but I just don't know. Things around here—"

"I know your time costs more than it used to, and I know you don't want to go because you have a lot of business and don't want to be out of town, distracted from it. So I'll pay you an outrageous amount of money, if you'll just help me out. Come on, Lydia."

"Who are we talking about?"

He said, "It's a young woman who committed suicide here a couple of days ago. The police haven't even got a name yet. I . . . met her before she did it. She was on the beach. She tried to drown herself, but I pulled her out."

Her voice changed. This time there was an unaffected curiosity in it. "You really care about this, don't you?"

"Yes."

"Where do you live these days? What's the address?"

"It's 2905 Boca del Rio in Santa Barbara."

"I'll be there as soon as I can get a plane."

"Thanks, Lydia."

Her voice hardened again, but unconvincingly. "Don't thank me. You're going to pay full price for anything you get, you rich bastard."

It was late afternoon when she arrived in Santa Barbara. Mallon watched her from behind the window blinds as she got out of the back seat of the cab, handed a bill to the driver, and waved him away from her wheeled suitcase. As the cab drove off, she slung her big purse over her shoulder, extended the handle of the suitcase, hung her carry-on bag over it, and pulled it up his driveway.

She did not look as he had expected her to, and he had not been prepared: she did not show the ten years since he had last seen her. Her face seemed nearly the same to him, although he knew he was probably not seeing wrinkles that were there, maybe now appearing at the corners of the big, light brown eyes. He could see that she still had the hourglass figure that, when Mallon had worked with her, used to cause whispered, longing comment among their colleagues in the overwhelmingly male office. The narrow waist curving out to wide hips and shoulders had, even then, been out of fashion with other women, but no man had ever agreed with that assessment. There had been a kind of defiance to her attitude about her appearance: the business suits she favored had seemed tailored to show the curves.

She walked with the same energy and determination that he remembered, her eyes making tiny restless movements to take in everything around her as she came. She did not knock at the door, because she had already seen him studying her through the blinds, merely waited for him to get there to open it.

They hugged wordlessly, and then she stepped in, bumping her suitcase up and over the threshold before he could get around her to reach it.

"Don't pretend you're a gentleman at this late date," she said. "I worked with you when you couldn't afford an extra pair of socks."

The voice, with its mock-sarcastic tone, made him begin to sense how much he had missed her. "You're looking great, Lydia."

"You're not. You look ten years older." She brushed past him and sat on the couch. "On the plane I used my laptop to read the Santa Barbara papers. It wasn't exactly page-one stuff. Tell me what wasn't in the papers."

He recited the story again, telling her everything he had told Detective Fowler. When he had finished, Lydia sighed and stared at the wall, her lips pursed.

"I didn't expect that you would approve," he said.

"I don't approve or disapprove," she answered. "I'm not your mother, and I never had any interest in you myself, except what I could get out of you as a parole officer, which was damned little. You were terrific at holding their hands and sympathizing, but not so hot at tracking them down when they got scarce. Since I've known you for a very long time, I will say that I had hoped that by now you would have outgrown having sex with any young thing who has the impulse, but there's no reason for you to be the first man who ever did. So let's get started on finding out who she was."

"How do you want to begin?"

"Where you did. Take me to the spot where you pulled her out of the water."

"All right," said Mallon. "When?"

"Now," she said. "Give me a few minutes to change. While I'm doing it, you can put on the clothes you wore that day. It will help me put together a picture of what happened."

Fifteen minutes later, she emerged from the spare bedroom dressed in a pair of shorts and a loose Hawaiian shirt with her long brown hair unraveled from its bun and tied back in a ponytail. Mallon drove her along the ocean to the stairway that led down to the beach.

As they walked, Lydia asked Mallon questions about his daily activities, about local real estate and weather patterns. She never showed a reaction to any of the answers except comprehension. She simply waited for a sign from Mallon that they had walked far enough.

Finally, Mallon stopped, looked at the cliffs to his right, the big rocks at their base, then up at the crest where the tops of a couple of eucalyptus trees were visible, and said, "This is it." He pointed at the spot in the ocean where she had gone in.

Lydia looked at the rocks along the upper part of the beach under the cliffs. "When she arrived, exactly where were you? Do you remember?"

Mallon started to point, but Lydia said, "Go there."

Mallon sat among the rocks, where he had been when he had first noticed he was not alone anymore. He watched Lydia walk to the spot where the cliff curved and came out near the water and the beach was only a few feet wide at high tide. She stopped at the spot where the girl had stood that day, staring out at the sea. Lydia turned to Mallon. Mallon nodded: that was where she had been.

"I'm not surprised that she didn't see you." Lydia took a slow, deliberate step toward the ocean, then another, a bit faster, and maintained a steady pace down to the hard, wet sand at the surf line. Then she stopped. She looked back at the beach above her, then began to walk in her own footprints, back toward the little point. Mallon stood up and followed her at a distance.

She was stepping slowly, dragging one foot sideways across the sand. Now and then she would go out of her path to the nearest part of the cliff face to delve in the sand around the base of a rock of a certain size, then return to the path she'd been making. It led her back the way they had come. After about fifty feet, she turned to look again at the spot where she'd left Mallon, and saw Mallon coming after her. It didn't seem to strike her as important. She had only wanted to know where Mallon had been sitting, and she kept looking back at the spot until she was around the point. Then, instead of stopping, she went to work even harder. This time she picked up a long piece of driftwood, an inch-thick branch of some drowned tree, and began to make grooves in a sweeping motion as she walked. After ten minutes, she stopped, dropped the piece of wood, and dug with her hands. She lifted something and set it aside on the sand.

Mallon came closer. "It's her purse, isn't it?"

"I think so." She was still digging, now lifting each handful of sand and sifting it through her fingers instead of merely pushing it out of the way.

"How did you know?"

"I didn't," she said. "She didn't have money or I.D. when you saw her, or any keys. She'd had them earlier, so she left them someplace. This is what they sometimes do."

"You have the purse. What are you looking for now?"

"Whatever she had that she didn't put in the purse."

She sifted some more sand, and then held out her hand. In the palm was a simple gold ring with designs etched on it. She looked at the place where she had been digging, then seemed to make a decision. She stood, taking the ring between her thumb and forefinger and looking inside it. "It's not a wedding ring. It's one of those rings men give a girlfriend."

Mallon said, "How could you know she buried these things?"

Lydia glanced at him impatiently, then looked back at the ring. "I've been hired a few times over the years to find out if suicides were really suicides. It's just one of the things they do sometimes."

"Why?"

"I don't know. It feels right to do it, so they do. By the time it happens, they're way past pleasing anybody else, or explaining themselves. Maybe they're not sure whether they want to destroy these things or just put them where they'll turn up someday and be wondered about." She thought for a moment. "And you can stop feeling bad, thinking that you said the wrong thing or didn't think of something good enough to convince her to stay alive. She was already gone."

"Why do you say that?"

"After you pulled her out, she didn't come back looking for these." She removed the wallet from the purse and thumbed through the credit cards and memberships and receipts, then opened the zipper on the cash compartment. Mallon could see a few twenty-dollar bills and hear a clink of change. She unzipped a compartment built into the silky fabric inside the purse. There was a sheaf of hundreds. She zipped it up again. "We'll have to stop at the police station on the way to your house."

"Maybe you ought to drop me off first," said Mallon. "For the moment, the cops here seem to have accepted the idea that I might not be a murderer, but the case isn't closed."

"Don't worry. We'll make it clear you didn't move this from your house or something. But this is the kind of evidence you have to get to them right away."

As she walked along the beach toward the steps, she took out each item in the purse, one at a time, examined it closely, then put it back. When she reached the driver's license, she held it out to Mallon.

Mallon reached for it, but she said, "You know better than that. Don't touch it, just look. I want to be sure it's her."

Mallon stared at the photograph, scanned the name, the birth date and description. "Catherine Broward," he said. "Cathy Broward. No, I think she wasn't a Cathy. Catherine."

"You didn't see her on her best day," she reminded him. "People who are in that kind of depression talk slowly and think slowly. And she had been unconscious. You'd have to hunt down some people who knew her before, if you wanted to know what she was like."

"I need you to help me do that," said Mallon. "I want to know."

She looked at him steadily. "What do you think it will tell you?"

"Why she was so sure she had to be dead right away. You can see from the picture that she was an attractive young woman. She looked healthy, and she said she was, too. She had some money—maybe not a lot, I don't know—but there was enough in her purse so she wasn't in danger of starving to death." He realized that he wasn't saying anything that mattered, and that made him try harder. "It was a calm, cool, hazy day. The ocean was glassy, the air was soothing. It was beautiful. Standing there and looking around her should have been enough."

Lydia cocked her head but said nothing.

"You think I sound like an idiot." It was an observation, not an accusation.

She said, "I think you sound like somebody who wants to know things that you're not going to learn by investigating a stranger who killed herself." She paused. "I know that sounds a little harsh. But I can tell you from bitter personal experience that having sex with somebody is not the same as knowing them. And unless she left a note that we haven't found yet, we're not likely to know her thoughts on any subject, least of all you."

"I didn't say this was about her relationship with me."

"What else, Bobby? What else could it be?"

After a few more steps he said, "I know I have no excuse for this, but I cared about her. I wanted to be with her for a longer time. If that turned out not to be something she wanted too, I wanted her to go off and enjoy the rest of her life. From a distance, the suicide looks unsurprising, even inevitable: she tried once, got stopped, then finished the job. But it wasn't, and only I know it. It was shocking: it didn't fit. Things like this—events that changed everything and just seemed to come from nowhere—have happened in my life before. This is the first time one happened after I had the time and money to try to find out what it meant. Maybe I want to know what I can't. Even if I can't, it's worth the effort because the death of a person you shared something with is important. Maybe all that's left to do for her is to care about why it happened."

Lydia kept walking for an interval while she considered this. Then she said, "It is in the interest of anybody in any business to convince you that spending your money will buy you important things, like wisdom or contentment, so I shouldn't say this. But I've spent a lot more time than you have looking closely into the secrets of strangers, including dead ones. I don't think that I've learned much that's made me any happier."

"I'm not sure that happier is what I'm trying to be. I want to know."

"But what do you—" She seemed to have a sudden thought, a suspicion. "This is your first, right? You didn't have a relative, maybe a friend, who did this when you were younger?"

Mallon hesitated, then said, "Yes. I did. It was my older sister. Her name was Nancy. She killed herself when she was away at college. I've thought about this a lot, and I'll admit that the similarities haven't escaped me: they were both young and apparently healthy, and seemed to have no reason for it. But I don't think that what I'm trying to do is wrong or irrational. I'm not asking you to look into something that happened over thirty years ago. I just want to know what happened three days ago."

Lydia looked up at him as they walked. "This looks like a fairly simple, straightforward investigation, Bobby. You and I used to do harder ones than this in a day. We've already got what looks like a real name and address. If we wait a week, the police will probably be able to tell us most of what we'd find out," she said. "For me, it's easy money. If you want to pay it, I won't turn it down."

"Thank you," said Mallon. He let those words close the topic. He suspected that the fact that he and Catherine had been in bed together made it all seem simple to Lydia: Mallon's interest during her life was romantic and his interest in her death is sentimental. He did not want to end the inquiry before it had begun simply because it looked like something Lydia found familiar. He was haunted by the feeling that he had faltered somehow and lost the one precious opportunity to save her. But as he walked, he noticed unexpected, contrary thoughts: maybe she had foolishly taken an action he had, at various times in his life, rejected. Or maybe she had gone ahead to show him the way.

When they had gone to the police station and surrendered the purse and the ring to Fowler, Lydia said, "Now we'd better go see your defense lawyer and let him know what's up."

"He's in L.A.," said Mallon. "My regular attorney—the one who handles my business stuff—hired a criminal lawyer, just in case the police were serious."

"I wouldn't be too quick to assume they're not. Who is he?"

"His name is Brian Logan."

"Wow," said Lydia. "Very impressive."

"You've heard of him?"

"Oh, sure," she said. "We're not buddies. The kind of people who can hire him don't need bail bonds much." She looked at him with sudden disapproval. "I keep forgetting you're that kind of people now. But he's known. Dropping his name might impress the other guys on death row when you get there. For now, let's just keep it simple and mention this to your local guy. Who is he?"

Mallon took Lydia to meet Diane Fleming. While Mallon explained to Diane what he and Lydia had found, the two women stood in Diane's office and eyed each other from behind wary smiles. Mallon suspected that neither had yet decided whether the other was someone to be trusted, ignored, or opposed. But when Mallon had finished, it was to Lydia that Diane spoke.

"I'm so glad you took the time to keep me informed. At first he seemed to be under the impression that this wasn't quite serious. He didn't even tell me about it until after he'd talked to the police."

"I know," said Lydia, and shook her head in frustration. "I've known him for years, and he's always been too dumb to get scared when it would still do him some good."

"For years? How did you meet him?"

Lydia glanced at Mallon. "Didn't he tell you? He and I worked together for three or four years. We were parole officers. Whenever somebody didn't show up for his appointment, Mallon and I would go looking for him. That's probably why we both burned out at about the same time."

Diane's eyes widened. "You did?" She turned to Mallon in amazement. "I never knew you were a police officer."

Mallon shrugged. "It was a long time ago."

"I thought you were a land developer," she said accusingly.

Lydia jumped in. "That was a long time ago too. From what I understand, he hasn't done one useful thing since I last laid eyes on him."

"That's not exactly the only possible view of the subject," Mallon told Diane.

"I thought you'd try to deny it," Diane said, then turned her attention to Lydia again. "But you became a private detective. How interesting."

"It's really just a sideline, now," said Lydia. "Years ago I became a partner in a bail bond business, and it's grown. Most of my time is taken up tracing deadbeats who don't show up for their trial dates. I still take a few outside clients now and then, but only cases I can do in my sleep. There's nobody in the world better at surveillance than a middle-aged woman. We're invisible."

"I know the feeling very well," said Diane, glancing at Mallon with exaggerated coolness.

By the time Mallon and Lydia left, the two women seemed to have formed an alliance that transcended him, and showed signs of going beyond his problems. They had exchanged business cards, implied that they would refer prospective clients to each other, and promised that they would talk often. As Mallon walked with Lydia to the car he said, "What was that all about?"

Lydia shrugged. "We hate each other, and we're making the best of a bad thing."

CHAPTER 6

‖‖‖

Lydia Marks sent Mallon out to do some errands and buy them some dinner, then called her office and listened to the messages on the telephone voice-mail system, mentally sorting them. She was busy for the moment with the matter of Catherine Broward, and in any event had no interest in taking a lost-husband case in Denver, or getting involved in a child-custody dispute in Phoenix.

She took down the numbers, but she was listening for something that would require her immediate attention. If she'd had to guess what that might be, it would have been Donald Finnan suddenly going to the safe-deposit box at the Bank of America branch near his house in San Jose. That was where he kept his passport, and probably the valuables he would take with him if he decided to skip and become a fugitive. Donald Finnan was awaiting trial on a manslaughter charge, and he was the type who might try to leave the country. But Donald Finnan seemed to have stayed put, and none of the messages had any urgency. When the last of them had played, she erased them all, set up her laptop computer on Mallon's dining room table, and connected it to the telephone jack.

Next she sat at the table and looked at the piece of paper on which she had scribbled what she had seen in Catherine Broward's purse before she had turned it over to the police: her New York driver's license number, credit card numbers, social security number, date of birth, address. She e-mailed them to her office in San Jose. She also retyped and e-mailed herself the strange little contract that Mallon had paid his lawyer to draft:

I, Robert Mallon, agree to pay Lydia Marks the sum of one hundred thousand dollars, in exchange for expending her best efforts to investigate the history and affairs of the young woman who took her life in Santa Barbara, California, on June 15 of this year, tentatively identified as Catherine Broward.

I, Lydia Marks, acknowledge having received and accepted, on June 19, a sum of fifty thousand dollars in partial payment for my services under this contract. In doing so, I agree to attempt in good faith to find out as much information as possible about the deceased woman and report it to Mr. Robert Mallon or his attorney, Diane Fleming.

The sum was very high for this kind of work, particularly when the client was no longer a murder suspect. But Bobby Mallon was an intelligent man, and Lydia had warned him that he might be wasting his money. It was even possible that she was wrong and he would get his money's worth by the time this was over.

The contract, Lydia suspected, had been the little blond lawyer's idea. Lydia had not expected to have an old friend put everything in writing. She had often signed contracts with corporate clients who needed something to show auditors and, ultimately, had to answer to stockholders. The oral agreements that were customary in her business were not acceptable in theirs. They had to make sure they could prove what they had hired her to do, and protect themselves from liability for whatever else she might happen to do. Contracts with individual clients where rarer. She kept a standard agreement on a disk in her office for the clients who wanted one. It was full of complicated clauses that put the two parties at arm's length from one another, declared that they held each other harmless for this or that. Some clients seemed to like that kind of thing, and Lydia didn't mind.

As she thought about it, she changed her mind and decided the contract must have been Mallon's idea. It had something to do with old times—maybe to reassure himself that he wasn't merely demanding a favor of an old friend, maybe to ensure that she would allow him to pay her at all—but she had not worked out the proportions yet.

Bobby Mallon's case had a great many aspects that she found depressing. She had always harbored a wish—not quite allowing it to grow into more than a pleasurable thought—that she and Bobby might someday meet again when they were both free. When she had first seen him in his doorway, it had come back more strongly than she had anticipated, a sudden shock to her chest, almost like air being forced into her lungs.

It had been looking into his eyes after all this time. Mallon had the kindest eyes she had ever seen in a man. They were watchful eyes, a little sad. She had once allowed herself to think that when they looked at her, he too might be entertaining a wish that he couldn't speak aloud: he had still been married to Andrea then.

She had to admit that she had caused the feeling of emptiness she felt now. After he had called her, sometime while she was busy packing and making plane reservations and rushing down here, she had allowed that part of her brain to awaken. But now it was clear that she had been foolish. He had become a rich old bachelor—too rich for anybody to marry without seeming to be after the money—and the case was about a little chick half her age that he had taken to bed with him. She had learned to live comfortably with the idea of Bobby Mallon as a missed opportunity from long ago. This was worse.

She forced herself to concentrate on her tasks. When she had finished sending her e-mails, she turned her attention to learning about Catherine Broward. Over twenty years ago, when she had started her own detective agency, she had also filed to give legal existence to a corporation called LJM Financial Systems, which she used as a front to request credit checks and other information on people. She set to work now and used the corporation to impersonate an insurance company sending an inquiry about Catherine Broward's driving record, including any cars registered to her, to the New York State Department of Motor Vehicles. She ran credit checks with the three major services. Finally, she logged on to the site of a company that collected public records. She began with New York and California and searched for any criminal judgments, civil lawsuits, marriages, divorces. Then she extended her search to Illinois and Texas because of their sizes, and Nevada because it was a stop that had often produced interesting surprises for her in the past.

When she had finished, she sent the information as an attachment to an e-mail to her computer in her office, then turned off the laptop. The part of this that she could do in Santa Barbara was done. She was going to need to travel. In a way, it was a relief.

It was nearly nightfall when Mallon returned with the food.

Lydia waited until they had eaten before she said, "I've got a place to begin searching, so I'm leaving."

"When?"

"Now would be pretty convenient." She glanced at her suitcase, which she had left in the living room. "I haven't unpacked."

"I'd like to go with you."

She sat completely still and stared at him. "Why?"

"I want the answer. I don't have any reason not to go find it myself. I just don't know how—even where—to begin anymore. I hired you because you're the only detective I know I can trust. You know how it's done these days. You're also a woman, and I think what we find may be easier for you to understand than for me. Maybe it would be better, simpler, if I didn't go, but I'll try to be useful instead of annoying." He stopped speaking and waited patiently.

It was the waiting that kept Lydia from delivering the automatic re-

fusal that had formed in her mind. Mallon had said everything he
wanted to say, and had then had the sense to stop talking and wait.
That was a rare quality, and she had missed it over the years. If she
looked at it from a pure business perspective, she was aware that Mallon had put up fifty thousand dollars in advance, which he had a right
to expect would buy him extraordinary tolerance from a detective. But
none of that would have mattered to her if it had not been Mallon. He
wasn't just a client, he was her old friend, her partner in the parole office when they'd both been young and had shared a belief in the fundamental goodness and perfectibility of human beings. Over the years
they had both learned to hide it—she more convincingly—but it was
still there. After all, that was what they were both doing in this Catherine Broward case: acting on the faith that things should have gone
right, and trying to learn why they hadn't.

She supposed she had just discovered the catch in the contract, the
unwritten expectation that would make this routine job maddening
and difficult. It was possible that at some time in the future, she would
remember this as the moment when she should have given Mallon his
money back. But she didn't. She said, "All right."

Mallon didn't thank her, just said, "I'll be ready to leave in twenty
minutes."

Lydia sat in the living room and read over her notes in silence while
Mallon quickly and efficiently moved from room to room, locking
windows, picking up small items like keys and sunglasses, then disappeared for a few minutes. For Lydia it was a pleasant surprise when
Mallon was at the front door with a small suitcase after only fifteen
minutes. Mallon was a rich man now. There were very few rich people who didn't speak about other people's time carelessly, and it was a
good sign to her that he still lived up to his word in small matters.

They got into Mallon's car and drove up the freeway to Fairview
Road and into the entrance to the small, quiet airport. Lydia and Mallon were on a half-empty commuter plane to Los Angeles Interna-

tional in another half hour. When they arrived, they were in time to catch the red-eye to Pittsburgh.

Lydia sat beside Mallon through the two flights and in the airport waiting areas, preparing herself for questions that never came. At first it seemed to Lydia that Mallon had assumed that questions from him would detract from the efficiency of her inquiry. Later, she wondered if maybe it was simply that Mallon had lived alone for so many years that he had grown comfortable with silence. Halfway through the flight to Pittsburgh, she decided to volunteer.

"We're going to Pittsburgh because I think Catherine Broward may have come from there."

Mallon looked politely interested. "Why do you think that?"

She said, "What you and I are working on now is an outline I got from a credit check. About two months ago, she was there. She flew to Pittsburgh from her last place in Los Angeles. She bought a plane ticket in Pittsburgh to fly back to Los Angeles after a couple of weeks. But while she was there, she didn't use a credit card to pay for a place to stay. She didn't arrive with a round-trip ticket. It all has a certain feel to it, doesn't it?"

"A man?"

She shrugged. "If she was visiting a boyfriend, she would have made a round-trip reservation, knowing when the visit would be over. If she had been coming to Pittsburgh to live with him, she would have given up her apartment in L.A. and put her stuff in storage or shipped it. Those are things that create charges, and there aren't any."

"So you're guessing she was visiting her family."

"Everything is a guess right now, except that somebody let her stay for free. This isn't science," said Lydia. "It's just like looking for parole violators. The method is still just using your instinct for recognizing something that's odd."

Mallon studied her for a moment. "Why did you start in Pittsburgh, and not L.A.? You think they'll know, don't you?"

She hesitated. "Maybe, if they are relatives. If she went home to see them for an open-ended visit, maybe what she was doing was something young people sometimes do. The world out there gets to be too much for them."

"What do you mean?"

"You know. She gets a job, and the job is low-paying and leads nowhere. She has a relationship, but the boyfriend isn't somebody she wants to marry. So maybe she waits until she can get some time off or, more likely, makes time by quitting, and goes back to where she came from. She knows she can't go back there to stay, because that would be the dead end of all dead ends. Her family is glad to see her, but even they know it isn't going to last. Still, she toys with the idea of staying in Pittsburgh. What she's doing, really, is playing that she can stay, pretending that she's younger and hasn't gone off on her own yet. It goes away." She sighed. "Or it takes a worse turn."

"Do you think it's possible that Catherine went to see them because she knew she was about to commit suicide? I mean, if that's who she saw."

She nodded. "It's entirely possible."

"Then what?"

"Then either she will have told somebody her troubles, or she will have lied through her teeth, smiled a lot, and pretended everything was just great. They do that, too."

They arrived in Pittsburgh in daylight, with the sun still very low and shining almost horizontally into the windows of the airport. Lydia rented a Lincoln Town Car and checked them into a large, expensive hotel downtown. While they were walking to the elevators, Mallon said quietly, "Everything doesn't have to be luxurious just because I came along. I'm still a pretty ordinary guy. Do whatever you normally do."

"I'm not wasting your money," she said. "When I hunt bail jumpers, I check into the cheapest, most anonymous fleabag in town, lie low, and start hunting for my guy in the neighborhood. In this kind of investigation I try to play against type a little. People who live in a town know the hotels better than we do. They form impressions of outsiders based on a lot of superficial things, including what kinds of cars they drive and where they're staying. Detective work is a trashy profession. Expecting that people will talk about personal matters to a private detective staying in a cheap motel by the tracks is asking too much."

"This hotel's fine with me," said Mallon. "I don't have any more nostalgia for cheap hotels than you do. I just don't want you to waste your energy trying to keep me pampered. I haven't changed that much. Where do we go first?"

"You can get yourself settled in now. I've got to go back to the car-rental agency, but I'll be back in an hour or two. If you can't sleep, maybe you can take a walk and get a swim. That's pretty much your regular routine, isn't it?"

"Yes," said Mallon. "That's why I don't need to do it here. What are we going to do at the car rental?"

"I'm going to get somebody to show me the forms Catherine Broward filled out to rent her car when she was here."

"How?" asked Mallon. "We're not cops carrying an arrest warrant anymore."

"What I usually try first is bribery."

"If the person turns you down, what do you try second?"

"Bribing somebody else."

||||||||||||||||||||||||||||||||||||||||||||||||||||||||||||||||||||

CHAPTER 7

They arrived outside the car rental just before nine. The sun was bright, but the air had a humid heaviness that made them glad to get into the small air-conditioned building. Mallon was silent while Lydia tried talking the pale, thin young woman behind the desk into showing them the papers, offering her one hundred, then three hundred, then five hundred dollars. As the young woman politely and cheerfully shook her head, the thin, faded blond hair flew into her face and she had to brush it away from her eyes in a practiced gesture that Mallon sensed made her feel unapproachable and yet alluring. It seemed to give Lydia an idea. She turned to look at Mallon.

Mallon stepped closer. "Miss," he said. "I'm Robert Mallon, the client who hired Miss Marks. Catherine Broward tried to drown herself on a beach in California where I live. I pulled her out of the ocean, but a few hours later she shot herself. She's dead. The police in Santa Barbara have not yet been able to find and notify her family. All we want to know is whether there's a local address on the form where she said she could be reached. It might lead us to her parents. They could be frantic with worry, trying to reach her right now, and there's no reason to make them go through that. They have a right to be told what happened."

The young woman was no longer smiling opaquely, but she did not offer to give them anything.

Mallon persisted, as though what needed to be prodded was her memory. "She was about your age, not blond like you but with long, dark hair. She was kind of pretty—I don't mean like a movie star, just a nice-looking person. Do you at least remember her coming in?"

The young woman looked worried, and perhaps even a bit irritated by his attempt to manipulate her. "So many people come in for cars, and I have to watch the paperwork so closely that I don't always even look close at faces."

"Honey, you look at their faces when they show you their driver's licenses," Lydia reminded her gently. "You have to be sure it's the same person."

The girl's smile came back. Mallon could see it was her armor. "Is there anything else I can help you with?"

Lydia would not be dismissed. "We're not from your company. We don't work for your company. Here's my identification. As you can see, I really am a private investigator."

The girl stared at the detective's license, but seemed unconvinced. She looked at Mallon expectantly. He pulled out his wallet and held it open while she examined the California driver's license behind the plastic to verify that his name really was what he had said. She sighed. "All right. I'll see what I can find."

Lydia reached into her purse. "Here's your five hundred."

"I don't want it," she said. "I just don't want to lose my job." She began typing on the keyboard of her computer terminal, staring at the screen. Then she took the pen that was lying on the counter tied to a string, scribbled something on the back of a company brochure, and handed it to Mallon. She did not touch the money Lydia had placed on the counter. "That's the address and phone number she gave."

"Please," said Mallon. "I would like you to take the money. If this is her family, the whole search is over, and you've saved me whatever I would have spent hunting for them."

She ventured a glance at the money, but she didn't move. She studied Mallon. "Why are you doing this—any of it?"

He shrugged. "I suppose it's because this is the only thing left that I can do for her. I had a chance to talk her out of it, but I didn't think of the right thing to say. I feel sad about it. I wish you would take that money."

"Why do you care whether I take the money?"

"So that somebody who showed compassion would get some small benefit out of it." He took the bills from the counter and added some from his pocket. "I'm rich now, but there have been a couple of times when a few hundred bucks might have changed my life." He folded the money, took her hand, and folded her fingers over it. He held the hand for a couple of extra seconds, until he felt her finger muscles tighten, then gently released it like a small bird. "Thanks for your help." He turned and walked out the door.

Lydia said quietly, "We really aren't from your company. And I really am a detective." She pointed up at the tinted glass half-globe on the ceiling above the door. "Don't forget to put a fresh tape in the security camera's tape deck before you leave. You can lose the old one on the way home."

⫲

The address belonged to a woman named Sarah Carlson. The house was a very small, narrow, two-story cottage painted a daffodil yellow with spotless white enamel trim. There was a small covered porch with a white railing that gleamed in the sunlight.

Lydia and Mallon stood on the porch listening to the soft footsteps moving toward the door. The woman who opened it was about thirty, with light skin and dark brown hair that she wore short, and Mallon knew that Sarah Carlson was not just a friend.

Lydia appeared not to have seen the resemblance. "Good afternoon. Are you Sarah Carlson?"

The woman looked at Lydia, then at Mallon through the closed screen door, and answered, "Yes." The voice was like Catherine's. It made Mallon feel the sadness again.

"My name is Lydia Marks, and this is Robert Mallon. Do you know Catherine Broward?"

She looked at them warily. "What is this about?"

Lydia said, "A few days ago, in Santa Barbara, California, Catherine Broward took her own life. We're trying to find her family, and—"

Sarah Carlson was crying. It had begun at "took her," the tears appearing in the eyes without the expression having time to change yet, so that it looked as though a cold wind had simply blown into her eyes and made them water. But then the eyes squinted, the shoulders came up in a cringe, the mouth quivering and the chin puckering before the hands could rise to her face to hide it. She began to wail, "Oh, no. Oh, no. No . . ."

Mallon watched, wondering. The girl he had saved had seemed to be healthy, smart, sure of herself. Now he could see that she'd had someone who had cared very deeply about her. He had heard or read somewhere, in the period after his sister's death, that sometimes people killed themselves in order to punish someone—their families, usually. As he watched this young woman behind the screen sobbing, he reflected that if this was a punishment, it was incredibly effective. It was hard to imagine anything a stranger could have said to this woman that would have made her dissolve into sorrow this way. It occurred to him that what he was seeing was probably like watching himself thirty-three years ago—not the tears or the exact expressions, but the utter devastation.

He turned to Lydia, at first only to keep from staring cruelly at the woman. Lydia's body was straight and rigid, her face solemn, but her eyes were in quick motion. She was looking past the woman, over and around her into the house, then to the left at the house beside hers, then to the right, and back at the woman. Now that she had temporarily forgotten the visitors, Lydia studied her pitilessly. After Lydia seemed to have exhausted the sights available to her, she asked, "Would you like us to come back later? We only need to ask a few questions. Her parents . . ."

Sarah Carlson forced herself to focus her attention on the two people still standing at her door. She raised her eyes toward them and seemed to see them as troublesome. She began to nod, but then appeared to remember something, or to discover it. "No, please," she said. "Come in."

She pushed the door open and held it, and it occurred to Mallon why Lydia's offer had sounded so perfunctory and insincere to him. Lydia had known Sarah would not send them away. If she did, she would be left sitting alone in this house grieving, but knowing nothing about what had happened.

Mallon followed Lydia in and stood awkwardly beside her in the small living room. Mallon liked the room as much as he had liked the outside of the house. Built-in bookcases covered two of the walls, all filled tightly, but without pretense. There were old leatherbound volumes stuck in among paperbacks, sets of faded clothbound books that looked as though someone had reread them many times beside bright-jacketed books he recognized from recent visits to bookstores. The framed pictures on the walls were all interesting rather than merely decorative. There were a couple of miniature portraits of nineteenth-century people who didn't seem to be famous and weren't beautiful, a couple of color plates of ferns from some forgotten botany text.

She said, "I'm her sister. Carlson is my married name. Our parents are dead, so I'm all she had. Tell me what happened."

Lydia glanced at Mallon. "Mr. Mallon spoke with her a few hours before she died. I think he can tell you more than I can."

Mallon turned toward her to speak and felt alarm, but he took a breath and began, trying to say enough words to fill the void between them. He told the first part of his story honestly and fully, describing what had happened at the beach, their walk to his house, everything that had been said. He spoke without lying about anything. He did not try to make himself seem less than quick and brave in saving Catherine, nor did he pretend he had not felt a stupid vanity at the thought that he'd been a hero. He talked until he came to the point when she reappeared at the top of his staircase wearing his robe, then began to leave out parts of it. "After her nap she said she was hungry. She didn't have any clothes with her that she was willing to wear to a restaurant, so I went out for food. When I returned, she was gone. I drove around the area searching for her, but never found her. I waited for hours, left the door unlocked and the lights on in case she came back. The next I heard of her was two days later, when the newspaper reported that she'd been found."

Sarah Carlson asked, "Did they find a note?"

Lydia shook her head. "No. They always look for one, but it's not unusual not to leave one."

Sarah narrowed her eyes at Lydia, but did not say what she was thinking. Mallon knew it was something angry about Lydia's way of talking. She implied that everything was something that had happened hundreds of times before. There was nothing special or new about what this woman's only sister had done to herself.

Mallon tried to erase the impression by giving the same answer to her question more gently. "I'm sorry. If she left a note, they haven't found it yet." He paused. "We'd like to help you. Are there any other relatives we should speak to, or do you prefer to call them yourself?"

She seemed to be listening more closely to Mallon now, as though she had detected something surprising in his voice. "You feel terrible, don't you?"

Mallon took two breaths before he answered. "Yes, I do," he said. He hesitated for a moment, wanting to tell her about his own sister. But he concluded that the impulse was misguided: this was about her sister, her feelings, not his. "I tried to get her to see a doctor at the hospital, offered to take her to a different one if she wanted. She refused, and I let it go. I tried to remind her that life isn't always the same, and that people get through bad times. I tried to convince her that if she let herself live for another day she might feel better. I failed. I didn't say enough, or I didn't say it well, or what I said was stupid and beside the point. I was the last chance, and my arguments weren't good enough, or I wasn't good enough. I'm very sorry."

Sarah Carlson shook her head, tears still running down her face. He could tell that what she was going to say was costly. "It wasn't your fault," she said. "Nobody could have said anything that would have convinced her." Mallon knew, rationally, that she could not possibly mean it. She must believe that if only she had been the one, it would have made all the difference.

He said, "I think you're very generous to say that. I wish things had been different."

"I meant it. See, Cathy had a problem with depression. Not a clinical imbalance or disease, where a doctor can prescribe something. It was sadness."

Lydia visibly straightened, her head held still, as though if she moved she might miss a word, or startle Sarah into silence.

Sarah sighed. "It was one of those things that you read about in the papers, or see on television. It must happen to lots of other people, but it still doesn't seem real to me. Cathy had a boyfriend. She was absolutely devoted to him, adored him. For about a year she was impossible to listen to. She wouldn't talk about herself, or what she thought or did, because he was what she thought about, and trying to please him was what she did. If there was something to have an opinion about, it was 'Mark thinks' this or that, or even, 'Mark knows about these things, and he says' this or that."

Mallon had lied. Neglecting to tell her about the sex made his whole story false. Mallon felt ashamed while he listened to her now, because listening this way was another act of deception, pretending to be receptive to every word, but really waiting to hear the secret reason that Sarah would divulge in a moment of weakness or misplaced trust.

Or maybe she would report with such perfect accuracy that she would describe the reason without knowing it for what it was.

He decided that to dispel the feeling, he had to make her remember she was talking to strangers. "Who is he? Does he live in Pittsburgh?"

Sarah shook her head. "She met him in Los Angeles. I remember there was a class she took in the evening. She wanted to get a master's degree in psychology, and this was an undergraduate class she wanted to make up. She met him at some coffee place on campus. He wasn't in her class; he was just having coffee. About a month later she wrote and told me she had moved in with him. I didn't think much of that, but she sent a picture of him in the letter, and I could hardly blame her. He was gorgeous. He looked like a model: tall and thin with black hair and blue eyes. He really did seem to be perfect, and she wasn't my baby sister anymore, she was a grown woman. She was happy, so I was happy."

"What happened?" asked Mallon.

"Everything was great for about a year. Then it wasn't, or maybe she was just beginning to worry that it wouldn't always be. She was kind of tense and irritable when I talked to her on the phone. About that time they moved to a different apartment. One day she left a message on my machine with a new phone number. A month later she called with another one. Then, six weeks after that, Mark was dead."

Now Lydia stopped hiding her interest. "Dead? How?"

"Murdered. Shot dead in his car in a dark alley behind their apartment, where their garage was. She came to see me the next week, and she had a newspaper article about it. There was a lot of vague stuff about how he spent a lot of time in after-hours clubs and was 'associated' with people in the designer-drug scene, and all that. If the reporter knew what he was talking about, the article didn't manage to convey it to me. People in their twenties go to clubs, and when they do, there are people who might be using just about anything. Of course, I asked Cathy."

"Did your sister explain it?"

"She admitted that she had been getting nervous about some of the people Mark seemed to know. And now and then he would be out all night, and when he came in it was pretty clear he had been partying."

"Other women?"

Sarah shrugged. "She didn't know, and she said she didn't want to know, but after all, he wasn't out all night alone. He must have been with somebody and it wasn't her, right?"

Lydia said, "Did he take a lot of drugs, or just know people who did?"

"She said she never saw him take *anything*. But she admitted that if he had wanted to, he could easily have fooled her. She didn't care. She was absolutely in love with him. When she came and told me all this, she hadn't slept in two days, and she talked just about all night, until she fell asleep. She woke up about fifteen hours later, and she had changed."

"How?" asked Mallon.

"She never talked about him much after that, but she was always thinking about him. I waited for a month, but she was still that way—mourning him as though he had just died. One morning when I woke up she was packing. She thanked me and said she was going to New York."

"Why did she pick New York?"

"I don't know. She lasted there a few months, working in a restaurant. Then she moved to Scottsdale, Arizona, because it was a change from New York. Then she moved back to L.A. After Mark died, she was never the same. She was nervous, restless. She went places, but it wasn't because she was hoping that anything was going to happen when she got there. It was more like a person pacing the floor, just moving because staying in one place was intolerable. She came here two months ago. She stayed here with me. She rented a car, the way she always had, but all the time while she was here she probably never went farther than the yard. I would come home from work and find her lying flat on her back on the floor, staring at the ceiling. She had no desire to see anybody from the old days, or to pick up the phone to talk to anybody in any of the places she'd lived. Not even L.A. She had always been the one who was athletic, but this time she seemed physically weak. She was unwilling to move, but she wasn't ever at rest. Finally one day, she packed up again to go home. That's what she said. That it was time to go home."

Sarah barely got the words out before she dissolved into tears again. Mallon and Lydia let their eyes meet while hers were closed. There seemed to Mallon to be nothing for them to do but wait. Lydia gave her only ten seconds before she said, "What was Mark's last name?"

"Romano."

Lydia said, "Do you know whether they caught the person who killed him?"

"No," said Sarah. "I don't think so."

"Did that seem to bother Cathy?"

She stared at the window for a moment, and her answer seemed to come as a mild surprise to her. "I don't think so. She talked about him, about good things they had done together. She didn't talk about the killer at all. I suppose that if the only man you ever loved that much is killed, then what matters is that he's gone. She never talked about the rest of it, the way some people seem to. Like they could never rest until the person gets punished. I think Cathy knew she could never rest no matter what."

Mallon said, "Maybe if I had somehow known all of this at the time, I could have said or done the right things."

"No. I knew everything, and I talked to her over and over for a year or more. It made no difference. The only thing that would have was bringing Mark back."

Lydia said, "I hope you don't mind if I give the Santa Barbara police your phone number and address. They'll need to talk to you, and there will have to be arrangements made."

Sarah looked at the floor. "I know. I'll call them right away. I'll have her brought back here so she can be buried near my parents." She seemed almost to be talking to herself. Mallon knew she was going to be talking to herself often in the next few days, reminding herself of things that needed to be done, people who needed to be called. Death wasn't just an event that happened by itself. It was a lot of work.

Lydia stood and said, "We'll be back in California tomorrow. If there's anything we can do to help, here's my business card. It has my number on it." Sarah accepted it, but placed it on a bookshelf without looking at it.

She said, "Thank you. And, Mr. Mallon, I thank you for trying so hard to help my sister. I don't think acts of kindness are wasted or lost. You made my sister's last memory of people warmer and brighter."

All the time she was speaking, they were advancing on the door, and then they were outside. Mallon looked for a last time at the yellow house. It was outdated now, the cheerful paint job and the neat interior all part of a phase of Sarah Carlson's life that had stopped existing at the moment when he and Lydia had stepped onto her porch.

He stood on her front walk, gripped by the impulse to go back up the steps and tell her the rest of the story. He asked himself what he was longing for. Could he possibly want sympathy from her for the sense of loss that he felt? No, it was something else. He had momentarily imagined that telling Sarah something so private—so damning, now that Catherine had proved that her consent could not have been the free choice of a person in control of her will—would make Sarah reciprocate and tell him things that were equally private: intimate details and secrets that would make him finally understand what Catherine had been thinking. He recognized that the urge was insane. If he told Sarah that he'd had sex with her sister a couple of hours before she'd killed herself, she could only loathe him. He had already heard everything she would ever tell him.

"Bobby?" Lydia's voice startled him. "Forget something?"

"No," he said, turning toward the car, and took a step. "Just for a minute, I thought I had."

"You're right," Lydia said softly. "We told her enough."

||||||||||||||||||||||||||||||||||||||||||||||||||||||||||||||||||||||||||||||||

CHAPTER 8

As Mallon drove the Town Car around the corner and pulled over on the next block, Lydia took out her cell phone and dialed a long-distance number. "Detective Fowler, please." She turned to Mallon. "You know we've got to do it."

Mallon nodded, then listened with undisguised curiosity.

"This is Lydia Marks. Robert Mallon and I are in Pittsburgh." She repeated, "Pittsburgh. We've managed to locate the sister of Catherine Broward. Yeah, the one who killed herself. The sister's name is Sarah Carlson and she'll be calling you shortly. Want her number and address anyway?" She recited them, spelling the street name. "You're welcome. Nothing you haven't heard before. There was a boyfriend, he died, and she never got over it. The only odd thing was that he got murdered." She rolled her eyes at Mallon. "Mark Romano. It was in L.A., about a year ago." She paused for only a second. "I doubt it, but I'm going to look more closely when I get back. Of course I'll let you know anything I find." There was another pause. "Oh? That's quick. I'd better let you take her call."

She avoided Mallon's eyes as she put the telephone away. "There," she said. "Now he's got nothing to bitch about, and if he finds out something we don't know, he might very well save us from wasting our time trying to get it too. In any case, he hasn't got the unpleasant suspicion that I'm a problem."

Mallon gave a single nod and a perfunctory half smile of acknowledgment, but he seemed not to have necessarily agreed. He remained silent as he pulled back onto the residential street and turned in the direction of the highway back to their hotel.

"Well, what do you think?" Lydia asked. "This might be a good place to quit."

Mallon looked surprised. "Why do you say that?"

"You tried to save a girl. You wanted to know why she wasn't willing to be saved. Now you know: her boyfriend was killed, she felt depressed, and she never got over it."

Mallon seemed to be comparing the assertion with some interior standard. "I'm not ready to quit. I don't think I know enough yet."

Lydia considered. "You don't think the sister told us the truth?"

"Well," said Mallon, "I think what she told us was true. I don't imagine for a second that she told us everything she knew to be true, and I think she suspects still more that she isn't sure is true, but maybe. All of it together doesn't seem to be enough."

"Has it occurred to you that some things can't be known so completely and in such detail that there are no mysteries left?"

"Sure," Mallon said. "But I don't think we've reached the end. We've just got one person's reaction, with one point of view."

Lydia said, "Let's look at it from another point of view, then: yours. We've just listened to her only relative. What did you hear that makes you curious? You tell me what to look at next."

"The relationship with Mark Romano."

"Fine," said Lydia. "That's L.A. We can be on a plane back to L.A. in an hour or two. We'll find out what we can about Romano, and see where that leaves us."

The flight back to Los Angeles seemed longer to Mallon than the flight to Pittsburgh. This plane seemed to be smaller than the last, and

Lydia had said little since the conversation in the car. Mallon opened the subject again. "I know I'm being self-indulgent."

"If you know, then why are you doing it?"

"I think it's because I realized that for the first time in my life I actually could. I've seen things happen to other people, had things happen to me. I don't think I ever really understood why most of them happened. This one I saw coming. I knew what she was trying to do, but I still didn't understand what she was thinking, why she was doing it. I don't, even now. This seems to me to be a chance to find out one thing that matters."

"I've known since the beginning that this isn't just about her," said Lydia. "When you first realized what she was doing, you felt as though you were reliving your sister's last day, when you talked to her and couldn't save her. You were trying to make sure that this time it came out right—that you said the right things, did the right things, and made it not happen."

"Maybe I was," Mallon said. "It didn't work. All that's left now is knowing."

"What you want isn't possible to get in one lifetime. It's omniscience. That's why people read books. Maybe you could take a night class or something."

"Night class," said Mallon. "That's where she met him." He was silent for a time. "What do you think of him?"

"Nothing."

"Nothing?"

"I heard what Sarah Carlson said. So far the only person who ever laid eyes on him seems to have thought he was a prince. I need to find out more facts before I start having an opinion of my own."

Lydia and Mallon rented a car at Los Angeles International Airport and drove it to the Hotel Bel-Air, then checked in. Lydia said, "I'm going to go to my room and see what I can get on the Internet. I'll call you later for dinner." Mallon followed a bellman to his bungalow. He unpacked his single bag, showered, changed, and went out.

Los Angeles was more crowded and intimidating than he remembered it. He knew that was a sign that age was advancing rapidly, making him not timid exactly, but prickly and unwilling to be inconvenienced. In Santa Barbara, people walked. Here, in order to go to a place where he could walk without appearing to be a vagrant or a criminal, he had to take a cab a couple of miles, past Santa Monica Boulevard to the shopping area of Beverly Hills. He walked up and down the streets pretending interest as he looked in famous windows at rather ordinary merchandise. The sidewalks and the fronts of buildings seemed to be particularly clean and mostly white. The blocks were short and required waiting for traffic lights to change, so he went around blocks in a series of squared loops.

When he returned to the hotel, Lydia was sitting at a table in the tiled patio dining area, sipping a tall glass of iced tea.

She said, "You must have walked halfway to Tijuana. I'm glad you finally made it back, because we're meeting somebody here in a few minutes."

"Who?"

"A cop. I looked up the article in the L.A. *Times* that Sarah Carlson told us about to get the name of the homicide detective who investigated the Romano thing. It turned out to be somebody I met while I was here on a case one time. It's a big favor to come down here to talk to us, so you're buying dinner. Better go put on a coat."

Mallon went to his room and returned wearing the only sport coat he had brought from home. As he approached the table, Lydia looked to her right, smiling. Mallon turned his head in order to see the cop's arrival.

She was blond and looked about thirty-five, with the raw, light-skinned sort of face he had always associated with the inland towns that were almost desert, skin that seemed to have been sunburned too many times.

Lydia said, "Here's Mallon, my client. This is Detective Angela Berwell."

She held out her hand to Mallon, but when he reached for it expecting her to grip too hard, as women in jobs like hers sometimes did, she surprised him by gently grasping his hand and letting go. She wore a blue summer dress with a pattern of white flowers, and high heels that were a bit too high. Mallon could see that Lydia was amused at her own cleverness in not mentioning that the cop was another woman. Mallon mumbled, "Pleased to meet you," and she gave him a display of even white teeth and sky-blue eyes.

Next she turned to Lydia and hugged her, both of them careful not to touch their cheeks and smudge their makeup. Then she pulled back with a wry look on her face. "Love your purse, Lydia." Mallon looked at it, a small, unremarkable black bag with a zipper on the side. "In fact, I've got one just like it."

"You do?"

Detective Berwell nodded. "I almost brought it tonight. It's the best I've ever found that was designed for the purpose. But I needed a bigger purse tonight. Want to show me a carry permit for the gun?"

"Sure." Lydia took out her wallet and showed her a card.

"Town of Stovall. Kern County, eh?" She handed it back to Lydia, then mistook Mallon's discomfort for surprise. "Nobody gets a concealed-weapon permit in most of the urban counties, L.A. County especially. So people who want one establish a residence in some rural county, and get a permit there. When they carry here, it's legal. We can't stop them."

Mallon nodded politely, as though that loophole in the law were not already familiar to him. He supposed Lydia must have decided not to reveal that she and Mallon had once worked together as parole officers. He spent only a second wondering why, and then reflected that knowing more than people supposed was a useful pose.

Lydia smiled. "Don't worry. I just got off an airplane. I'm not carrying. I just didn't change purses when I left home." She slipped her wallet back into the purse, then looked at Detective Berwell. "Did you bring the tapes?"

"Yes," she said. She patted her oversized purse. "That's what's in here."

"Would you like to have a drink out here first?" asked Lydia.

She shook her head. "No, I don't think so. I'd like to get this over with, and do it where we can talk a bit in private."

Lydia said to Mallon, "Let's go to your room."

Mallon led them past the open doorway of an interior dining room that was painted a pinkish color. They could see thick, starched white linen and heavy silver and quiet, unobtrusive waiters. Mallon waited until they were walking down the quiet garden path toward his bungalow before he spoke to Detective Berwell. "I appreciate your willingness to meet with us."

She said, "It's not entirely out of the goodness of my heart. This is partly for me. Lydia always says she's the best, but the truth is, the worst I can say is that she's only one of the best. I wouldn't be upset if you paid her to turn up something that I missed and solve the Romano case for me."

"Did she tell you how I got involved in this?"

She nodded, and her eyes stayed on him. They weren't quite as cheerful. "I've been through that. Almost everybody I know has. When you lose one, you go over and over it for a while. I'm not sure what I have will help you: I don't really know much about Catherine Broward. She just came up in the investigation with a few dozen other names. What I know about is Mark Romano."

They had reached Mallon's bungalow. Mallon sidestepped ahead of the others on the narrow stone walkway and opened the door. They stepped inside, and Mallon closed it. He gestured toward the couch, and Lydia and Detective Berwell sat. He pulled out the desk chair, turned it around, and sat facing them. Mallon said, "The newspaper implied he had been involved with the drug trade. Is it true?"

"Not exactly," Berwell answered. "The way he first came to the department's attention was on a surveillance. There were some gentlemen who were being watched by the D.E.A. The agents were taking videos, and the department was cooperating—running license plates, identifying people these guys met with, and so on—and he got himself on a couple of tapes. We identified him, so he got a file. Nobody ever got anything on him to add to the file, and certainly there was nothing illegal about what he was doing on the feds' tapes: he was talking to people in a bar. So he was forgotten until he was murdered."

"Do you have any idea who killed him, or why?" asked Mallon.

"You can die just by hanging around with the wrong people," she said. "The men Romano was seen with had arrests for drug possession, some trafficking charges that didn't stick, some suspected extortion, some assault, some domestic violence stuff. It wasn't one crime, it was a pattern, a lifestyle." She looked at him curiously. "Are you understanding this?"

"I think so," he said. He understood it perfectly. What she had said applied equally to most of his old clients and all of their friends. This was a logical time to tell her that he had once been a parole officer, but he decided he would learn more if he left things as they were.

"Romano hung out with a social set who knew one another slightly because they went to the same clubs, used drugs, liked certain kinds of cars, and so on. As far as I could tell, the investigation fizzled because it was a search for organized crime, and all they found was a bunch of lowlifes. Most of the connections weren't even between the men. They were between the women, who stood in front of the mirrors in the ladies' rooms of bars, talking while they put on way too much makeup. If one of them had been dumped by a boyfriend, one of the others knew somebody who would be interested in taking her out. They invited each other to parties, probably shared drugs. Maybe a couple of them bought and resold small amounts."

"That's it?" asked Lydia. She looked disappointed.

"Don't get me wrong. Some of those people had connections with big, ugly drug networks, and some of them had committed real crimes. But Mark Romano wasn't one of them. When you ask me if I think I know who killed him, I have to say yes: one of those people. I don't know whether it was one of the ones he knew who got mad at him, or another one who happened to run into him and didn't like him. And I don't know why, exactly. My guess is that it was over a woman, because he was very popular with women, and jealousy is always a potent motive. But sometimes when there's an investigation, even if it's done perfectly and there are no mistakes or leaks, the bad guys seem to sense it. If Romano got killed because some criminal guessed there was a surveillance going on and thought he might be a police informant, he wouldn't be the first. And there's evidence to support that view. Within a minute or two after Romano was shot, the killer or killers walked into a house nearby and shot a family of four who must have seen what was going on. Jealous boyfriends don't usually do that. They might open up on whoever they see right afterward—especially friends and relatives of the victim—or even turn the gun on themselves, but they don't go looking for witnesses."

She spoke in a tone that seemed designed to make Mallon see the futility of his inquiry, but he became even more attentive. "A whole family?"

"A mother, a father, and two kids, aged ten and six. They were the nearest neighbors who were home at the time, and there was nothing about them that could have gotten them killed except seeing too much."

"That's horrible," Mallon said. He seemed lost in thought for a moment, then looked at Detective Berwell again and asked, "Where does Catherine Broward come in? I assume you interviewed her right after the shooting?"

Detective Berwell shook her head. "No. She wasn't living with him at the time of his death. The neighbors said there were frequent female guests but no roommate right then. Catherine Broward was not around, and he'd had at least one regular girlfriend for a couple of weeks after her."

Mallon frowned. "Are you sure?"

She looked at him steadily. "It was a homicide investigation. We do try to get the easy facts straight."

"It's just that her sister seemed to be pretty sure that she still loved him. She said that his death was what threw Catherine into a depression, and she never recovered."

Detective Berwell sighed. "I never met Catherine Broward. She came up only after we searched his apartment." She looked at Lydia. "Think it's time?"

"I'd say so," said Lydia. She stood and waited while Detective Berwell pulled a videocassette from her purse and handed it to her. Lydia stepped to the television cabinet, slipped the tape into the VCR, and started it. The screen showed a few seconds of snow and static, then resolved itself into a dimly lighted bedroom.

Mallon watched while a young woman came into the room. A few seconds later, a young man came into the frame from somewhere in the vicinity of the camera. The woman switched off the bedside lamp, but the man turned it on again, then pushed her onto the bed. He said, "I want to be able to see you," and she giggled and turned her face away from his, in the general direction of the camera. She did not seem to see it.

Mallon said, "That's her. That's Catherine." He turned to Detective Berwell. "What is this? Can this be a surveillance tape?"

She gave her head a little shake. "Uh-uh. The man is Mark Romano. This is a tape he made himself. We found it when we searched his apartment."

Mallon watched the screen for a minute or two. The couple were already naked, and caressing each other passionately. The sight made a wave of heat spread up the sides of his neck to his temples and his scalp: he sensed feelings of shame, anger, loss, and jealousy, all asserting themselves in shifting proportions. He turned away from the sight toward Detective Berwell, and saw that she was staring intently not at the television, but at him. He said, "I'm not sure I understand. He made tapes of himself and Catherine. Did she know?"

She shook her head slightly. "Not just her. There were a number of women. There were some tapes where we had a question about whether the woman was fully aware of what was going on. They were all conscious—more or less—but some were obviously under the influence of something. We got the best stills of faces we could from the tapes, identified the women, and asked them about it." She gave Lydia a tired look and rolled her eyes. "I got to do that, of course."

She returned her gaze to Mallon. "By the time we obtained Catherine Broward's name, I had interviewed at least twenty. None of them had known they were being taped, but none of them claimed it was anything but consensual sex. Catherine Broward was out of town while that was going on, and by the time she got back, I had moved on to follow other leads, so somebody else interviewed her, but there are no revelations in the file. It was a pointless issue by then, anyway. None of the women knew about the tapes, so the tapes weren't a motive for the murder. And even if we'd found a woman who had been drugged without her knowledge or something, we weren't going to prosecute a dead man for rape." She looked at the screen again, where Catherine Broward and Mark Romano were now having intercourse. She displayed no discomfort or embarrassment at the sight, only impatience. "Seen enough?"

Mallon nodded. "More than enough."

Lydia stood up again and walked to the television to stop the tape. She pressed another button, and they could hear it rewinding.

"Her sister was under the impression that this Mark was the love of her life, and that his death caused the suicide," Mallon repeated.

Berwell leaned forward and patted Mallon's arm. "I know. Things aren't always just one way. I'm sure that Catherine probably did tell her sister all of that, and meant it. When things were going well in the relationship, he was her true love, they were going to get married, and all that. But after the investigation, I can tell you it was never going to happen. She was kidding herself. He had a long history. He used his looks—which were really something, as you just saw—to attract women. And he could talk very convincingly. He would go wherever he could find women: college campuses, coffee shops, food courts at the big malls. He got their confidence, their trust, and then took advantage. He treated them like slaves, and spent their money as though it were his. When he was tired of them, he dumped them. In at least a couple of cases, he passed them on."

"To whom?" asked Lydia. She handed Berwell the videotape, and Berwell put it back into her purse.

She looked at Mallon while she answered. "Now we're back to the beginning—the people the feds were investigating. That seems to be the reason he was popular with creeps. He was somebody who knew a lot of attractive, available women. He had the temperament of a pimp."

Mallon asked, "And the women put up with that?"

"Some of the women we interviewed weren't exactly squeamish about it. They were basically no different from him. They used him too: got a place to live for a while, went to all the parties, and met people who had a lot of cash and were willing to throw it around. When Mark Romano moved on, they considered a change to one of the bigger creeps a soft landing, or even a step up. Who has a better supply of money and drugs than a guy who sells drugs?"

Mallon shook his head. "Catherine wasn't that way at all. Why would she kill herself over a man like that?"

Angela Berwell's lips formed a half smile, but her eyes were sad. "The reason somebody like him can exist is that some women are really good at convincing themselves of things that aren't true. It's entirely possible that when he kicked her out, she told herself they were just having a spat. And when he was with another woman he was just trying to make her jealous. I've seen people who have ignored everything they knew about some jerk, and spent years mourning the person they wished they had known. It's possible that she even blamed herself for his murder. I can see a whole train of thought for that. She tells herself it's her fault that he threw her out. She wasn't pretty enough or compliant enough or giving him enough money. And it never would have happened if she had still been in his good graces that night. He wouldn't have gone out at all, or she would have been with him and the killer wouldn't have shot him in front of a witness, or whatever. I've spent hours listening to this kind of thing from other women. Maybe that's what made Catherine Broward kill herself."

"But she didn't do it right away," said Mallon.

"Right. It's been about a year since he died. Lydia tells me she drifted around from city to city after that, not really accomplishing anything or taking hold. She showed up at her sister's. That's not an unusual thing, making a last visit."

"I suppose not."

"They're not exactly saying good-bye. That would tip their families off. They're just sort of taking a last look. Sometimes they say something revealing. In this case, it seems she had convinced her sister that what was wrong with her life dated from the death of Mark Romano. All I can say for sure is, if he was a loss to anybody, he was no loss at all to her. They had broken up at least a couple of months before he was killed. She wasn't living with him. She wasn't even in L.A. She'd left about six weeks before he was shot."

"Before?" asked Mallon. "Are you sure?"

"I told you," she said. "We don't know everything, and we never find it out. But what we do know, we try to get right. She had been out of L.A. for six weeks before."

"Where?"

"Up north, staying on a ranch somewhere above Santa Barbara."

Lydia checked her watch. "We owe Angie a nice dinner, and our reservation is for eight. We'd better get back down the path before they give our table to some congressmen on a relief mission to Beverly Hills."

Mallon stood up. "You're right, Lydia. I'm getting hungry." He went to the door and opened it for her and Detective Berwell. For the rest of the evening they were surrounded by strangers, so the conversation became light and pleasant, and was limited to comments about the preparation of the food, the beauty of the hotel, and the gentle, cool June weather the city was having. Mallon joined in as well as he could, but now and then one of the others would notice that he was staring down at the table, his brow furrowed in thought.

||||||||||||||||||||||||||||||||||||||||||||||||||||||||||

CHAPTER 9

Mallon and Lydia walked Angela Berwell to the end of the wooden bridge, where the valet-parking attendant brought her car, and then watched her drive off into the night. Lydia was grateful to her for coming: she had wanted Mallon to hear the details directly from the investigating officer. She knew that at some point she was going to have to repay Angela's favor in some way, but she sensed that this was in keeping with this phase of her life. She seemed to have moved entirely into the realm of repaying favors, incurring new ones to repay the ones she had owed for years.

She had wanted very much to help Bobby Mallon, had an urge to reward him for being the kind of person he always had been, by finding the answers to his questions about Catherine Broward. But now it seemed clear what the rest of the revelations would be like. What she had just seen on tape had also raised a confusing mixture of feelings that were making things more difficult for her. She couldn't quite banish from her mind the wish that Bobby's concern had not been devoted to a young stranger who was already dead. Seeing the tape had raised feelings of jealousy, but also had given the girl a reality she had never had before. Lydia felt terribly sorry for her. She turned to Mallon. "Kind of a depressing story, wasn't it? Think you've heard all you need to hear?"

Mallon and Lydia walked back toward Mallon's bungalow. "What if she was afraid? What if the reason she left was that she sensed the danger, or even knew about it, and didn't want to be killed?"

"Maybe if we knew why he was killed, that would be a good theory," said Lydia. "In my experience, people aren't very good at sensing danger in advance. If they're scared, it's usually of the wrong thing."

"If he saw one of these guys commit a crime, and told her about it, she would know he was in trouble," said Mallon. "Or if he heard there was a big drug shipment coming in at a particular place and time, and he wasn't supposed to know. She might have panicked, run away, and regretted it later."

She looked at him with mild skepticism. "Nobody can rule any of those things out, or any other story we dream up. But if she knew Romano had seen or heard something that put him in danger, he should have known too, and run away. And you heard Angie," said Lydia. "The tape we saw was one of dozens. It's a hundred times more likely that he got killed for fucking somebody's girlfriend."

Mallon walked along for a few steps, then stopped. "Look at her behavior afterward—all of it. Maybe it was aimless, but maybe it wasn't. She moved from one city to another, got low-paying jobs, stayed a few months, and each time, she suddenly packed up and moved on again. She could have been wandering, but what she did was also exactly what you might do if you didn't want to be found. It's what parole violators used to do after they skipped out."

She shrugged. "Still do. Know of any reason why she wouldn't tell her sister she was afraid?"

"Not offhand."

"Know of any reason why she would spend all that time running to save her life, and then suddenly change her mind and kill herself?"

"No. Maybe she realized running was futile. Maybe there was a reason not to be caught alive."

"You saw her go into the water. Was there any sign that she thought somebody was after her, or that she was in any hurry?"

"Not then," Mallon admitted. "But she didn't seem to be willing to put it off for one more day." He shook his head and walked on. "But no. I specifically asked her if she was running from something, and she denied it. There was no reason not to tell me the truth."

"I'm not so sure about that," said Lydia.

Mallon unlocked the door of his bungalow and they entered. "I don't get it."

"I understand your attraction to her better now that I've seen her in the buff," said Lydia. "Since I was forced to watch that tape, it kept occurring to me that this was a woman who was sincerely interested in the man she was with. I think it was true that she was in love with him, and doted on him, and would have cared about his every move. It's hard to believe she wasn't curious about what he was up to. What else do we know? We can be pretty sure that whatever got Mark Romano killed, it wasn't innocence."

Mallon tried to formulate a suitable answer, but he found that he had nothing to say. He nodded, to acknowledge that he had heard.

"That would be a motive for Catherine to not to tell you the truth about things, to open up to you." She waited, then said carefully, "I'm not saying she was involved in something illegal, but maybe something was worrying her that we don't know about. Maybe we've made some false assumptions about her. Think back on how she behaved with you. I mean, she hopped right into bed, but wouldn't tell you her name."

"I'm sorry," said Mallon. "I know you're right to bring it up, but I don't think so. And I don't think I'm fooling myself about her. One of the things that you're thinking is that she had sex with me for some hidden reason, some practical reason, like money or a place to hide. But I had offered her money and a place to stay hours before that. Yes, the sex happened, and it was surprising at the time. But it's a kind of information that seems at first to be important but, finally, isn't."

"How can it not be important?" asked Lydia.

"Because I understand it, and it leads nowhere. She had complicated reasons for doing it, but none of them were causes of her suicide—just the opposite. The sex was possible because the suicide was already a certainty. She knew that I had made a big effort to save the life of a complete stranger and asked nothing in return. She saw that I was a middle-aged heterosexual guy who lived alone and had spent his day alone, and realized that a convincing and generous demonstration of her appreciation would be to seduce me. I also like to think that she told me the truth, and really did feel an unaffected urge to do it. Since she knew she was going to die that night, she thought, 'Why not? What have I got to lose?' And she did it. Do you see? It wasn't for gain, because she didn't accept anything from me—not even dinner. Having sex with me didn't obligate her to tell me anything, not even her name. And none of this tells us why she killed herself."

She studied him for a moment. "I suppose it doesn't. I guess we know why she did it: Mark Romano broke up with her."

"I don't," said Mallon. "Just because Mark Romano broke up with other girlfriends, it doesn't mean he broke up with Catherine, does it? We assume that's what happened, that she lied to her sister out of embarrassment, or that she deluded herself into thinking he didn't mean it or something. What if the reason she never told her sister is that it never happened, that he never broke up with her?"

"Well, for one thing, she gave her sister a new phone number, then another one six weeks before he was killed, remember?"

"One was probably the ranch where she was staying near Santa Barbara."

"Maybe," Lydia conceded. "But the rest of what she told her sister was a fantasy. This guy was a slimy little character who preyed on women. He got killed because he was a bum who hung around with bums. He pissed somebody off. No mystery there. But she told her sister what a great catch he was."

"I can imagine her telling her sister a reassuring lie that would keep her from worrying. But Catherine didn't seem like a person who would delude herself to that extent."

"Okay," said Lydia. "I guess she preferred the delusion that Mark Romano would treat her differently from the way he'd treated everybody else. I'm not sure that we're ever going to know exactly what she thought, but—"

"I get the point," Mallon interrupted. "No matter what she thought, being with him is evidence of some delusion."

Lydia sighed as she sat on the couch. "It's my professional opinion that we've reached the point of diminishing returns. Whatever nuance you read into the story, the essentials are not going to change: she ran into a guy who was very good-looking, who knew how to be charming, and fell in love with him. I think the fact that he had her tape among a couple of dozen others indicates that she was nothing special, and I accept Angie's theory that he got tired of her and broke up with her. But I don't insist on it. Even that doesn't matter. Either way, we know she was deprived of his company forever by the shooter. She was depressed about it—felt guilt for running away, or regret for not letting him take even more advantage of her, or sadness at being dumped, or shame for being with him at all—and took herself out."

"But which story is it?" asked Mallon. "We still don't know, and it makes a difference."

"You're the client, Bobby," said Lydia. "It's still your money and your choice. If you want, we'll keep looking into it until we can determine which it was, or until we find that we can't. But if you're ready to quit now, I'll refund the part of your advance we haven't already spent and call it even."

"I want to keep looking," said Mallon. "I have the feeling it's not over, but I don't know where to look next."

Lydia sighed. "If you're trying to find out some single fact that changes everything, that will make you feel satisfied that things happened for the best, you're going to be out of luck."

"Don't you really mean that I'm out of luck if I'm trying to convince myself that I did and said the right things?" asked Mallon.

"I guess I do," said Lydia. "Look, I've known you forever, Bobby. I understood from the beginning that you're not just a rich guy who's got morbid curiosity about some young girl. You cared about her a lot. Probably in about a month, she could have gotten you to marry her if she'd wanted. I'm just reminding you that no matter what we find out, we already know there wasn't a happy ending." She squinted her eyes for a moment, then said wearily, "But I suppose you still want to do it."

Mallon nodded. "I still want to do it."

"Well, there are things we can still look into. I might be able to find out more about these guys Romano knew who were involved in drugs."

"That's about him. It doesn't tell us anything about Catherine," Mallon said. "I need to know what she was thinking."

Lydia looked up at him and nodded. At some point, Lydia supposed, she was going to have to fire her client.

"Maybe I'll check with Detective Fowler in Santa Barbara and see if there's anything new he can tell me," she said. "They've had a chance to look around in Catherine's apartment here in L.A., and maybe something turned up there. The apartment has been locked up, but as soon as her sister gets here, that's over. Unless there's some indication that it's not a suicide after all, they won't hold anything. Sarah will probably retrieve a few family mementos, dump the rest, and take her sister home to bury her." She stood up. "Well, I'm tired. I'll get started on all of that in the morning, and I'll give you a call before noon. In the meantime, don't be too hard on yourself. The more we learn, the clearer it is that this had nothing to do with what you did or didn't do. You couldn't stop it, because you didn't cause it."

He studied her. "You don't just mean Catherine's death, do you?"

"I mean both of them." She suddenly leaned close to him and gave him a kiss on the cheek, then went to the door and let herself out.

As she drove away from the hotel, she glanced at the address she had retrieved from her computer earlier in the day, and headed east on Sunset toward Hollywood. Many times in the past twenty years she had been down to Los Angeles looking for clients who had decided to lose themselves. She knew the area between Franklin and Santa Monica Boulevard well, and when she had seen the address in the purse the day after Catherine's death, she had thought she could even place the building in her memory. She had been right. It was not one of the old apartment buildings with decorative 1920s facades that had been refurbished in the past few years. It was a nearly new four-story stucco rectangle with rows of identical balconies and rows of identical aluminum windows that did not fit the neighborhood, a structure that managed to be ugly in spite of its simplicity. It was a bit after midnight when she came to the door of Catherine Broward's apartment. She had considered doing this later, when the neighbors would be in their deepest sleep, but she had decided that coming later raised the stakes too high. If someone heard her at midnight, they would hear other sounds too, sounds coming from other parts of the building and sounds from the street. At twelve, she was probably a resident coming home from a party. At three, she was a burglar.

Lydia was glad to see that the locks on the doors along the corridor were a cheap, standard five-tumbler model that she was comfortable opening. She rechecked the apartment number, removed the pick and tension wrench from the lining of her purse, and began to work the lock. It took only a few seconds, and she turned the knob and entered.

She closed the door quietly, locked it, and stood still, letting her eyes adjust to the dim light from the sliding glass doors on the balcony and listening for sounds that would indicate that someone had heard her. When she was ready she went to the glass doors and closed the drapes, then turned on her small flashlight and let its narrow beam show her the general structure of the place. She was in a compact living room, with an off-white couch and matching chair probably bought from Ikea. Beyond this room was an alcove that served as a kitchen, furnished with a table and four chairs. She let the light play on the counter surfaces for a moment, then opened the refrigerator to confirm her theory: it was empty. Either Sarah had already gotten here and thrown out everything, or Catherine had decided to quit the world without leaving a mess behind.

She looked in a drawer to see which it was, and found silverware and kitchen knives, all clean and neatly arranged in segmented trays: Catherine. Sarah would have packed those. She felt forebodings of failure—messy people and ones who did not know they were about to die were more accommodating than ones who planned suicide. They left things around that would answer questions. But she also felt a kind of guilty relief, since she would be able to tell Bobby Mallon that she had risked a burglary charge to get in, and then found nothing. She moved into the single bedroom.

The bed was a platform with a futon covered by sheets and a quilt in bright colors that she guessed had probably come from Ikea too. There were a small dresser and a simple desk with four drawers. She moved immediately to the desk and opened them, knowing before she did that she was simply looking in all the obligatory places. The drawers were three inches deep, not big enough to hold a large collection of old papers. The top one held pens and pencils and paper clips, the second stationery. The rest were empty.

It was like a man's apartment—a dull man, at that. Catherine Broward had been a woman who traveled light. Or at least, she had ended as that kind of woman. Lydia suspected that no woman began that way. Happy women accumulated troves of things—furniture, cosmetics, clothes, useless trinkets, pictures, china, souvenirs. They were always adjusting their surroundings to suit them ever more closely. Even when they lived in apartments like this one, the kind of disposable architecture that any sensible person would know was doomed in the next earthquake, even when they were nomads who moved every year, they collected. She and all of the women she knew had a special energy for this incessant and pointless settling.

That was what was missing from Catherine Broward, that energy. Whatever it was that had really happened to her, it had left her depleted. And Lydia suspected that as she had moved from city to city, she had jettisoned things. Probably the first she would have thrown out were the very things Lydia could have used: receipts, canceled checks, letters.

Lydia opened the dresser drawers, but found nothing except the usual clothes, folded as though for display. She looked in the closet. The clothes were all hung with the same care, the shoes lined up underneath. On the shelf above, her light settled on some shoeboxes, so she reached for one. It did not feel as though it contained shoes, so she brought it down and opened it. The box was filled with bank statements. She looked at the front one, then at the one in the back, and saw that Catherine's filing system must have been determined by the size of her shoeboxes. She had kept her statements as long as they still fit, which was about three years. Lydia looked in the next box, which was full of canceled checks.

Lydia held the light in her mouth and fingered back through the checks to last August, when Mark Romano had died. But Catherine had been gone a couple of months before, so Lydia pulled out July, June, and May too. She put the stack of checks into her purse, then reached up for the third box. It was full of photographs. The oldest were from Catherine's childhood. The later ones had more clarity and the color got better and better because of the improvements in technology. There were a few of her as a teenager clowning with friends, then a prom picture, and a few of Catherine as a college student with some different friends. Lydia had no trouble identifying Catherine's sister.

When Lydia reached Mark Romano's era, she recognized him from the dim videotape. She studied the pictures to get a clearer look at his face. Sarah's description had barely done him justice. For the first time during this case, Lydia understood what had happened to Catherine Broward. A man that handsome would be nearly impossible to resist.

A woman with any imagination at all would be able to think up enough excuses for him to keep herself fooled for years. She sighed. A boyfriend who was too handsome was not a problem Lydia Jean Marks was going to have in this life. If this one was what they were like, maybe it was just as well.

She leafed through more photographs, and began to see more pictures of Romano and Catherine together: the dead couple at play on a beach, in a park, at a party. Instinctively—maybe because she knew a bit about him, and maybe because she identified with any woman who had been treated that way—she found herself hating Mark. She liked Catherine. In the pictures she had a good-natured face rather than a beautiful one, and the tapes had shown a body that was nice, but not spectacular. She looked like a good companion, a person who could tell a funny story.

As Lydia looked at the pictures, she noticed that she was feeling sleepy. If she had known she would be doing this, she would not have had wine with dinner at the hotel. When Mark's time was up, the pictures ended. There were none that seemed to have been taken after that. She selected the photographs she wanted and put the rest back.

She kept searching the apartment patiently and carefully, but increased her pace. When she ran out of shoeboxes she stood on a chair to be sure she had found everything on the upper shelf. She looked under the frame of the futon, in the cupboards of the little kitchen. All she found confirmed the sparse and frugal tone of the place: a set of four plates, a set of four glasses, a set of four coffee cups and saucers. There were no more papers.

Lydia took a final look around her with her flashlight, wishing she had brought Bobby Mallon with her to see this place. Maybe he would have understood the girl better. Catherine had prepared everything she was leaving behind, absolutely certain that the next visitors would arrive after she was dead. By the time Bobby Mallon had seen her, there was nothing he could have done that would have changed anything.

Lydia used her flashlight to take a last look in her purse, ticking off the things she had kept: a good, clear photograph of Mark Romano and a good one of Catherine Broward, both from sometime late in their relationship; one of them together taken at a beach; the most recent bank statement from the shoebox; a stack of checks. She told herself that taking these things didn't matter. The negatives for the pictures were still in the box in envelopes, the bank statement could be duplicated, and the checks were a year old. Taking them was a felony, but so was being here at all. There was no use for them except to somebody who was examining Catherine Broward's death in detail, and nobody seemed to think there was anything left to know except Robert Mallon.

卌

"You were in her apartment?" Mallon was incredulous. "You broke in?"

Lydia said, "Breaking in sounds a lot more interesting than what I did. Nothing is broken. Nobody will notice I was there, and what I took is of no value to anyone but us."

Mallon watched as Lydia opened the plain manila envelope she carried, and began placing things on the table near the window that overlooked the bungalow's little garden. "Here. Take a look," she said.

Mallon studied the photographs. The two with Catherine Broward in them were painful to look at. This was a version of the sensation he had sometimes felt when he saw pictures of happy Europeans taken just before World War II. In the midst of this happiness, did they have any tiny feeling that something was coming, any fear that something about this day wasn't quite right?

He took his eyes off Catherine Broward and studied the boyfriend. The photograph was clearer and brighter than the videotape had been. Romano had been tall, lean, and well-formed, his face almost too good, too big-eyed and perfect, so his looks almost crossed the line and became feminine. He had the sort of appearance that teenaged girls liked—the look of a boy, really, because boys weren't as frightening as men.

There was a bank statement. Mallon looked at the address of the branch in West Los Angeles and saw that the date was only a month ago. There were about fifteen checks written for sums that invited him to identify them. Eleven hundred near the end of the month was her rent, because it was even. Thirteen hundred eighty-two and forty-nine cents on the third was a credit card bill that had arrived on the first. One twenty-seven thirteen was probably electricity. It couldn't have been gas because it was summer and she would have used no heat. His eyes stopped at the balance, a bit over one hundred and twelve thousand dollars. There had been one deposit: twenty thousand even on the first of the month.

Lydia seemed to have read his expression. "The balance?"

"That and the only deposit."

"The deposit is the same every month. I think it's a trust fund. She and her sister probably each got twenty thousand a month. I could see from the apartment that she didn't spend much, so the balance tended to grow on her. Now and then she would write a check to move some to a savings account. If she moved it from there, I didn't see the record. She doesn't seem to have been an investor: she didn't have much interest in the distant future."

Mallon was silent.

"What are you thinking?"

"I'm trying to catch up. I guess I never thought of her in those terms. For a young woman who worked as a waitress, she was pretty wealthy."

Lydia hesitated. She was not sure whether she wanted to show Mallon her next exhibit. She knew that if she showed it to him, Mallon would jump to conclusions again. The ironic part of it was that Lydia knew any detective should be eager to show it to Mallon. It would make Mallon want to keep paying her for the next year. Delving for ever-more-minute details of Catherine Broward's short life was a lot easier than going back to the bail bond shop to begin hunting down the next violent jerk that Harry managed to bail out of jail. But Lydia was determined not to take advantage of Bobby Mallon's guilt. She let herself think wistfully for a moment of putting it all back in the envelope and saying, "Well, that's it. That's all she left lying around." Instead, she reached into the envelope again and produced one of the canceled checks she had stolen.

She laid it on the table beside the photographs. It was for forty thousand dollars, and the date was last July 15. It said, "Pay to the order of Safe-Force School of Self-Defense," and the notation written on the line in the lower left said, "July 15–August 15." She said, "There are two of these, both to the school, to pay up to September fifteenth."

She watched Mallon bend over it and stare. He picked it up and turned it over to read the stamped endorsement. "Deposit only SF Self-Defense." The bank was in Ojai, California. Mallon placed the check back on the table and stared at Lydia impassively.

Lydia said, "Don't read too much into this."

Mallon's left eyebrow arched. "July fifteenth through September fifteenth, Lydia. She was off taking a self-defense course when her boyfriend got killed. How can that be a coincidence?"

"I'm not saying it was a coincidence. I'm just not assuming it means she knew he was in danger."

"Then what was she afraid of?"

"It doesn't even mean she was afraid."

Mallon's other brow rose. "Forty thousand bucks a month?"

Lydia shrugged.

Mallon pressed her. "Forty thousand bucks for four weeks at a self-defense camp, and she's not afraid?"

"It's not much time if you're not doing anything else, and forty thousand is not much money if your trust fund brings in twenty thousand while you're gone."

"Forty thousand is not much money compared to my bank account either, but forty thousand bucks is still forty thousand bucks. It has an objective value. I know that most people work a long time to get that much, even if I don't. To throw it away is disrespectful to them."

"You worked most of your life, built a couple of businesses. You learned young. She probably didn't."

"She worked as a waitress, not once, but several times in different cities. She wouldn't have to do too many shifts on her feet to get the idea."

"Maybe it was a lark," said Lydia. "You know: go to some fancy ranch with a couple of girlfriends, learn a few judo moves, and discharge a firearm at a target a couple of times."

"That's not a lark. For forty grand she could have gone anywhere." Mallon frowned at the check. "Depending on who you talk to, she was either in the midst of the love affair of her life or she had just been dumped. Either way, it doesn't sound like a time to go out of town for intensive self-defense training, does it?"

"It could be a response to her boyfriend's social set. Maybe they just gave her the creeps."

"Then she was afraid, exactly as I said," Mallon insisted. He looked at Lydia expectantly.

"All right. We're never going to figure out what she was thinking by sitting here and making up stories," said Lydia. "We've got to go back up to Santa Barbara anyway if we're going to get anything out of Detective Fowler. Why don't we drive up? On the way we can take a detour, have a look at this self-defense school. Maybe they'll be able to tell us what the hell she was doing there while her boyfriend was down here getting himself killed."

CHAPTER 10

||||||||||||||||||||||||||||||||||||||||||||||||||||||||||||||||||||||||||

The Safe-Force School of Self-Defense was not easy to reach. Mallon followed the route with a road map while Lydia drove. They were over forty-five minutes north of Ojai on the winding highway into Los Padres National Forest before they spotted the turnoff on the right. They followed the smaller tributary road eastward into the rising, tree-covered hills as the pavement narrowed into something under two lanes. At several points, flat spaces beside the shoulders had been cleared to provide turnouts so a driver could pull over and let vehicles behind him pass.

The first sign of habitation on the road was a high chain-link fence that began before Mallon noticed it. Mallon had simply tired of looking to his right into some woods that ran up a slight rise and left no view. He stared ahead at the road for a time, looked to the right again, and saw that a fence had begun. He turned around in his seat and verified that it stretched back for some distance. It had not caught his attention at first because there was tall brush on the inner side that had grown through the wire, keeping the fence in shadow, muting the metallic gleam and keeping the eye from perceiving the straight boundary line. The coiled razor wire along the top was above eye level, and in some places climbing plants had grown into it as though it were a trellis.

After a time an open gate interrupted the fence. There was no sign, but an oversized rural mailbox at the first gatepost had the stenciled words SAFE-FORCE SCHOOL. Between the posts was the beginning of a long, straight gravel drive that led into the property, past some low wooden buildings and one in the distance that looked about the size and shape of a barn. A short way in there was a parking lot on one side of the drive that held about fifteen cars, and on the other, a sprawling one-story ranch house with a rough board exterior and a large roofed-over front porch above a row of benches and a drinking fountain.

Lydia drove into the parking lot and glided to a stop between two freshly painted white stripes. She turned off the engine and opened her door. In the sudden silence they both heard a distant report of a gun. As Lydia stood, she turned her head and listened. There was a rapid *pop-pop-pop.* She pointed up the long, gradual slope of the hillside beyond the driveway. "Sounds as though the rifle range is over there someplace."

"Yeah," said Mallon. "Only that sounded like a pistol, didn't it? Maybe a forty-five, or a nine-millimeter?"

"Sounds about right to me," she said.

They closed the car doors and walked across the driveway toward the low ranch house. As they approached it, a tall, lean man in a khaki shirt with button pockets and tinted aviator glasses stepped out of the building onto the porch to wait for them.

𝍸

The gunshots had come from the other side of the long hill, where a young woman named Marcia Teller held her nine-millimeter Smith & Wesson pistol at her side, muzzle downward, as she walked carefully along the path at the bottom of the arroyo. The combat range was supposed to be a simulated battle, but the battle had rules. There could be no accidental discharges, no wild shots of the sort that indicated she was afraid of her weapon, and if a round misfired and jammed the gun, she would have to stop, flop to her belly, and clear it before she showed herself again.

As she took her next step, another target popped up to her right, a cardboard cutout in the shape of a man's head and torso. She went to a two-handed grip and a bent-kneed crouch, fired three shots into the target's chest, then pivoted to face forward again. The targets were spring-loaded on their own stands so they could be moved to different hiding places each day. The range master triggered them with a remote control.

She walked up the arroyo another hundred feet, watchful and tense. She knew she had gotten the first two with something close to perfection, and it made her feel more serious, more committed to the game.

The third one popped up ahead and to her left, so close it made her jump. She let a small involuntary cry escape as she dropped to one knee and fired twice through its chest. She stood and advanced again. The third target had been good for her. It had reminded her that all the speed necessary was in efficient, deliberate movement: it pops up, you aim, you fire. When she had come out here the first time, she had mistaken the course for a quick-draw contest, and she had failed humiliatingly. Now she was calm and unhurried, and she was splendid.

The next ambush was especially devious. The target came up behind her: how had she passed that bush without seeing it? She did as her instructors had drilled her to do, not shuffling to turn in place but stepping, bringing her foot around with her so that before she faced the target she had already moved a pace to the side. She fired too low this time, maybe not a fatal first shot, but she compensated by bringing the barrel up, and when she fired again she saw a spot of light open in the center of the faceless head.

Marcia remembered to repeat the step-around to face forward in time to see the next target appear ahead of her, as though the two targets had been trying to get her in a crossfire. She placed two rounds into that one, and dropped to the ground to reload. She pressed the catch to release the magazine, removed it from the bottom of the grips, and put it into the pocket of her canvas jacket. Then she inserted a new clip and used the heel of her hand to push it home. She pulled the slide to cycle the gun and put a round into the chamber, then looked up, rose to her feet, and stepped forward.

There were ten targets—assailants, enemies—and she spotted all of them, one after another. Sometimes, as in the fourth and fifth, more than one came up in rapid succession, as real enemies did, ganging up, taking advantage of the very ability to focus and concentrate that she had so laboriously developed to become a competent pistol shot. Everyone had been told that a "pass" was to get all of them. Wasn't that what would have been required in real life? The one you missed would kill you—a "fail." There were no grades beyond those.

At the end of the arroyo she leaned her backside against a big sandstone rock, released the magazine, and cleared the round that was left in the chamber, then stood waiting for Parish to come up and congratulate her.

It was Spangler, the firearms instructor, instead. He was striding up the arroyo in his khaki shorts and hiking boots and red sleeveless T-shirt. "Good shooting, Marcia!" he called. "It's a pass!"

She looked up from her weapon and smiled diffidently to hide her disappointment. "Thank you, Paul," she said. Her eyes moved beyond him and flicked here and there to interpret distant shapes, searching for the tall, thin shape of Parish.

Spangler read the expression. "Michael had to run off ahead of us a minute ago. He got a call to tell him there were some visitors."

"Did he see the shooting?"

"Oh, sure," said Spangler. "Practically all of it. He said to tell you he would speak with you later." He looked back up the long, twisting streambed, glanced at his watch, then turned to her. "Come on. Let's go look at your targets."

They walked to the last one, and he used his index finger to poke each of the holes she had put into the effigy. "Here's your fatal shot, to the heart. This one down here would be very painful and incapacitating, but not a kill." He took two gummed squares of paper from his pocket and stuck them over the bullet holes so the enemy was healed, then pushed the metal rod that held the target back into its trap so its catch held the target down. He placed a few cut boughs over it, stared at it critically, and moved to the target she had shot before that one.

At each stop, as he patched and reset the target, he gave an evaluation. "This one you got four times. That's what I like to see. This hit to the head was your third or fourth round. If you hadn't taken that shot, who knows? Your earlier shots are keeping him from killing you, and maybe he'll bleed to death, but this is what we're after." They went on.

"Now this one is a bit thin, just two hits in the chest, but no sure fatals. I made the other one pop up across from him right away, so you had to turn around and get him too. In the street, what do you do? They're both down. You come back to the first and put a hole in his head, and then the other."

Marcia listened attentively and seldom spoke. Spangler was the firearms instructor, the one who had given the classroom instruction and taught the mixed group of men and women how to break down a weapon, clean it, clear jams, and recognize worn or damaged parts. Then he had taken them out to the range and taught them how to fire effectively. But somehow, she had expected that Parish would stay to see her test this morning, and that he would be the one to talk to her about it afterward. Spangler was a technician. He was an expert, but he was not the master. She had looked for the quiet, brooding presence of Parish this morning. She felt almost as though she had gotten less than her money's worth because he had not watched all of her test.

When Spangler had reset the first target she had hit, he glanced at his watch again. "Where do you go next?"

"Hand-to-hand is in about a half hour."

Spangler grinned. "Drink plenty of water before. It's going to be hot today, and your stomach won't hold what you'll need if you take it in all at once." He paused, then said, "And rest a bit. You earned it."

Spangler patted her shoulder, and Marcia began the walk back to the main lodge. The dry brown hills were dotted with short, round California oaks with dusty leaves. Beyond them to her right was a wooded area, some parts of it tall pines, and the rest thick with a growth of bushes and deciduous trees. Here and there among the rocks on the high ridges above the ranch where trees would not grow were a few shin-high paddle-shaped cactus plants that had grown in to fill the gaps.

She came to the beginning of the path. This was the way she had always been led back from the firing range after group instruction, but today a new thought occurred to her. She would be testing soon in the hand-to-hand combat class too. What if they were planning to spring another test on her today? This would be the perfect moment, when she was feeling overconfident about her skills, and preoccupied thinking about the test she had just passed. It would be just like them to do something like that.

As soon as Marcia thought of it, she was sure of it. She would be walking along the familiar path, probably with her eyes on the ground ahead to be sure there were no snakes, and out of the bushes would come Debbie Crane, probably wearing olive-green cargo pants and top, but she would not neglect to tie on her black belt. She would throw Marcia to the ground just hard enough to hurt her, and then put some hold on her that was incapacitating and humiliating. That would be Marcia's martial arts lesson for today: be alert at all times, especially when you were walking a familiar, predictable route. Hand-to-hand class was not a place, a gym with mats on the floors. It was a discipline for life.

Marcia stopped and listened. It would be both of them, Debbie Crane and Ron Dolan too. If there weren't two of them, who would serve as the witness to her failure? But if it was both of them, maybe she would hear them whispering while they waited for her. No, she thought. They could hardly not have noticed when the shooting had stopped. The memory of the shooting made a horrible thought occur to her: what if it was Parish too? What if he had skipped seeing her triumph so he could be in position to watch her humiliation and then lecture her about it?

What could she do? Debbie was not somebody Marcia could defend herself against. When she was demonstrating something on the mats, she would allow herself to be thrown, or put down, or blocked, but always her movements were a parody of a big, dumb attacker. There would always be some movement—a startling roll and jump to recover, or even a flip—to remind the class that she had been playing. Sometimes when she was having them repeat some kick or blow over and over, she would begin to do kicks and punches or combinations of her own, at twice the speed, to keep time with them. It appeared to be the result of nervous energy, a kind of athleticism that was uncontrollable. But it was frightening. The kicks and punches were always hard and fast, and it took no imagination to judge where they would catch an opponent. Sometimes Marcia would feel a phantom pain in the spot Debbie was aiming at, like a warning.

Ron would not be the one to ambush Marcia, because that would be too extreme. He would be the witness. He was about six feet four and very muscular. She had thought, when she first saw him, that his being a martial arts instructor was incongruous: what opponent could he ever face that he couldn't simply beat up without using all the throws and holds and secrets?

She wished it would be Ron. He would be gentle, to keep from harming her. He would only need to put a hand on her to control her and make his point. That would not be what Debbie did. For the first time after a month of study, Marcia gave herself permission to admit that she hated Debbie. There was something sick about the way she treated the women. She always implied that they had gone through life using their sex out of laziness, to avoid effort, and out of cowardice, to avoid danger. But she was here to unmask them and force them to experience what they feared. Look at you, and look at her—the tiny waist, the round breasts under her sports top, the firm, rounded bottom—wasn't she as much a woman as you?

Marcia stepped off the path to her right and made her way through the grove of oaks that bordered the pine woods. She walked as quietly as she could, straining her ears to hear any sound from the direction of the path, and keeping her eyes in motion to watch for any sign of human beings ahead.

She concentrated on staying about fifty feet to the right of the path. She desperately wanted to foil their plan, but she also wanted to keep from missing the set of low wooden buildings that made up the main part of the camp. The few times she had been inland from the ocean in California, she had learned that hiking wasn't the way it had been in the East. If you took a shortcut or walked away from a road, you might have to walk a hundred miles before crossing another, and that wasn't something you could do. The camp was inside an area called Los Padres National Forest, but when she had looked at a map it had seemed that beyond the forest was not a populated area, only even emptier wilderness. If she walked in the wrong direction, she had no idea whether she would ever be found.

Her ear caught a faint rustling sound to her left, and she stopped. She could see along a narrow gully that formed a break in the low, thick trees. She had been right. Debbie Crane was crouching there waiting for her to come up the path. Ron Dolan walked up the gully toward her, zipping up his pants. He was walking through thick brush, and Marcia knew he had left the ambush to urinate in privacy. The noise of his return seemed to infuriate Debbie. She waved one hand at him, while her other held a finger to her lips.

He stared up the path in the direction of the combat firing range to verify that Marcia was not nearby, then sat down with a bored expression to wait.

Marcia remained still until he turned his head to look up the path again, then she hurried across the gully and off into the cover of the trees. She felt elated as she approached the compound. She had passed two tests today. She emerged from the trees far from where she had expected to. She realized that she must be near the road, because she heard the whispery sound of a car moving along on pavement. She followed the sound until she reached the high chain-link fence, and followed it to the gravel driveway that led to the main lodge.

As she walked past the veranda in front of the lodge, Parish stepped out of the doorway, followed by a man and a woman she had never seen before. The man was maybe forty-five and tanned, like an outdoorsman. The woman was only a bit shorter and wide, not soft the way an overweight woman usually was, but big like a woman who did physical labor—or maybe a policewoman. Marcia wondered if they might not be new instructors. She stopped to drink from the water fountain near the door.

Parish's eyes widened slightly as he saw her, and she knew she had surprised him, but for the moment he ignored her presence and spoke to the man. "I was very sorry to hear it, of course. Any person you've spent time trying to know and trying to teach becomes a special friend."

The woman said, "Did she seem to be afraid when she arrived?"

Parish said, "Afraid?" He paused and squinted into the distance, as though that were where the past could be found. "No. She didn't." He focused on the man. "You met her, Mr. Mallon. Did she strike you as a fearful person?"

The man he had called Mr. Mallon said, "No. But I wonder if a young woman would spend that kind of time and money on self-defense unless there was a clear reason."

Parish looked at him thoughtfully. "There is a reason. As a rule, the students come here because they want to learn something new. They want to improve themselves. Virtually all of the older ones have already achieved a great deal in their lives, some in business or the professions, a few in the arts. It's a certain kind of person who does that. He works terribly hard for all of his life to be better than his competitors, but even more, to be better than he was yesterday. After the initial goal is achieved—he's a success—he doesn't stop. The need isn't imposed by circumstance, it's internal. It doesn't matter whether we meet them at Catherine's age or seventy, it's still the same kind of person."

The woman said, "It's a lot of money to pay unless there's a reason that's a little more tangible, don't you think?"

"Our guests are the elite, people who are used to certain standards. The surroundings are intentionally kept rustic, but the amenities are expensive."

The woman persisted. "They must be, for over a thousand a day."

Parish seemed surprised at her attitude. "Our students receive a great deal of individual attention. This isn't just a guest ranch with a theme. We're dedicated to teaching a discipline that's difficult to learn properly, and can be terribly dangerous unless it's studied under the strictest supervision." His eyes were on their way to the man when they stopped. "Excuse me," said Parish, and held up a hand. He quickly glided to Marcia's side, leaned close to her, and murmured, "This isn't on the way from the range. Is something wrong out there?"

Marcia smiled slyly and shook her head. "I decided to take a different way back, just this once."

Parish grinned and gripped her shoulder. "Good instinct. Exceptional. I'll talk to you about this later." He glanced at his watch. "You just have time to beat them to the gym." He launched her up the gravel driveway with a gentle pat on the shoulder.

As she strode off toward the gym, she heard Parish saying, "I apologize for not introducing you, but my policy is to protect my students' privacy and anonymity to the extent that I can. What were we saying?"

As soon as Marcia was around the bend in the drive, she broke into a run. Five minutes later, she was lying comfortably on the thick mat, staring at the bare beams of the barnlike roof, when she heard the door open. Ron Dolan walked to her feet and looked down at her. When she met his eyes, she saw him smile. As he walked away, Marcia sat up. Debbie had silently stepped in the door after him. She was standing to the side of the doorway, contemplating Marcia with her eyes narrowed and the full lips she was so proud of compressed into a thin, pale line.

Marcia stared back at her for a few seconds, her eyes wide with false innocence and expectation. Finally, Debbie spoke. "Congratulations. You're beginning to get the idea. Let's do some stretches to warm up before the others arrive and we can get started."

━━━

CHAPTER 11

The fire in the fireplace had been allowed to burn out when the rest of the guests had gone to their cabins for the night, but Marcia could see the reflection of a row of red embers in Parish's eyes as he turned toward her and began to speak. "Before we go out into the field, it's essential that you understand how the hunt works, what everyone does." Parish sat in a hard, straight-backed chair just like Marcia's, his knees almost close enough to touch hers. He leaned his tanned face forward as he spoke, his light hazel eyes never blinking or straying from hers. She had sometimes thought she detected a faint remnant of a foreign accent when he spoke, and this felt like a foreign mannerism. An American would have placed a desk between them that had no function except to be between them.

"This is going to be your hunt, but with you will be a team to en-sure that your hunt is successful and safe." He paused, and she de-cided that during the second's delay he was studying her to be sure that she had heard and understood the words precisely as he had meant them. That was another hint, just a small indication that he was not a native English speaker, did not have the native speaker's certainty that his words had been the right ones, spoken perfectly. They had been.

Parish turned to look away for the first time, and glanced at Emily Lyons. "Your tracker will be Emily. She will be doing precisely what it sounds like. She goes out ahead, and finds the target. When she has, she signals the party to come ahead. She stays on the scene, keeping him in sight."

Marcia looked at Emily Lyons, who nodded and gave a quick, businesslike smile. She was about thirty and small, with dark, curly hair and very white skin, and a compact body that looked as though she had done some gymnastics when she was young. Her face was pretty, and it made Marcia feel jealous and defensive, and that made her feel stupid. She had tried to break herself of the habit of looking at other women that way. Was she engaged in a competition with Emily Lyons over Michael Parish, for Christ's sake? Hardly. She nodded at Emily Lyons and turned back toward Parish in time to see him point at the other woman in the room.

"Mary will be your scout."

This one was, if anything, a bit scarier to Marcia, because Mary O'Connor was attractive in the same way that Marcia was. She was tall, thin, and athletic looking, with long red hair that had gone to strawberry in highlights from the sun. Marcia forced herself to stop thinking about her and listen to Parish.

"But it all starts with the tracker. The tracker finds your target and immediately signals the main party. While the main group comes up, the tracker stays with the target. She's prepared to move with him, to note exactly where he's going. He remains her responsibility all the way through. If he smells trouble and bolts, she stays on his trail. If the client takes a shot but only wounds him and he keeps running, she stays after him and follows him to ground. She never loses sight of him, if she can avoid it. Do you understand?"

"Yes," said Marcia.

"Good. Now, the main party comes up. Its purpose is to bring the hunter—that's you—into close proximity to the target so you can get a clear, unimpeded shot that will result in a clean kill."

"The main party? How many?"

"Usually it's just a scout and a professional hunter. The scout on this hunt is Mary. She stays a bit apart to watch and handle any external factor on the scene that might interfere with the hunt. If the target seems to be in a good place for a shot—say, alone in the middle of a field—but then a group of picnickers comes along and gets in the way, she would have to handle that. The easiest way to think about it is that the tracker's responsibility is the target, and the scout's responsibility is the place: seeing and averting external problems. She's a lookout."

"What about the professional hunter?"

"This time that's me," said Parish. "My sole responsibility is the client, the amateur hunter. I stay with you at all times. I help you move into the best possible position. I provide you with the proper weapon, check all conditions with the tracker and the scout, get the all clear, and give you the go-ahead to fire."

"I get it," Marcia assured him. "The tracker shows up first, spots the target, then calls in the rest of us. The scout comes up separately, checks out the area, and the two of us come ahead together."

"That's right," said Parish. "It takes a little patience. We give the tracker and the scout as long as it takes to find the target, assess the conditions, and signal us. Only when everything is right do we commit ourselves."

She looked at him closely. "You're not really just there to say go, are you?"

Parish returned her gaze for a moment. "No. The professional's responsibility is the client, the person whose hunt this is. Sometimes the client will commit himself, then freeze. Sometimes the game doesn't simply take the shot and die. Sometimes he runs, or even charges. The person any mammal will attack is the one he recognizes as a threat. It will not be the tracker or the scout, whom he's already seen and discounted as innocuous. The client will not be used to that sort of thing, and may hesitate. At that point, the professional hunter must try to bring him down before he harms the client." Parish smiled. "None of those things are what usually happens. But the system allows the hunting party the flexibility to handle all the likely problems—not the least, worrying about them—and it leaves the client free to concentrate all of her senses on the pure enjoyment of the experience."

"It sounds very . . . effective," said Marcia. She didn't know whether that was the right thing to say, but it was all she could think of. She wanted him to know that she was smart enough to have understood, and that she would not be one of the ones who collapsed, who stepped out of cover and did not have the guts to fire, or did not have a steady enough hand to hit anything.

Parish went on. "That's the basic hunting party. Under difficult conditions we might add people. Usually it would be extra scouts, but if there is a need for special equipment, we might lay on a bearer or two. The essentials are the same. The method has been widely used over a two-hundred-and-fifty-year period of big-game hunting in India and Africa, and has worked on a hundred species, with surprisingly minor variations. What that indicates, at least to me, is that it takes advantage of fundamental aspects of the nature of all consciousness that has been developed on this planet. It works both on the vulnerability of the prey to an attack that comes from multiple hunters, and a peculiar ability in predators—lionesses, wolves, humans—to hunt cooperatively. The prey is confused and disoriented, but the hunters are each made bolder, quicker, and steadier."

Parish leaned back in his chair and the intensity left him. His body acquired the studied quiescence and ease that Marcia had noticed in the rest periods during the first month she had spent at the camp. At some periods of her life, she would have found his looks and his ways of moving and carrying himself intriguing. She knew that the relationship he had with the two women, Emily Lyons and Mary O'Connor, was, among other things, sexual. She did not have the patience to begin examining exactly why she knew that, and since she never intended to tell anyone, she did not bother to assemble proofs. She just knew it. At one time she would have vied to be the third. But not now. She had watched him all this time, thinking not that she wanted to be with him but that she wanted to be like him.

A second later she realized that this was exactly how the other two women had gotten here. They carried themselves in imitation of him, but a special kind, as a dancer is a mirror imitation of her partner: he steps back, she steps forward; he turns, she turns. The two women looked not at all like each other, but in motion they looked like his sisters. She did not feel jealous, and she did not want him. She wanted only to be the hunter he was for a time.

She gave in to an impulse. "When can we go? I'd like to do it as soon as possible."

"I know. That's the kind of spirit we like." He glanced at Emily and Mary. Both nodded at him and smiled knowingly, their eyes on him. They never looked at her. She suspected that they felt contempt for her, the sort of contempt that a woman feels for a potential rival, built of the competition rather than any real quality of hers. She did not care, and she did not detest them in return. She merely noted that they would do their jobs flawlessly, if they could. They would do anything rather than forfeit his confidence.

Parish said, "We'll go hunting tomorrow, for practice."

⊞⊞⊞

She awoke in her cabin before dawn, dimly aware that something had occurred, and that she needed to know what it was. She sat up quickly, and in the still-darkened corner of the room she saw a tall, silent figure standing. Marcia gasped and her muscles locked, while her heart seemed to skip, then pound. "What?" she rasped.

Mary O'Connor moved closer. Her red hair was tied back tightly. "It's time. Get up and get dressed. We're waiting outside." Then she turned, opened the door, and stepped out into the dark.

Marcia got up. She had seen in the dim light from the window that

Mary O'Connor had been wearing hiking boots, khaki shorts, and a sweatshirt, so she hurriedly put on a tank top, a sweatshirt, shorts, and her hiking boots. Then she stepped outside.

Mary O'Connor and Michael Parish were standing very close inside the shadow of the cabin—closer than two people intent on business would be—whispering. Marcia coughed just loudly enough to be sure they were aware of her. Mary's shadow separated from Parish's and floated quietly off up the dry hillside behind the cabin. Parish came close.

Marcia said, "What's happening now?"

"This works the way I described last night," he said. "Emily has gone out ahead of us to some likely places, tracking. When she finds the deer, she'll signal Mary to start up and bring us."

Marcia could see Mary O'Connor's tall, thin body kneeling near the top of the hill, one arm across her stomach with the other elbow propped on it to hold the small radio to her ear.

"Here." Parish picked up a rifle she had not seen leaning against the cabin wall and handed it to her. When she ran her hands along its stock and trigger guard, her fingers recognized it as one of the Remington Model 710 .30-06 bolt-action rifles she had used at the practice range. There was no scope on it today. He seemed to be watching her hands. "Use the factory sight. Put the bead in the notch, and the shot will be true."

Marcia saw Mary pop up suddenly. Her long arm waved once, and she turned and disappeared over the crest of the hill.

"Let's go," said Parish. "She found it."

They walked in silence for a minute or two, achieving the top of the hill without stepping on sticks or dislodging stones. Parish broke the silence, whispering. "Now we get ready to kill. Part of it is seeing. Part is feeling the shot in your own body as you take it. Big mammals are all pretty similar. You aim for the parts that you feel in yourself are vital: the head, heart, lungs. Here to here." Marcia felt his hand tap her on the side of the head, then again on the ribs, his hand just brushing the bottom of her right breast.

They walked on for a time. Marcia held the rifle diagonally in front of her, the left hand on the foregrip, and the right clutching the polymer stock just behind the receiver. Now and then she let her right index finger slide ahead of the trigger guard to touch the safety, or moved the hand forward to grasp the bolt for a second. She was rehearsing, trying to be sure she would get it right in the darkness, to be sure she would not fumble or hesitate.

They walked as the sky began to change, the light turned blue, and objects sharpened from dark blots to shapes that had definite boundaries, and then three dimensions. It was another half hour before the old, complicated oak trees began to have their deep green, and the sage and chaparral had lightened to gray and brown.

She noticed now that Parish had been looking past her to his left, not at her, and she followed his eyes to see that Mary O'Connor had reappeared. She was giving Parish some kind of arm signal again.

Parish stopped, touched Marcia's arm, and whispered in her ear. "It's just ahead, in a clearing by a narrow streambed. In the dry season they find small puddles to drink from. When we come into sight, it will go to your left. Lead it. You'll take one shot only. Get ready."

She lifted the bolt handle, pulled it back, pushed it forward and down to put a round in the chamber, pushed the safety off with her trigger finger, and moved forward slowly. She was aware that Parish was not walking beside her anymore but a few steps behind and to her right, then far enough back to be entirely out of sight and hearing, the space that mattered. He had removed himself. As long as she looked ahead, kept her ears tuned to hear the prey, she was alone.

She climbed the gradual rise, searching the landscape. She could see the tops of the first string of oak trees in a long line beyond the hill, and she knew they would grow that way along a streambed. As she reached the crest of the hill, she bent lower, then went to her belly and crawled, keeping her head from coming above the low weeds. She came forward until she could stare down the far side to see the green stripe across the brown field.

She saw the deer. It was standing perfectly still, its head up and its ears twitching, its eyes like big black marbles against its tawny fur. There was a moment of joy and gratitude at being permitted this sight, this beautiful wildness still there in front of her. But even in her first glimpse she could see it was edgy, nervous. It turned its body so it was facing left.

She formed a crook of her left elbow, propped the rifle on her left hand and stared through the notch sight, along the gleaming blue-black barrel to the bead above the muzzle. The deer's haunches bunched up suddenly, its back legs bent, and she knew it had to happen now.

She saw and felt the smooth, beautiful chest expand, and moved the bead in the center of the notch onto the spot where she could feel the heart beating, and squeezed the trigger. The rifle kicked hard against her shoulder and cheek, and the noise seemed to slap her ears and her stomach at the same time. She found herself standing, staring down toward the creek, but she couldn't see the deer. She took a step, but her arm was held in a tight grip. She turned. Parish was beside her. He took the rifle from her hands.

She could see Mary O'Connor off to the left, running at full speed down the hill toward the creek. In a second, she saw Emily Lyons stand up from the middle of some chaparral on the far hill, a rifle in her hand. She was pointing.

"Hurry," said Parish, and began to run.

Marcia launched herself forward, and the slope of the hill carried her down. She had to run a few paces, then dig in with her heels to stop herself, and then she was bounding forward across the short stretch of field. When she was at the streambed—no more than a narrow trench with a few muddy spots—she saw it. She stepped closer, but Parish gripped her arm again.

"Don't get in front of it. They sometimes get up and run."

"It's . . . alive?" she whispered.

"Come this way," he said. He pulled her closer. She was behind the deer and to its right. She could see the rib cage rising and falling, and hear a deep *huff* sound. There was blood on the animal's muzzle and on the ground. "See the blood—how red it is, and the bubbles? You hit the lungs. Maybe got enough of the heart to make it die."

Marcia looked up from the deer, and she could see Mary O'Connor coming closer. Marcia turned toward Parish, who nodded at Mary.

Mary O'Connor reached to her back, lifted the sweatshirt, and pulled out a pistol, then held it by the barrel, so the grips were toward Marcia. "Do you want to do it?"

Marcia turned, her eyes on Parish. "Yes," she said. "I should be the one."

Parish seemed unmoved, unconvinced. He didn't nod or show her his approval, just looked at his wristwatch. For a second, she hated him. She wanted him to do it. He should do this. No, she knew, he shouldn't. She took the pistol. She kept her eyes on it so she would not have to see the contemptuous look on O'Connor's face. She aimed it at the deer's head just behind the ear, and fired.

The sound of the pistol did not seem loud, and she realized that the rifle shot had made her ears feel stopped. She could see the deer give a reflexive kick, but it was dead. She reversed the pistol and handed it back to O'Connor. "Thanks," she said, her eyes on O'Connor's forehead.

O'Connor put the pistol away and pulled her sweatshirt over it again as Emily Lyons came up.

Parish said to Marcia, "It was a fair shot. Any time you put a deer down with the first one, and you don't have to tramp all over creation tracking it while it bleeds to death, it's a fair shot."

"What do we do with it?"

"Right now, we hang it from one of these trees and gut it, then let it bleed out while we walk back to get the pickup truck and drive it home. Then we'll butcher it, refrigerate some for dinner tonight, and freeze the rest."

She stared down at the deer. "It looks bigger up close."

He stared down. "It isn't bad." He seemed to be consciously, willfully evading what she had meant. "This is a pretty good buck for these hills." He took the pack off his back and produced a nylon rope. "May as well get started. Where's the best one, Mary?"

"There's an oak with a good horizontal limb right over there," she said, pointing.

He tied the rope around the rear hooves and dragged the carcass to the tree, then threw the rope over the limb and hoisted the deer off the ground upside down. He tied the other end of the rope around the trunk to hold it, then produced a long fixed-blade knife from his pack. He looked over his shoulder to be sure Marcia was still watching, then inserted the blade at the groin and, with a slight sawing motion, began the first long incision downward toward the center of the rib cage.

Marcia watched from beside him, because she knew that if she didn't he would tell her to. The other two women had walked off toward the camp carrying the rifles. She said nothing to Parish, asked nothing because it was all obvious. She knew why she'd had to come out here at dawn and hunt with these three. She knew why they had wanted her to have the feel of killing. Now, as she watched Parish making a slice and then pulling the intestines out of the animal, she knew why it could not have been a rabbit or something. It had needed to be nothing less than a full-grown buck.

CHAPTER 12

||||||||||||||||||||||||||||||||||||||||||||||||||||||||||

Marcia sat across the table from Michael Parish, drinking the bubbly water. She wanted a real drink—a strong one—but when Parish had ordered water, she'd had no choice. He had not ordered for her, and she could not remember his ever having said anything about alcohol. But she knew that what would get her through this was to do exactly as he did. Her gift for sensing what men expected and yielding to it was quicker, more reliable than her ability to figure out what was really required by the circumstances. She had to put faith in her alertness and in the subtle mimicry she had practiced all her life. They could be counted on because they were a weakness, and took no effort.

Sitting with him was disconcerting. His face was turned toward her, but his eyes kept focusing on a point beyond her left shoulder, as though he were a sly enemy watching someone sneak up behind her and trying to keep her from noticing. His conversation made the feeling stronger, because he was only prodding her into talking, to keep her calm and distracted, while he kept refocusing his eyes on Mary O'Connor, who was sitting alone in a booth thirty feet away.

"Did you come to this restaurant when you worked in Washington?"

"No," she answered. "It's a nice place, but most of its business comes because it's in the hotel. I think I was here maybe twice, just to meet out-of-town clients who were staying here and get them to pretend to read something and then sign it."

"Pretend to read it?"

She nodded, then realized that he was looking past her again, so she said, "Yes. Nobody can eat a meal and really read a legal document while a lawyer is sitting across the table providing helpful offers to explain anything that's not clear. If a lawyer really wanted him to understand it, the document would have been sent to him in advance. So they just pretend to read all of it, trying to buy the lawyer's respect by seeming to read rapidly and understand instantly. But they're distracted by the food, which is tantalizing, and it's also threatening because they want to eat it and are afraid it will get cold or the waiter will take it away, but they can't. They have to listen to what the lawyer is saying so they won't offend her or make her think they're stupid. And they're concerned about how they look."

"How they look?"

"Sure. Vanity. They're afraid to spill something on themselves. And do they look important to the strangers around them, reading contracts at lunch, or do they just look crude and commercial?"

"And how they look to the lawyer?"

"Of course," she agreed.

"When we talked before, you always seemed to resent that you were treated differently from the men," said Parish. "But it seems to me that what you're describing is you using your sexual attractiveness to confuse the other party in an agreement."

Her face flattened. She felt a wave of hot irritation at the nape of her neck. "My using it is different. It's mine to use. Mine," she repeated. "Not theirs."

"When a firm hires a lawyer, aren't they hiring the whole person?"

He was looking closely at her now. She wished he would look at O'Connor again. "That depends," she said firmly.

"Education? Grammar and diction?"

"Yes," she said. "Those things."

"Manners?"

"Sure, but—"

"Voice?"

She gave him a glare. "Within certain limits. If you had an irritating way of speaking that wasn't the product of a handicap or something, it probably would be legal not to hire you."

"And if you have a soft, musical voice that men find pleasant, it would be legal to consider that an asset, wouldn't it? Surely when you went in front of a judge and jury you used that voice."

"This isn't about me."

"Of course it is," Parish insisted. "What about your eyes and your hair? Your complexion?" He smiled. "Your figure?" He seemed to know she was about to interrupt, so he dropped the smile and spoke more quickly and seriously. "Suppose your company did a study to find out a jury's reactions to a group of lawyers. I've heard there are companies that do that kind of research."

"There are," she said tersely.

"Well, suppose they did one and found that a jury's reaction to an attractive woman was more positive than their reaction to an ugly one. Wouldn't the company be foolish not to hire her and use her in difficult cases?"

"Why are you trying to make me angry? Do you think I'll fall apart if I'm not?"

"No," said Parish. "I'm just curious to know what you're thinking. It's important to me that I understand you."

Marcia's heart gave an odd little flutter at that, and she cursed herself for it.

But he went on. "You are extremely attractive."

She rolled her eyes and let a breath out through her teeth. "Please."

"I'm not trying to insult you," he said. "It's an advantage—an enormous one—and you've shown me that you're aware of it, at least in certain circumstances. If you can confuse a person at lunch, you can get a client to hire you. You can charm a jury, make a judge want to help you. It would seem to me that it's a gift, like being born intelligent or healthy or strong. In fact, beauty—sexual attractiveness—is made of those qualities."

"What's your point?"

"You have these advantages, but you complain. It would seem more sensible for someone to complain who had been deprived of them."

Marcia's eyes narrowed. "If I succeeded, people would think I batted my eyes at a judge. If I was promoted, people would think I slept my way to the next level, or just that my boss hoped I would be grateful for the favor. No matter what I did or didn't do, I could never get credit for earning it with my work. Is that fair?"

"That's a false question," Parish said. "It's probably possible to figure out which lawyer won a case, even if her side consisted of a team of three or four. But it's not possible, even for her, to determine exactly how she won: what proportion of her victory was caused by the cold logic of her presentation, what proportion by how appealing she looked while she was giving it. In every instance, it was both." He paused. "The only place where fairness comes in is whether she—a person—gets rewarded for using what she had to win."

"But part of the reward should be the respect. You shouldn't win and then have people feel contempt for you."

"People don't feel contempt in that situation. The only negative feeling is jealousy," he assured her. "The women feel you don't deserve to have what you've been given. The men see that you have powerful magic that's not available to them."

"I earned what I have."

He looked at her, his expression intrigued, but said nothing to contradict her. His eyes refocused, and she knew he was studying Mary O'Connor again. At first Marcia was relieved. But after a time, she realized her irritation would not let her leave the subject. She needed to deliver a rebuttal.

"All right," she said. "I'll tell you why it was unfair. I was interviewed by the senior partners, and they asked difficult questions. I was hired, and was given no special privileges that I know of. I worked for three years, as hard as anyone. By then I thought I had become an important part of the team, a member of a group that valued me because I knew some things that the others didn't, had experience that was different from theirs, was willing to devote as much effort as anyone did to succeed on a case. It was a shock to learn otherwise. It was a sudden dose of reality that I'd never had before. And do you know what? When the time came, my reaction wasn't 'They have it wrong.' It was 'Of course.' It had never happened before, but it felt familiar, as though it had happened a hundred times. I'm bitter, but what I'm bitter about isn't the world we live in. It's the loss of the brighter, better, fairer world I imagined and lived in before."

"What did you learn about the real world?"

"It's a hard, harsh place."

"Why?"

"You have to study as hard as I did and work the same hours, but you also have to work to be attractive. And you can't decline to use it: all you can be is pretty or ugly, not somebody who refuses to be either. And you have to be very calculating about everything you do, including sex. You have to make self-serving decisions about who you will sleep with, but also who you won't sleep with. And you have to be very careful never to let them know that 'no' is permanent, that you won't ever sleep with them, because then they'll stop pleasing you and begin to punish you. And . . ." She let her voice trail off.

When she stopped talking, Parish looked at her sharply. She began again. "I wasn't prepared. On an impulse, I had an affair with a partner. David. He was cruel to me. I broke it off. He made it clear that I didn't have that option. I was afraid, but more afraid of giving in to him than of being fired. So he had me fired. When I told them I'd fight, they produced a file full of fake negative performance evaluations. In the meeting, in front of all the senior partners, one of them said, 'You're a disruptive influence. Who you fuck or won't fuck is taking up billable hours. You're not good enough as a litigator to make up the lost money. Nobody is.' "

Parish was looking past her again. "It's time." He stood up and she glanced over her shoulder to see Mary O'Connor put a cell phone into her purse and walk out of the restaurant into the hotel lobby. Marcia turned toward Parish, but he was heading for the door that led through the garden to the street.

She followed. He had done it. He had gotten her to talk through all of the waiting, and had gotten her to talk about her injustice, to make her pick at the sore until she felt the hatred like a stab. She saw Parish come close to Mary on the street, and saw her tell him something. He waved his hand at a cab, and when it stopped, Mary got into it. Parish walked back to join Marcia. "The place is a bar in Georgetown. It's called Handel's. Have you been there?"

She shook her head. "Uh-uh. Never heard of it."

"Good." He took her arm and looked at his watch, then conducted her toward the Metro stop. "We'll take the subway."

In the Bethesda station, Marcia watched Parish step up to one of the big automatic ticket machines along the wall at the bottom of the long escalator, push the plus and minus buttons until he got the right fare, then slip a bill into the machine, take the tickets, and scoop up his change. She had thought she would be the one to do that, because she was the one who had lived in Washington. But Parish seemed to have been everywhere and to know how all systems worked. He repeated the process. Four tickets? Return, of course. She would not have bothered.

They took up places near the tracks and watched the lights that were set into the pavement blink on and off to signal that a train was coming. The train slid into place at their feet and they stepped through the doorway and sat together in one of the orange plastic benches near the front of the car, but they did not speak. She realized that she missed being one of the people who came down into a station and stepped onto one of these trains that used to take her to work.

Everybody in the Washington subway seemed to wear a plastic pass on a long lanyard around his neck. It was a status symbol that had started with government workers and spread. Like all status symbols, it had a reverse effect. Marcia had always worn a smooth, tailored suit and kept it fresh by never sitting down on the train. An attorney for Spailer, Creeden and West didn't have anything as common as a security pass around her neck, any more than a cabinet officer did. She could feel a tight, angry knot in her stomach.

She looked at Parish, who was staring straight ahead, his expression vacant and his body at perfect rest. It was his fault that she felt the bitterness so strongly tonight. He had reminded her, and now each step was one more familiar sensation that she had not felt in over a year, and had missed.

The vibration of the Metro train that she felt under her feet reminded her that she would never ride it again, not all dressed up on her way to that beautiful office in Georgetown. Even the hotel restaurant near the Bethesda station had set off feelings of loss. She wondered if Parish had known before he had asked.

The ride took only twenty minutes, and as the train pulled in briefly at each of the familiar stops, she felt the intensity of her anger growing. Her life had been destroyed. She was willing to concede that what she was most angry about was that a whole system of false beliefs had been wrecked, shown to be untenable. But anyone could have seen that she had needed those illusions. She was also aware that billions of people in the past had lived and died without ever being disabused of similar beliefs. Why could hers not have been preserved?

When she had been at school, she and some friends had spent hours discussing what the unforgivable sin was, the one that could never be erased by absolution. The majority had said it was witchcraft. Marcia had thought it was destroying another person's faith. What had set that off? Oh, yes. A Hawthorne story they had read in class. Things were so much more complicated in girls' schools than mere philosophical inquiry. The witchcraft answer had gained adherents because one girl had been having a feud with two others, and burning candles in her room with ominous incantations. The faith answer was not free from outside influences either. Tanya Holbrooke had recently scandalized a few classmates by referring to born-again Christians as "fooled again," and they spent most of the time during the discussion giving her side-long glances.

That had not been what Marcia had meant when she had chosen that position. She had meant someone like Hitler, who had done something so evil that a person who had seen it happen would find the world intolerable and the idea of a loving God laughable.

The train began to slow as it approached Farragut North, and she stood up. Parish remained seated until it stopped, then joined her. The door slid open and they walked to the escalator and came up on I Street.

The night was warm, but it was beginning to rain now, a soft, persistent rain that had already made the streets shine with reflected headlights and taillights, and made Marcia stay close to buildings to take advantage of awnings and overhangs.

This part of I Street had a few old, quiet, pretty hotels and restaurants, a lot of businesses that sold clean, small things like watches and invisible things like travel and investments. A couple of blocks south, the diagonal of Pennsylvania Avenue marked the busy, faster-paced zone where a small, quiet bar was an impossibility. She had never been to the bar that Emily Lyons had tracked him to, although she had walked that part of Washington completely a number of times when she had lived here. A person didn't have to be away for long before things began to change, and there were few places left for memory to hang on to.

She saw the corner coming up, and confirmed her impression. This was a bar that had not existed when she had worked for the firm.

But there was a new, nagging sadness. She could not remember what had been on this spot before. She could not bring back any image of what had been, only look at the windows and the doorway of the place, and see a business that could as easily have been on an intersection in Cincinnati or Philadelphia.

She slowed and began to watch Parish. He had put an earpiece into his right ear, and he was listening as he walked. It occurred to her that he looked like a Secret Service agent, with the thin wire the color of a doll's skin leading to the single earphone, and the raincoat that might cover a gun. Tonight it covered two of them: his, and hers.

He said, "Emily says that he's in a booth with a young woman. We'll have to wait."

She let a frown show, then worried that he might have seen it.

"Does that bother you?" he asked. His curiosity seemed intrusive, voyeuristic.

"The woman?" she asked. "Believe me, it's not jealousy. I'm just frustrated that I can't get it over with. She's an inconvenience."

"Emily says it won't be long."

"What won't?"

"They finished dinner a while ago, and they're drinking. She'll go to the ladies' room, or he'll go to the men's."

"What will happen then?"

But he had his hand over his free ear, and he was listening to the earpiece, nodding and smiling. He turned to her. "They're ready. Are you?"

She nodded. "Yes."

They moved around the building to the rear, and stopped at the edge of a paved alley that held a dumpster. She could see a back door that opened onto a short corridor with a telephone and rest rooms. Parish opened his raincoat, reached to the inner pocket, and handed her the gun. It was a nine-millimeter semiautomatic pistol like the ones she had practiced with on the ranch. She could feel Parish watching her closely, so she performed all of the necessary motions deliberately and efficiently. She checked the safety to be sure it was engaged, released the magazine and withdrew it to verify that it held a full load, then pushed it back up into the butt until it clicked in. She pulled the slide back to cycle the first round into the chamber, then flipped off the safety again. Her eye passed across his, and caught there. "I have good reasons," she said.

He smiled broadly, amused. "The only reason you need is that you want to."

He held his hand to his ear again. "All right. The woman has gotten up and is walking toward the ladies' room. She's inside. Mary is moving in to keep her there. Now Emily is going to his table. She says the woman asked her to tell him she needs him outside. It sounds as though he's coming. Yes. Get ready. The first one out that door will be Emily. Did you hear me?"

"Yes. I heard you." She held the gun behind her back as he'd taught her, not in a pocket where it could catch on the lining or come out too slowly. The door opened and out came Emily, stepping into the circle of light from the overhead flood over the door. Emily did not look in their direction but took a wide, leisurely turn out of the door and held it open.

The man who came out after her was David. He glanced around under the light for his new girlfriend. He looked good. He seemed to have lost five or ten pounds, and his hair was a little gray at the temples now. It went well with the dark gray suit.

"David," she said. "Here."

He turned his head, saw her female shape in the shadows, took a step toward her, then stopped. He seemed to know the voice. He half-turned, but Emily was leaning against the closed door.

Marcia brought the gun around her body at shoulder height. David pushed Emily aside so he could tug on the door, but she had engaged the lock when she had closed it. He whirled toward Marcia, and she fired. The gun kicked upward a few inches, but she brought it down and fired once, twice more at his chest. Her aim had not been perfect, and he was sitting on the ground now. She could see a hole in the suit up near his left shoulder—not his heart—and another in the middle of his belly. He had both his hands clasped over that one, and his mouth was clenched in a bare-toothed grimace. She knew now why they had made her kill the deer. The size and the look of dazed agony were about the same.

Parish said, "Marcia, we're just about out of time."

Marcia stood over David, staring at his eyes. She wanted to say something to him that would make him hurt more than the bullets and teach him that he deserved this.

She heard footsteps behind her. Parish appeared on the left side of her peripheral vision, pulled his gun out, held it near David's temple, and fired it through his head. The body toppled sideways onto the pavement as though pushed by a wind.

Then Parish had her by the arm, and Emily Lyons was striding off along I Street to the west. Parish's legs were much longer than Marcia's and they were stepping along at a pace that forced her to trot to keep up, but she knew that his coat shielded her so that together they would look like any other couple going home in the rain.

Then they were down under the street in the Metro station again, boarding a train. "Doors closing," said the soothing recorded female voice, and they were away. They sat together. She looked up at Parish's face for the first time, but he seemed unaware that she was looking. She turned to stare out the window into the darkness of the tunnel.

He had even done the last thing better. She had seen it on David's face. She had already shot him two or three times, and he had been in pain. But she had watched his expression change as soon as he had seen Parish step out of the shadows with a gun. It was then that she had understood.

She had been staring stupidly down at David, trying to think of words. Words! But then she had seen David's eyes. He knew what Parish was about to do, and it meant everything to him. She could tell that somewhere, deep in his mind, hidden from her, had been the thought that this would be over: an ambulance would come and take him to a hospital, and the surgeons would save him. He would somehow live on. All the time while he had been watching Marcia standing there over him, trying to choose between ways of saying "I hate you" and ways of saying "You deserve this," he had been thinking, She'll go away soon, because she has to, and I'll get through this. I'll live. But when he had seen Parish with the pistol, stepping up to him, he had felt much more than the pain she had caused. David's eyes had said that he now knew that this moment was absolutely his last. There would be no ambulance, no surgeons. He was going to have a bullet through his brain.

She even understood the deer better. The reason they were dangerous when they were wounded was not that they were trying to fight. They were trying to get up and run. They still had hope. Parish had taken David's hope.

Suddenly, Marcia was terribly tired. She felt as though she were weightless, but she could barely lift her arm.

"Well?" said Parish.

She cocked her head and looked up at him.

He asked, "Was it what you expected?"

"No."

"Not disappointed, are you?"

She looked down at her hands. To her surprise, they were not clenched in fists, or shaking. They were merely her hands, at rest on her lap, the fingers a bit too plump for her taste, the nails too short to be very pretty. "No," she said. "It was exactly what I might have wished for. I just couldn't decide how it should end. But you knew. You ended it perfectly."

CHAPTER 13

When Lydia had driven Robert Mallon down from the self-defense school to his house in Santa Barbara in the late afternoon, she had stopped the car in the driveway without turning off the engine. Mallon had said, "Aren't you going to stay?"

Lydia had answered, "No. I'm going back to L.A to spend a few days asking around, and see if I can find some more people we can talk to. I'll get in touch as soon as I do. In the meantime, check in with Diane and let her know you're home. Fowler may have asked about you."

Mallon had returned to his routines. In the mornings he walked on the beach. Since Catherine's death he had not wanted to walk near the spot where he had pulled her out of the water, so now he usually walked down to the foot of State Street and followed the coast to the east toward Montecito. Each time he returned to his house, he immediately stepped to the kitchen counter to see if the red light on his answering machine was blinking, but always it glowed steadily.

On the eighth day, the telephone rang, and he picked it up to hear Lydia's voice. "Bobby?"

"Yes, Lydia."

"I'm in the car right now, but I wanted to tell you I'm interviewing somebody tomorrow, and I thought you might be interested in joining me."

"Who is it?"

"It's a woman who knew both of them. It took me a while to hunt her down, because she's moved a few times since those days, but I just talked to her and she's agreed to meet me in a bar on Abbot Kinney Boulevard in Venice at one o'clock. You don't have to decide right now. I'll be there either way."

"I would like to join you, I think. Thanks."

"I do have to warn you that I can't guarantee she'll show up," Lydia said. "They don't always, and it's not like being their parole officer, where they have to make up some kind of an answer when you ask them a question."

"Do you have the address of the bar?" asked Mallon.

"Not on me. I thought it would be best if you'd just take a morning commuter flight down here tomorrow. There's one that leaves around ten. I'll pick you up at the airport, and we'll go to the bar together."

──────

The woman was strikingly attractive, but not what Mallon would have called pretty. Her face looked triangular, the large dark eyes making the upper part seem very wide. She had a nose that was wide at the bridge and seemed to narrow, and below it a set of lips that he guessed had been treated to make them fuller, then a tiny pointed chin. Her eye shadow was too dark, the liner too thick and black, the lipstick too starkly outlined for daytime. The tight pants and the top that tied in the back, Mallon knew, were what was in store windows this month, but intended for teenagers, who were slightly younger and a bit skinnier. On her, they seemed to be a costume, something she was always thinking about, touching and readjusting. It made him think about them too.

They sat at a table near the windows that looked out on Abbot Kinney Boulevard. Mallon wondered why they had not met at one of the bars a few blocks closer to the ocean so they could see it. There was enough light streaming in for her to see the photographs that Lydia had stolen from Catherine Broward's apartment. The woman squinted at them, then pushed them toward Mallon. "Yeah," she said. "Markie was the one I knew, really. The girl was only with him for a while. She's dead, too?" Her perfectly outlined Cupid's-bow lips pouted while she waited for an answer.

"That's right," said Lydia. "She killed herself."

"Oh," said the woman, tonelessly. "I only saw her a few times." That seemed to be her explanation for her utter indifference. Then she said, "I remember I was working on the video for Alien Steam's first CD at the time, so it would be . . . about two years ago."

"I'm sorry," said Mallon. "Working on the video?" His confusion was sincere. All Mallon could tell was that she was dropping an impressive name. "Are you a musician?"

Lydia said, "Miss Gracely danced on that video. I've seen it. She was the principal dancer, really." Lydia turned to her. "Did you meet them at a party?"

She nodded, picked up her glass, and brought it toward her mouth, then pantomimed her surprise that it was empty. Mallon waved to the bartender. "Three more, please." He returned his attention to her. "I know the police probably drove you crazy with questions about all this at the time, but can you tell us anything about the party? Where was it?"

"It started at the ballroom of the Millefleurs Hotel. It was for the release of Juan-do Ward's last CD—he was already dead—and the company invited, like, the whole industry. I got a lot of work from that party. Later it overflowed and kind of oozed from one place to another. There were a couple of suites in the hotel, and some people went to the company offices, and there was a kind of after-party at a club. Alien Steam had a limo, and we traveled from place to place."

She chuckled at the memory of it. "Nobody was any good at opening champagne bottles, so it kept shooting all over the windows and the seats and us."

Mallon nodded in a sympathy that he did not feel. She was a person with obvious attractions, but her evaluation of them seemed to be too high: they did not dazzle him and make him unable to form unflattering thoughts. She said, "I remember first noticing Markie at the hospitality suite. He was really something. Those eyes, the expression on his face." She gave a little shiver of appreciation, then seemed to return to the present, where he was dead and could be of no use. The look immediately changed to boredom. Then she saw her next drink arrive, and she brightened. "He was at the bar. I went over to him, and asked if he would get the bartender to make me a Cosmopolitan. I was with a couple of the guys from Done Deal right then—Fred Howard and Mickey Dill—but I just had to get a closer look at him. He hit on me. He asked my name, and phone number. I gave, but then there's this girl."

Lydia pointed at the picture of Catherine on the table. "This girl?"

Del Gracely nodded. "She had been in the bathroom. When she got back, I kept right on flirting with him, because it never occurred to me that he could be with her. He was the most beautiful man. She was . . . she had kind of stringy brown hair and a sort of ordinary face. She had kind of an okay body, but come on. That room was full of women who made her look . . . Well, I thought he must be in the business, and she was his agent, or an executive or something. She had good clothes—very expensive—but she wasn't good-looking enough to be there unless she was something like that."

"Did he introduce you to her?" asked Lydia.

"Sure. He was one of those guys who never slips up, never forgets anybody's name, always looks at every woman in the room as though she's the special one and he just came there on the off chance that he might run into her. He said, 'This is Cathy,' then 'This is Del Gracely.' I gave her my best smile and everything, because I figured that she must be somebody, a behind-the-scenes person. But she wasn't." Her mind seemed to shift. "About that time was when Irwin Rogow noticed me. I saw he was looking, so I went over to talk to him. The party began to move again, so we did too."

"But you saw Mark Romano again?" asked Lydia.

"Lots of times. Maybe once or twice a month until he died."

"What about Catherine Broward?"

She seemed taken aback. "Oh, I thought you meant alone. Her, I saw only once more. I was at a club. I was leaving with a bunch of people because there was going to be a party at Wilfred Fillmore's house in Malibu."

Mallon knew who that was. He was a basketball player who seemed to spend his off-seasons getting arrested for felonies, then having the charges dropped or reduced to minor infractions.

"Mark was in the parking lot and she was with him. I had gotten the impression that they had broken up, but I think I got it from him, so it probably wasn't true yet. They were having a fight." She stopped, looked out the window, and sipped her drink.

Mallon's muscles tensed as he waited for the woman to put down the glass and say more, but she seemed to think that she had already told them the whole story, that the few words she had said would evoke for Mallon and Lydia exactly what she had seen and heard. She placed the glass in front of her and looked at them expectantly.

Lydia leaned forward. "Can you remember anything at all about the fight—what was said?"

She seemed surprised. "Oh, sure. She was trying to move close to him and talk quietly, but he pushed her away, so her voice got loud, and it wasn't hard to hear. She said he'd taken some money of hers, and that it was okay, but he should come home. He brushed her off, and got into his car. It was embarrassing him, because the valet had just brought it up, and we were all waiting for our cars. She reached in the window and snatched the key out. He got out of the car and tried to get her to hand the keys back, but she wouldn't do it. Meanwhile, we're all standing around watching this, while the valets went to pull our cars up so we can go to the party. People started making funny comments and laughing. These are guys who are cool and important, people Markie would have wanted to impress. And the girls are . . . well, guys like that don't hang with second-rate girls. Everybody's laughing, and Cathy is making him look stupid. He reaches for the keys, and she twists around and keeps them out of his reach. He grabs her wrist, but she's already moved them to the other hand. She says they need to talk, and she won't let him go. He says, Give me the keys, Cathy. She says, It's not even your car. I bought it. He's intensely aware that this little scene is ruining him. He twists the wrist around behind her back and reaches for the one with the keys. Instead of letting it happen, she tosses them into the sewer by the curb."

"What did he say?"

"Not much," she said. "He was still holding her arm, so he jerked her around with it. Then he hit her, right in the mouth. Twice, real quick, and let her go. She dropped on the ground. That was when I could see her arm was actually broken, because it was kind of hanging limp, and looked wrong. She tried to talk, and her mouth was all bloody, and I could see these two front teeth right here were out."

Mallon winced. He could see her in his mind, intuit the emotional pain she must have been feeling, the sheer amazement that someone she loved would hurt her that way. "What happened then?"

"By then our cars were there." She shrugged.

A few minutes later, Mallon and Lydia were on the street making their way to the parking lot where Lydia had left her car. Mallon said, "Did you know about this before?"

"I had some suspicions," said Lydia. "The autopsy report in Santa Barbara said that two of her upper incisors were dental implants. In a girl her age, that usually says car accident, but there was nothing conclusive about that. The arm didn't show on the autopsy, so if it really was injured it was probably a dislocation, and after the doctor popped it back in there wasn't anything."

Mallon felt a wave of horror that threatened to turn into nausea. He tried to make his mind form another image to replace Catherine's agony. "How did you come up with Del Gracely?"

"Angie interviewed her in the homicide thing."

"Did you really see the rock video she was on? Should I know her face?"

"I saw several she was on. She's probably twenty-five years old and she's already past it without having gotten anywhere. There's an endless supply of girls who gyrate around behind some group. You have to listen for clues. The one she was talking about—Alien Steam's first CD—made them rich. Not her. It was their first CD, before they were anything. She was on one for Done Deal, a couple other name groups. She's not exactly a show-business legend. She goes to parties. She hooks up with various guys for various periods. Including Markie Romano. The reason she got interviewed in his murder was because she was in some of his nonmusical videos."

"After she saw what he did to Catherine?" Mallon sat in the passenger seat of Lydia's car.

Lydia got in and started the engine. "Before, or after, I'm not sure which. Probably she isn't either." She drove up Abbot Kinney to Washington Boulevard, then turned right onto Lincoln.

They drove in silence, moving south. Finally, Mallon said, "Do you think that was why Catherine went to the self-defense camp— because she was afraid Romano would hurt her again?"

Lydia hesitated for a moment, overcame her reluctance, then spoke carefully. "I think we've been looking at this wrong from the beginning. We've been acting on the strength of things we thought we knew before we started. Everything we saw or heard, we just used to revise the story we started with. We knew Catherine was bent on killing herself. Her boyfriend was dead? Then she must have been depressed because her boyfriend died tragically while she was waiting for him to come home. Oh, she was out of town at some resort north of Ojai at the time? Then maybe she left L.A. and went there because she knew he was going to get it soon, and she was scared. The resort isn't a resort, but a self-defense boot camp? Then she really must have been scared, and trying to learn enough to protect him. He had already dumped her, beaten her up, and thrown her out on her ass? Then she was trying to learn to protect herself from him, or guys like him. You have an excuse for that. I don't. I still do this for a living."

"An excuse for what?"

"For starting out with a story that had to be true because that's the way things usually happen, and just fitting everything new that we hear into it. I think we need to throw out the old story and start with a new one."

"We've been trying to figure out why Catherine got into a depression and committed suicide," said Mallon. "I didn't hear anything today that wasn't a reason for her to be depressed."

"Yeah," said Lydia, "but the story doesn't fit together. At least not the way we've been looking at it."

"Of course there are contradictions," said Mallon. "I started out wanting it to be neat and logical. But nobody's life is neat and logical. I know the sister told us she was still madly in love with this guy, and everybody else agrees that they'd already broken up, but—"

"Not just broken up. He punched her front teeth out."

"But it wouldn't be unprecedented for her to hate and fear a guy like that and still love him too, would it? Or maybe just be heartbroken that he had turned out not to be what she'd thought?"

Lydia was silent.

Mallon added, "And it wouldn't be odd not to tell her older sister all about it, but instead to let her keep believing that everything had still been beautiful. After all, the truth was ugly and humiliating. And for what? Why would her sister need to know all the tawdry details?" He paused. "And it's even possible that the sister knew everything, but had no desire to tell two strangers all about it." He waited, then seemed to run his own arguments through his mind again but be dissatisfied. "Do you have another way to look at it?"

"I might," said Lydia. She took her eyes off the road for a moment to look at Mallon, then looked ahead again. "Let's think about the things we didn't know when we started two weeks ago. We know that Markie was not a nice man. He was a lowlife. We know that when she tried to talk to him about their personal disagreements, including his having a car she paid for, and her money, he beat the hell out of her in a parking lot. We know that sometime later—a month or two, after her teeth had been replaced and the arm healed—she paid forty grand to spend four weeks at a self-defense camp. That was in July. A month after that, Markie gets shot. At that moment, where is Catherine? She isn't even in town. She's—still—at the self-defense place in the woods."

"Right," said Mallon. "Is there some way to make it all fit with the rest of what we know?"

"Yeah, there's a way: she killed him."

"No!" Mallon said immediately. Then he cocked his head as though listening while he soundlessly tried the tone of it. He said, more quietly, "That's crazy."

"She had a hell of a motive."

"Well," said Mallon, "all right, he was a bum. Some women might respond to that fact by wanting to kill him. But even if she did, wanting to is a very long way from actually doing it."

"You know what they study in that self-defense school? I took a brochure. There are courses in the technology of self-defense, which is about pepper spray and Tasers and alarms and locks and security cameras, and so on. That's standard stuff, but there's a high-end tilt to it because the customers are rich and worry about kidnapping and protecting big houses. The second course is hand-to-hand combat, taught by male and female instructors who have black belts in aikido and karate, among other things. The third course is firearms training, including work on a combat range. That was why we heard pistols the day we were there. So Catherine had a pretty good introduction to ways of hurting people, and enough knowledge to understand that the only realistic way for her to get Markie was a shot to the head. She also, after you stopped her from drowning, killed herself with a pistol, which means she was capable of getting one when she needed it. We have enough of a motive, I'd say. How hard do you think it would be for her to get an opportunity—maybe slip out of that camp at night, drive to the apartment where she used to live with him in L.A. and do him, then drive back?"

"Okay," said Mallon. "Crazy wasn't the right word. I just don't think she was the kind of person who would kill somebody."

"You knew her for a few hours," said Lydia. "And spending time naked with somebody isn't the same as reading their innermost thoughts. I'm not saying this to be cruel, but that's one of the mistakes Catherine seems to have made."

"And now I'm making it about her?"

"All I'm saying is that the whole story about her going to a self-defense school because she was afraid her boyfriend was in danger makes very little sense. It makes no sense at all once you know he'd already beaten her up and thrown her out," said Lydia. "It makes perfect sense if she was the one who killed him."

Mallon glared at her. "I'll admit that your theory is logical. But I talked to her, and we've both talked to other people about her, and I'm just not prepared to say that she would kill someone, even someone who deserved it."

"Neither am I," said Lydia. She turned right at Century Boulevard and headed toward the airport. "I want you to take a plane back to Santa Barbara. I'll get in touch in a few days."

"What are you going to do?"

"I've got to take care of some other stuff: you know, check in with Harry up north at the office, then try to figure out who else to ask questions down here. I'll call you."

╫╫╫

As afternoon was ending and the sun glared brightly from a low angle above the ocean in preparation for the change into evening, Mallon stepped off his plane and into the Santa Barbara terminal. His lawyer, Diane, was already walking toward him, smiling. Her short blond hair was perfectly brushed and shining, and she wore a tailored navy blue suit, as though she had been in court. He looked at her and held his hands out in confusion.

"I was trying to reach Lydia Marks, and when I did, she told me your flight number."

"So you're here for me?" He realized that he had asked the wrong question. What he wanted to know was why she had called Lydia.

"Sure. She said you would tell me what's going on."

"I'll try."

They waited a few minutes in the baggage claim area for his single suitcase to appear on the metal ramp and slide down to the carousel, and then she drove him to a restaurant on Stearns Wharf, where they could look out and watch the yachts and fishing boats putting slowly into the harbor for the night. She listened patiently to his recitation over dinner. Finally, he asked, "What do you think?"

She sipped her coffee, looked out the big window at four blue kayaks coming into the harbor. "I think it's getting to be time to move to the next phase."

"What's that?"

"First, you record everything you've learned in a journal: what you observed, the evidence you found, what each person told you, and when. You read each entry over to be sure it's absolutely accurate. Then you write down what you think actually happened, in chronological order. Draw a conclusion. If the story is convincing enough so that you're sure you know the truth, then you go to the police."

"And if it's not convincing enough?"

"Then you put it at the bottom of a drawer, and concede that there are some questions that just can't be answered."

He stared at her uncomfortably. "You think I'm out of my mind to do this."

She returned his stare for a moment. "Not at all. When this first came up, it had not been established that Catherine Broward's death was a suicide. If it turned out to be something else, you were a potential suspect. In those situations it's not a bad idea to have experienced defense attorneys and private investigators visibly working on your behalf. I also knew that you'd had a weird, unsettling experience. I thought it might be therapeutic for you to go find out what had caused it. And, frankly, I expected that when you found out, you would come to the conclusion that you had done all you could to save her, but she was not somebody who could be saved. You've done that. I think at some point, you stop. Now would be a good time."

He looked out the window again, and stared across the harbor at the thicket of white masts of the sailboats moored at the slips. "I don't know enough yet. We've found things that I think we have to resolve first."

She studied him with benign tolerance. "You have to drive on the right side of the street and pay your taxes. You don't have a civic duty to spend hundreds of thousands of dollars trying to uncover every nuance of the reason a stranger killed herself. It happens. It's always partly obvious, because there's always some real reason to be unhappy, and it's always partly mysterious, because we can never know what anybody else is thinking." She saw the expression on his face as he impatiently waited for her to finish. "I'm trying to do you some good here."

A smile raised the corners of his lips, faded, and then returned. "I know that. I'm not sure I can explain why I'm going on with this, because the reason keeps changing. At first I wanted to know what I could have said or done to stop it. I realized—maybe while I was listening to her sister—that it was incredible egotism to think that just by saying some words I could induce a person I'd just met to reverse the biggest decision she had ever made. But it happens. It happens all the time. Somebody on a suicide hotline talks a young woman like her out of it every night."

"She has to call the hotline first. They don't wait until she's drowned herself, pull her out, and make her come to the phone. Maybe that's the difference. Or maybe she was nuts. Delusional. Yes, I'm being flippant. I hope you know that if she were here now, I would be the last person you know to say, 'Who cares?' But now that it's over, I have to say, 'Who still cares?' because the second that life left her body, all of this became a nonissue. Nothing you do will help her, or anybody else."

"You're not even curious?"

"Of course I am," she said. "I'm the biggest gossip in town. You know that. Right now I spend a few minutes of each day spying on the tax attorney who has an office down the hall, because just about every day at lunchtime, a good-looking young guy shows up with take-out food, and she closes the office for an hour and a half. But he doesn't leave until she reopens at one-thirty. I want to know all about it: who he is, where they met, what they're doing—specifically and in detail—and how she's keeping her husband from catching her." She paused. "See? It's titillating, it's interesting, it's not especially sad, and I don't have to hire an expensive detective to interpret it for me."

He grinned. "You keep returning to the money. You think I'm wasting it, don't you?"

"You're not the only rich client I have, thank God, and you're not nearly the silliest. Usually, I include you in the other group, the ones I don't worry about because they still have their first dollar. But right now, you have a certain quality that appeals to the motherly side of my nature, so I'll give you a motherly lecture. Money can have some traps. It allows people to do surprisingly dumb things without obvious disastrous consequences. That can be a danger. You can get the idea that your money buys you everything you want, and will protect you from anything you don't want. It can't always, and when you reach the limit, it can be a nasty shock."

"I'm not sure how this applies to me," said Mallon.

"I don't think you can find out everything about another person's life just by paying a fortune to investigators. And I'm not sure that if you could, it would be a good bargain."

"Lydia is an old friend of mine, and I have more money than I need," he said.

"You don't have unlimited time," she said. "Nobody has. It's hard for a person who cares about you to see you obsessed with a dead woman."

"She wasn't dead when I met her." Mallon paid for their dinner, and they walked along the harbor breakwall, watching the last of the boats coming in just after sundown.

"Is it the boyfriend's murder that's keeping you involved?" she asked. "Do you secretly think her death was a murder too?"

"I don't know what to think," Mallon replied. "We know she went to a self-defense school. What for? Lydia thinks she went there to learn how to kill somebody, and then did—that she killed Mark Romano herself."

"And then what? Something drove her to suicide?"

"I don't know. Guilt, maybe, or regret." They walked along for a few yards, and he said, "I keep wondering about that self-defense camp. Have you heard of it?"

"I don't think so," she answered. "But you have to remember what kind of place Santa Barbara is. It's always been a place where rich people came to live after they stopped doing whatever it was that made them rich—sometimes a generation or two after. And it's drawn more than its share of strange characters of one kind or another, who have something specific in mind, some way of taking advantage of that potential. A friend of mine used to say that there are five thousand living religions, and thirty-eight hundred of them were started within a hundred miles of here. This is also one of the places you come if you want to hold a class in yoga, or start a health-food store, or push some kind of self-improvement. This self-defense school seems to me to fit into that mix—on the fringes, maybe."

"I suppose," he said.

They walked back to the parking lot, got into Diane's car, and she drove him to his house. He took his suitcase, leaned in the open window on his side, and said, "Thanks for picking me up, Diane." Then he added, "And thanks for listening to all this."

"Thanks for dinner," she replied. "If listening helps you get over this, I'll listen anytime."

"It's not a complete waste. Lydia and I may have solved a murder."

"And found a murderer who's mostly a victim and who is, incidentally, dead."

"The truth matters."

"Some truths matter more than others. Spend your time thinking about living women. They sometimes repay your interest." The window on Mallon's side slid shut, and she drove off into the night.

Mallon unlocked his front door, turned on the lights, and carried his suitcase up to his bedroom. He began to unpack, hanging up the clean clothes he had packed this morning. He was frustrated. Nobody seemed to understand that what he was looking for made a difference. He was sure that the girl who had been in his house had not been seeing things in a distorted way.

She had been clear-eyed and sane. Maybe the one who killed Mark Romano had tracked her to his door, taken her out, and shot her. Maybe she had known that Mark Romano should die, had gone out and learned how to kill him, and then done it. And maybe she had discovered something he could not quite know, but suspected: that killing another human being had changed her into someone she did not want to be.

CHAPTER 14

||||||||||||||||||||||||||||||||||||||||||||||||

As Stewart Markham walked along the sun-dappled path through the woods above the main lodge into the outer reaches of the self-defense camp, he could hear Coleman's footsteps behind him. He had met Coleman here over three years ago, on his second stay at the school. Since then, they'd had the sort of relationship he'd had with a number of other men. When they didn't happen to be around, he never thought about them, and didn't have any impulse to stay in touch. Now and then one of them might call to mention something like a change of address or, only slightly more often, out of hope that a bout of extreme boredom would be relieved by a little cheerful banter. But whenever they were in the same place at the same time, they were instantly close friends—not merely as close as the last time but even closer, because now the friendship would have been extended by a year or two and by one additional reunion.

Stewart was forty-two now, and the number of friends who turned up like this had grown large. There were old classmates from Etheridge School in Massachusetts, others he'd known at Princeton. There were not more than two or three from his business career, maybe because Stewart had needed to endure the brokerage, to satisfy his grandfather, for only five years before the old man died and could no longer change his will. The people around him in the brokerage had been a mix of women, men too old to share his interests, and foreigners.

Marshall Coleman, however, was a kindred spirit. Stewart had sensed that almost immediately. Coleman had the friendly ease of manner, the familiar, hearty tone that Stewart had been trained in childhood to recognize. These were the qualities shared by men who had been to the right schools and the right colleges, and had not been suffering outcasts there. But Marshall also had the reserve that had always been the sign in the English-speaking world of people whose families meant something.

Coleman was strong and in good shape this time. Markham could tell by listening to the quiet evenness of his breathing and the pace of his steps as they climbed the first ridge. Coleman had been a ranked tennis player in college, so it was no surprise that he still took care of himself. Markham habitually made critical observations of every person he met, and had never found any reason to amend what he had known was true in eighth grade: there were humans, who looked like what they were—straight and strong and healthy and energetic—and there were subhumans, who had started out small and ugly and inferior, and whose innate weakness would, through adulthood, make them degenerate even more. Marshall Coleman was one of the humans. He and Markham could have been mistaken for brothers.

Markham reached the crest of the ridge, once again heard the sharp crack of a rifle, then silence. He stopped to listen.

Coleman came up behind him and said, "What do you think? Did that sound like it came from the range?"

There was another crack. "Got to be. If he was out popping deer or something, he wouldn't get that many shots."

They followed the path over two more low hills, then came up to the range. Parish was wearing shooting glasses with yellow lenses and earphones. He was behind the high wooden shooting bench with a rifle propped on sandbags, staring through the telescopic sight at a target on the five-hundred-yard mark. He made a small adjustment to a thumbscrew on the scope.

Spangler was up on the raised platform with a big spotting scope on a tripod, staring into the eyepiece at Parish's target. Parish fired again, then raised the ear protector off his right ear to hear Spangler. "That one's dead on, Michael. The elevation is perfect for that ammo." He took his eye away from the eyepiece to look down at Parish and saw Coleman and Markham standing below. He waved his hand at them, and Parish looked over his shoulder. He gently placed the rifle on the felt pad that covered the bench, and turned to shake hands with them.

His grip was firm, two hard shakes for each of them. Parish's tanned face wrinkled at the corners of the eyes as he gave them a closed-mouthed smile. "Marshall, Stewart. Good to see you." He looked up at the platform, where Spangler waited, and called, "Thanks, Paul." Spangler came down the ladder with the spotter's scope, folded the tripod, and busied himself putting the pieces of equipment in their carrying cases.

Parish began walking downrange toward the paper target, waiting for the others to speak.

"I'm surprised to see you doing that," said Markham. "I mean, sighting it in yourself."

Parish reverted to his pedagogic tone. "Sighting a rifle isn't just to get the rifle's sights adjusted to a particular distance. It's also to improve the shooter. Spangler cares for the weapons his students use on the firing range, and he shoots every day. He can drive nails at two hundred. I'm the one who needs the practice. A good rifle is a reliable device, always the same, clean and flawless like a sword. Achieving a dead aim is a perfection of the eye, the hand, the will."

Markham was reminded of why he admired Parish so much: he was the master, but he had a respect for standards that gave him a special humility.

Coleman's question was jarring. "Have you thought at all about what we were saying before?"

Parish kept walking, and he raised both hands a few inches and rocked his head from side to side in a gesture of indecision and frustration. "Of course I've thought about it," he said. "This isn't like the shoe business. You're not just customers. When a person has succeeded in passing my course, he's somebody I'll listen to. If he's gone beyond courses, and put what he's learned into practice on a hunt and never wavered or panicked or lost his nerve, he's reached a different level."

"That's really good to hear," said Coleman. "It means a lot." Markham muttered assent: "Yeah, it does."

"So I've taken it seriously and thought about it," Parish continued. "I have questions. If you two want to go on a hunt together, why haven't you? Why are you here? Do you want me to help you sharpen your skills a bit first? Is the target somebody who is likely to be beyond your capability?"

Markham said, "That's part of the problem. We don't know."

Parish reached the five-hundred-yard mark and stepped to the post where his target hung. "You don't?"

"No," said Coleman. "This time it's not that there's somebody either of us hates and needs to kill. It's not a personal thing. This time it's . . ." He glanced at Markham.

Markham said, "It's not about the target now. It's about us. It's about how we go about it, how we can improve ourselves, how we react to the pressure and the risk."

Parish turned to examine them. "Sport," he pronounced. "It's a sport hunt."

"I guess you could say that," Coleman admitted uncomfortably.

"I can understand that," Parish said. When he noticed the relief on their faces as they glanced at each other, he said, "It's something I respect. The rule for a target here is that the client wants to kill him. I don't judge whether or not the target deserves it. I don't shoot a deer because the deer deserves to be shot. I do it because I want to. Have you picked the target?"

"No," said Coleman.

"Why not?"

"We thought maybe it would be best if you did it. That way, it would be more of a test, a challenge: the professional hunter chooses, and you take the game you get."

Parish took the paper target off the post, held it up to let the others see the pattern of holes around the bull's-eye. "See, the first one was way up here, the second down here. I overcompensated for the distance by raising it before the shot even missed, and then did it again in the other direction. Then the wind kicked up, and the shots drifted to the right. I had to teach myself how much to adjust for it at that range with the new rifle."

Coleman and Markham looked at the pattern of bullet holes with unfeigned admiration. Markham said, "But then you drilled it. The rest are all in the black, over and over."

"Yes," said Parish evenly. "It's a good rifle, made to do that. The rifle is always the same. It's the shooter who changes." He folded the paper and stuck it into his back pocket, took another from the wooden box at the side of the range, and pushed it onto the post so the nails went through it. Then he walked off the range and up the bank of the dry riverbed. "What kind of hunt do you two want? You said it was for the risk and action. Do you want a target that might shoot back, or a harmless one that's going to be in a difficult spot for hunting? If I'm going to plan your hunt, I'll need to know."

Markham hesitated. He had not anticipated the question, so he had to evaluate its terms. He had pictured the adventure as the two of them—Markham and Coleman—killing someone in plain sight, in a city. He and Coleman would be walking down a crowded street in a place like New York, and the prey would be ahead of them. Maybe the guy would start down the steps to a subway station, and as soon as he was below street level they would drop him and go back up, maybe looking down at the fallen man with distaste, as though he were an unconscious drunk. Maybe they would do it in an elevator in a big office building.

But Coleman answered eagerly, "One that might shoot back. We're looking for a challenge."

It was too late. Markham could not contradict him once it had been said. His fantasy had been the challenge of doing it in a public place; the risk had been in being seen. What he had relished was fooling both the target and the bystanders, and getting away with it. Never had he imagined placing himself in a position to be shot at. It was a new idea. He tried to envision such a thing, but it brought him no pleasure. Things had gone so slowly until now—the long, deliberate walk across the ranch, then waiting for Parish to give them his attention—but he sensed that a crucial part of the conversation had just come and gone, and what had been pronounced was irrevocable. His heart beat faster, and his breaths were shallow.

Parish was walking on a path now, and Coleman was beside him. The path was unfamiliar and it was too narrow to walk three abreast, so Markham had to hang back alone. He heard Parish say, "I'll have to give this some more thought." Then, a few steps up the first hill, he said, "No. No, I don't. I have a perfect target for this kind of hunt." He turned his head to look at Coleman, then turned his torso far enough to bring Markham into view. "You two did well enough in classes and on your first hunts, so I don't have any doubts about your knowledge. But have you stayed sharp?"

Coleman grinned and nodded emphatically. "Always."

Markham tried to formulate a way of amending the impression that Coleman's brusque overconfidence had left. He wasn't soft and flabby, but he did not think he was what Parish meant by sharp.

Parish said, "Good. Then we'll get started right away. I'll pick a tracker and a scout today. Anybody you'd especially like to work with?"

"Maybe Spangler?" Markham suggested quickly. He hoped the

others did not suspect his reason for the choice, but Parish glanced at him and gave his thought a generous interpretation.

"It's possible he would be best. Having Spangler gives you an advantage in a firefight."

What Markham had been thinking was that Spangler looked formidable enough so that he probably would draw most of an opponent's fire, leaving Markham a bit safer. He began to feel better.

"But it might be better to have someone who won't make the target suspicious," said Parish, "somebody who can keep you out of a firefight until you're ready to open up. We'll have to talk it over."

—||||||||||||||||||||||||||||||||||||||||||||||||||||||||||—

CHAPTER 15

Markham sat in the back row of the theater, staring at the movie without comprehension. It was as though he were not in Los Angeles but on an airplane, watching the movie without headphones. The actress who was on the screen eighty percent of the time was one who had been in many movies he had seen, and in this one she had already shown the camera all of the expressions her face would make. She and the lead actor had moved more quickly and abruptly at the beginning, but now they often lingered in the same frame for a while, so he assumed they'd discovered the reason why they had been put in this story together.

Markham was clutching the pager in his hand, so that when the signal came there would be no doubt that he would feel the vibration. His mouth was dry and he was sweating, although he had just finished a big cup of cold cola and other people in the air-conditioned theater were wearing jackets. His was on his lap.

He had approved Parish's plan to split the hunting party this way. If Markham, Coleman, and Parish, all of them tall, noticeable men, were simply loitering on the street, someone might wonder why and would certainly remember them. But this way, Markham was invisible in the dark theater, and Coleman was in a coffee shop around the corner and down the street with his face hidden behind a newspaper. Parish was in a car with tinted windows driving around within a few blocks of here.

The only one in view of the target would be the tracker, Debbie, whom Parish had hired in the three years since Markham's last visit to the camp. He had tried to be friendly when Parish had introduced her, but his approach had elicited a particular kind of smirk that he'd decided meant she was an angry lesbian. It was all right, he supposed. Parish had assured him that she and Emily, the scout, were good at what they did, and their competence was far more important to him tonight than any interest they might have shown in him.

He knew that Debbie was undoubtedly with the target now, and that Emily was near here, probably in the restaurant or the street outside, making sure the scene was secure. When she saw the target and the tracker arrive, she would make the three calls. He corrected himself. She would make the calls if, after they arrived, it was safe. Parish had assured him of that, and repeating it to himself made him feel better. The scout had been there long before anyone else. She would already have studied the entrances and exits and every person there to be sure there was no threat, and she would make sure everything stayed that way.

He jumped as the pager in his hand began to vibrate. He had tested it before he had come, but now it didn't feel like a machine: it felt alive. He barely kept himself from throwing it. He sat up straight and looked at the display in the little window on top. He hoped it would be a line of dashes, the sign that he had accidentally triggered it, but he could see 6543210, the number she'd told him to expect. It was real. She was calling them in.

He put the pager, very deliberately, into his pocket before he stood up. He had to get each stage of this out of the way in its turn. He moved to the aisle and out into the lobby. The lights made him blink and the strong, greasy popcorn smell nauseated him, but he made his way through quickly enough, and as soon as he was out of the splash of light the marquee threw onto the sidewalk, he felt stronger and more purposeful again. He didn't like Los Angeles, but these warm summer nights made walking easy and quick.

He walked with brisk, powerful strides and took deep breaths to force extra oxygen into his lungs, and it made him feel even better. As he came around a corner to a darker street, he ventured to touch the pistol hidden under his jacket at the back of his belt. He began to prepare himself by visualizing what was going to happen. As he did, he tensed each muscle he would use. He would arrive, and all of the others would be in position in view of the target. The target had been patiently stalked for days, and tonight, lured into a small, almost windowless restaurant on a side street. Markham would walk in, take a safe position a distance away, and pull out the gun to fire. The target might see the movement in time to duck or crouch, but it would do no good.

The thought made Markham walk faster. As he approached the restaurant, he could see without being seen, as though he were a ghost materializing out of the darkness. There were Parish and Emily, the scout, outside the front door, and there was Marshall Coleman strolling toward them from the opposite direction.

He stepped up to Parish, who said quietly, "It's a go." Markham moved to the front door, and heard Parish behind him repeating to Coleman, "It's a go." Markham opened the door and held it so Coleman could go first, then slipped in behind him.

Markham could see the target instantly, because Debbie was at the table with her. The target's face had the round, pushed-in look of the lower classes, with a short, characterless nose and small, darting eyes.

Coleman was already reaching into his coat, covering his motion with the newspaper he carried, and Markham hesitated in confusion: had he missed some signal, not known of some change in the plan?

Markham saw Debbie stand up and heard her say, "I'm going to the ladies' room," looking down to fiddle in her purse. That distracted the target for only a fraction of a second. All of the unexpected motion seemed to alarm her. She was on her feet instantly, and she made the one move Markham had not imagined in advance. She backed up toward the narrow corridor, retreating toward the rest rooms ahead of Debbie, so that Debbie would be between her and the shooters. Suddenly she was staring past Debbie at Markham and Coleman and reaching into her purse.

Debbie's left hand jerked up and efficiently swatted the target's hand away from the purse, while Debbie's right hand stopped in front of the target's face. Then Debbie whirled to the right, away from the target, and went low.

Markham saw that the target's face had suddenly become wet. The target winced and blinked and ducked down, her mouth open and gasping, and clapped her hands to her eyes: pepper spray. The target was in agony. She rocked from side to side, tried to turn and make her way blindly down the hall toward the parking lot.

Markham quickly pulled out his pistol and fired without aiming, trying to catch up with Coleman, and the restaurant sounds were obliterated by the noise. Which shot cut flesh first scarcely mattered, because Parish had taught them not to fire once and wait. Coleman and Markham each fired rapidly four times, watching the target's body jump and buckle. When she was on the floor, Markham stepped forward. The target was dead, but Markham had been taught that the coup de grâce was the professional way, so he aimed at the target's forehead and fired once more.

He stepped back, because there was a blood rivulet heading along a crack in the floor toward his left shoe. As he looked up, he could see that Debbie had made it down the corridor to the back door. She opened it and slipped out.

He jumped when he heard the next shot, and involuntarily glanced down at his gun. The scout, Emily, had stepped inside. She was shooting the bartender and the waitress, then the two customers at the bar, then the one at the table. He had forgotten that the scout's responsibility was the place, choosing the spot and keeping it safe. She looked down at each of the bodies, then moved out the way Debbie had gone.

Markham turned on his heel and stepped toward the front door. He felt numb, slow and clumsy. The sudden silence left a ringing in his ears that seemed to rise and fall with his heartbeat. He saw Parish standing just inside the doorway, and held a picture of him as he stepped past him out into the night. Once again it was Parish, the instructor, looming silently on the periphery, watching everything with concentration and coldly evaluating it. His face was unreadable. As Markham turned on the sidewalk to look back, he saw Parish step calmly out the door after him.

Markham saw Coleman a block ahead of him, and he felt his pace increase in a canine eagerness to catch up. He had to keep himself from bounding up the street or calling out to him. They had done it. The hunt had been successful. They were outside now, the target was dead, and there were no living witnesses. He shivered briefly with residual fear, almost a physical memory of how he had felt. Now that his fear was only a memory, it was pleasant, titillating. He and Coleman had done it, gone up against an armed adversary, who had actually tried to shoot first. They had bet their lives, taken their chances, and won.

The feeling was better than the first time he had gone hang gliding, better than rock climbing. He had killed an armed enemy in a gun battle. After all, he was pretty sure that his first round had been the one that had done the trick. It was a shame that he couldn't tell anyone about it, at least not for a lot of years. And there was no trophy for this kind of hunting. The rewards were all internal. Now that the target was dead, he wished that the target had been a man, not a woman. But that made little difference, really: Markham would have been just as dead if the target had fired first. He knew that no matter how long he lived, he would never forget the name: Lydia Marks.

CHAPTER 16

Mallon squinted against the morning sunshine as he walked up to the office on De la Guerra Street holding a folded newspaper under his arm. He stepped inside, looked at the seats along the wall where clients were supposed to sit and wait, and approached Sylvia, the secretary. She said, "Good morning, Mr. Mallon. Can I get you something to drink while you're waiting, maybe a cup of coffee, or . . . ?" Her voice trailed off as she saw the expression on his face.

"No, thanks," he said, then turned to see Diane coming out of her inner office.

She looked at Mallon, then quickly at Sylvia, a question in her eyes. Sylvia gave a tiny shrug, and Diane's eyes snapped back to Mallon. "Robert!" she said, with a large, fixed smile. "Come on in." She stepped aside to let Mallon in, then lingered, her eyes on Sylvia again. But Sylvia only slowly moved her shoulders up and shook her head, her eyes wide.

Mallon stood waiting in the center of the carpet until Diane had closed the heavy office door. "Lydia is dead."

She froze. "What do you mean, 'dead'? How?"

"She's been murdered. Somebody killed her last night. It's on the news on the L.A. television stations. It's even in the early edition of the L.A. *Times.*"

"Oh, Robert, I'm so sorry," she said. "I can't believe it."

Mallon handed her the folded newspaper, with the article facing up. She stared at it, her eyes picking up disconnected phrases, which she said aloud—"evening shootout," "unknown assailants"—then she lowered it. She tried to hand it back to Mallon, but he would not reach for it.

"Keep it. I bought that on the way for you. I have one at home."

"This is terrible." She dropped it on her desk and turned away from it, toward Mallon. "Tell me what happened."

"Somebody killed her in a little restaurant down south of the L.A. airport. They shot her, it says, 'numerous times.' They also killed a bartender, a waitress, and three customers. It says the police aren't sure who was the intended victim, or if it had something to do with the restaurant—maybe a robbery. They had to be after Lydia."

"They did?"

"Look at the place. She wouldn't go into a place like that all by herself unless she was on business." He picked up the newspaper from her desk, turned it over, and held it in front of her face. There was a picture of some officials pushing a wheeled stretcher into an ambulance. The building was low, made of stucco, with a big sign and a satellite dish, and only small front windows high on the wall.

"It looks like a dive," she agreed. "So what was she doing there?"

"She must have been meeting somebody, probably another one of the women who knew Mark Romano. When we met with people, if she couldn't go to their homes or businesses, she would suggest a place that was expensive. She said it helped her to get people to open up to her. She even stayed in big, fancy hotels, because she figured local people knew the hotels and judged strangers by where they stayed." Mallon stared at the picture again. "Not this time, though. The person she was interviewing must have picked that place."

Diane looked at the picture again, then leaned on her desk and read the article. She seemed to be concentrating, so Mallon sat in a chair by the wall and waited. After a minute, she looked up. "It doesn't say she was meeting anyone."

"No," he said. "It doesn't. They don't seem to know that she was working, or that what she did when she was working was talk to people. I need to tell them."

Diane stared at Mallon, an expression of curiosity on her face. "They know who she was: it says she was a private detective. I think they must know how detectives work. They're investigators too, after all. They know the mechanics of the job better than we do." She paused, then said uncomfortably, "How well did you know her, really?"

"About as well as I know anybody," he said. "What are you getting at?"

"I'm just wondering. You said you hadn't seen her in a long time. She also had other cases, a bail bond business to run, undoubtedly a lot of personal relationships that you can't know about." She looked at him defensively. "I'm just saying, it may be too early to imagine that we know why she was killed."

"I called the bail bond office and talked to her partner. He said she'd called in every day to check with him, and all she seemed to be working on was Catherine Broward."

"Do we know she would tell him if there was something else?"

"I'm not sure what I know anymore," Mallon said. "Before I talk to the police in L.A. today, is there anything else I need to keep in mind?"

"Yes. Don't," she said.

"But they'll need to know about the case she was working on for me, and what she was investigating, and so on."

"You're right," she said. "We've got to do that. But I think you'd better let me make that call."

"You do?" Mallon was surprised.

Diane nodded. "I do. After all, I wrote up her contract, and kept in touch with both of you all the way through. At the moment, I know what was going on as well as you do. I have a responsibility as an offi-

cer of the court to come forward whether you do or not. I also am unlikely to whet their appetites for a suspect. If, after I've told them what
we know, they still want to talk to you, we'll go there with Brian
Logan."

He squinted at her skeptically. "I'm just trying to help them solve
the death of an old friend who was doing me a favor. Why so cautious?
What have I got to be worried about?"

"Let's see. You hired Lydia originally after you spoke with the Santa
Barbara police about a woman who had died of a gunshot wound
right after she was with you. Once her death was declared a suicide,
you and Lydia both went across the country to conduct a private investigation of her life. You then started in on her boyfriend's murder.
Now Lydia has been murdered. I don't know everything there is to
know about homicide cases. It's not my field. I do know that every
now and then, a person who has been talking to the police, giving
them leads, will be arrested for a murder. And the next thing you
know, the police are building a case based on the fact that he's been
around when several other people were murdered, sometimes a few
people going back ten or twenty years. It's hard sometimes for the police to believe these things are coincidental."

"I don't believe for a minute that they're coincidental," Mallon
insisted. "That's the whole point of going to talk to the police."

"I know, I know," said Diane. "And I'll try to convey that. But another thing we want to avoid right now is giving them the impression
that you're one of those people who are eager to spend a lot of time
hanging around the police and guiding them in one direction or another."

"I don't see how they could imagine I killed Lydia." He had let his
irritation creep into his voice.

"I'm not comfortable saying what they might or might not imagine," said Diane.

"But it's silly."

"Silly is no defense. Let's just keep this simple. Right now you're upset because of the death of a good friend, and probably don't really feel like talking to the police. I've got to call them anyway, so I'll start out by speaking for both of us. If they need more information from you directly, we can cooperate fully without acting strangely." She stood straight, glanced at her watch, and then met his eyes with a benevolent stare. "That's my legal advice. Do you disagree?"

He shrugged. "All right," he said reluctantly. "Go ahead."

She picked up the paper. "Then I'd better call them while it's still believable that I just saw this." She walked him to the door. When they reached the outer office she said, "Sylvia, can you please get the Los Angeles Police Department for me?" She set the newspaper on Sylvia's desk, tapped the article, and said, "Find out what division this was in, and call them." Then she looked up at Mallon, patted his arm sympathetically, stepped back into her office, and closed the door.

As Mallon walked along De la Guerra Street, then up Anacapa toward his house, he kept feeling an urge to stop and go back. He wanted to wait for her to finish talking to the L.A. police so he would know right away what he should be doing. It wasn't possible that what he was supposed to do was simply sit at home and wait. Lydia Marks had been a friend of his. She had been shot to death working for him. How could he do nothing?

As soon as he reached his house, he called Diane's office, determined to tell her that he was going to call the Los Angeles police himself. Sylvia said, "I think she was just getting ready to call you."

Diane's voice came on the line. "Robert?"

"Yes," he said. "Did you get through to them?"

"Sure," she said. "They're a police force. Somebody's always home, and they can't just not answer the phone. I told them what we know."

Mallon waited for a second or two, but she did not go on. "What did they say?"

"I talked to one of the detectives who's working on the case. He was very polite, and very appreciative. He took my name, address, and phone numbers. I gave him yours too, of course, but I also got him to agree to call me if he needed to talk to you."

"He didn't think that was odd?"

"No," she said. "Because it's not. Everybody is familiar with the right to an attorney—the Miranda warning and all that. But there's a part that not everybody knows. If they've already been notified that you have an attorney, then they have to include the attorney. That doesn't mean they won't talk to you anytime they feel like it, but it does mean they'll let me know, so I can get Brian Logan to go with you and protect your rights."

"I guess that's reasonable," said Mallon. "But what I meant was that people who just want to give information to the police don't usually do it through a lawyer, do they?"

She sighed. "You just never learned to behave the way people with your kind of money do. I guess that's why I like you. But people in your situation don't usually deal with authorities in person, and they never do it alone."

"Did you tell them everything?"

"Sure," said Diane. "I think I already said that."

"Aren't they going to call me?"

"Maybe," she said. "I think it will depend on what direction their investigation takes. You have to remember that even though Lydia might have been working on your case at the moment when she died, her death might not have been connected with it. Over her career, she must have worked on hundreds of cases, and a lot of them left some-body angry. She was the one in the bail bond business who traced the clients who skipped out on their bail, wasn't she? If the police think we can help them, they won't be shy. But I don't know what the evidence they have in hand tells them. They may already have found out that it's not related to your case, and they would not have told me at this stage." She paused. "They may be tying up the last loose end right now."

¶¶

CHAPTER 17

Parish had quietly appeared in the gym so that he could look in on Ron Dolan's early martial arts class. Today was this group's last at the camp, and he liked to leave them with the impression that they'd had more of his personal attention than he had actually given them. He had left the gym and was on his way to the firing range when it occurred to him that he had not seen Debbie or Emily this morning. He walked into the cabin at the end of the long path, and saw Debbie barefoot, wearing sweatpants and a tank top, perched on a chair hugging her bent legs so her knees came up to serve as a chin rest.

He said, "What's up?"

She turned her head farther than it seemed she should be able to and looked over her shoulder at him. His eyes moved to see Emily lying on her back on the single bed in the corner, with her hands clasped behind her head. She said, "We came together to bitch, Michael. You should get out while you can."

"It sounds like something I should hear." He stepped up to Debbie, took one of her hands, and gently tugged as he walked toward Emily's side of the room. Debbie let the arm straighten, then yielded to the steady pressure and brought her feet to the floor to walk with him.

When he reached the bed where Emily was lying on her back, staring up at the rafters, he sat on the very edge, then moved his hip against hers and pushed. "We're joining you." She slithered closer to the wall, and he and Debbie sat.

Emily rolled to face them, lying on her side. "She could kill you with her hands," she said thoughtfully.

Parish looked at Debbie, put his arm around her waist, and said, "So? You could kill me in some other way."

Emily persisted. "Even lion tamers sometimes go into the cage at the wrong time and get torn apart."

"And while it's happening, maybe what they feel is . . . ecstasy. That's what their lives were all about, isn't it—that the danger was real all along? And just being near those beautiful creatures, tempting them and teasing them." His eyes glittered as he smiled, reached out a hand, and softly touched Emily's cheek. He let his hand linger there for a second, but when she brought her hand up to brush it away, it was already gone. Her laugh seemed to escape in spite of her.

He said, "You both have legitimate complaints. Which one are we talking about?"

Debbie said, "Last night, Michael. The idea was to have those two do their own hunt, wasn't it?"

Parish nodded. "Yes. It was."

"Well, what I was doing wasn't what a tracker usually does. I had to take a big risk to lure that target into the restaurant in the first place. She wasn't some man I could get to follow me by batting my eyelashes. When I got her there, I had to find a way to signal Emily without her sensing that I was doing it, then sit there for fifteen minutes talking about the camp and about Catherine before anybody else even arrived."

"You did it brilliantly," he said. "I heard every word over the radio. That little bit of an implication that you were a bad girl but you regretted it, and that you needed her protection, I think that was what kept her there."

Debbie gave an embarrassed smile, but she knew she was being seduced, so she gave his shoulder a push. "I did what was necessary. But at that point, my part should have been over. I signaled Emily, I gave her fifteen minutes to bring the two all-stars up and point them in the right direction. I waited, and talked. When they got there, I was supposed to get up and go to the bathroom, wasn't I?"

Parish nodded. "That was certainly the plan. I know it didn't go smoothly—I was there—and I'm very sorry." He turned to Emily, waiting.

Emily said, "I did everything the scout is supposed to do. I found the restaurant, I got the two of them into safe places where they could wait, then brought them forward when it was time. So what do they do? They fuck it all up. They burst in there while Debbie is still at the table. Coleman was already reaching for his gun when he stepped in the door. If Debbie hadn't been the fucking martial arts nightmare girl, she never would have been fast enough to keep the target from turning the hunt into a slaughter."

Parish looked apologetically at Debbie. "She's absolutely right," he said. "You kept the target's gun out of her hand and disabled her with that pepper spray. I'm still amazed at how quickly it happened."

Emily went on. "And *then* they open fire. Debbie's lucky they didn't shoot her too. And what do they do next? With the bartender and the waitress gaping at all of us, they turn around and start to leave!"

Parish nodded. "I saw you drop the witnesses before you left. I admired your presence of mind. I was as disappointed as you are that Coleman and Markham didn't do it themselves."

The two women looked at each other and rolled their eyes, then stared at Parish.

He said, "They asked me for a challenge. I knew that bagging a private detective in public was sure to be exciting, but I didn't anticipate that Miss Marks would be that challenging. I took into account the possibility that she might be armed in some way, but I didn't know she'd be alert enough to her surroundings to cause a serious risk. She was very good."

Debbie's eyes narrowed. "But did you know how bad *they* would be? She saw them pulling out guns as soon as they were in the door, but it took an eternity for them to fire. I practically had to kill her myself—hold her there, disarm her, and disable her before they could even pull a trigger. Did you know they were that bad?"

"No, never," said Parish. "But I knew if it turned wrong, then you would be up to it." He tightened his arm to give her an affectionate squeeze. "I also knew that, from looking at you, she would never imagine that you would be capable of doing much harm. So if she had managed to get off a shot, you were not going to be the one she aimed it at. She would shoot Mr. Coleman or Mr. Markham."

Emily eyed him suspiciously. "You're not putting up much of a defense."

Parish half-turned to see her better, leaned down, took her hand in his and kissed it. "I'm sorry. I apologize again for my mistake. I don't think excuses are what you want, really. I have none."

"You could at least offer a little resistance."

He shrugged. "You're both describing this situation accurately, just as you read the situation correctly last night. The tracker and the scout were in position and prepared. They saw that the clients weren't going to be able to handle things, so they stepped in. The tracker took responsibility for the target, and made it an easy kill. The scout took charge of the environment and kept it safe: no interference, no witnesses left alive. You forgot nothing, and we all got home. It's the way the hunting party is supposed to work. I'm very pleased with that part of the experience. It confirmed my faith in the professionals I chose to run this hunt. But I can't defend my decision to let those two clients go after big game."

Debbie put her arms around Parish and placed a kiss on his cheek. "Oh, Michael. You're such a weasel." She stood up and stretched, then stepped into her sandals and said over her shoulder, "I have a class to teach." She slipped out the door silently.

Parish turned to Emily. "I have to go speak to the two clients. They're probably already waiting for me. Do you want to come along?"

She lay on her side and squinted up at him as though judging his sincerity. Suddenly she sat up. "All right."

They left the cabin and walked across the field and down the paved road toward the main lodge. "We have to keep in mind," Parish said, "that these men are our customers. They pay us for all of this."

"The customer is always right?" She watched him closely.

"We run a service for spoiled, childish people who have lots of money. Most of them have never done anything useful to get it. When they're tired of their houses, they hire an architect and a decorator, then go off to Europe. When the house is done, they come back and tell people they did it all themselves. And this is the part that you need to know: they mean it. They believe what they're saying. If you understand that, then you own them. Right now those two are probably very pleased with themselves, unaware that you and Debbie did everything for them. They should be aware that you and Debbie performed valuable services, but they're feeling very potent and brave right now. That's the way we want them to feel when they leave."

"Whenever you talk about clients, you sound as though you don't even like them."

He glanced at her in surprise, then laughed. "Let's just say the customer is limited in experience, but perfectible. You can't judge him by the standards we use for ourselves."

She muttered, "I'm not likely to get that mixed up."

"I want you to remember that signs of contempt from a beautiful young woman might be particularly unproductive when I'm trying to teach these two clients."

"Debbie's right. You are manipulative."

"I'm trying to be perfectly transparent right now. And I'm sincere about teaching these two. They're strong, athletic, and eager. They're both developing a taste for killing—a need for it that we can fulfill—and they'll get better and better at it if we keep training them. People like Markham and Coleman are everything to us. They pay us. They share secrets with us. So let's be careful what we say."

They had nearly reached the lodge. Emily could see that the two men's cars were parked in the small lot across the gravel road in front of the building, a new two-seat Mercedes and a new BMW. The two men were flawlessly true to type. She stepped up onto the porch, but Parish held her arm. "Give me a couple of minutes alone with them first," he whispered, and stepped inside.

Emily walked to the water fountain, took a drink, then moved past it and sat down on the edge of the wooden porch, watching a hawk circling in a warm updraft high above the arroyo.

Inside the building, Parish pulled three chairs into a triangle, sat down in one, and looked at Markham, then at Coleman. He lifted his right hand in a gesture to the two men to sit down facing him. He said, "Before we get started on the critique of the hunt, I want to say something about a side issue that I never brought up with either of you before. I almost hesitate to say anything about it, because I should already have taught you the etiquette of the hunt."

"What is it?" asked Coleman. "We're here to learn everything we can."

"Let me say it as a story. Two amateurs go on a big-game hunt in Africa. They hire a professional hunter, who provides an expert tracker and an experienced scout. The hunt is set up competently. The tracker finds the game—say, a lion—and keeps close to it—maybe dangerously close—so it won't disappear into the tall grass. The scout brings up the hunters, covers their backs, makes sure they're safe. But the lion spots them too soon, and prepares to charge. The tracker jumps up and distracts him. The hunters shoot, and get their lion. Everything seems to be over. But suddenly, out of the grass nearby, come two more lions. The hunters aren't prepared for that, so the scout takes dead aim, and drops the two lions with two shots." He paused, scrutinizing them. "Everybody gets to go home." He waited.

"What?" asked Markham after a few seconds. "I don't think I understand. That's us, but what am I missing? That's how it's supposed to work, right?"

"The two hunters. What do you think they should do, as a matter of etiquette?"

"A tip?" gasped Coleman. Markham winced, but Coleman did not stop. "We paid you fifty thousand for this hunt. Are we supposed to tip you, too?"

Parish stared at him coldly and in silence until Coleman's eyes found their way to his feet. "I wasn't referring to myself. You don't tip the owner of a hotel or the captain of a ship."

"It's for the girls," Markham announced, as though he had discovered something nobody else had seen. "They took a risk, too. At least until we got there and killed the target." He turned to Parish. "You're right. We should give them something. What would be appropriate?" He grinned. "We don't want to spoil them for you."

If there was anything in Parish's eyes that could be called amusement, neither of them saw it. He appeared to be considering. "Twenty percent should do it."

"Ten thousand dollars?" Coleman said. His eyes looked thoughtful. "Do we split it so they each get five?"

"No," said Parish. "So they each get ten."

Coleman and Markham exchanged a quick glance. Markham said, "Well, thanks, Michael. Last night we were wondering if there was something we ought to do for them, weren't we?" It was obviously a lie. "And then it kind of slipped."

"Then I'm glad I brought it up," said Parish. "Now, I'm going to bring Emily in to help with the critique. The scout sometimes sees things the professional hunter misses, because she's in closer. This is for your benefit, so don't be shy about asking questions." He stood and carried a chair from the wall to a spot beside his own. "Emily!" he called at the open doorway. He turned to the two men and said conspiratorially, "You might want to say something about your gift."

Emily stepped into the doorway, and the sun glowed through her dark hair for a second.

Coleman said, "Hi, Emily. You know, Markham and I were talking, and there's something we'd like you to have, to show you we appreciate the good job you did on our hunt. We didn't know we'd be seeing you today, so you'll have to give me a minute to write out the check."

Markham said quietly, "If you're doing that, I may as well write the one for Debbie. Maybe we can give it to her after we're through here."

Markham noticed that when Emily saw the number Coleman was putting on her check, she looked quickly at Parish, and her blue eyes were different. They were bright and intense, and her lips were turned up at the corners, but only a little, and they were tightly closed. Markham supposed that she was feeling gratitude, mixed with a bit of awkwardness, as people sometimes did in situations like this, but it didn't exactly look like gratitude. It looked as though she thought something was funny and was having a difficult time keeping from laughing out loud.

She took the check. "Thank you," she said, and she seemed more attractive to Markham than before. He could see that Coleman could barely keep his hands off her. It was typical that Coleman would jump in early to be sure he was the one who gave Emily her check, leaving Markham to track down Debbie and face the barely veiled hostility he and Coleman both remembered from their first meeting, before the hunt.

He decided it would serve Coleman right if he got Emily interested enough to have a relationship. He could end up married to a woman who was accustomed to killing people for money, who was comfortable with it. Coleman had more than enough money to make her consider dropping something heavy on his head as soon as the marriage certificate was filed in the county courthouse.

The thought pulled Markham into new territory. He found himself considering what sort of target Coleman would make. It would be amazing, incredible, to hire Parish to set up a hunt with Coleman as the target. This time, Emily could be the bait, and take him to a quiet, private spot. Markham, the old friend, would arrive unexpectedly. For a moment, Coleman would wonder if it was a practical joke, a surprise party. Markham pushed the idea out of his mind. He signed the check to Debbie, tore it out of the book, and set it on the table where it could be seen. Then he went back to his chair.

"Let's start with your reactions," said Parish. "Did you feel that your hunt was worth the time, the money, and the risk?"

"It was the best," said Coleman. "It's the most intense activity that human beings do. It has anticipation, bravery, cunning, camaraderie . . ." He looked at Emily. "Even temptation."

Markham detested Coleman for his eagerness always to jump in too quickly, leaving him nothing to say. "I agree."

Parish did not seem to notice. "Fine. We wanted you to have a good experience. The rest of what we offer is training. We want you to improve each time out. That's the spirit in which we make these critiques."

"Fire away," said Coleman.

"First, when you stepped in the door of the restaurant, you took the wrong approach to the target. What happens in this situation is, two men walk in the door. In a restaurant, bar, or small store, the target will always feel a blast of air from the door opening or hear it and look, or see it in his peripheral vision. He will make an evaluation. It's primal stuff: Do I know these two men? No. Are these two going about business that has nothing to do with me, or are they a threat of some kind? Once you pass this examination and the target determines that you're not interested in him, he won't stare at you for a time, because it's rude."

"But this was a woman," Coleman said.

"All of this works even better if the target is a woman. They're not subject to instinctive rivalry if they see men, and they're more likely to worry about being rude, so they stop staring sooner. But you didn't give this target a chance to reassure herself. Instead of going to safe positions off to the side, you faced her table directly, and began to reach for weapons when you were still too far away to use them. And most importantly, you forgot to wait until the tracker, Debbie, had moved out of the way."

"We knew we wouldn't hit her or anything," said Coleman. "She stood up as soon as we came in."

Parish appeared to be considering the argument, then spoke quietly and carefully. "It seems to me that you may have underestimated the target because she was a woman. You knew that she was an experienced professional detective. You knew that Debbie had lured her to that restaurant by posing as an informant. Now, the conclusion I wanted you to draw from that information was that this target knew she was in a situation that had great potential for danger. She might be armed—as, in fact, she was. If she realized that she had been set up, then she would know it was Debbie who had done it. If you'll remember, the plan was for Debbie to get physically out of sight before anything happened that might make the target feel threatened. Debbie was to see you come in the front door, and excuse herself to go to the ladies' room, remember? That would get her away from the table and behind the target, to control the back corridor and the rear exit. Her act of standing up and walking back there would also distract the target from whatever was going on at the front entrance, which was your taking positions. Done right, it makes all three of you safe: the target can't figure out whom to watch, so she tries to swivel her head to see where Debbie's going, and back up front to see what you're doing. But it wasn't done right."

"I'm sorry," said Coleman. "I guess I was the one who got too eager."

Markham didn't contradict him, or chime in to share the blame. It was true. He even knew what Coleman had been trying to do. He had wanted first blood. Probably he had even hoped his first round would be fatal, so he would get the kill, and Markham would have paid twenty-five grand to fire shots into a corpse.

"I'm not looking for apologies," said Parish. "There were errors, and if I fail to point them out, you won't improve. This time we had the target five ways, so no matter what she did, she was going to be ours. But she could have gotten off a shot and hit somebody. We didn't have to give her that chance. Fortunately, Debbie took it away from her."

Coleman shifted uneasily in his seat. "Watch the timing, and make sure the tracker is clear. That's it, right?" He put his hands on the arms of the chair as though he was ready to stand up.

"Not quite," Parish said. "When the target falls, you're not home yet. There were other customers in that place, the waitress, and the bartender."

"Well, yeah," said Markham. "But Emily took care of them, so we didn't need to."

Emily said, "What were you waiting for?" Her voice was strained, as though she was trying to keep it calm but couldn't quite do it.

Parish warned her with his eyes, and turned to the men. "Emily is right, of course. Once a gun appears, anyone in the place is justified in killing you, and some of them get over any reluctance very quickly. Some bartenders hide a gun near the cash register. Emily perceived that this one was moving in that direction and needed to be dead before he got there. You didn't." He let them think about it for a moment, then stood. "That's it." He smiled. "Otherwise, it was a perfect evening." He held out his hand so Coleman could shake it, then turned to Markham and let him shake it.

Markham muttered, "Thank you, Michael. Thanks, Emily."

"You're welcome," said Parish. "If we can do anything more for you in the future, get in touch."

He walked them out to the porch and watched them cross the road to get into their cars. As they backed into the driveway, Emily joined him. "Wave to them," he said. "And smile. The man just gave you a ten-thousand-dollar tip."

Emily waved her hand. She could see Coleman waving energetically back to her as he drove out the gate. "No, he didn't," she said through her false smile. "You did."

As soon as the two cars had gone around the first bend, Parish said, "Where to next?"

She grinned, and this time the expression was real. "I want to be the one to give Debbie her check. I'd like to see the look on her face. Do you mind?"

"Not at all." He watched her slip into the lodge and snatch up the check that Markham had left, then hurry toward the gym. He walked across the long drive toward the hill in the direction of the firing range. He had problems to consider, and he welcomed the solitude. He had managed, by force of will and self-discipline, to control several unsatisfactory situations at once, but he had not yet had the time to consider what they had to teach him.

Parish had designed last night's hunt to provide a specific experience for two paying clients. He had assumed that when Lydia Marks was made to believe that an informant had come to her, she would do as she had done in the past: show up with her client, Mr. Mallon, and they would interview the informant together. Parish went over his reasoning again: they had come to the self-defense school together, and while they were talking to Parish, they had said they'd gone to Pittsburgh together to interview Catherine's sister. They had also said they were fresh from interviewing some woman in Los Angeles together. Parish had been perfectly justified in drawing the conclusion that if he presented an informant as bait, two targets would appear, not one. He had chosen those two targets over all others precisely because he had wanted to provide each of his two clients with a kill of his own.

Parish strode up through the dry brown weeds that covered the hill, considering. When he had heard Debbie's first radio transmission making it clear that there was only one target, he had dreaded the dissatisfaction of his two amateur hunters: they would feel cheated with only one kill between them. But he had overestimated them. They

were too arrogant to have noticed that their challenge had been in-
sultingly easy. They had been so spoiled and flattered all of their lives
that whatever meager achievement they accomplished was magnified
to heroic proportions. There had been nothing for Parish to worry
about. He had greatly overestimated them.

But that thought brought its own worries. Their mistakes on the
hunt had been gross and shocking. He had seen at the time that most
of the mistakes had come from pure selfishness. Coleman and Markham had each wanted to beat the other to the kill, each rushing to get
his money's worth and the other man's too. Their greedy competition
had been carried out in a mental vacuum, so that they had eagerly
fought over one target, and left five equally good targets—the bartender, the waitress, and the three customers—completely alone. In
their minds, only Markham, Coleman, and their designated target
existed.

Parish never let his discoveries go unconsidered, and he sensed that
this one had great potential for the future. The key to a new source of
profits might be contained in the single word *competition*. There had
also been other discoveries that cheered him a bit. He had watched his
staff react instantly and expertly to salvage the hunt. And although he
may have misjudged Markham and Coleman—their experience, their
sagacity, their technical competence—he had not been mistaken in
choosing to exploit them. They were acceptable.

The camp's prices for the initial training, in money and in time, ensured that all of his guests were wealthy and idle. Month by month, the
classes came and went, while Michael Parish watched and listened.
Some clients were plagued by a fantasy that strangers would steal their
money or take them hostage or rape them. Some of the middle-aged
men who had been born too rich and protected to have been forced
into military training when they were young seemed to thirst for it
now, to feel their incompleteness and inadequacy and want to patch it
up. But among the legion of silly, frightened, or bored people who paid
him over a thousand a day for simple shooting lessons, he would see a

few who had real potential. It was a small group, and they were very precious to Parish. What they wanted was the real thing.

Often he could see it in their eyes. On the range, they weren't aiming at targets, they were aiming at a person, and he knew that the person had a name. When they were in martial arts, they were the ones who went into a strange reverie when they punched or kicked the heavy bag. The clenched teeth, the fixed, determined stare, the strain when the blow connected told him that they were seeing a particular face.

He waited, and eventually the hints would start. The student would ask where to hit to cause the most damage, what it took to make the heart stop beating. The ones he wanted had no interest in self-improvement. They only half-listened to lessons about anything but firing the fatal shot or striking the deathblow. Their ears merely monitored the stream of talk for tips that might help them fulfill the dream of the avenger that their minds were forming.

Parish never approached any of the guests to offer special services. He simply answered questions, admitted the truth that the lessons of self-defense were the same as the skills of an aggressor: a bullet could do nothing but punch a hole in what it hit. The bullet did not distinguish between an opponent who was about to attack and an unsuspecting enemy who had committed his offense five years ago. The methods, the lessons Parish taught, were the same.

Parish accepted only a very few, the ones who were right for his needs. They had to be reasonably good at their lessons. They had to be haters, but they had to hate in the right way. Parish could not be involved with lunatics who were afraid of whole races, or wanted to kill politicians or other public figures. He could not accept the sort of emotional, undisciplined person who would go into it in a hot rage, without considering what killing a human being would be like or what it would mean after it had been accomplished. Students he found acceptable had to embrace the hunt, not see it as a sin or a crime that they were driven to take on themselves. If they saw it as a sin, they might later decide that the way to lift the burden of the sin was to confess it. What he needed were people who were immune to seeing their acts as infractions, because they could not imagine why they should ever be denied any possession, or any pleasure.

Parish was patient, and Parish never compromised. He observed, and then he waited until the right students came to him and tried to persuade him to give them the chance they wanted. After he was convinced that they were the right ones, he did not assume that they were ready. He had to impress upon them the seriousness, not only of the act they contemplated but also of sharing knowledge of the act. Anyone who knew of a kill was dangerous to the others and, therefore, was in danger if he seemed unreliable.

Parish had not yet failed in choosing clients who would not compromise the hunt. He had also prohibited hunting anywhere near the self-defense school. Almost every hunt had taken place in some distant part of the country. Over the years, he had permitted only two expeditions anywhere within the state of California, neither within eighty miles of here.

The clients were satisfyingly malleable. They were so egotistical that they could easily be made to believe that what they wanted was their birthright, simply because they wanted it. The logic was irresistible because it was familiar to the rich. They believed they had more of everything than other people because they—or more often, their ancestors and consequently they themselves—were superior. They had done more for society than their inferiors: they had tamed a wilderness into a sprawl of shopping centers, or created labor for the masses, or developed some innovation into a corporation. It was simply the law of nature that they should be richer, because they were better.

Parish professed to agree with their deeply held belief in their superiority. It made no sense, he repeatedly declared, that in the United States the upper classes should have to suffer offenses at the hands of nobodies. It was an outrage that such a perversion had been allowed to grip this country. In other parts of the world, these incidents were not tolerated. The authorities would simply have made these vermin disappear. Parish had traveled in certain circles with access to inside information, and take his word for it, even in some countries he could name that professed egalitarianism, the ruling class was not subjected to insult, insecurity, or harm. The authorities knew whom they were working for. They took care of such matters efficiently and quietly. Parish's flattery always worked, because his customers were so convinced of their superiority, so cushioned from reality by their money, that they didn't know they were being flattered.

The secret that Parish never revealed to anyone was that the reason he knew how to instill in his chosen students the taste for killing was that he had it himself. It was a kind of addiction, a gnawing need that had afflicted him since the Africa days. After he had come to this country, it had taken him years to find a way to feed it.

He had managed to do very well. Here he was, training his killers openly, without having to hide anything from anyone, because he was operating a legitimate self-defense school. He had little to fear from the authorities in the distant places where the hunting parties took place, because there was no connection to make between the targets and Michael Parish. There was nothing to fear from the authorities in California, because he and his people never did anything illegal here. As soon as his mind had formed the thought, he remembered the exceptions. He should never have allowed Catherine Broward to hunt in California.

He reached the end of the dry arroyo, opened the steel door of the storage building at the end of the firing range, and took out a rifle. He loaded it and fired a round at one of the targets placed at two hundred yards, then cycled the bolt. Dead aim was not just a matter of practice— of training hand and eye. It was a matter of calm, of control. It was character. He had, narrowly and provisionally, kept Emily and Debbie happy. But he would have to try to restore balance, and keep the other instructors involved. He had one more loose end to clip.

—————————————————————————

CHAPTER 18

Parish stood at the side of the main lodge's meeting room, his back to the night-darkened windows, holding his wine glass in his left hand. He kept his right hand empty so he could offer it to the men to shake, or put his arm around the women. The glass held an inch of red wine, and always stayed at the same level because he never drank any of it. He never approached anyone at these final-evening farewell parties, merely oversaw them as he oversaw everything else at his school. The students came to him—first in greeting, simply acknowledging him as they arrived, and then again singly, as they saw their chances—to smile and talk.

"I've loved my time here," said Helen Corrigan. She had a habit of lifting her shoulders and compressing her face in an ingratiating smile during her pronouncements, then simultaneously releasing both sets of muscles in a gesture that signaled both her satisfaction and her intention to stop talking.

Parish bent his head lower to nod slightly. "I'm very glad. Tomorrow, as everyone in your class goes home, you'll be given a questionnaire about your experience. Sometime in the next few weeks, maybe you'll share any ideas you have for improving things: the courses, the accommodations, the food, or anything else. Now that this little group has spent a month with us, you're all a very valuable resource."

"We are?" She was flattered.

"You're experts," he said. "You've learned what we were intending to teach, and now it's your turn to teach us by telling us what we could do better."

As her face grew sincere, it went slack and allowed a few of the wrinkles that had been surgically erased to reveal their shadows. "I'll try," she said. "But this has been a life-changing experience I wouldn't tamper with too much. I've always been a little afraid, without really being aware of it. That's not entirely over, but the stupid part is, the part that's almost like a superstition: you're scared, but you don't know what you're scared of, and it doesn't matter, because whatever comes along, you're not capable of thinking of anything to do about it. Now I know there are some things I can do that will help."

Parish lowered his voice and leaned down again. "I sensed that we were succeeding with you, Helen. I've kept an eye on you, and I've been very pleased with your progress."

"So have I." She giggled. "I've even lost fifteen pounds." She raised her hands to her shoulders and half-jokingly twirled around.

Parish chose to take her seriously. "We've all noticed that, too. It's not uncommon. Our guests eat a nutritious, balanced diet and get a great deal of exercise without giving either much thought."

"After the first few days, I began to think of friends I'd like to talk into coming here. One look at the weight I lost would be enough for some of them."

"I'd love to see a few of your friends here," he said. "If the physical program is what attracts them, fine. Come back with them, and you can help them learn. As you know, we have to keep classes very small and personal, but with enough notice, we might be able to arrange something just for you and your friends."

"I'll think about that. I will." She repeated her gesture of lifting her shoulders and tightening her facial muscles, then settling again, and moved on to let others pay their respects.

Parish let his eyes wander around the room without letting them focus on anyone. This class had consisted of six men and women in their fifties or sixties. Because the basic course at the camp took a month and started at forty thousand dollars, it was inconvenient to the lower classes: all of these people could afford to come back when they wished. He had seen on the first day that there was only one who had any potential whatever as a hunter, but the rest were useful in their way: there had to be some harmless self-defense students or it would be hard to account for Parish's income, or the existence of this place.

He watched Christiana and Edward, two of the customers, engaged in a whispered conversation across the room. After a moment he saw that their hands were touching. Suddenly Christiana seemed to sense that she was being observed, and turned toward him, so he smiled and drew his eyes away. Excellent. Those two people would leave with this camp experience mixed up in their minds with sex, remembering it with the same irrational glow. Maybe they would return, and they would both be very sincere in their praise of the place to their friends.

"I wanted to thank you, Michael."

Parish turned his head to the left. David Altberg was beside him. "You're welcome, David. It's been a pleasure to have you in our program." He had been watching Altberg for weeks, and he knew that Altberg was not here just to take the obligatory leave of his host. Women who wanted to talk to him about something in confidence or speak seriously always planted themselves in front of him and looked into his eyes. Men stood beside him and looked at whatever he was looking at. Parish was ready for what Altberg would say: he had been waiting.

"I . . . have a couple of friends who have been through the program with you in the past, and we've talked about it some," said Altberg. He glanced at Parish's face for signs that he should not proceed, but Parish looked politely interested. "I got the impression that you also sometimes offer . . . advanced instruction, for people who have been through the general course and want to do more?"

Parish nodded. "That's true. We can offer training at any level. Who are your friends? It's likely I'll remember them."

"Well, Ray Darville? Carl Fortin?"

Parish leaned closer and dropped his voice a bit. "I think I know the sort of thing you had in mind. We can talk tomorrow about arranging something, if you'd like. You could stay on after the others leave."

"Great," said Altberg. "I'll do that."

"Why don't you meet me here in the lodge tomorrow at, say, two o'clock, after I've seen the others off?"

"I'll be here," Altberg said. "And thanks." He stepped forward, turned to face Parish, shook his hand, and moved off.

In a moment, Debbie was at Parish's side; she stood on tiptoes to put her face close to his ear. "Don't tell me you're arranging another expedition already." He glanced at her and saw that she was wearing a long yellow summer dress with thin straps. The effect was disconcerting, because the dress revealed her soft, curved feminine silhouette, but the upper part left bare the lean, sinewy muscles in her upper back and shoulders.

Parish shrugged. "We'll see." He turned to watch her face. "Interested?"

She pursed her lips and squinted. "Not right away." Her voice dropped to a whisper. "And not with creaky old geezers like David Altberg. Would I have to?"

He shook his head, and whispered too. "No. It's nothing that's likely to demand your skills. There's a loose end that I could take care of, and give David his thrill at the same time."

Parish watched her move off into the party. He was often intrigued that there were people who thronged around Debbie. Some were women who seemed to ignore her acerbic manner and see her as a heroine, a big sister. She demonstrated throws in her class by using the most formidable male students as opponents, and some of the women had never imagined such a thing before. Other admirers were men, who seemed to see only the curves she had accentuated in her body through fifteen years of brutal workouts, and not understand that what she had been doing was fortifying herself against that kind of attention. People understood parts of Debbie. Parish suspected that he was the only one who knew that her indifference to men applied equally to women: she had no interest in sharing her bed with anyone, and not much interest in talking to them.

In the corner of his eye he caught Mary O'Connor's red hair. Her head turned, she walked past Christiana and Edward, then stopped in front of him. "Michael, will you help me with something out here?"

Parish nodded, then followed her out onto the porch. When she was sure they were alone, she said, "Debbie says you're going out again right away."

Parish smiled. "I was going to talk to you about it later. It's just come up in the past few minutes. A client came to me."

"You're using them to get rid of your own problems, aren't you?"

"It wasn't about me at all," he protested. "The detective came here asking about Catherine Broward's suicide. Catherine seems to have had a kind of inner weakness that we didn't detect while she was here with us."

"She was sorry she did it," said Mary O'Connor. "She told me the next day, and I guess she never got over it. Is that so hard to understand?"

Parish looked at her with detached interest, then scanned the area around them to be sure none of the guests were close enough to the porch to overhear. "To be so eager for the hunt one day, and then be consumed by regret the next is certainly not a sign of stability. But she obviously couldn't help it. I think we owed her at least enough to protect her memory from some kind of accusation, don't you?"

She laughed, her eyes glittering, and pushed back her long red hair. "Oh, Michael. You're so good at this. You don't care about her, but you think I do."

"You're wrong. I feel terribly sorry about her," he said. "We made a commitment to her to protect her privacy. That isn't over, is it?"

"I suppose not," said Mary. She looked at him over the edge of her glass. "Debbie told me you got her a ten-thousand-dollar tip."

"Did she tell you why?"

She ignored his question and pursued her own train of thought. "And Emily too."

Parish nodded. "That hunt was a mess. The careful plan we laid out for them was just an inspiration for an evening of improvisation. They opened up while Debbie was within a foot of the target, Emily wasn't in position yet, and I was still outside. Ten thousand wasn't enough."

Mary looked at him for a moment, turned and took a step, then stopped and said, "Keep me in mind."

"As soon as it came up, I was thinking of you."

"Who else?"

"I'm not sure at the moment. Emily to handle the client. And I think Spangler."

She cocked her head, thought for a moment, then nodded. "Spangler would be fine with me. We could be a couple. We'd look good together." She turned and walked back in to the party. After ten seconds, Parish followed and took his place along the wall.

Mary joined Helen Corrigan and two other students across the room at the hors d'oeuvres table, tolerated a few minutes of their chatter, then stepped over to Edward and Christiana to distract them from each other long enough to get them to include David Altberg. Then she made her way through one more circuit of Parish's admirers stiffly, her face held in a fixed smile that made her facial muscles tired after a few minutes. She was taller than most of the guests at this party, and her bright red hair was easy to spot above the other heads, so she felt conspicuous.

She acknowledged the women's compulsive but vague politeness: "I enjoyed the experience very much," rather than "Thank you so much for" this or that. All of the students had met her, because she filled in and helped out in the classes, sometimes working the firing line on the range, teaching students to clear jams or rearranging their limbs in proper shooting stances. She often worked with Debbie, assuming the various fighting *kamae,* or showing students how to roll and recover. Debbie needed to perform the roll, but she never let a student throw her. Mary supposed few of the guests knew what she was doing there. They probably thought she was some sort of advanced student who stayed on and on.

In a way, that was exactly what Mary was. She had been Michael Parish's first friend in this country. She had met him before he was Michael Parish, when he was still only Eric Watkins, and she had been the one who had known things. She had been sixteen, having for the first time gotten too far from North Carolina to be found and dragged back home. She spent time with a changing group of acquaintances, all of them young and from someplace else. Most of them slept in abandoned buildings south of Hollywood, and spent their days trying to get enough money for food and drink. When they did, they sometimes shared, and when they didn't, they sometimes traded.

Mary O'Connor fit into that world easily. She had already learned that accepting the affection of boys came easily to her. It had always seemed to be the generous thing to do. And now when she did it, they shared their food, drinks, and even their money with her. It wasn't ever a transaction; it was just that human beings were herd animals, and they accommodated each other's needs to get along. Often, after she and one of the boys had formed a temporary alliance, she found that the affection she had been feigning had actually come to be.

For the year before she had met Eric Watkins, she had been living most of the time by shoplifting with two other girls, Darlene and Wendy. They would find a fresh shopping bag from a good store or two, then go into another store. Mary would step into the dressing room with one item to try on. On her way in, she would search the nearest stalls to find clothes that somebody had tried on unsuccessfully and left there. She would use a pair of wire cutters to remove the electronic tags from some of them and slip them into her bag. When she came out, she would very visibly return to the rack the single item she had tried on, and then leave. Darlene would be doing the same, while Wendy kept the clerk busy with requests and complaints.

Mary and her two friends would then station themselves beside an expensive, sporty car they found parked at a different shopping mall, usually near a music store. Mary would accost girls who passed and tell them wonderful stories. Sometimes she had driven a hundred miles from home against her parents' orders, spent all her money on clothes, and discovered she was out of gas. Another time, she said she had been at a movie with a boyfriend, and he had gotten angry and left her there. She had no money, so she had charged some clothes at the mall, and now she was trying to convert them to cash to get home.

Some of the young girls she chose to hear her pitch were eager to help her because she seemed to be like them, and others were simply eager to take advantage of her misfortune. Even when they suspected she was lying they bought the clothes: the goods were the most desired and sought-after styles and brands, certified by the fact that they were the ones that girls before Mary had selected from all others in the store and wanted badly enough to try on. And they really were bargains. They had real price tags from fine stores to prove it.

One night she was with several acquaintances who had been sleeping in the back of an abandoned camper one of the boys had found parked on a side street a few days before. When she saw them on the street, they were on their way to buy dinner, so she went along. Then Eric Watkins turned up. She did not see him arrive. He just materialized in her peripheral vision on the street among the others, and they began to talk. He seemed to be no more than two or three years older than the oldest boy, maybe twenty-six or twenty-seven, but he had a kind of self-assurance that made him a hundred years older than anyone.

After that evening, Eric Watkins showed up on the street twice more. Nobody in the group expressed much curiosity about what he was doing there, but when one of the boys asked where he was from, he said he had come from Australia, and had "gone walkabout." Mary had pondered the phrase for a few days, partly because she liked the sound of it and partly because it meant that he was probably going to move on soon, and she was not sure how she felt about it. But the next time someone asked, he answered that he was from Canada and had registered at UCLA. The third time Eric Watkins simply came and took her.

He had always come on foot before, but this time he pulled up in a car, as she had known he would sometime. She was walking on Sunset with her friends Wendy and Darlene, and when he pulled up and stopped the car, all three of them stopped walking and looked for a moment. Then the other two had turned and walked on, while she had stepped to the curb and gotten into the car.

She had sat in the front seat beside him. Although she'd had no idea where he was going, or what he intended to do with her when he got there, she had sensed that all uncertainty was over. She had known from that moment not that she would be okay, because nobody could know that, but that she would be possessed, told what to do. The car door had slammed shut, and she had been home.

She and Eric Watkins had traveled for a time. Sometimes he would stop to work just long enough to buy them some new clothes and the next few tanks of gas, and then they would move on. Sometimes they would both get jobs and stay for several months. She would clean hotel rooms in the morning while he sold cars. He was very good at selling things, she supposed because he had a slight accent that sometimes sounded British, and the snobs would buy anything they were told to buy in an accent like that. In the evening she would wait tables at a restaurant while he worked as a bouncer in a bar. It seemed to be a job he had no difficulty getting, because he was an expert at unarmed combat. She had known when she had met him in Los Angeles that he had been a soldier for some extended period, because when everyone else was slouching on the street, maybe leaning on things as they talked, he would often slip into a stance with his hands clasped behind him and his feet exactly as far apart as his shoulders. You couldn't grow up in the part of North Carolina where she had, surrounded by military bases, and not recognize parade rest.

She had been the one to pick up Emily. Mary had been in a laundromat in Phoenix, washing her clothes and Michael's—he had just become Michael—so she could pack them clean before they went on the road again. She had noticed Emily, because Emily was not happy. They were about the same age, and Mary could see that Emily was washing some clothes that were hers, and some that belonged to a man. The place was hot as only a laundromat in Arizona—with eight commercial dryers going on high heat and surrounded by a mile of blacktop on every side—could be.

The sweat was making Emily's curly, dark hair hang in ringlets. Mary said, "Hot in here."

Emily turned her head quickly, startled. "What?"

Mary guessed that Emily had been so completely locked in her reverie of dissatisfaction that she was not actually sure that Mary had spoken. She looked relieved when Mary answered, "I said it was hot in here," then giggled. "Did you ever notice that when you have to re-peat something like that, you feel really dumb? Both of you listen to it very carefully while you're saying it again, and when it's over, it wasn't actually telling anybody anything they didn't know."

Emily's expression turned into something better than relief, a kind of fellow feeling, as Mary had hoped it would. Mary instinctively knew it was time to wait, so she picked up a magazine that somebody had left on the blue molded-plastic seat next to her. It was an issue of *People*. The cover had been torn off, but she could still tell. It was so old that the story the pages naturally opened to was about a hot new TV star—a pretty blond girl like all of them were—who had by now been around forever. Mary had never picked up the habit of reading for pleasure, but she did not mind looking at photographs, so she began to leaf through the magazine from back to front, letting her eyes trace the contours of the beautiful faces. After a few minutes she could sense that Emily was becoming increasingly agitated. As Mary serenely stared at the pictures, Emily's movements became more quick and fluttery. Finally, Emily blurted out, "I'm Emily. What's your name?"

"Mary. Do you live around here?"

Emily nodded. "If you want to call it living." She pushed the wheeled basket that she had been loading from the washing machines over to a dryer and began pulling out big male shirts and pushing them in. "My boyfriend was coming out here to the university. I decided I'd come along, get a job, maybe pick up some credits in night classes." She shut the door and moved to another dryer and began loading it. "How about you?"

"No. We're just here for a day or two. Is it nice?"

Emily sat down on one of the plastic chairs near her. "I don't know. It might be okay in the winter, because it couldn't be this hot all year round." She was watching Mary's face, as though waiting for confirmation of the theory.

"I suppose not," said Mary. "Where were you from before?"

"West Virginia," said Emily. "As if you can't tell from my accent."

"I don't think I've ever heard one from there before," Mary said truthfully. "I think it's nice." Her mother had not permitted her to know people from the other side of the small North Carolina town they had lived in, let alone anybody from West Virginia, and she could not remember meeting any West Virginians since then. She supposed there just weren't many.

"You said you were only here for a day or two. Are you and your husband on vacation?"

Mary smiled. "He's not my husband. And we're just here because we—he, really—is closing a deal. Then we're going to California. We're gypsies, I guess."

"God, I envy you," said Emily. Then her eyes looked surprised, and

Mary knew that it had just slipped out. She had not intended to say it aloud.

"Why?" asked Mary. "Aren't things working out here for you?"

Emily's eyes were suddenly brimming, but the tears weren't from sadness. They were tears of frustration and anger, the tears of a stubbed toe. "We've been here for three months—since June twenty-seventh—and it's been exactly this hot. From the minute my parents found out we had left together, they've hung up on me. The only time I've heard my mother's voice, she called me a whore, and my father won't even do that. Danny, my boyfriend, is this big, dumb kid. He thinks that since the coach said he's going to start on the freshman squad at tackle, he's set for life, so he won't even crack a book. He sits in front of the TV, because he'd rather see it than me. I can't do night school this semester because the only job I could get was at night. If I'm not at work I'm here, or at the grocery store, or in that hot little apartment cooking." She looked at the floor as though she were talking to herself. "I've got to do something, find something."

Mary said, "I'm sorry Phoenix didn't work out for you, but there are lots and lots of places." She tried a bold experiment. "If you could get a ride to California, would you go?"

Emily stared at her for a moment, her mouth half open. "With you?"

Mary nodded. "We're leaving tomorrow morning, and it takes about seven hours of driving to reach L.A."

"What about your boyfriend? Will it be okay with him?"

Mary nodded. "You'll like him a lot." She looked at Emily judiciously. "I can't promise anything, but he's about to start a business, and he's looking for people to work there."

"I ought to go," said Emily. "I really feel like it."

Mary wrote down the name of the hotel, the street, and the room number on the margin of an advertisement in the *People* magazine, then tore it off and handed it to her. "Come tomorrow morning."

"What time?" Emily asked anxiously.

"I wouldn't come much after seven. Michael likes to get on the road early. And he's not my boyfriend. Please don't say that he is in front of him. He wouldn't like that."

"I really feel like it," said Emily. "I'd love to walk out of here and never see Danny again. He thinks I don't have any choice but to stay with him, because my parents have dumped me and I'm not in school or anything, so he treats me worse and worse. I'm beginning to hate him."

"If you don't want to go back there, you can come right now," said Mary. "You can spend the night with us."

Emily studied her, a bit uneasy. "Is this something weird?"

Mary shook her head. "It's pretty straightforward. He's been buying up land, and he's going to build something like a dude ranch, a self-defense school for rich people. He knows about that."

"I don't mean the business," Emily said. "I mean you and him. And now me."

Mary said, "Not to me. I'm not interested in you that way. He might be, but since he hasn't seen you, I can't really predict. I just thought you looked like you could use a friend, but that you didn't look as though it was all your fault. Sometimes you meet people who are all alone, but they also look like they're mean, so it shouldn't be a big surprise to anybody. You don't. But if you're worried about it, there's no pressure. Ours isn't the last car out of here."

Emily opened a dryer and began to fold her clothes. She did it with the hasty efficiency of a person who was not devoting any thought to it. Mary returned to her magazine, holding her hand over the captions and trying to guess what they would be. Then Mary's dryer stopped. She pushed one of the rolling baskets over to the machine and emptied it. When she returned, she saw that Emily was finished. She had packed up her laundry, and left Danny's neatly folded on a counter. She helped Mary fold hers, and then followed her to the car.

On the way to the hotel, Mary tried to prepare Emily for Michael

Parish. She did not tell her that he had still been Eric Watkins when she'd met him, but she did tell her that he had been born in South Africa and had started out as a soldier there. She told her that he had been in lots of armies of African countries after that. She went no further, because the details were all vague and probably jumbled in her mind. He had mentioned Uganda and Zimbabwe. He talked most often about the Congo, but it seemed to be both a place and a river, both of sizes that kept changing, and part of the river was not even in the country. There was no way of sorting out in which places he had been part of the government and in which an invader, or part of a group chasing invaders into another country.

She knew that the rank got higher each time, and it had not surprised her, because he was ambitious. Sometimes he had been a captain, sometimes a colonel. Unless colonel wasn't a real rank, but was an honor the way it was in the South, where *Colonel* was just a name the chamber of commerce or even a club could give a man. He had once said he'd left South Africa because of the blacks. She had at first assumed it was because the change in the government had left the blacks in charge. But they were also in charge in Uganda, Zimbabwe, the Congo, and everywhere else he'd chosen to go, weren't they? She had not pursued the issue very far.

She had helped him invent the name Michael Parish. He had not said why he didn't want to be Eric Watkins anymore, but she knew it was for reasons that had to do with the U.S. Immigration and Naturalization Service, and with the banks and licensing authorities in California. She was not sure whether the fault that had been found with Eric Watkins was something that had happened since he had come to the United States, or something he feared might have stuck to him from his early days in Africa.

Tonight, as Mary suffered through the farewell party, she still had not settled those details, although a good ten years had passed. They did not seem any more important now than they had then. She looked across the main lodge at Emily, who was surrounded by Helen Corrigan and her two classmates. Mary had been a good judge of character. She had also known from the beginning that Michael would find her attractive: Emily was so perfectly the opposite of Mary that he could hardly fail to think of her that way as soon as he saw them together. She had never doubted for a moment that Emily would acquiesce as soon as Michael signified a desire. Emily had as much as asked in the laundromat whether that would be part of it, and Mary had as much as confirmed it. She certainly had not denied it. She and Emily had at least shared some intelligence that included an understanding of what men were like.

That was before Emily had even met Parish, had him look at her in that way he had, in which he devoted every bit of his attention to her, studying her and giving her the impression that he was seeing things about her that she had always wished men would notice but was convinced that none of them ever had. And even more to the point, she had not yet heard him. His talk was what was impossible to withstand. He used his foreignness, the fact that he had seen the world and knew things, to make people want to know them too. But he also used it to ask questions. It was as though he were a man not from across an ocean, but from across the galaxy, that he was a sublimely benevolent being who was deeply fascinated by every detail about a person but did not know anything about petty provincial rules against asking very personal questions. Talking to him for an extended period was like being slowly, gently, but relentlessly stripped.

Michael had found Mary at sixteen, and she had found Emily at nineteen, and Michael had raised them. They were his apprentices, his partners, his first and best students, so perfectly schooled in his ways that they were inheritors of his experiences as well as his knowledge.

She had never stopped being the same girl she had been when she'd left North Carolina, the girl she thought of as the basic human being. But when she wanted to, she could also be like him, someone who had hunted on veldts and fought in jungles. In becoming his second self, his reflection, she had acquired the power to kill. That was something she could never repay him for.

Mary looked around her at the small group of students. As soon as this lot had drunk too much and gone back to their cabins, she would take off this uncomfortable dress and begin to look over her gear to prepare for the next hunting party.

CHAPTER 19

This morning Mallon walked the route he had usually taken during the years after he had first come to Santa Barbara, past the tourist hotels along Cabrillo Beach. The other direction—westward along the beach toward Hope Ranch and Isla Vista—would have taken him to the spot where Catherine had gone into the water, and he had not been able to bear it since her death. He was agitated, anxious, pacing along looking down at the sidewalk, going over and over the details of Lydia's murder and trying to decide what he should do next. Diane seemed to have anticipated the restlessness he would be feeling, the urge to do something. She called him every couple of days to tell him that the Los Angeles police had not yet been able to provide new answers to her questions about Lydia's death.

Mallon needed to do something about Lydia's death, but he had to be smart: what else could he do that wouldn't just distract and delay the police? Mallon tried to distinguish what he knew from what he felt. He knew that Lydia had begun to favor the theory that Catherine Broward had not exactly committed suicide: she had committed murder, sentenced herself to death, and carried out her own execution. Lydia had told him that much. What else did Mallon know? Lydia had said she was going to try to find out more about Catherine Broward. She had not said that she was going to do it that night, or how she would go about it when she did. But everything Mallon knew made him believe that Lydia had gone with the wrong person to the wrong place in order to ask questions about Catherine.

Mallon walked onto Cabrillo Boulevard, above the ocean, and kept going, past the zoo and the bird sanctuary, across the street and onto East Beach. The volleyball game that had been going on the afternoon when he had arrived ten years ago was still going on, all of the players still in their early twenties. They had been replaced many times since the first time he had seen them—always just at physical prime, a little too old to be spending business hours playing a game on a beach, already late at starting real work, already late at beginning to see each other as future husbands and wives, if not for actually marrying and having families. Within a few months, if not tomorrow, this set would be gone, replaced one at a time by others exactly like them.

He walked on, assessing the progress of the tide. This was a walk that took him to several spots where the high tide would swallow the whole of a narrow beach and the waves would roll into the cliffs. He judged from the thin strip of dry sand above the breakers that he might get a bit wet today, but it did not matter.

He went a quarter mile and came to the first of the small points that jutted out into the sea. He liked the stretches between these points, scallops of beach cut off by the rising waves. The power of places like this was not in vastness—a stretch of empty beach did not have to be long—but in seclusion. It made them seem prehistoric: human beings had not yet come. A gang of white seagulls hung in the air above the point ahead, showing him the way.

He walked along the beach toward the white gulls, thinking of his walk on the beach with Lydia Marks three days after Catherine had died. Lydia had been very astute and perceptive, searching in the right spot for the purse. It had never occurred to either of them that day that Catherine might have killed herself because she could not live with something she had done. Guilt was such an odd—what was it, an emotion? A judgment? It seemed to be both—an affliction, debilitating as a disease. He had felt it; he felt it now, but he didn't understand it. And even if Lydia had been right about Catherine, if guilt was a way to understand Catherine perfectly, he still did not know who had killed Lydia Marks. He did believe he might know why.

He tried to separate the logical question from his grief and anger, but he could not. The part of the story of Mark Romano's death that he and Lydia had both ignored was that Mark Romano had not been the only victim. When Detective Berwell had told them that a family nearby had been killed the same night, he and Lydia had let it go by; it was sad, but it had not seemed to have anything to do with Catherine Broward. But if Lydia's final theory was right, and the person who had killed Mark Romano was Catherine, then it was a crucial fact. Somebody had shot four innocent people to keep them quiet, and Catherine would never have done that.

He was looking down again, so he was a bit surprised when he raised his eyes and saw two people walking along the wet sand toward him. One was a man in late middle age, dressed in baggy shorts and a nylon jacket, his head covered by a cap of netting with a bill like a baseball cap. The woman with him was half his age and attracted Mallon's attention because her features seemed to be slightly exaggerated: she was short and had wide hips and large breasts, and her face had a wide mouth with full lips, and big eyes.

He stared at them while they were still far enough away so that he was sure they could not tell he was staring. They seemed to be opposites: the man was all bundled up to keep off the sun and the wind, but the girl was walking along comfortably in a black two-piece bathing suit, letting her curly dark hair blow in the wind as she approached.

Mallon felt frustrated when they came too close to permit him to stare anymore. Even with his eyes hidden by his sunglasses, it would be too obvious. He directed his gaze out past the next curve in the shoreline, toward the sea. It was then that he thought about the boat. It had been out there since the man and the woman had rounded the point, moving so slowly that Mallon could sometimes hear an unevenness in the distant engine sound that indicated it was running just above a stall. It was a small cruiser with a low, streamlined profile, a white hull, and a cabin that probably held only one bunk on each side. He could tell by the deep register of the engine that it was overpowered, and part of him was waiting for it to do something to justify the power: drop a pair of skiers into the water, or suddenly roar out toward the islands. As it bobbed on a wave, he saw a glint of glass near the stern that must have come from binoculars.

He constructed a story to make sense of it: the old boy was very rich, some billionaire who was well known to people who kept track of billionaires, but whose existence was absolutely new to Mallon. People like that visited Santa Barbara all the time, and quite a few of them had houses there. That explained the young girlfriend or wife, and it explained the boat out there, moving along at a slow walk with the couple. It carried servants with the old man's heart medicine and Viagra or, more likely, security people who were using binoculars to study the shore for danger. From out there it was easy to see everything before, behind, and above them, while still preserving the illusion that the two were alone. He glanced to his left at the man and the woman as they passed.

His eyes, by preference, moved to the girl, but the man was in motion, and that attracted Mallon's attention. His right hand, the one in his jacket pocket, was coming out. The girl reacted in a surprising way: she grasped his biceps, as though to keep the man from falling. The hand came out anyway. The man twisted away from her toward Mallon, and she lost her grip.

The man started to bring his hand up across his belly, toward the side Mallon was on. The girl was behind him now, and she was backing away like a wary cat. Then Mallon saw that the hand held a gun. It was a heavy, solid-looking chunk of metal, a semiautomatic pistol with square corners and a muzzle that looked huge to Mallon, like the end of a pipe.

Mallon was instantly aware of the vast emptiness around him. The distance to the next point was a hundred and fifty feet, the backtrack to the last one was twice that far, and he would be running in loose sand. Behind Mallon was the Pacific, a stretch of empty horizon that stretched around half the planet. The only place for Mallon to go was toward the man.

The man was still off balance, and he brought the gun around his body clumsily. Mallon leapt, both hands in front of him. He struck down the man's forearm with his left fist, and brought his right into the man's face. It landed on the man's cheek with a smack, and he punched again quickly and reached for the gun.

The man's body abruptly jumped and contorted, and Mallon got the impression he had heard the bang only afterward. The man dropped to the sand on his arm, covering the gun hand, but Mallon had the thought that he must have accidentally shot himself instead of Mallon. Then the body jumped, and Mallon heard the second shot.

Mallon looked up toward the young woman for an explanation, but she was doing something unexpected. She lowered her arms, and only then did he realize that what she had been doing behind the man during the struggle was waving them. She was looking at the ocean, and he followed her eyes to see what she was staring at.

The boat was moving closer now, roaring toward the beach. He saw a figure kneeling low near the bow, resting a rifle with a scope on the gunwale. He felt a moment of gratitude: the sharpshooter had undoubtedly saved his life. But then the rifle fired. The shot plowed into the cliff behind him, and he dived to the sand beside the body. He saw a hand move from the trigger to grasp a bolt and cycle it to put a new round in the chamber. The boat was pounding over the waves, the bow rising on each crest, then slapping down with such a jolt that the man in the bow could not hold the rifle steady.

Mallon looked to see if the girl was taking cover, but she was sprinting into the ocean. She had already made it down the beach and was still running, her knees high and the water nearly to her waist. She used the last of her momentum to dive over an incoming wave, and then swam. The boat swung in close to shore just beyond the line of breakers. The man crouching in the bow put down his rifle and moved along the rail to the stern as the boat glided close to the swimming woman. He rested his chest on the gunwale, took both the woman's forearms, held her as though they were two trapeze artists, and pulled her up into the boat. Both of them lay low, nearly hidden by the side of the boat as it quickly swung out toward the sea, accelerated to full speed, and angled around the point out of Mallon's sight.

Mallon looked down at the man in the sand. He knew he had to find out if the man was alive, but he did not want to touch him. He turned his head to stare around him—up and down the beach and out onto the water—at first to verify that it was really over, and then in the hope that people had heard the rifle and were coming to help him. He was alone. He knelt down.

He touched the man's back, felt no breathing, then moved the hand up to his neck, with the vague intention of feeling the carotid artery for a pulse. But the man was lying face down, and Mallon wasn't sure what he was touching. The neck seemed loose, like the neck of a dead chicken. He pulled his hand away and it was covered with a bright streak of blood. He looked at it, wiped it on the back of the man's jacket, then realized that new blood appeared there. Pushing it down saturated the cloth.

Mallon slid one hand under the shoulder and the other under the hip, and rolled the body over. The man's eyes were open and the jaw slack. The front of him had sand stuck to it from the forehead to the feet. Mallon could see down the half-open front of the jacket that the rifle bullet had torn through him and emerged, spraying blood and bits of flesh into the lining.

Mallon stood and looked away for a moment, then looked back and noticed the gun pressed into the sand. The sight brought back his confusion. At first Mallon had been sure that the man had been bringing the gun around toward Mallon's chest when the rifle shot had killed him. Maybe he had been wrong. Had the man seen the rifle appear on the boat and tried to defend himself by firing a few rounds at it? And who was he? Why had he been carrying a gun on the beach? Mallon stepped closer to the body, then dropped to his knees on the sand again. He took two deep breaths and began to search the body. He patted the pockets of the man's shorts, and then the jacket pocket, and reached inside to be sure. There was no wallet. There were no keys.

Mallon stood and looked out at the ocean again. Far off, nearly at the horizon line, there were tiny white specks that he knew were boats. Probably one of them held the woman and the man with the rifle. He had to get to the police. Mallon turned and began to run back up the beach toward the city.

When he reached the turn around the point, the tide had already come in far enough to have completely covered the sand. Now the waves were breaking against the big rocks at the base of the cliff. He ran into the surf and came to the curve. The next swell was bigger, and it came at him from a different angle, whipped by a strong west wind. It lifted him off his feet and pushed him sideways into a rock. He took a step ahead as it receded, and felt it tugging hard at his legs, drawing him out to deeper water with it. The second wave collided with him and tumbled him over so that he sat down and rolled once as it hissed and sizzled over his head. He held to the cliff and waited, then lunged forward around the point.

The going was easier now, and the waves hit him from behind, propelling him more quickly up onto the wet sand at the high-water mark. He broke into a run again, staying on the hard, wet stripe where he could run without digging in and fighting loose sand. The tide was coming in fast. At the next curve, when he ran down into the surf the water reached his chest, but he pushed off, let the first wave float him, and swam around the point, then sloshed out and resumed his run.

He reached the wide, dry section of beach. Ahead of him and to the right he could see the volleyball nets, and beyond them, the cars gliding along Cabrillo Boulevard. He turned toward them and strained to keep up his speed, trying to reach the grassy area near the road, where there were people. But now he was winded and the sand was loose and dry. Running on it was harder and slower. Once his foot didn't clear the sand and he tripped, but he got up and ran on.

He came to the volleyball nets. He shouted, "Hey! I've got an emergency," as he came to the back foul line, but his voice was breathy and strained, and it sounded to his own ears like a casual comment rather than an alarm. The young man who had just served stole a quick glance in his direction, but his eyes did not seem exactly to see Mallon, only to note his position as a possible obstacle, then return to the ball. The other team tipped the ball up once, then again, this time lofting it above the net to set for their center forward man to spike.

Mallon kept going. At the edge of the grass along the road, he saw three young women getting out of a car. He was afraid to run at them, because he knew he must look wild and deranged. He walked toward them and said, "Please, if one of you has a cell phone, please call the police. I've just seen a murder."

CHAPTER 20

━━━━━━━━━━━━━━━━━━━━━━━━━━━━━━━

One of the cops was about forty, and the other was in his twenties. Mallon had seen him before, a blond man riding a bicycle on State Street in a uniform with short pants and short-sleeved shirt that showed chunky reddish forearms and calves covered with fuzzy blond hair. The purposeful way they got out of their car and stepped toward him, fiddling with the gear on their black leather belts, made it look as though they were preparing to subdue him.

They both stood close to him and the older man said, "Did you place an emergency call, sir?"

"Yes," Mallon answered. "I asked this young lady if I could use her phone." He turned to indicate to her that she should join them, but he didn't see her. "She must have left."

The two cops looked around them, and seemed to notice the volleyball people who had gathered on the grass nearby. The older cop put a big hand on Mallon's shoulder and conducted him closer to the police car, while the younger cop took a step toward the gaggle of young people, not saying anything, just swinging both hands, palms upward, in a sweeping motion. They turned and walked off toward the volleyball court marked on the sand, having understood from the young cop's signal that order had been restored and nothing else of interest was going to happen.

Mallon fought to overcome the air of imperturbability that he sensed in the police officers. "I was walking on the beach, maybe half a mile up that way. A man—an older guy—and a young woman were coming toward me from the other direction. The man pulled a gun out of his jacket. There was a boat offshore, and somebody with a rifle shot the man. He fell down, and the person shot him again. The woman ran to the water, swam out to the boat, and they took off."

"Why?" asked the older cop. "What was going on?"

"I don't know," said Mallon. "I don't understand any of it."

"Is the man who was shot alive?"

"No," said Mallon. "Not alive. He's definitely dead. There's a big hole through his back and out his chest."

"Where's the body now?"

"I left it there. He was dead, and I knew you wouldn't want a murder victim moved."

"Let's go take a look." He opened the back door of the car.

Mallon stood still and shook his head. "It's down there. On the beach."

"We can get there from above."

Mallon got into the car. The older policeman drove, and the younger one sat half-turned in his seat to stare at Mallon. He had a pen and a small notebook. "Let's get some preliminaries while we're on the way. Your name, sir?"

"Robert Mallon. M-A-L-L-O-N."

"Address?"

"It's 2905 Boca del Rio."

"That a house or an apartment?"

"House."

"Age?"

"Forty-eight."

"Phone?"

When Mallon gave him the number, he asked, "That home or work?"

"Home. I'm retired."

The young policeman moved down his dull list, merely extending it into the crime seamlessly. "And you did or didn't know the victim?"

"Didn't. It's the first time I've ever seen him."

"What was he wearing?"

"A jacket. Like a windbreaker. It was tan, that material they make trench coats out of. Khaki shorts. A pair of sneakers."

"What about a hat?"

"Yes. A baseball cap, with a crown that was made of netting. It's white."

"And you said he had a companion?"

"A young woman. Twenty-five, thirty at most. Maybe five feet three. She was wearing a black bathing suit. It was a two-piece, but not like a bikini. There was a little more to it."

"Can you describe her?"

"Yes. Dark hair with sort of a curl to it, so it wasn't quite frizzy, but kind of stuck out. It was about to her shoulders when she was in the water and it was wet."

"How old was the victim, again?"

"I don't know. At least fifty-five, but I would guess closer to sixty-five."

The older policeman had driven them up along the road beside the cemetery, and now he slowed down and turned into it. He said, "We can see down to the beach from up here."

They got out of the car and walked past gravestones toward the trees at the end of the last row of graves. Mallon oriented himself by the sun, and marveled at his not thinking of this. Of course the beach would be somewhere beyond the edge of the cemetery. The ocean didn't stop because there was a cemetery, and then resume later along the road near the Biltmore Hotel. They reached a bluff above the ocean. The older cop said, "Watch your step."

Mallon walked up beside him and they approached the edge together.

"Tide is way in now," said the older cop. Mallon looked down. The tide had risen, and seemed to have eaten up the rest of the beach.

"Is this about where you left the body?" the younger one asked.

Mallon did not like the question, but he was aware of seconds passing, and insisting on certain ways of saying things was not going to help him with these two men. "Things look different from up here." He stepped closer to the edge and looked along the shore toward the city, then in the other direction. "I think this was about it, though."

"Where do you suppose it went?"

"I don't know. It's probably under the water."

The young cop turned and trotted back toward the car. The older cop stayed with Mallon. "There's no chance he just got up and walked off?"

"No," Mallon insisted. "No chance."

"You ever see anyone shot before?" He was staring hard into Mallon's eyes.

Mallon returned his gaze. "Not close up. I never saw anything like this."

"What did the wound look like?"

"He was shot through the back. It was a hole in his jacket, and his chest was blown open right here." Mallon touched his own chest at the sternum. "And there was lots of blood, and more stuff from inside that came out with it. It looked like pieces of the heart or something. I tried to feel a pulse, and couldn't. I think he was hit twice, because there were two shots, and he kind of jerked at the first one and fell down. The second was the one through the back, after he was on the ground."

The older cop nodded and they walked back into the cemetery, toward the police car. The younger cop was standing beside it, still talking into the radio microphone. He ended the call and said to his partner, "We're going to have some help looking. They'll be here in a few minutes." He turned to Mallon. "What we need to do is get a really good description of the boat. Did you see the registration number?"

Mallon stopped for a moment, and tried to bring it back. He could see the boat, but the numbers he knew had to be painted in black letters at the bow were just not in the memory. "I should have looked for it. I just didn't."

"Any name painted on the stern?"

"I didn't see one."

"Any commercial number along the hull near the stern?"

"No, there wasn't. It was a pleasure boat, like a small cruiser. About twenty feet long, at most. It was white, low near the stern, high at the bow. There's a closed cabin, but low, so the guy steering the boat was standing and he was looking over the top of it. As he was coming in, I could see his head over it."

"What did he look like?"

Mallon shrugged helplessly. "Just a head. He had sunglasses on, a black baseball cap. And his hair was—I guess—reddish, but mostly hidden by the cap. I didn't notice much about the clothes. They were dark, maybe jeans and a sweatshirt or jacket."

"So let's put this together," said the younger cop. "Small private cruiser, twenty feet, white hull, low cabin. Two males and a female. That's all we've got."

"I'm sorry," said Mallon. "I was scared, and it was so confusing and weird that I didn't think to look for more. I don't know what happened, really, or what it was about. I didn't know where to look."

There were engine sounds, and two police cars pulled into the entrance to the cemetery, then up the drive to join them. The two police officers conferred with the newcomers for a few seconds, and then both of the cars drove out of the cemetery and off toward the east. When the two cops returned, the younger one said, "Let's go."

Mallon got into the back seat, and the older policeman drove them to the stretch of road just west of the Biltmore Hotel, and parked behind the others. There were already a paramedic truck and a red utility vehicle from the fire department. Down on the beach, there were policemen and firefighters forming a line.

Mallon said, "Can we help?"

The older cop said, "You'd better leave that to the people who get paid for it. If they find him they'll let us know at the station."

Mallon had no idea when the next low tide would come, and it surprised him. He was amazed at himself for not knowing, not having bothered to pay attention to something so big and fundamental that he saw twice every day. It was a few minutes later, after he was at the station, that he heard another cop say it was over four hours until the next low tide.

After a while, Mallon called Diane. He simply asked the older cop if it was all right if he used the telephone, and the cop nodded. Diane's machine answered, and he left a message for her, then returned to waiting for the police to announce that they had found the body. Just as he was getting restless, another police officer came to the bench where he was sitting, invited him to a back office, and asked him the same questions the first two had asked. Then he too went away. Mallon felt like a person at a party who didn't know anyone. People talked to him until they simply ran out of questions to ask and then drifted off.

After three hours, a policeman wearing a tan blazer came to his office and stood in the doorway. "You're the same guy who saved the woman on the beach and then found out she killed herself."

"Yes."

"I'm Detective Long. What else haven't you said?"

"I don't know," said Mallon. "Have you found the body?"

"Not yet. The ocean sometimes drags things out from shore for a while, if there's a big tide. But they come back. They get washed up somewhere."

"The gun. The man had a gun. When he was shot—the first time—he fell down on it. When I was alone I rolled him over, and I didn't pick it up. The ocean shouldn't have moved that."

The detective expressed no opinion. "Do you want to go home?"

Mallon said, "I don't know."

"You don't?"

"I've spent a lot of time thinking about what happened. I still can't be sure I know what was going on. But I think that I might be in danger."

"Why?"

"I don't know. I think the older man on the beach was trying to shoot me. Or maybe the one in the boat was. I don't know. But I can't see how this can possibly not be related to the death of Catherine Broward."

"Why is that?"

"I have no enemies. There's no other reason for anybody to try to harm me."

Detective Long looked unconvinced. "I don't understand what you think this has to do with a suicide."

Mallon took a deep breath, released it, and said, "I kept Catherine Broward from drowning herself. Then she went off, and the next day I learned that she had shot herself with a pistol a couple of hours later. It seemed odd to me, but it didn't bother any of the people who know more than I do about such things: Lieutenant Fowler, the coroner's office. So I accepted that version of what had happened. But I couldn't get her out of my head. I wanted to know what had made her do it. I hired Lydia Marks, a private detective I'd known for years, to help me find out."

"How did she go about that?"

"We investigated, interviewed people—Catherine's older sister, whom she had visited in Pittsburgh only a month or so before, a woman who had known Catherine and her boyfriend, the L.A. police detective who had looked into the boyfriend's murder, the owner of a self-defense school she had gone to just before the boyfriend was killed. I don't even know who else Lydia talked to, because when I wasn't with her, she was often on the telephone or on her computer finding things out. After we had completed an interview, she left me here and drove back to L.A. to do some more digging. A couple of nights ago, Lydia was in a restaurant late in the evening, and she was murdered."

"That's quite a story," said Detective Long. "Do you know what she was doing there? Was she alone?"

"I'm almost positive she was working. When she was killed, so were a bartender, some customers, and a waitress. I've been trying to figure out what the connection would be, and I just don't know enough. Maybe it was a place where Catherine and her boyfriend used to go. Or maybe the waitress was a friend of hers. Catherine used to work as a waitress. I just don't know. But I think that's what got Lydia killed."

"How do you know the Catherine Broward investigation was what she was working on?"

"She had just formed a new theory, and she said she was going back to L.A. to find out more, so she would know whether or not it was the right one. I think somebody she talked to led her into an ambush."

"Okay," said Long. "Then what? They waited a couple of days after they killed her, and then set up a second ambush on the beach in Santa Barbara to kill you?"

"Yes."

"If they lured her to a restaurant and killed her to keep her quiet, why not kill you too? Why not lure you both to the place? Or maybe kill her and then drive up here to kill you the same night? It's only a two-hour drive."

"I don't know," Mallon answered. "We had been interviewing people together. Maybe they thought I'd be there with her."

"But waiting all this time to find you gave you the opportunity to tell the LAPD everything, right?"

"I suppose it did. My lawyer told them everything we know."

"So whatever damage you could do to these people is already done."

"Maybe they don't know that," said Mallon.

Detective Long leaned against the wall near the door. "It occurs to me that what they know might be a subject worth thinking about. Do you always walk along that same beach at the same time each day?"

"I walk almost every day, but usually not there. Until recently I've usually headed in the other direction, toward Hope Ranch and Goleta. I suppose they could have simply been watching me, and waiting for a time when I was really alone. I can't really even say I know that they were trying to kill me. The man on the beach may have been planning to shoot at the man on the boat. It's possible that the man on the boat was aiming at the man on the shore all along, and never at me. I grew up with rifles. I could easily have hit what I was aiming at from that distance, but he was trying to fire while the boat was moving, coming up over waves and slapping down again. It must have been hard just to stand on the deck. I don't know what he was trying to do. I just think it's extremely unlikely that suddenly, after all these years, people should begin shooting that close to me, and it would have nothing at all to do with the death of Lydia Marks, or that her death had nothing to do with Catherine Broward's."

"We'll keep everything you've said in mind. If we need anything more, we'll get in touch."

Mallon looked at him in surprise. "You mean just go as though nothing happened? Or is what you're saying that nothing did happen?"

Detective Long sat down across the desk from Mallon and leaned closer on his elbows. "Look, Mr. Mallon," he said. "I can't really keep you here. The only place to sleep is a cell. I can't give you any answers unless something you described—the body, the boat, the two men and the woman—turns up. Do you have any friends you can call, and maybe stay with them tonight?"

Mallon watched him stand up, so Mallon stood up too. "Maybe I will." He felt the detective's hand on his back. He was ushering him in a slow, affable way, toward the lobby.

"Do that," said Long. "We'll let you know as soon as we find anything out."

The detective walked Mallon to the front door like a host, opened the door for him, and gave him a little wave as Mallon descended the front steps. When Mallon had walked fifty feet, he turned and looked back to verify that the detective had gone back across the lobby into the office. He had not asked Mallon to call in and let the police know where he could be reached. He was probably already filing a report that said Mallon was a harmless local eccentric who had lately gotten into the habit of making false reports to the police.

|||||||||||||||||||||||||||||||||||||||||||||||||||||||||||||||||||||||||||||||||||

CHAPTER 21

It was easy to tell from the row of lighted windows visible through the trees that the house David Altberg had lived in was large. Like the others that lined this part of Benedict Canyon, it was set back from the steep, winding road behind an eight-foot wall with an electric gate. Mary O'Connor slowed down as she came to it, then pulled the car to a stop beside the wall, turned off the headlights, and waited.

Debbie slipped out her door, climbed onto the hood, then stepped onto the roof, pulled herself over the wall, and was gone. Emily stopped beside Mary's window long enough to make a long-suffering face to show her distaste for this job, then repeated Debbie's climb to the top of the wall. She paused there to watch Mary's departure.

Mary stared into the rearview mirror to be sure there were no cars approaching. She pulled back out onto the road and drove off, reached a comfortable speed, and then coasted down the slope toward the Beverly Hills flats.

Emily looked at her watch. She had twenty minutes before Mary would turn around and begin the drive back. In forty, Emily and Debbie should be outside again, waiting. She swung her legs to the inside of the wall, turned, and lowered herself partway, then dropped to the ground.

Emily crouched in the dark and stared at the house. This was not a job that Michael could charge some amateur for the pleasure of performing. David Altberg had been sixty-three years old, so his wife was probably about the same. Customers wouldn't pay for the sport of blasting an old lady.

Through sliding glass doors she could see broad, well-lit interior spaces. There was a big foyer that led into a living room with a wide stone fire pit in the center and a copper hood that vented it, the sort they had in some ski lodges. Two walls had bookcases to the ceiling, but in each, only the bottom shelf held a row of coffee-table books. The rest of the shelves were filled with little statues, baskets, framed photographs, vases. Emily had been to rich people's homes in L.A. before. If they owned any real books, they were always placed in some closed room where they would not pollute the decor.

Emily looked into the darkness among the dwarf evergreen shrubs along the path from the garden to the house and made out Debbie's shape. She was stretched and flattened in a posture from one of the innumerable martial disciplines she had studied. This one made her look very feline: she had the cat's ability to remain motionless and simply not look like something that was alive. After a time, Emily's eyes adjusted to the darkness, and she could see that Debbie's eyes were on her, waiting for her to move.

Emily stayed low and advanced on the sliding glass doors. They were often easy to force because the locks were not good, and even if she decided they were not the best way in, they would give her a good view of the whole first floor. She stopped at the side of the glass, her body shielded from view by a solid stretch of wall about three feet wide. She looked in, making her eyes move carefully along the walls she could see, noting everything. The chairs and couches showed no signs that anyone had sat in them recently, and nothing was left out of place near them. The fresh flowers in the purple vase on the table meant that the wife had not gone away during the extra week her husband had been at the self-defense camp for the "advanced course."

Emily kept the palm of her left hand pressed lightly against the wall as she looked, so she could feel any small inaudible vibration in the building. When she had satisfied herself that nobody was in sight, she stepped quickly in front of the glass door and stopped. She looked at the alcove near the front door and found the alarm keypad. It was turned on, its red light glowing steadily in the upper left corner. But the display on the right side was blinking.

She glided quietly along the outer wall of the house until she reached the next set of windows, then looked at the keypad again. The display was blinking a succession of numbers: 8, 39, 41, 8, 39, 41, 8. Emily understood the common alarm systems. This signal meant that the perimeter was armed, and an alarm would go off if any of the doors or windows were moved, but there were three points that had been left only partially closed. Alarm installers labeled the access points starting on the ground floor, making the front entrance number one. Thirty-nine and forty-one were undoubtedly upstairs windows. Eight intrigued her.

She looked at the front door. To the left of it was the hallway leading to other rooms. To the right was a small, high window. That would be number two. The first set of floor-to-ceiling windows with a sliding door where she stood was number three, the second four. She moved quickly back along the side of the building, counting. Five was the solid door that probably led to some kind of service room or pantry, and six was the small louvered glass window beyond. Seven was the first set of bay windows on the back side of the house. Through them, she saw eight.

Eight was a set of floor-to-ceiling windows with a slider to match the ones on the opposite side of the house. She could see that there was a set of extra contacts on the inside of the sliding door's track, so the door could be opened a few inches and the alarm turned on. If the door was opened any wider than it was now, the alarm would be triggered.

She could feel her heart beginning to beat more quickly, and an excited flush came to her cheeks. She had been feeling despondent and irritable since the problem on the beach in Santa Barbara today. The first mistake—when David had suddenly reached for his gun in Mallon's sight—had taken her by surprise. She had tried to stop him, but he had been unwilling to be stopped. After that, the errors had piled up so rapidly that there was nothing she could do. Spangler had seen that there was a problem, tried to get David out of trouble by firing from a rocking boat, and hit David instead of Mallon. Emily had considered snatching David's gun to dispatch Mallon, but she had seen Spangler aiming for a second shot, so she had moved back out of the line of fire. She had stepped back, but Mallon had not. In a second he was already kneeling over the body, presumably to get his hand on the gun. All Emily could do was escape. She'd had to sprint down the beach to the water, and hope he didn't have the presence of mind to kill her while she was fighting her way through the surf to the boat. Everything had gone wrong on the hunt. Since then the balance had begun to be restored, a bit at a time, each step bought with extra care and work. First they had needed to remove David Altberg's body. Now they must clean up the rest of what he had left behind.

Emily had found what she needed. She turned around to scan the foliage behind her. A bit of darkness seemed to coalesce and become a deeper bit of darkness and then Debbie stepped closer, and passed through the light to Emily's side. Emily pointed at the partially opened slider, so Debbie could see it across the room. "See the two extra magnetic contacts?" Emily whispered. "Too narrow for me. If we move it any wider the alarm will go off."

Debbie whispered, "Let me see."

Debbie walked around to the spot. She looked closely at the narrow open space between the door and the end of the track, did a quarter turn to put herself beside it, as though measuring, then faced it again.

226 | ||| THOMAS PERRY

She put her right arm inside and let it go in up to the shoulder, rounded her back to get her right breast in past the door, then placed her chin on her shoulder, shrugged, and twisted. Her knees bent, her legs spread apart, and her right side was in. As she slid inward her ear brushed the door, but she continued her turn. It looked to Emily as though she were stepping through the glass instead of past it.

Emily hurried to whisper through the opening into Debbie's ear. "Find the alarm circuit box. It will be in a closet or cabinet, but it has a green glowing light on the door, so you'll see it. The key will be hidden near it. When you find the key, unlock the box and flip the off switch on the lower left side. The green light on the door will go out."

Debbie nodded and set off. She opened the entry closet and closed it, then another near the kitchen. She moved down a hallway, and Emily saw no more of her for a few minutes. She reemerged through the dining room, and quietly climbed the stairs.

Emily leaned on the wall and prepared for a long wait. She stared at the alarm keypad by the front entrance, and as she stared, the red ARMED light and the green POWER light went dark. She took a deep breath, and pushed the sliding door open far enough to slip inside. No alarm rang out. She pushed the door shut and listened. She advanced deeper into the living room, tuning her ears to any small sound.

She climbed the stairs and found Debbie standing motionless at the top, gazing up the hall toward the end. The door was closed, but there was a faint light beneath it.

Emily looked away from it to Debbie and saw a look of distaste on her face. She moved close to Debbie's ear. "What's wrong?"

Debbie whispered, "She's not alone."

Emily's eyes widened. It was not unusual, and it was certainly not unimaginable. She should have thought of it, but she had not. It made perfect sense. David Altberg had been a sixty-three-year-old man with a balding head and a pot belly. His conversation had been dull and self-absorbed. The only thing that had made him bearable was his money. At frequent intervals, he had gone off without his wife. He'd mentioned hunting in Alaska, fishing in Florida. And of course, the past five weeks at the ranch. His wife had probably been delighted.

As Emily tried to think it through, she began to hear sounds. There were little cries, moans, and then the sound of a bed squeaking.

Debbie's lips beside her ear tickled and irritated her. "Let's kill them both."

Emily shook her head hard, to cover the shiver. "No. Let's turn the alarm on again. We'll hide and wait."

"What about Mary? She'll be back in a half hour."

"She knows enough to keep going if we're not there. We'll call her when it's done."

She followed Debbie to a room off the upstairs hallway. It was dark, but she could tell that it had been decorated as a kind of sitting room. Debbie went to the closet, opened the metal box on the wall, and reached up to flip the switch.

"Don't!" Emily said it aloud.

Debbie's body whirled to face the danger. When she saw nothing she remained with her body tensed, but her face looked puzzled.

Emily stepped closer. "I forgot I closed the sliding door downstairs. She has it programmed to be open to the first contact. If we turn on the system now, the alarm will go off. I'll go open it." She slipped out. She could hear the sounds from the bedroom, louder and wilder now. She waited until the noises convinced her that there was no chance that they would hear her, then moved down the staircase, pushed the slider to its former position, and slowly began to make her way back toward the stairs.

She heard footsteps above her head. They couldn't be Debbie's. She wouldn't make any noise. Emily slipped into the corner of the room and hid behind a couch. The sounds resolved themselves into two sets of footsteps. One set was soft and light, and the other heavier, a man's feet. She waited for a few minutes, then heard them again.

At the top of the stairs she heard the woman's voice. There was a pouting quality to it. "Are you sure you have to go just like that? David isn't going to be home until late tomorrow."

"Sure, that takes care of him," said a man's voice. "But Marian isn't out of town. By now she's wondering where I am."

"I'll call her as soon as you leave, and chat for a while, so she won't be in such a snit when you get there," said the woman's voice. "She won't be thinking about you at all. But I will be."

Emily lay behind the couch and waited. She heard them come down the stairs. There was a curious silence. She moved forward a few inches and looked beyond the edge of the couch. It was no surprise that they were kissing. The surprise was that the woman was so young. Mrs. David Altberg was no older than Emily.

Emily pulled her head back and remained still. The kiss ended, the woman pressed her code on the keypad, making eight beeps. The front door opened, and in a few seconds it closed. Emily heard the electric motor of the door opener spinning the screw to slide the garage door up. That was smart, she thought. They had parked his car in the garage, where David's car usually went. Nobody who came by would see his car parked here. Emily heard the car pull out, and the garage motor hum as it brought the door down again. She waited until the woman walked across the room to close the slider, then returned. Emily slithered to the end of the couch to watch while the woman pushed the keys to engage her alarm again. Then she ducked back.

Emily hoped that Debbie had the sense to be patient. If she appeared before the woman was far enough from the keypad, she might get back in time to push the emergency button.

The woman turned off the downstairs lights and climbed the stairs toward her bedroom. The darkness was reassuring to Emily, because it meant everything had gone perfectly. The sensation was refreshing, a physical release that made her feel free and energetic.

As soon as Mrs. Altberg disappeared at the top of the stairs, Emily began to move toward the bottom step. But then she heard the sounds above her. They came much sooner than she had expected. There was no scream, just an indrawn breath like a gasp, then a heavy thump, a knock as the woman's head hit something, and a softer, heavier noise that Emily knew was Debbie letting the woman's body drop to the floor in the upstairs hallway.

Emily took the steps three at a time, pulling herself up with the railing, then dashed past the landing into the hallway. The woman was lying on the hardwood floor, and Debbie was looking down at her, cocking her head to get a look at the face.

"Is she dead?" asked Emily.

"Sure. I thought I'd put her out quickly." Debbie looked at Emily and shrugged. "I mean, why not? This wasn't her fuckup, was it?"

"No," said Emily quietly. "Thank you for taking care of it."

Debbie gave her an annoyed glance and walked down the hall toward the bedroom. "What now?"

Emily followed her. "Now we pack a suitcase for her, as though she and her husband went away together." She stepped in past Debbie and looked at the bed, which was in extreme disarray. She moved closer to it. "I guess I'd better make the bed first."

"You think the boyfriend won't go to the police?"

"Probably not. But if he's not calling them right now, it doesn't matter what he does, as long as we don't leave any prints."

Debbie nodded. "I'll go see where she kept her luggage and get started with the packing."

"Make it real. There will probably be a few cops here the day after tomorrow who will notice if we forget her makeup bag."

"I know that," muttered Debbie. She disappeared into the long walk-in closet. Emily could tell that she had not enjoyed killing Mrs. Altberg and was feeling resentful about this evening. Being alone with Debbie made Emily uncomfortable sometimes, but tonight was worse. She was a little bit afraid of her.

They did not speak again until the bag was packed and the bedroom straightened. Then Emily took out her cell phone and dialed Mary's number.

"Hi," said Mary.

"Hi," said Emily. "We're going to open the gate. When you get here, pull all the way down the driveway to the house, and then turn off your headlights and pop the trunk. Okay?"

"I'll be there in about five minutes."

Emily and Debbie lifted the body and carried it down the stairs in the dark, then outside, where they laid it on the grass next to the driveway. Emily went back inside, pressed the remote control to open the gate, picked up the suitcase, and turned off the last of the lights. At the front door she set the lock, pushed the code she had memorized to turn on the alarm, then stepped out and closed the door. She sighed. It was going to be a long drive back to the ranch, and then a couple of hours of digging before this awful day would finally end.

#####

Paul Spangler was packing his belongings when he heard the familiar flat-handed slap on the door jamb that was the military knock. He simply turned the knob so it was unlocked and let it swing open as he turned away and walked back to the bed, where his suitcase lay open.

Parish stepped inside and closed the door, then stood with his back against it. "I wish you wouldn't do this."

"I know you do, Michael," said Spangler. "Thanks for that." Both men let their voices relax, as they always did when they were alone. The old, natural South African way of pronouncing English words came back, the traces of Afrikaans thicker on Spangler's tongue and palate than on Parish's.

Parish said, "The girls will have the whole business cleared away by dawn. There won't be a trace. They're like deer, their eyes always open, and their ears twitching. They already feel what you feel about this. They'll never blame you, or even remind you of it."

"Nah, old friend," said Spangler. "I know they wouldn't. I know you wouldn't either." He stepped to his closet, took a handful of hangers with shirts on them, and laid them on the tightly made bed beside the suitcase.

"I've made a few bad shots myself, Paul," Parish said quietly. "You might remember one in Uganda."

Spangler sat on the bed, both legs stiff and his heels touching the floor. "I remember." It had been a deep forest patrol along the border between Uganda and Zaire, searching for rebels in a place where all of humanity seemed to have spun off into violent factions, so the problem was not merely sighting groups of armed men but identifying their political affiliations before they opened fire. Spangler had been in command, a captain when Parish was still a lieutenant. That had been when Parish had still been called Eric Watkins, but when Spangler looked back on those times now, Parish always came back to him as Parish. The name Eric Watkins had only been a stage he had passed through.

Parish had been walking point for the patrol, with three soldiers. Spangler had known that Parish would be farther forward than was necessary or advisable in this thick bush, sometimes two or three hundred yards, where if he met resistance the straggling column that Spangler was leading along the jungle track could do little to help him. But when the two had arrived to enlist, Spangler was given the superior rank because he was older, so he did not exercise his nominal authority over Parish unduly. Parish liked adventure, so he could have it. Spangler listened to the sounds of the forest: the calls of birds, buzzing insects, the whispering of billions of leaves and stems—what Spangler thought of as the sounds of heat.

The noises were abruptly replaced by the hammering of an automatic rifle. Before the first burst ended there were others, overlapping. Spangler's men had already split apart to crouch in the bush on either side of the trail, listening, but Spangler had held his ground. He had instantly identified the shots as Parish's troops firing their FN

FAL paratroop rifles. He waited for answering fire, rounds of a different caliber or automatic fire of a different frequency. The rebels they had encountered in this district had been traveling in gangs of forty or sixty, and when they opened up it was a cacophony of Eastern-made AK-47's and SKS's, sometimes a few British or American-made hunting rifles, even a shotgun or two.

He sorted the possibilities, then signaled his men to spread wide and advance toward the sounds. The silence could mean either that Parish's men had gotten jumpy and opened fire on imagined enemies or that real enemies had ambushed and killed them. Either way, Spangler had to bring his men through the thick vegetation toward the spot.

When they reached a clearing, on the other side he could see Michael Parish and his men standing around looking peculiarly grave. He halted his troops, sent word to maintain their cover, and proceeded alone. Parish met him in the middle of the clearing. "Paul," he whispered. "It seems we've made a slight error."

"What is it?"

"We heard fairly serious sounds of brush being pushed aside, some branches breaking and all that, so we opened up. It turns out we've killed a troop of gorillas."

"Have you identified what army they belong to?"

Parish leaned closer. "No. Gorillas. Apes. A silverback, about four females, a couple of young ones. Concentrated fire. As long as we saw any bushes moving, we kept it up."

Spangler had looked around him, over his shoulder, to be sure his men were still in position. "What do your men say?"

"They're no more eager to let the others know than we are." He shrugged.

Spangler assessed the situation quickly. He and Parish had come here together and enlisted. They had verified each other's lies about their former ranks in the South African army and their time in service. Their troops were not all volunteers, and the ones who were tended to be the sort who couldn't return to their villages. If he and Parish allowed these men to believe their two officers were buffoons, their lives would be in danger.

Spangler said, "How about this? You caught some poachers in the act. You fired on them and chased them off."

"It's the best we can do."

"Then I'll go and brief the noncoms while you talk to your men and get the story straight."

Spangler had been especially long-winded in his briefing, then posted pickets and gave his men a rest to allow Parish and his men the time to mutilate the gorillas' bodies a bit with knives. By the time the main column was allowed to advance to the spot, it appeared that the animals had been butchered for the lucrative trade in their hands and feet. Since the missing parts were not to be found anywhere, it was clear that the poachers must have gotten what they wanted before their escape.

Many years had passed since that day in the forest. Spangler marveled at the way looking at Parish and listening to his voice seemed to bring it all back in absolute clarity.

"We've been in some scrapes," Parish said. That was the other part of the story, and Parish needed to say nothing more to trigger Spangler's emotion. They had been in battle together.

"We have," Spangler agreed. "And your bringing me along on this has got me permanent residency in the States and a good supply of dollars. I thank you for it. I've tried to be sure you didn't regret it. And this is the time when I think I'd better save you the work of asking me to leave."

Parish said, "If I wanted you to leave, I know that I could ask you, and you would go. I also know that I would never have to wonder if I could trust you to keep still about our business here."

"Of course," said Spangler.

Parish continued. "What happened today was that you, as scout, had to step in to protect the rest of us, because the amateur hunter fell apart. You had to fire from two hundred yards out standing on a moving boat in a heavy sea. When Emily and Mary told me what had happened, and that you had shot Altberg twice under those conditions, I was planning to congratulate you on your fine shooting."

Spangler looked surprised. "What? Why?"

"I figured you must have made the determination to drop the client and scrap the hunt. Once he'd had his chance and ended up grappling with the target for the gun, it was a perfectly reasonable decision." He smiled. "I didn't suspect that the first hit was a wild shot until I asked where you were and Mary told me you had gone off alone."

Spangler shook his head and chuckled sadly. "When I squeezed off that shot and saw the wrong one go down, I was paralyzed for a few seconds. Mary kept her head and brought the boat around, and all I could think of was to fire a second round into him on the way in, rather than leave him wounded and ready to talk. I hauled Emily up over the side and fired once at Mallon on the way out to sea, to no purpose. It was a balls-up debacle. I made a bloody ass of myself. After thirty years of shooting, I was useless."

Parish began to pace the floor. "I won't deny that I'm speaking as your friend, and I certainly won't deny that I've owed my life to you on more than one occasion. If you were past usefulness, I admit that I would surely try to find you something to do around here where you wouldn't hurt yourself. But it isn't that way. You're the best sniper I ever saw, and the only combat pistol instructor I would have around me. I don't want to lose that. I can't run this place with teachers who've done nothing but shoot at paper targets and beat up punching bags. I need a professional soldier who stood when the blood flowed. You know that. You also know that David Altberg isn't the first friendly-fire casualty either of us has had. There were times in Africa when I would send my men into the bush, set my rifle on full auto, and kill anything that came back at me."

"Michael, it's not remorse or something," said Spangler. "It's a different kind of feeling." He looked anxious, tormented. "You've seen it, just as I have. A man's luck will be wrapped around him like a coat. Then one day, it's gone. He seems to wake up one morning, and the day looks different to him. The next thing anybody else knows, his mates are toting him back in a body bag."

"Are you getting superstitious?" asked Parish.

He shook his head. "All I know is that things have started to go wrong."

"Paul, you've devoted years to this business. You and I built this building we're standing in. I'm sure you were right before when you said you had a supply of dollars, because God knows, you've never stood any man a drink. But now is when it's starting to pay off. You can't walk away now. You'll be rich in a year."

Spangler said nothing for a moment. He knew he was being manipulated. He had seen Parish do it to other people many times before. He always did it in a respectful, distinct, earnest voice, looking and sounding so sincere that it seemed to the listener as though the words were forming in his own mind. Michael's alert eyes were unblinking, watching the listener's face to determine which themes provoked signs of resistance, and which caused the impervious will to weaken. When Michael talked about money, he did it in a way that made Spangler's chest tighten with greed, and his heart sink at the thought of revenue forfeited. When he invoked loyalty, Spangler found himself gripped by a surge of it. Even when Parish said something badly, a listener would not resist him, but feel sympathy for him, convinced that he was simply a soldier after all, and capable only of plain speech.

"You remember what it was like in the old days, Paul. We would see those rich bastards like Bill Finney pass us by in their sports cars, and just marvel at the way the world worked, that it would put scum like them on top. Well, it's our turn now. They're lining up to come here. If you'll stay on a little longer, you'll be as rich as any of them."

"Michael, what happened today was a mistake," said Spangler. "If we make mistakes, it's over. I just don't want to ruin this for you and the others."

"Don't worry. It's safe. We've been doing the hunts for years without trouble, haven't we? I almost never agree to do one in this state—until Mark Romano, they've been spread over the country, everywhere except California. And he was more than a year ago."

"And because of him, this Marks woman, and now Mallon. All of those hunts had problems," Spangler reminded him.

"And all of the problems have been solved—or they will be soon."

"Well—"

"They have," said Parish. "And you've been part of that. The truth is that I need you. I've always thought that you deserved more, and I've intended to be sure you got it. You should be rich, and I don't want you to leave until you are. It would kill me to see a man like you going off with your hat in your hand, knocking on doors looking for a job. When you retire from this, I want you to never have to work another day."

"If I get us caught, that's about what will happen."

"We should get a medal for this. We're just giving rich bastards permission to kill other rich bastards. We're purifying the race, getting rid of the weak and credulous."

Spangler chuckled as he thought, This is what makes it work. It's the fact that Michael can persuade people that they are deserving, that they must do everything they can to protect and preserve their precious selves. He could convince them that they were too important, too valuable, to have to tolerate the existence of enemies. As Spangler listened, he felt calm. The best argument for staying with Parish was Parish. He could convince people that whatever resentments they had were righteous indignation. The slights and insults they had suffered were capital offenses. Spangler had no problem with that. He had become a soldier at seventeen because he had felt that killing people was not a big price to pay for being freed from a life of farm labor.

He looked once more at Parish, his misgivings gone. "Thanks, Michael. You don't need to spend the whole night telling me this. If you want me to stay, it's good enough for me."

Parish clapped him on the shoulder. "I'm glad." The two shook hands once, hard. Then they turned away from each other. As Spangler faced the bed to begin unpacking, he heard the door open and close, and Parish was gone.

Parish walked on the damp grass away from Spangler's cabin, into the field, where the flow of the lights did not reach. He came to the edge of the woods, where thick bushes had begun to grow in to replace the trees that had been cut. The forest was always trying to expand onto the clear-cut hillsides. He said, "Let's go."

There was no rustling as Mary stood up. She held one of the new rifles that Spangler and Parish had been sighting in all week on the range. She said, "I assume Paul has decided to stay?"

Parish answered, "Yes. He hasn't lost his nerve. He was just upset with himself for hitting David Altberg on his first shot when he was aiming for Mr. Mallon. He'll be fine. He'll probably be on the range every spare moment for a time, giving himself the illusion that he'll never miss again."

They walked in silence, moving along the ridge toward the firing range. Mary asked quietly, "Would you do this to me?"

Parish looked at her blankly. "What?"

"If you thought I had lost my nerve and wanted out, would you let me go, or would you kill me?"

Parish took the rifle in his right hand and put his left around her waist as they walked. "I didn't tell you to kill him."

"You sent me out there to watch for your signal. And it's exactly the way he was supposed to shoot Mallon when he missed."

"Oh, is it?" he asked without interest. "I'll have to take your word for it. I wasn't there."

"You would kill me, wouldn't you?"

He pulled her close and laughed. "Don't be ridiculous." He leaned down and gave her cheek a kiss, then released her and held his watch close to his face so he could make out the faint glow of the dial. "This took longer than I expected. Would you mind putting the rifle back in the rack before you come down? I told Emily and Debbie that I would help with the rest of this." He held the rifle out to her. "Unless you'd rather do that?"

"I'm not digging any graves," Mary said. "I'll put the rifle away." She took it from him, stood still, and watched him moving down the hill toward the lodge. She turned and walked in the other direction, toward the storage building at the end of the firing range.

||||||||||||||||||||||||||||||||||||||||||||||||||

CHAPTER 22

Mallon had been awake in his hotel bed for hours, waiting for daylight. At five A.M., he got out of bed, stepped to the window, and opened the curtains. Across the road, he could see the small stucco building with a tile roof that housed public rest rooms, and beyond it, the white beach and the blue ocean. The hotel was quiet.

He put on a pair of jeans, a baseball cap, and a sweatshirt, went down to the beach, and began to walk, staring at everything washed up by yesterday's high tide. He tried to force himself to stop imagining that each of the big bundles of kelp was a man, but he walked close to a couple of them to be sure.

Mallon was trying to keep himself from being angry. He knew that the police department couldn't afford to have every cop out on the beach all night waiting for the body to wash in, but now that it was dawn they could at least try using metal detectors to find the gun. Otherwise some two-year-old with a sand shovel was going to dig it up and take it home in his plastic bucket. He walked at a steady, quick pace along the same route he had taken the day before. When he got to the stretch of beach where the man had been killed, he saw that there wasn't even a marker or a line of police tape.

Mallon reached a spot that looked to him like the place where the older man had pulled the gun out of his jacket. He looked at the point he had just passed and judged the distance to the next one, then looked out to his right at the ocean. There was nothing on that side that he could use to take his bearings: the Pacific was an unchanging expanse of blue that met the horizon, but he could tell that the tide was low. The surf line was at least fifty feet farther away than it had been when the man was shot. He turned to his left and used the cliffs to verify the distance.

Mallon walked back and forth on the beach, digging his feet into the sand, kicking it out of the way, sometimes dragging one foot sideways to plow a little deeper. He remembered that it was the way Lydia had searched for Catherine's belongings the day after she'd died, and it made him feel sadder and more hopeless, and yet more desperate to do something about their deaths. He was the first to walk on this stretch of beach this morning, so the trails he was making were clear and easy to see. He kept widening the area of his search, staring hard at the sand in case he uncovered some part of the pistol without feeling it.

A wind came up, and he looked back and realized that a lot of time had passed. The places where he'd brushed the surface and exposed the wet, mortar-like sand were dry and powdery now. The wind was blowing the sand smooth again, so he could no longer be sure where he had searched. The sun was much higher, and his sweatshirt was wet with perspiration. He looked at his watch: he had been here for nearly four hours. He turned to look back the way he had come. There were local people on the beach now: adults lying on blankets, children crouching just above the surf, digging. He had seen a few of them on his walks, knew which parts of town they lived in, but had never spoken to any of them. Seeing them made him feel isolated and vulnerable. He had lived here for ten years, but he was a stranger.

He looked at the sand around him to measure how much of the area he had searched. It was hopeless. He began to walk back toward the hotel. It was still early, but usually Diane was in her office by nine. If she had heard his recorded messages, she would be trying to reach him at home, and failing.

At the hotel he called her number, but there was no answer. He showered, and dressed in some of his most respectable-looking clothes. He had bought the sport jacket on a trip to New York because he had seen it in a window. Mallon had packed in a hurry last night, anxious to get out of his house and into the safe anonymity of a hotel, and he had taken the coat because it had been visible in his closet and had not required evaluation.

He tried calling Diane again, but there was still no answer. He looked at his watch. It was after ten. Even if Diane was in court or something, surely Sylvia, the secretary, should be in. He paced back and forth a few times, and on the fifth trip across the room, he simply kept going out the door. There was no point in waiting in the room. He took the elevator downstairs to the lobby, went out the back, and walked to the lot to find his car. He drove to the municipal parking structure on Anacapa Street, then walked down De la Guerra to Diane's office. Even though he had come in person to give Diane time to return to her office, he found himself hurrying.

As he walked along De la Guerra, he noticed a young woman with long red hair getting out of a car not far from him. She was tall and lean and had a pretty face. He took the risk of a second glance, but at that moment she was not walking, as he had expected. She was still by the car, facing him. She held a camera up before her face, using one hand to focus a big lens.

Mallon's spine straightened and his brain sent an impulse to turn away and appear not to be staring at her, but he heard the click. He faced forward and forced his muscles to relax. He felt foolish, and hoped she had not seen his clumsy attempt to keep from being caught staring. But then, before his mind had quite worked out the words that went with his new feeling, he had begun to be uncomfortable again. Why did she have a camera? Had she been taking his picture?

He looked in the other direction and realized that he had been between the woman and the county courthouse. It was a pretty building, famous for being pretty, in fact, and he supposed she had taken a picture of that.

When he reached the low white office building, he stepped into the hallway and walked to Diane's door. He turned the knob and pushed, and to his relief, the door swung open. But when he went inside, he could see that things weren't right. The overhead fluorescent lights weren't on. The place had a different feeling. It seemed lifeless, silent.

The door to Diane's office opened, and Sylvia came out. She was holding a potted plant, staring down at it as she walked. She looked up to see Mallon standing in the office, gasped audibly, and gave a little jump. Then she seemed to go limp. "Oh! You really scared me." She glared at him for a second, then looked down past the rim of the pot fretfully, and he could tell that she had spilled a little dirt on the rug.

"I'm sorry," he said. "The door was unlocked, and I didn't think that I would startle you."

She had restored her composure. "That's all right, Mr. Mallon," she said. "But I'm afraid that Miss Fleming isn't here. She won't be in today."

"Do you have a number where I can reach her? It's very important."

Sylvia looked past him instead of into his eyes as she said, "I'm afraid I don't have a number for her yet. She had to leave suddenly, and she hasn't given me one. But if you'd like to leave her a message, you can either put it on voice mail, or you can leave it with me and I'll let her know as soon as she calls in."

His eyes wandered around the room as he composed a sentence that was short enough and clear enough to get to Diane intact. "As soon as she calls in, please let her know that I've got to speak with her right away." His eyes had passed over the office, but now they returned to Sylvia's desk. There was a box there, the kind of carton that held reams of copying paper, and it sat in the center of the blotter.

"You're taking the plants home," he said.

She shrugged uncomfortably, went to her desk, and carefully set the pot in the box. "She said it might be a week or two, so she gave me the time off. It's not a big practice, and it's usually not very busy. I'm going to send a note to all the clients today, before I go home."

Mallon said, "Can I see it?"

She shook her head. "I haven't written it yet." She added, "It will say pretty much what I've just told you. That's all I can say. There will be a list of three attorneys who have agreed to stand in for her if any client has anything urgent."

Mallon tried again. "Is she here, or is she in some other city?"

"She's out of town." Sylvia stepped away from her desk and got another plant to put into the box.

"I can't believe this," he said. "Is she on a vacation, or sick, or going out of business, or what? I really need to know."

"Honestly, Mr. Mallon," said Sylvia, "I have no reason to think anything at all is wrong. She hasn't said anything like that to me, and I don't know of any reason to keep it from me. But I know that if you have an urgent need for an attorney, she would never want you to lose anything because of her. I can retain one for you, and Miss Fleming can take over when she returns. I know she had placed Brian Logan on retainer for you. Let me get you his number."

Mallon wanted to protest, to tell her the solution she was offering had nothing to do with the problem, but he could see it was pointless. He waited while she looked in her Rolodex, scribbled the number down, and handed it to him. "Thank you." He managed a faint smile that lasted only a second, then turned and left the office.

As Mallon walked toward the parking structure on Anacapa where he had left his car, he felt more and more uncomfortable. He stopped and turned around, then walked to State Street. He stopped at one of the banks where he had an account and withdrew five thousand dollars in cash. The hundred-dollar bills made a big, satisfying lump in the envelope in his inner jacket pocket. He was not sure that he understood his reasons for wanting the money, but this morning as he'd gone from the hotel to Diane's office and out again, the town had begun to seem smaller. It was a narrow place sloping down to the edge of the vast, empty ocean on one side and hemmed in by a wall of mountains on the other. The money made him feel as though he were ready to leave instantly if he wanted, and that seemed to help.

He went back to the hotel where he had spent the night, and checked out. Then he drove home, went into the kitchen, and checked the answering machine beside the telephone. There were no messages.

His confusion about Diane was growing. Was he becoming suspicious of everyone? He had retained Diane a few years ago, right after she had come to Santa Barbara from an enormous law firm in Los Angeles. She had been young but seemed a little tired, as though she had burned herself out, and that had endeared her to him. He had already found that his retirement did not, as he had hoped, allow him to dispense entirely with lawyers, and she was smart and inoffensive. His requirements for legal services had been small and intermittent: he needed a local tax attorney to be sure that he stayed out of trouble with the I.R.S. and to handle the certifications and agreements that were occasionally necessary to the financial management of a fortune.

He made an effort to think clearly about Diane. Taking off like this without warning, without revealing a destination, and without even a prediction as to when she might return seemed strange. What could be said in her favor was that she had provided for professional services for her clients. But what he needed was not her professional services. She was simply the only one who knew everything he knew, and he wanted to verify that he could reach her if he needed to.

He had a very strong feeling that she would call him. He stared at the telephone for a few minutes, then played back the messages he had already heard to be sure he had not missed her voice. He made breakfast, washed his dishes, and did his laundry, always staying where he could reach the telephone quickly. When afternoon came, he called

Diane's office again to see whether Sylvia had left yet, but wasn't surprised when the telephone wasn't answered.

Late in the afternoon, Mallon's phone rang. He picked it up, his ear tuned for the high pitch of Diane's voice. It was a woman's voice, but a different one. "Robert?"

"Yes?"

"Robert, this is Laura Amester at Wells Fargo Private Banking."

"Hi," Mallon said, manufacturing a convincing imitation of patience and calm. "How are you?" Laura was the administrator in San Francisco who controlled his investment accounts at Wells Fargo.

"Well," she said quietly, "I guess that was what I was calling you to ask."

Mallon had begun to dread this conversation as soon as he had recognized her voice. Laura sometimes called to plumb Mallon's deepest feelings about some prospective investment decision, and Mallon had no feelings about investment decisions. But this was not how those conversations usually began. He said, "I don't understand."

"I just got your order to liquidate about twenty minutes ago. To tell you the truth, it took me a few minutes to recover from the shock, collect myself, and decide to ask you why. You hadn't said that there was something that you were dissatisfied with. I wondered what—"

"Hold it," he interrupted. "I haven't sent you any order to do anything."

"But . . . are you sure?"

"I could hardly forget something like that. What does this order say?"

"It says we're to sell all of your holdings and wire the money to your account at Moncrief and Tydings. It's signed by your attorney, Diane Fleming. I tried to reach her first, but I missed her, I guess."

"You haven't sold anything yet, have you?"

"No. The markets were already closed for the day when we got this."

"Then don't. Don't do anything," he said. "Let me make this absolutely clear. I didn't approve this. I didn't even know about it. She never had my permission to make any decisions, or to send you anything without my seeing it. I don't know if she was even the one who did this, but don't pay any attention to it. I want my investments left where they are. This seems to be some kind of fraud."

"I'm amazed," said Laura. "This is one of those times when I'm glad I called before I did anything."

"What do I do now, to be sure something else like this doesn't happen?"

"I can guarantee it won't now that we've talked. The next thing I'm going to do is turn on the recorder." There was a pause.

"Have you done it?"

"Yes," said Laura. "It is now July the seventh at four-sixteen in the afternoon. I am Laura Amester, and I am speaking with client Robert Mallon, and recording our conversation. Mr. Mallon's voice is known to me, and I've reached him by calling his home number. Is that right, Mr. Mallon?"

"Yes, it is."

"Can you tell me the last four digits of your social security number?"

He recited the number.

"Thank you," said Laura. "Can you repeat what you've said about the withdrawal order we received today?"

"Yes. I did not authorize any withdrawal of funds from my account. I do not believe that my attorney did either. Just to be safe, I am now revoking the power of attorney I granted to Diane Fleming. Please make no changes to my account unless you have verified it with me first."

When the conversation was over, Mallon made a list of the other banks and brokers that held investment or savings accounts for him. He had once signed a power of attorney authorization for Diane for a specific, limited set of circumstances: she had needed to withdraw money from one of his accounts from time to time to pay taxes and fees. But if something dishonest was going on, someone might have altered that authorization and sent it to other institutions to gain control of other accounts. He began making telephone calls. Most of the offices were closed, but even those had voice mail. As soon as he had gone down the list, he went to his computer and wrote a letter that repeated the same information. He strongly suspected that e-mail had no legal status, so he customized his letter twenty times with different addresses and account numbers, printed out and signed the copies, then made out the envelopes and went out to mail the letters. As soon as they were in the mailbox, he made his third trip to the police station on Figueroa.

He stepped into the too familiar lobby of the station and up to the counter. The desk sergeant had an exaggeratedly respectful expression on his face as he said, "Mr. Mallon. How can we help you today?"

Mallon's stomach tightened. He said, "Is Detective Fowler in? Or Detective Long?"

The sergeant shook his head. "No, but I can take a message for you and make sure they receive it."

They were all convinced he had lost his mind, but he had to try. He said carefully, "I think something strange is going on with my attorney, Diane Fleming. She may be in danger, or threatened in some way. And she's disappeared."

The sergeant squinted at him. He said, "What makes you believe that?"

"She suddenly took off this morning, or maybe yesterday. I'm not sure, but probably it was then. An attempt had been made on my life, and I called her a number of times, but she didn't return any of my calls."

He stopped and blinked his eyes. He sounded crazy. He paused, trying to think of a way to repair the impression. There was no way, so he pressed on. "A couple of hours ago, I got word from Wells Fargo

Bank in San Francisco that she had requested that an investment account of mine there be liquidated and the proceeds wired to another account at Moncrief and Tydings."

"In her name?"

"I don't think so. They said, 'to your account at Moncrief and Tydings.' So it must be in my name. I don't know of an account at Moncrief and Tydings, but it's possible one has been opened there."

"Why would she do that?"

"I don't know, really. It appears to me to be an attempt by someone to embezzle the money. It's possible that they were doing it just so I wouldn't have the use of it. Do you see? It would be hard for them to withdraw it, but if it were simply moved to another account in my name that I didn't know about, I couldn't use it."

"Does she usually handle your money? Can she move it around like that?"

"Well, she has—had—a power of attorney that allowed her to move money to pay some bills and taxes and so on. But this is different."

"How?"

"It's a lot of money. It's about fifteen million dollars."

He had lost the sergeant. He could see that. Maybe the idea that he had that kind of money created a gulf between them that precluded sympathy or even understanding. Maybe the other policemen had not talked about him as a wealthy man, and his throwing these numbers around convinced the sergeant that he was hallucinating. He tried to keep his dignity. He tried to summarize his complaint. "She has left—left town, supposedly—with no notice, and is now—again supposedly—doing things she's never done before, and which I don't believe she would ever do, at least voluntarily."

"Mr. Mallon," said the sergeant. "Have you ever been to court with Miss Fleming?"

"No," said Mallon.

"You're sure."

"Yes. I only saw her in court once, but it was because I was meeting her for lunch. It wasn't anything she was doing for me."

"You don't recall ever hearing the word *conservator* or *conservatorship*?"

"Of course I've heard those terms," he said angrily. "But they have nothing to do with me. Nobody has ever thought I needed a conservator. I'm not deluded or something. I'm telling you that a young woman, a respected attorney in this city, has abruptly disappeared, and now there are papers appearing with her signature on them that she would never sign. In other words, either she's suddenly become an embezzler or she's in trouble."

"Why do you think she's disappeared?"

"She left without telling her secretary where she was going or when she'd be back."

"Who is the secretary?"

"Her name is Sylvia."

"Is she worried too? Did she come to you to tell you this?"

"No. But she doesn't know any of the things I've told you about the money. She was in the office to take the plants home because Diane told her not to bother coming into the office until she returned. If it was Diane. I'm beginning to think it couldn't have been."

"Can you give me Sylvia's full name?"

"No," he said. "I'm sorry. I've never heard her last name."

The sergeant looked at his watch and wrote something at the top of a form, then glanced at Mallon. "Seven o'clock. Do you happen to know the date today?" He held the pen above the line for the date.

It was the question doctors asked old people to see whether they had dementia. Mallon felt hot panic. "July seventh."

"I'm going to make a full report, and make sure it gets to the detectives. They'll let you know what they find out, I'm sure. But it'll take a while. You may as well go home and get some rest."

Mallon stood in silence for a moment. "I'm not insane, you know."

"Of course not."

Mallon stared at him for a moment, but his eyes were on the paper. He was busy writing, filling in blanks on the form. Mallon desperately searched his mind for something tangible, some piece of evidence that the police couldn't ignore, couldn't dismiss as either a delusion or a magnification of a routine event into something sinister. He was aware that time was passing, and that while the cop was pretending to pay attention to the form he was observing him, waiting.

Mallon said earnestly, "I know that this sounds vague, and I have no single piece of physical evidence that I can use to prove what I'm saying. But honestly, none of what's happened is normal, or within the usual range of behavior for Diane Fleming. I need to have you take this seriously."

The cop looked up from his paper, his clear, benevolent eyes wide open in a look of innocent surprise. "I assure you, we are taking it seriously." The fact that he was lying was completely undisguised, and there was absolutely nothing Mallon could do about it.

He had nothing more to say that would convince anyone. He reluctantly turned and walked. Mallon left by the side door and stepped out into the sunlight. The exit he had chosen gave him a short, shaded passage to walk before he reached Figueroa Street. He walked slowly, his shoulders hunched and his eyes studying the ground ahead. At the sidewalk he turned to the left, away from his house. He needed to walk and to think.

He was in trouble. Somebody—either the man walking on the beach or the man in the boat with a rifle—had tried to kill him. Now it was clear to him that the police believed that he had imagined the whole episode, or made it up. His lawyer, the only one who really knew what had been going on since the death of Catherine Broward and could verify the details, had suddenly vanished. What Mallon decided to do next would very likely determine whether he lived or died. As he walked, he began to feel more and more alone and uneasy.

He used the intersections as opportunities to turn and look back at the streets behind to detect followers. People were driving past on their way to stores or restaurants on the streets surrounding State. As they passed, he studied the faces of the drivers, looking for something out of the ordinary, some peculiar look, some expression that would give him a warning.

Yesterday, the man on the beach had been striding along, his eyes focusing on Mallon and then moving away, then returning to check on him, as though to see how close he was getting. During those minutes, those steps on the beach, the young woman had been leaning close to the man, talking. She had slid her eyes to the side to keep Mallon in sight while she talked. She had looked like a person whispering secrets, although normal speech would not have been audible to Mallon over the surf. Mallon had never imagined that the older man and the young woman in a bathing suit were dangerous. The change had come suddenly.

It was a strange look that had appeared on the man's face. It had in it a preoccupied concentration at the brow. The eyes had been sharp and alert and hot with eagerness for what was about to happen. On the lips had been the beginnings of a smile. Could it have possibly been pleasure? No. It was excitement, anticipation, the certainty of winning. He had thought a lot about the expression on the man's face, but it still made no sense to him. Was this the man who had killed Lydia? Had he been trying to kill Mallon next, because Mallon knew something that would help catch him? Was there some price on Mallon's head that he had been sure he was about to collect? Then who were the others—the girl, the man with the rifle? There was simply no answer.

When he got back to his house, Mallon quickly went up to his room and packed what he considered to be essential—a few sets of clean clothes, the cash he had withdrawn from the bank—then went down the stairs and out the door carrying his small suitcase. As he walked, he felt a tightness in his spine. He was expecting at each step to hear a shot, or a set of quick footsteps on the pavement behind him.

The feeling that someone was watching, preparing to stop him never diminished, but he did not dare turn around and look back. He placed his suitcase in the trunk of his car, unlocked his door, sat in the driver's seat, drove off, and hungrily searched the mirrors.

The world was curiously indifferent to what had happened. He could see women at the supermarket lot unloading grocery carts into their car trunks, couples walking together along Anapamu Street. Cars were coming up from the direction of the ocean and the freeway, as others came down from the residential areas. Nobody had been affected by the death of Catherine Broward, the murder of Lydia Marks, the shooting on the beach, the disappearance of Diane Fleming. They had not even heard of them.

Mallon drove along Anapamu to State, then down toward De la Guerra to coast past Diane's office. He could see that the windows were dark and there were no cars in the tiny lot. He accelerated again, and in a few minutes he was on the freeway, heading south.

He was going to do what he should have done two days ago: find Detective Angela Berwell and talk to her in person about everything that had happened since he and she and Lydia Marks had spent the evening together in the Hotel Bel-Air.

||||||||||||||||||||||||||||||||||||||||||||||||||||||||||||||||||||||

CHAPTER 23

I t's going to be a special kind of hunt," said Parish. "I've selected only the four of you to participate." He surveyed the four young people sitting before him in the main lodge. They were all under twenty-five, all clean looking and physically fit. They were perfect, the sort of postadolescents that advertising agencies assembled for a television commercial, with teeth that had been straightened and polished, hair kept trimmed by expensive stylists. "You can hunt as a team or in pairs, or you can go out alone. It's absolutely up to you. I trust each of you to that extent. You are among the very best hunters I've trained, in this country or elsewhere. I'll be completely candid with you. The staff of the school will try to help by getting information to you in the field, but we will not be there to hold anybody's hand during the hunt, or to get you out afterward." He turned his head slowly to look at each of them.

"I can't emphasize that enough. It's your hunt. You have to do your own thinking. That means thinking ahead. You do your own tracking to find the target. Before you do anything to reveal yourself, and especially before you take your shot, you'll have to do your own scouting. Think: Is this the best spot for taking down the target? Do I have a path out that will get me away before any curious bystanders arrive? Do I have a second way out if that one is unexpectedly blocked or proves dangerous? You all know what the considerations are."

A hand went up, and Parish was pleased. He liked it when his students seemed eager. "Yes, Kira?" He could tell she was doing this to draw attention to herself, and he admired her for it.

"What can you tell us about the target?"

He smiled, then said quietly, "I was just coming to him. Mary will pass out photographs of him now." He nodded at Mary, who had been leaning against the wall behind the four students. "She took them yesterday morning, and they came out very well. You should have little trouble recognizing him in most situations. He's six feet tall, forty-eight years old, and looks trim and fit. He has brown hair with a bit of gray around the temples. He's spent much of his life in the sun, so his skin has a slightly weathered look, and it's tan. He's divorced, and has lived alone for about ten years, so he's comfortable without companions, and that's the way he's likely to be when you find him."

Parish watched Mary handing out copies of the pair of photographs she had taken in front of the Santa Barbara courthouse and in the parking lot nearby. Each person would hold a photograph up for a moment, scrutinize it, and then lower it. He waited until all four listeners had looked at both pictures and then raised their eyes to him again.

"His name is Robert Mallon. He is, at least so far, unarmed. He's a retired contractor and real estate developer. The bad news is that he got into the real estate development business at a time when it was about to boom, and he's quite wealthy. As we all know, that gives a person flexibility, some experience in traveling, and possibly some allies or resources we don't yet know about. He has also been hunted before." He watched the faces suddenly become alert. "He has been here, and he has seen most members of the staff, which is why none of us will be going with you on this hunt.

"You're all wondering about him now—how he survived that kind of attention, whether there's something terribly important about him that I've neglected to mention. Very good. I want you to think that way. You want to know what I'm holding back about him. The truth is, there's not much. He has an honorable discharge from the military, but so do half the men his age, and as far as we know, he didn't see any combat. He didn't perform some physical feat to keep from being killed. In fact, he didn't even run away. I think that the reason he's alive is luck." He chuckled, shaking his head and lowering his eyes to the floor. There was a smattering of nervous laughter in the room.

He looked up suddenly. "I'm very serious. Luck is not always just an excuse we make up to account for poor planning or stupidity. In the first attempt he was out for a walk alone on a beach. There was a scout with a rifle in a boat a couple of hundred yards offshore, there primarily to keep the surrounding area secure while the hunter and the unarmed tracker approached the target on the beach and killed him. The hunter was too eager. Mallon saw the gun and attacked the hunter, and they began to struggle. In order to end it, the scout was obliged to fire from a boat rocking in the surf. Just as he squeezed the trigger, the boat moved, and Mallon was not hit. Do not underestimate luck. It's very real."

He brightened. "I also happen to know that it doesn't last forever. His changed the moment you four arrived. You're as unlike the people he's expecting as you could possibly be. You're superbly trained. You have each killed before and shown an aptitude for it. Your youth is an immense advantage. Your senses are at their sharpest, and you can easily move faster, and keep going longer, than anyone Mr. Mallon's age. Mr. Mallon is now on the run. He left Santa Barbara in his car—the one he's standing beside in the first picture—at three-fifteen. Right now he is on the Ventura Freeway heading toward Los Angeles. Emily Lyons and Paul Spangler are following him. You can call them on the road to learn where he is." He was pleased to see that people in the room were fidgeting, anxious to leave.

"Take a last careful look at the faces of the people around you. One of the reasons I brought all four of you together was so you could see the people you don't know. If you see any of them again later, don't mistake them for some inconvenient bystander and open fire." Parish turned his wrist to bring his watch into view. "It is now four thirty-nine." He lowered his arm, pivoted, and walked toward the door. He stopped, turned his head, and said, "Good hunting."

Kira squeezed her eyes closed and then opened them again. It was humbling. It almost made her cry. She could hardly believe that she was even here, that Michael had allowed her to be one of the people to play this game. She raised her left hand quickly to flick the curtain of blond hair from before her left eye so she could see Michael disappear.

She had been sure that while he had been talking, he had been looking right at her. Of course, he had looked at the others too—the three boys—but he had been looking at her more often, and for longer looks, than one-fourth of the time.

She stood and turned her head toward the window as though to look outside. There was nothing out there but an evergreen, but with the sun at this angle in the late afternoon, she could step into a beam of sunlight and see her reflection clearly.

She was pleased. The halter top revealed the slenderness of her waist and the outline of her breasts, and it let the definition of her arm muscles show. That was good for this group, because they probably wanted to be near a woman who was kind of buff. Some limp flower of a girl might get them blown away with her. She half-turned but kept her eyes on her reflection. The leather pants were great, too, maybe even better than the top. The window gave everything a greenish tint, so the burgundy leather looked black, but the effect was the same. There were so few people who could wear leather pants like that without looking as though their asses were crammed in and ready to explode. As the others moved to the door, she pried her eyes away from the window with a little trepidation to see whether she had attracted the kind of attention she needed.

She saw that it was the one with reddish-yellow hair who had responded first to her telepathic signal. He was looking at one of the photographs and listening to what one of his friends was saying, then suddenly he raised his eyes and turned to face her. One of his friends, the tall, thin one with the black hair, saw him do it, and moved his eyes to see what his friend was looking at. The third, a shorter, stockier one with a shaved head and a bull neck, turned to her last. He mumbled something that she hoped was "In your dreams," instead of something nasty, but the one with strawberry-blond hair was already making his way toward Kira.

He smiled shyly. "My name is Tim. I was wondering if you would like to hunt with us." He swept a hand in the general direction of his two friends. They were waiting for him by the door, pretending to be deep in discussion of some unrelated matter.

Kira tentatively imitated his smile, making sure hers was a bit smaller than his, and artfully made a slight shrug. She liked his eyes. They were clear blue. She looked warily at the two by the door. "Are you sure your friends wouldn't mind?"

"They'd be glad. Having you along would make us look less like a hunting party." He glanced around the room impatiently. "That's why Parish hires all those babes to be his pros. It makes everybody safer."

Kira did not like the sound of that. It was a bit too pragmatic and cynical, and not at all respectful. But at least it sounded to her like honesty, and it acknowledged that he had been looking at her in that way. He had ungrudgingly conceded to her that much—that she was too pretty to appear dangerous. She looked around the room very much the way he had, as though she were considering his invitation. "All right," she said. "My name is Kira."

"I know," said Tim. He led her to the others. "This is Kira," he said. "This is Jimmy." He indicated the tall one, then pointed to the shorter one. "And Lee." The shorter one, Lee, smiled and muttered something about being pleased, and the taller one merely nodded and stared into her eyes, but he did take her hand and give it a little shake.

She went outside onto the porch and they followed. At least they

258 ||| THOMAS PERRY

knew enough to let her go first, she thought. They knew she was a girl. She walked to her car, opened the trunk, lifted out her overnight bag, and slung the strap over her shoulder. Tim was at her side in a moment. "Take that for you?"

She slipped the strap and let him take it. Things seemed to be going exactly as she had planned: better than she had really expected. Since before the first time she had come to the camp, things had been going very badly for Kira, and this seemed to be a good indication of impending improvement.

Kira had first started thinking about taking some kind of self-defense class because a boy she had met at a party had tried to force her to have sex. It had been scary, and she had reacted by kicking and screaming for help instead of trying to reason with him. It had worked, but afterward she had been depressed, and there was nothing to do about it. It wasn't that she didn't know what was bothering her. It was that there were simply too many problems to solve at once, with one solution. One was that she had picked the boy out. She had liked him. She spent some time afterward looking back on the whole evening and wondering whether she had made his moves seem scary when they weren't, and whether maybe if she had been a bit more tolerant at certain stages, it might not have worked out all right—been a nice experience, even. But another problem was a dissatisfaction with the small number and low quality of options she'd had at the time.

He had seemed to think she was saying, "No, no, no," and meaning the opposite, as people sometimes did. She had decided to make it clear what she meant, but as she prepared to do that, she was aware that he might not care. With that thought had come her objective assessment that if he decided not to stop, she was not going to be able to do anything about it: he was much bigger and stronger than she was. He had stopped. He had apologized profusely. He had kept apologizing for so long and with such sincerity that he had become boring, and then annoying. She had not let him know that this was the meaning of her scowl, but had let him assume it was simple, unambiguous, out-raged innocence.

Of all the uncomfortable feelings that night had caused, the only one she could find a solution for was the inability to defend herself. Over the next few weeks she had talked to a few boys she knew, the ones who owned guns and took karate lessons. One of them had told her about the self-defense camp in the forest north of Ojai.

Kira had called the camp and asked if they would mail her an appli-cation. When it arrived, she had carried it to her father. Kira's father was the president of a boring company that made computerized de-vices that controlled car fuel intake, but he had once been a marine. Actually, he had been a captain in the Marines, but to him rank was not the distinction that mattered. To him, men were marines, or they were not.

He had stared at the brochure and at the application with the stony face he used for business. When he had looked up at her, the pale gray eyes were soft and concerned. "Baby, has something happened that you haven't told me?"

She had been prepared for this. She had giggled and shaken her head hard. "Of course not. It's just that when I come home late, the street near my apartment sometimes seems so dark and empty. I thought it might make sense to, you know, learn to take care of my-self."

He had nodded and handed her the brochure. "Go do it. I'll pay."

She had gone to the camp. She had always been good at classes like dance and gymnastics, and the hand-to-hand combat classes that Deb-bie taught had been like seeing the final picture in a set of assembly instructions: this was what all the work had been about. Spinning, kicking, and assuming exact postures correctly were precisely what she had been taught to do in dance classes. Doing handsprings and flips, balancing and rolling to recover from falls were just gymnastics exercises she had been trained to do since she was a toddler. After a month with Debbie she had become quick and wily. But a month had not satisfied her. It had only been enough time to stimulate her imagination. She had called her father and asked if she could stay on for another month.

She referred to him as "Jonathan" when she talked about him, but never when she spoke to him. She called him "Daddy" and told him that she was getting so good that he would be amazed. She talked to him about her work on the pistol range. She knew that Jonathan Tolliver had a deep skepticism about how much a hundred-and-ten-pound girl could ever learn to do in a hand-to-hand fight with a two-hundred-pound man, but he had great faith in firearms. He had always kept a few of them around his house: an M1911A1 .45 sidearm like the one he had been issued in the Corps, a .44 Magnum revolver that looked a lot like the guns cowboys used in movies, and two semi-automatic nine-millimeter pistols that he kept as a greeting for burglars. He fired them now and then to keep his aim sharp.

He had tried to interest Kira in shooting as a hobby when she had been fourteen and painting signs of future trouble on her face, because he considered shooting clean and wholesome. At the time, Kira had considered shooting "something farmers do when the 4-H Club is closed." This time, when she began to tell him about going onto a combat range and firing tight, rapid groups into man-shaped pop-ups, she knew she had him.

He had paid for psychiatry since she was eleven, paid unwittingly for drugs and tattoos, then for drug therapy and tattoo removal. He had paid her tuition to schools that were ever more geographically and thematically distant from the main thoroughfares of human activity. Self-defense seemed to him to be a simple, practical matter, like bread or a roof. The fact that she had expressed interest in something practical was a sign of better times. That she had stayed interested for so long was a hint of character that had previously been hidden from him. He paid.

Kira had been keeping a secret. It was not what had brought her to the camp, but it had been one of the things that had kept her here, working on marksmanship and tactics from dawn until dark every day, then doing exercises and practicing kicks and punches with Debbie until she needed to sleep.

Kira wanted to kill somebody. It was something she had thought about often since she had realized that it was not impossible. She had already chosen Mr. Herbick. He was the headmaster of the Shoreham School. The policy at the Shoreham School had always been to respect the privacy of others. But he had waited until Kira's class was at an assembly, and then searched their lockers. It had been an educational experience for Kira. She had learned that at a private school, there were no such things as a right to privacy, freedom from capricious search and seizure, or due process. Within ten minutes of the discovery of a plastic bag of white powder in her locker, she was no longer enrolled in the Shoreham School.

The pleasant part of the lesson was that the officials of the Shoreham School didn't feel that they owed the Commonwealth of Massachusetts any more attention to legal customs than they owed Kira. Headmaster Herbick and his assistant, Miss Swinton, called her mother in to witness a short, informal ceremony in which they flushed the white powder down the toilet in the headmaster's private bathroom and moved her permanent record file from the N–Z filing cabinet in the back office and into a file box in a storeroom marked "Inactive." At the time, she had been a year and a half from college. Mr. Herbick said he wished her luck, but of course she should not expect letters of recommendation from any school personnel.

It was late January. She could not transfer to another private school for the rest of the year, so she had been forced to go to a public high school. It took a day to find one that had space for her and a day to register, but the following Monday she found herself in a huge hallway that smelled of Lysol, jostled and pushed by the sort of crowd she had never seen anywhere but at a rock concert. She had to get used to bathrooms that were filthier than those at a turnpike rest stop, and so dangerous that she had to plead with girls she met in class to go with her and guard the stall door. This change had been educational, too.

Kira had lasted the year and a half, and had been admitted to a small women's college in Vermont. From then on, her higher-education career had been a constant unsuccessful search for a new school where she would be happy. When she dropped out of the last one, she had already wanted to kill Mr. Herbick for over three years. He had changed her life. But it wasn't until she actually had been trained in ways of going about it that she decided it must be done. She confided her fantasy to Debbie, the instructor she liked best, and Debbie accompanied her to Michael Parish. He placed her in a chair at the main lodge and spoke with her for hours, then dismissed her. It took four meetings held at two-day intervals before he agreed to arrange a hunt.

Herbick was easy. Kira had imagined a scene in which she would corner him somewhere and hold a gun on him, and he would weep and beg for mercy in a very satisfactory way. When it came to the actual event, it was less dramatic. It was like walking across a pasture and shooting a cow. She decided it was actually better that way: simple removal.

The problems came later. She had changed herself, which was what she had intended, but the change was of a slightly unexpected character. She had found that she had lost her capacity to have relationships with people who did not understand. They were living passive, uneventful, unimaginative lives, like the one she had lived before. She spent a year going on dates that always began with promise and retained exactly the same promise to the end. It was as though she and the boy were separated by a panel of perfectly clear, impenetrable glass. One of them would begin to talk, but the message would never quite reach the other. She would hear the boy talking about himself, but she could not respect his experiences or share his feelings, because he had never done anything as big and risky as what she had done. The problem became worse after her second hunt, and still worse after the third. She came to love killing. She had found the ultimate pleasure, the power to simply look at someone and think, I can easily kill you. The only reason you don't fear me is that you are too unimaginative to know it. The fact that nobody could look at little Kira Tolliver and realize that she was a killer added to the feeling of power, but it also isolated her.

She had realized that the best place where she could attempt to find a full and open relationship with a man was among men who had done exactly the same thing she had done. She had come and asked Michael Parish if there was any way she could come to work at the camp, or buy a long-term membership to make her regular visits at a cheaper rate. He had said he would think about it and keep her request in mind, so she had gone home and waited.

She had waited for weeks without hearing his reply, but then Michael had called unexpectedly and told her about this hunt. He had said he would let her join it for free while he thought about her request. She was becoming more confident by the minute. After all, who was either of them kidding? He knew that someday, she was going to inherit a whole lot of money. And she would probably, in the meantime, marry a man with some money. Parish knew he would get repaid with interest. He wasn't being so magnanimous.

Today she was taking advantage of something practical that she had learned over the past couple of years: that of all human beings, the only ones who were welcome everywhere, at all times, were beautiful young women. She looked up at Tim through her lashes as he shoved her bag into the back seat, then held her door open for her. She climbed in. As Jimmy, the tall dark one, drove the car down the gravel driveway toward the gate, she opened the bag and pulled out her new Beretta S9000 with the short barrel, slipped it into her purse, then found two full magazines and put them into the compartment beside it. She was aware that two of the three men in the car were staring at her in fascination. She thought that was just about right.

CHAPTER 24

As the car moved along the winding road toward the coast, Kira studied the photographs. She could see that the guy was a bit tired and a bit worried, not aware in at least the first shot that anybody was taking his picture. She put them into her purse and when her hand emerged again it held her cell phone. "Think it's time to call Emily and Paul?"

Tim wobbled his head noncommittally, but from the driver's seat came Jimmy's voice. "Yeah, you can try. He's had enough time to check in at a hotel, if L.A. is as far as he's going."

She dialed the number they had been given. "It's busy," she announced.

"Okay," said Tim. "We know we've got to drive an hour and a half anyway. Parish will probably hear where he is by then and call us."

"Right," said Lee. "There's no need to nag them."

Kira put her phone away and stared out the window. Coming down through the national forest made it seem later than it was. There was always a hill baking in bright late-afternoon sun on the east side, and another in deep shadow on the west. She waited until she judged that she had let the right interval elapse before she spoke again. "Are you guys friends from before, or did you meet at the camp?"

In the front seat, Jimmy and Lee turned their heads, and she could see their eyes meet. That look passed between them, that awful look that said, We knew it: we knew she would turn out to be stupid.

Tim turned his blue eyes to her and said, "Lee and Jimmy knew each other before. I met them at the camp about six months ago. They haven't said their last names or where they're from, and neither have I."

She felt a gush of gratitude to him for answering. She knew the others would have left her question hanging in silence, and she would have hated that. Tim's eyes were even better than she had thought at first. She did not even bother to construct a formulation in words. She acted on it, setting him apart from the others, making a distinction in her mind. She gave Tim her very best smile. She had known she would have to choose. When a girl was with three boys, they would eventually force her to, even if it was something they would all do together. They always had to know. She pursued his attention, to keep him looking at her. "But have you hunted with them before?"

"No," he said. "We've all hunted, but we each went solo. With the safari crew, I mean."

She laughed, making her eyes flash at him and throwing her hair back to show her perfect skin. She let the laugh become a lingering smile to let him see her small, perfect teeth. "It's pretty funny when you say it that way."

"That's what it is," said Tim.

"Not today, though. This is a party, and we get to do our own party planning. How do you think we should get him?"

"Beats me. Depends on where we find him, I guess."

The conversation wasn't very promising. Maybe Tim was feeling self-conscious because the other two were up there listening, and he couldn't see their faces. "I think I'll try calling again."

This time she heard only a partial ring, and then Emily's voice. "Yes?"

Kira clutched Tim's forearm. "It's me, Kira. Do you have a location?"

"Affirmative. He's checked in at the Beverly Towers on Sunset, room 1503."

"Great," said Kira. "Thanks."

"Good hunting."

Kira turned off her telephone, and sighed. "He's at the Beverly Towers on Sunset. Room 1503."

"Wow," said Lee. "That was easy."

"Yeah, but popping him in a hotel isn't. Whoever does it will be stuck way up on the fifteenth floor. If there are shots in a hotel room, somebody hears them. Then you only have three or four ways down, and the only place you can end up is the lobby," said Jimmy.

"We'll think of something," Tim assured them.

"Yeah?" Jimmy's voice was contemptuous. "Like what?"

"I don't know yet. It's early. He's checked in, but probably he won't stay in his room all the time. He drove to L.A. for some reason. Maybe there's somebody he wants to see, or something he wants to buy. Anyway, he's got to eat. Maybe he'll go out for that. Anything can happen."

Kira decided to stay in the conversation to establish sides. "Tim's right: anything can happen. We could get him just by being near his car."

"It would have to be better than that," Lee scoffed.

"The car was just an example," Kira said. "Tim's saying that it's too soon to say it's not doable. We'll think of something. We will."

The talk was an irritant, not quite an argument, just a general peevish dismissal of anything anyone said. But Kira didn't allow herself to feel weary or discouraged. The talk was an annoyance, but she had used it to delineate the sides. By the time the car came to the top of the long hill that rose above Camarillo and over the invisible line into Los Angeles County, the distinctions had been made: Jimmy and Lee, the two friends from somewhere or other, were in the front seat sharing contemptuous glances and patronizing smirks about Kira and Tim, thinking they couldn't see from the back seat.

She had become Tim's ally. He owed her more than he probably had yet understood. The other two could make the cleverest sarcastic remarks about Tim that had ever been heard, and it meant nothing. The contest was over, and they were the losers. They knew it. She could tell that they knew it, because she could hear it in the bitter, disappointed tone of their voices. They were trying to convince themselves that it wasn't a real loss because Tim wasn't as cool as they were and Kira was too dumb to be credible, but the defeat was primal. The desirable girl—the only girl—had picked Tim, and not them. It didn't matter whether her criteria were fair or wise: her choice was absolute and irrefutable. She could also tell from the disproportionate level of their irritation that they had each understood that this had not been an empty contest. There was a prize, and they were imagining exactly what having that prize would have been like.

She returned her attention to Tim. She had moved closer to him, and sometimes touched his arm or his hand as she made a point. She was secure now, and she could concentrate on the hunt. Soon they were off the freeway, going south over a winding canyon road down into Beverly Hills. When they reached Sunset and she saw the wide avenues lined with tall coconut palms, she began to watch for the hotel. She saw it coming from a distance. After a few seconds' thought, she said, "Anyone have a plan besides me?"

Ten minutes later, Kira and Tim entered the lobby. Tim was carrying his suitcase and had her overnight bag strapped over his shoulder, but he was strong enough so that it looked effortless. Kira scurried to the counter ahead of him and said, "We just called a few minutes ago and had a room set aside for us."

The clerk was a girl about Kira's age. "Mr. and Mrs. Wilson?"

"That's right."

"And how will you be paying for your stay with us?"

Kira placed on the counter one of the two credit cards she had bought before the hunt. It had been sold to her for two thousand dollars as a spree card. It was a perfect clone of a real card belonging to a real Mrs. Wilson, who was supposedly in Europe for the summer, where someone had gotten the card's information when she had used it. Kira had bought the clone because she had known that on this hunt she would have to make her own arrangements for getting out afterward, and, with the fake Massachusetts driver's license she'd had made to order, the card would allow her to rent a car or buy a plane ticket.

She held her breath as the clerk swiped the card on a magnetic reader, looked at a screen, and frowned. She swiped it again, and Kira began to feel the hairs on the back of her neck rise. She slipped her hand into her purse, grasped the pistol's grips, and let her face go blank. The clerk turned the card around to face her, and began tapping keys on the card reader. There was a pause while the machine communicated over a telephone line with some other machine, and then a sudden clackety-clack as the reader printed out a receipt. The clerk smiled, and Kira slowly pulled her right hand out of the purse. She took the clerk's silver pen and signed, then accepted the little folder with the magnetic key cards, turned, and walked to the row of elevators in an alcove.

As soon as they were inside, Tim leaned close and whispered, "I didn't see any sign of him in the lobby or the gift shop." She felt the soft puffs of his breath on her ear, and it made delicious chills go down her spine. She pulled away, and gave a little shimmy. "That tickles." Then she raised her eyes to him. "No. But let's talk in the room."

She had asked for a room as high up as possible, where there would be a view, and she had scored the fifteenth floor. She had told the others casually, without making too much of it, and left it to them to remember their negative comments and to consider whether they could have gotten so close to Mallon's room so effortlessly.

She had turned to Jimmy and said, "You two will have to find a way to watch his car without getting noticed." She had been aware that she was making the estrangement between them complete. Jimmy and Lee would be outside somewhere, or possibly in a dark, damp underground parking structure, while she took Tim upstairs to a comfortable hotel room with her. She and Tim would probably be the ones to get Mallon, and Jimmy and Lee would get nothing.

She gave Tim one of the card keys to their room and whispered, "1509," then slipped the other card into a pocket of her purse, where she could find it easily. As the elevator stopped and she walked out, she thought about the fifteenth floor. No hotel ever had a thirteenth, so they called that the fourteenth, and the fifteenth was really the fourteenth. She had traveled with her father and mother enough to know that she would almost certainly be able to get a room up high. That was because business travelers all knew that no fire department in the world had a ladder that went up above the sixth floor. If Mallon had unexpectedly shown up an hour ago and been given the fifteenth floor, chances were that she would be too.

She let Tim go ahead of her past 1503, his heavy feet made heavier by the luggage he carried. She used the noise to cover her while she stopped by the door. She placed her ear to the wood and listened. She heard Tim open room 1509. She knew he was standing in the doorway holding the door open and watching her from behind, so she tried to look dangerous and alluring at the same time, making her leg muscles tense and sucking in her abdominals to prepare to spring.

She held her pose for fifteen or twenty seconds, but she could hear nothing. She turned her head slightly and brought her eye to the corner to see Tim. He was no longer holding the luggage. He had his jacket over his left arm, and the other hand hidden, obviously on his gun. He was staring at her hard.

Kira stayed still for another few seconds to give Mr. Mallon a chance to move or cough or snore. Then she straightened and walked silently, as Debbie had taught her, placing her weight on the outer edges of her feet. She slipped through the doorway of 1509 past Tim, and waited for him to close the door quietly.

"I'm pretty sure he's out," she said. "It's too early for dinner."

Tim nodded. "Best thing to do is wait for him." He sat down on the bed.

She stood in front of him so she could look into his eyes. "Do you want to see if we can get into his room and wait there for him?"

Tim said, a little too quickly, "I don't see how."

"You're right," she said. "That was a silly idea." She sat on the other side of the bed. "It's just that these magnetic key cards sometimes don't work right, and you can open more than one door with them. I don't suppose it happens very often."

He seemed a bit more interested. He stood and picked up his jacket, then quickly went out the door. She was amazed. He had not said anything to her about joining him or anything. She picked up her purse and went to the door. She opened it a crack to look down the hall, but he was already on the way back. He brushed past her into the room, then went to the windows. He said, "So much for that. Not even any balcony, so that's out too."

"I don't think it would be much fun to climb from one to the other way up here, anyway," she said, then gave a little shiver. He didn't seem to have seen it, or to be listening to her.

Kira walked toward the cabinet that held the television set, but when she reached it she didn't feel like opening it. She was aware that time was going by, and the time was precious. It was nearly dark outside, day turning to evening. She knew it was likely that if Mallon was out now, he would probably be out for the evening. If he came back, the others would be watching for his car. He was dead without knowing it. What was bothering her was that she had gone to a lot of trouble, taken a lot of chances, and used up some luck to get where she was at this moment, and her forward motion seemed to have stalled.

Each of them seemed to be letting sentences die off at the end, and then turning their attention inward, wishing that they liked each other better, wondering what had gone wrong. She stole a glance at Tim. He was lying on the bed with his hands behind his head, staring at the ceiling with a pouting expression. People in situations like this wore out their enthusiasm; they just got tired of smiling, tired of thinking of the right things to say, tired of listening.

Kira couldn't let it go that way, let this chance turn into a failure that would gnaw at her later, just because of shyness, or passivity, or laziness or something. She heard herself whispering, "I want this." She hesitated, glancing at the television cabinet. Finally she took two deep breaths and walked around to the other side of the bed.

She sat down, then swung her legs up, lay beside him, put her hands behind her head, knitting the fingers as he had, and stared up at the smoke detector on the ceiling. "I guess all we can do now is wait."

"Guess so," he said.

"Any ideas about how we could pass the time?"

She caught a swift movement as he turned his head toward her abruptly, so she turned hers more slowly and looked into his blue eyes. She saw that they had suddenly become inquisitive. She turned her body toward him, crooked her elbow, and leaned her head on her right hand. She gave him a mischievous smile.

He rolled, almost a lunge toward her that startled her a little, and put her on her back. He hovered above her as he kissed her, pressing his mouth against hers too heavily. His tongue pried open her lips and came inside, searching, and then his right hand was groping, moving to her left breast. He was eager, she told herself: passionate, not rough. She began to need to stop for a second, because it was hard to breathe, but he didn't stop for that. She turned her head to break off the kiss, and took three deep breaths, and then she was feeling better. It was easier now, nice, really. He was kissing her neck, and he didn't have the weight of his upper body on hers anymore.

Then he was undressing her, but so quickly that she was afraid he was going to rip her top, or maybe tear the zipper of the leather pants. "Wait," she whispered. "Let me."

At first there was an instant when she was not sure that he would, but his hands stopped. She sat up, took off the top, and she could see the blue eyes staring in appreciation. She was beautiful, and she was glad that he knew it. She swung her legs off the bed and laid the top on the chair, then took off the leather pants. She left her underpants on and walked to the counter by the television, dug into a pocket of the purse, and found the condom. She stepped to the bed, holding it up and smiling.

He was beside the bed, quickly stripping off his clothes. As soon as he was naked, he stepped closer and pulled her to him. He kissed her and then pushed her onto the bed, and continued what he had been doing before.

"Here," she said after a few minutes. She pushed the condom into his hand.

He tugged her panties off. He obviously had interpreted her gesture as a signal that she was ready to accept him, but she noticed he had tossed the condom aside.

"Aren't you going to use it?"

He shook his head. "Don't like them."

"But we should. Would you please do it anyway?"

He stopped and held her at arm's length, staring into her eyes. "What? Do you have AIDS or something?"

"No," she snapped. "Do you?"

"What do you have, then?"

"Nothing!" she said angrily. "It's just a normal precaution."

He let go of her, then turned to pick up the condom, and sighed heavily as he tore the wrapper off and put it on. "There. You happy?"

She quickly made a decision. She lay back on the bed. She wriggled a bit to get closer. "Yes," she said. "Very happy."

She wanted it to be true, but something had turned sour. He had seemed a bit too rough and hurried before, but now he was distant, uncaring. He was very strong, and he made sudden, almost violent movements, grasping her too tightly and then thrusting too hard. She said, "Wait, be a little more gentle."

"If you'd relax, you'd enjoy it."

"Please."

He seemed to get more quick, more violent, ignoring her voice. She decided that what he had said might actually help if she could do it, and it was all she could do, so she tried to relax all her muscles, to offer no resistance. She only had to endure it for a few more minutes, and it was over. He disengaged himself from her, and she kept still, staring at the ceiling. He lay beside her for a few seconds, then got up, walked into the bathroom, and closed the door.

Kira wanted to cry, but she knew she shouldn't, or everything would be lost. A minute later, he came out again. Maybe he had been just so filled with lust, so sexually hungry for her, that he had needed to do it that way. Maybe that part was over now, and they would be closer to each other than before, and he would be kinder and in less of a hurry. She had proved she was not just a tease, getting him aroused and then not letting him find release. Maybe he had even been a little bit suspicious of her before, and resentful in advance, and now he would be okay. She cleared her throat and found her voice. "Come back and lie down with me."

He looked at her. He didn't smile, but he went back to the bed and lay there obediently.

She did not feel as though anything she tried was working, but she had decided that the only way was to advance, not retreat. "That was really nice. Thanks."

He looked at her again, more curious than warm. Then he seemed to remember something. Before he said it, she knew what it meant. "We'd better see if he's back." He got up and rapidly pulled his clothes on.

She had known it would be something that required him to go away from her for a bit. That way, before he saw her again she would be dressed, and he could pretend nothing had ever happened. She watched him put on the jacket with the gun in it and slip outside.

Kira remained on the bed and considered. Ordinarily, a girl would be happy to acquiesce in the deception, dress while he was out, and by the time he got back, have her makeup fixed and be demurely brushing her hair. A girl would wait for him to speak before she would say anything about having had sex, and maybe he would never mention it again, just assume that the next time he wanted sex, she would agree. Maybe they would part, and never speak again about anything.

Kira sat up. She was proud of the way her body looked in the big mirror across from the foot of the bed. She instinctively did not want to let this incident be over, just out of some misplaced modesty or a fear of awkwardness. Tim would realize in a minute that room 1503 was empty. She was positive that Mallon could not have come back onto this floor and gone into his room without her hearing it.

She was beginning to feel frustrated about Tim. He was attractive, he was strong, he was a person who should be able to understand her, a person she didn't need to lie to. She looked into the mirror again and fluffed her long blond hair. This should have worked better. He should be in here with her now, seeing what she saw, and marveling at his good luck.

——————||||||||||||||||||||||||||||||||||||||||||||||||||||||||||||||||——————

CHAPTER 25

Kira pulled the halter top on over her head, brushed her hair a few times, angrily, and then put the last touches to her makeup. She had given Tim a half hour, but he still had not come back to the room. She was going to have to find him. She made sure her bag was packed and locked, took her purse, then went out and closed the door behind her.

She stopped at the door of 1503 and listened for a moment, but then she heard the ding of the elevator bell, announcing that it had arrived. She quickly moved away from 1503 and took the final fifteen feet to the elevator doors so she would be there, face-to-face with Tim when the door opened. She had time for an instant's regret that she had not brought her overnight bag. The sight of her standing there with her bag—or maybe just brushing past him into the elevator without speaking—would have forced him to think quickly: if he wanted her, he would have to acknowledge it and make her know it, or she would be gone. She had not brought the bag, so she would have to do without it. She stood a pace back from the door, her head up and her shoulders back, and an expression in her eyes that would freeze a bird in flight.

The door slid open: no Tim. Instead, there were two men in their thirties who looked to her like businessmen. She lowered her eyes to avoid theirs and waited for them to move past, and as they did, she could detect the smell of liquor. They must have been sitting in the bar having a few drinks before dinner. She stepped into the elevator and pressed and held the "Close Door" button, pushed P2, the lowest button in the row, and felt the elevator begin to sink.

Kira was tired of men right now. Some time ago, she had discovered that after having acceptable sex, she often didn't think about having it again for days. That had not seemed surprising. What was odd was that having really bad sex had nearly the same effect. Afterward, she imagined she should have been prowling around trying to satisfy unfulfilled desire, but she found that even desire could be used up, depleted. Either way, men seemed unappetizing until the clarity of her recollection of the experience receded.

She wanted to find Tim right now and salvage the investment she had made in him. There were not going to be that many get-togethers where she could meet young men, and most of the young men she had met at the camp had not seemed promising. She had bet the whole hunting trip on Tim—she could hardly expect to meet someone else now—and gone to the trouble of separating him from the herd, seducing him and then enduring him. She had a sudden vivid memory of how awful he had been in bed, but she did not linger on it. She could teach him to be better at it. She turned and stared into the mirror at the back of the elevator car, straightened her hair, pulled her halter top down a little and her pants up on her waist a bit. The elevator stopped. The door opened on the lower parking level.

Kira saw all three boys instantly. Jimmy and Lee were seventy or eighty feet from her, both crouching behind parked cars, one on either side of the aisle ahead of her. The spaces in this underground parking area were all diagonal; the cars on both sides of this aisle were angled away from Kira, so each was squatting behind the rear tire of a car. Tim was much farther from the elevator, nearly at the far end of the next aisle, but his reddish hair made him easy to see and impossible for her not to recognize. He was sitting behind the wheel of the car in which Jimmy had driven them all here. She stepped out of the elevator.

She heard the elevator door slide shut behind her. She tried to read the sight, to extrapolate from the positions of the three men what was going on, but she could not. Certainly Jimmy and Lee could not have been crouching there for all this time, with their backs visible to the elevator door. And what was Tim doing way down there in the car, not even in the same aisle as the others? Something had begun.

Her legs seemed to be acting on a decision she had not consciously made. She had started to walk quietly to the right, away from Jimmy and Lee, and toward the aisle where Tim sat in the car. Her eyes kept returning to Jimmy and Lee, because she did not want to startle them, but she wanted a chance to be in for the kill.

There was the faint sound of an engine. It was idling, just coasting slowly down the ramp from the level above them. She realized that she had been hearing it since the elevator door had opened, driving up and down the aisles above, searching for a space. Jimmy reached into his jacket and pulled out a pistol. Lee had been watching him across the aisle, and now he did the same.

Kira's legs moved faster, carrying her to the beginning of Tim's aisle. Her right hand reached into her purse and closed around the new Beretta pistol. She could feel the rough pattern of the knurled handgrips, and she lifted it just a little off the bottom of the purse to feel the comforting weight of it as she walked. Kira craned her neck to look to the left, toward the aisle where Jimmy and Lee crouched. The sound of the car grew just a bit louder, and then it appeared. It was Mallon's red Toyota. She could feel her heart speeding up.

She was still too far away to open fire. She checked to be sure the others had not moved. Tim was all the way at the end of her aisle, at least two hundred feet from her. She decided that all she could do was stay in plain sight. She kept walking toward Tim, a little faster now.

She lowered her face toward her purse, as though she were a woman searching for a set of keys, but she held the red car in the corner of her eye.

She heard a car's starter turn over, then the hum of its engine. It was Tim. She saw him back the black car out of its space. Her heart stopped, then started again, faster. She gave the fingers of her left hand a little flutter, trying to get his attention, but he didn't seem to see her. She had expected him to move into the third aisle and drive toward her, but he steered the car around the end of the first aisle.

He had moved into the other aisle behind Mallon's car, and she understood. He was blocking the aisle, keeping Mallon from backing up. She heard his door open and slam shut.

Lee and Jimmy suddenly stepped into the aisle in front of Mallon's car, and opened fire. The noise of each report was a sharp bright clap that pounded her eardrums, then seemed to take a second to fade as it echoed around the concrete surfaces. She raised her pistol, but she could already hear Mallon's car.

The car's tires screamed, the engine growled. She stopped and pivoted, then dodged to the left, trying for a clear aim to the left of the nearest concrete column. The car's front end seemed to rise as it shot forward. The safety glass of the rear window was spiderwebbed with cracks radiating from bullet holes, and much of it had been pulverized into a milky translucence, so she could not see anyone inside. She saw the car hit Lee and throw him forward through the air, then hit Jimmy, drag him under it for a few yards, then bump over him.

The taillights came on and the tires screeched, trying to grip the pavement before the car reached the end of the aisle, turning sideways and sliding. Kira fired twice at the car as it rocked to a stop, but then it moved ahead around the end of the aisle and fishtailed toward Kira, heading for the ramp back up to the next level. Kira sidestepped out of its path into the aisle where Lee and Jimmy had ambushed it. As she ducked down, she took note of what she saw. Lee had flown most of the way to the elevator, and he lay near it with his head turned at an angle that meant he had to be dead. She ran past Jimmy. He was the apex of a long wet triangle of bright red blood that was flowing down the gradual incline of the floor.

Kira could see Tim clearly. He was all right. He was standing by the black car, his gun in his hand. He was staring at the car Mallon was driving up the next aisle, turning his whole body as he watched it. He made no attempt to raise his gun to shoot at Mallon. He made no attempt to move the black car again to block Mallon's way to the ramp. Kira could see that his eyes were not angry or calculating. They were open wide, staring with weak incomprehension.

Mallon sped up to the next level, and it was as though a door up there had closed. It was very quiet now. Kira moved toward Tim quickly, running on the balls of her feet, the soles of her shoes making a chuff each time they hit the textured concrete. Tim seemed to hear the sound. He turned to look up the aisle in her direction, but Kira could not tell whether he was looking at her or the crushed bodies of Lee and Jimmy. He put the pistol back into his jacket, then got into the driver's seat of the car and slammed the door. He began to back the car and turn the wheels to swing around.

"Wait!" she called. "Wait, it's me!" She watched him as she ran, hoping to see his head turn to look in the rearview mirror, but it never did. The car glided forward and turned up the ramp and out of sight.

Kira stopped running. She turned and looked back toward the elevator doors, past the two bodies. She was aware that the whole incident seemed to have taken much longer than it really had. It had taken less than half a minute, she was sure, but there would be people here soon.

She stepped quickly to the stairwell, making her plan by instinct as she climbed. She emerged, not at the lobby level but on the second floor, where she knew there would be fewer people to see her. There were none. From there she took the elevator to the fifteenth.

She was through with Parish, through with hunting. She was going home to Massachusetts. By the time she had reached her room, wiped it clean of her fingerprints, and checked her overnight bag, she could look down at the street through the window and see police cars and ambulances. She sighed. She knew she would have to drag Tim's bag home with her too. He had turned out to be a lousy lover and a coward too, but she couldn't take the risk of letting him get caught and questioned by the police.

CHAPTER 26

|||||||||||||||||||||||||||||||||||||||||||||||||||||||||||||||||||||||

Mallon felt light and cold now, his body no longer reacting to the sudden rush of adrenaline, but to the fact that it had stopped. The emergency was over. He walked along the street for another block, feeling his strength returning. He stopped to look behind him, but he could see nobody who might have followed him.

Mallon stepped into the first lighted doorway he saw. It was a small coffee shop that looked as though half of its business came from homeless men who cadged change from people on Sunset Boulevard and came here to spend it. A pay telephone hung on the wall, where everyone would hear him talk, but he put in two quarters and dialed 911.

When the emergency operator came on, his quarters came back. He said, "My name is Robert Mallon. I've just been attacked by two men with guns in the parking garage under the Beverly Towers Hotel. They shot at me, but I ran over them with my car."

The operator sounded strangely calm, almost sleepy. "And where are you now, sir? Where are you calling from?"

"A coffee shop on Santa Monica Boulevard, a few blocks from the hotel. I drove away because there were two more with them."

"All right, sir," she said. "I want you to stay on the line now, and I'm going to send officers to come and pick you up. All right?"

"I guess so," he said. "Sure."

The time seemed to pass very slowly. He was aware that several people in the coffee shop had heard his conversation, and they were watching him. The waitress kept glancing at him and wiping the counter with a rag so filthy that the surface looked gelatinous. At last, through the front window, he saw the police car come up Santa Monica with its flashing lights on, then swing around in a wide turn to stop at the curb just outside.

Mallon said into the phone, "They're here. Got to go," and hung up. On the way to the door he said to the waitress, "Thanks for the use of the phone."

She shrugged and muttered, "It's not mine."

He stepped outside as the two cops got out of their car. They both wore body armor under their shirts, so they looked big and square as they moved to intercept him. "Are you Mr. Mallon?" asked the nearest one. The other stood to the side, and Mallon knew he wasn't supposed to be aware that the man had his right hand resting on the grip of his gun while they waited for him to answer.

"I'm Robert Mallon. Thank you for coming so quickly."

The two moved in. The one who had not spoken said, "I'm sorry, sir, but we've got to see what's in your pockets. Can you turn around for me and put your hands up on the wall here?"

"Sure," said Mallon, but he didn't need to do anything. The two were already turning him and pushing him into position.

One of them said, "Am I going to find any weapons?"

"No."

He kept up the questions as he reached into Mallon's pockets and turned them inside out, then began efficiently patting his ribs, his legs, his ankles. "Anything that might cut or poke me, like a knife or a needle?"

"Nothing."

They finished quickly, and the other cop pulled him back from the wall. "Now, why don't you tell us what happened?"

Mallon carefully repeated the story he had told the operator, and the two cops listened intently, their faces expressionless. It occurred to Mallon that he had spent more time with police officers lately than he had when he'd worked in the parole department. In those days he had spent most of his time alone with the parolees in his caseload.

"Where's your car?"

"Back there about two blocks." He pointed. "I parked it so I could look for a phone."

"Why did these guys pick you? Were they trying to rob you?"

"I don't think so," said Mallon. "I think they were just trying to kill me."

"Why would they do that?"

Mallon looked at him, and began his story for the first time that evening, wondering how many times he would have to tell it again before morning.

He told it four times, to four different sets of interrogators. After one of them called Detective Fowler in Santa Barbara, their demeanor changed slightly. He was placed in the third small room of the evening, and this time the detective was a sad-looking man named Diehl. He brought Mallon a cup of coffee.

He said, "The two dead men's hands tested positive for gun powder. Before you hit them, they both discharged their weapons. Yours tested negative, so there isn't much argument about who put the holes in your car windows. You're no longer a hit-and-run. Now you're a self-defense."

"Do you know who they are?" asked Mallon.

Diehl shook his head. "No, do you?"

"No."

Diehl took the top off his own cup of coffee and sipped it, then set it on the table in front of him and leaned back. "Detective Fowler in Santa Barbara says this seems to happen to you a lot. Why is that?"

Mallon answered, "I've told everybody else the same thing. I don't know for sure. About a month ago, I saved a woman named Catherine Broward from drowning herself in the ocean. While I was out getting us some dinner, she apparently walked to her car, took out a gun, and shot herself. I hired a detective named Lydia Marks to find out why she did that."

"Why?"

"I'm not positive that she did. Lydia had a theory, but—"

"No," Diehl interrupted. "Why did *you* do that?"

"I happened to see her while she was trying to kill herself," said Mallon. "I thought I had stopped it, but I'd just interrupted it for a few hours, while I talked to her, got to know her a little, came to like her a lot. It was like holding a bubble in your hand: if you stop thinking about keeping the bubble intact, turn your eyes away, make a move, the bubble is gone. I turned my back on Catherine Broward for a short time, and she was gone. I needed to know why she would try so hard to kill herself. I thought if I found out about her life, it would tell me the answer. So I hired somebody who knew how to find out about people. I picked Lydia Marks because I knew her—used to work with her years ago—but also because she was a woman. I thought that maybe she could help me understand Catherine better."

"You didn't answer my question," said Diehl. "Why did you care?"

"That's one of the things that I'm learning. After she died, I tried to convince myself that it must be just detached curiosity, like science, because I wouldn't be foolish enough to care so much about somebody I didn't actually know very well. Then I decided that it must be some kind of midlife crisis—that it was about my own mortality. But it was Catherine. I liked her. For a few hours she made life surprising and mysterious again. I wanted her to live, and if she had, I would have tried to know her better. I'm still not sure whether that would have worked out, but I wanted her to live."

Diehl's melancholy stare did not change. He had tired eyes that looked red enough to hurt. "You found something about her that somebody didn't want known, or somebody thinks that you did. That's your theory now, I take it?"

"It's not just me they seem to be after. It's everyone who was trying to find out about why Catherine Broward died. Lydia Marks is dead. My attorney, Diane Fleming, seems to have gone somewhere—maybe into hiding, maybe kidnapped. I came down here to see if I could get help from an LAPD detective named Angela Berwell. She knew Lydia, and we had talked to her about Catherine's death. Before I got a chance to talk to her, these people found me."

"We'll be looking into all of that. Right now I'd like to find out more about you, Mr. Mallon. You're the sort of guy who stimulates my curiosity. You seem to have a whole lot of money, but you retired some time ago. Is that right?"

"Yes," said Mallon.

"At what age? About thirty-five?"

"Thirty-eight." He resigned himself to the fact that he was going to have to go through all the details. "I worked in the parole office in San Jose, for about four years."

"You were a cop? What happened?"

"I decided it wasn't for me. I went into it with the idea that what I was going to do was help people who needed it. After four years, it still didn't seem to be happening. So I quit."

"I can understand that," said Diehl. The expression on his face was ambiguous.

"Then I went into construction. It was a good, steady business for about twelve years, and it was getting better. I got into developing housing projects. Then my wife started divorce proceedings. Her lawyers wouldn't accept a half interest in the company. They insisted that I cash her out. I had already borrowed all I could to finance the projects I was doing, so there was nothing I could do but sell, and divide the proceeds. We happened to be at the beginning of a boom, and at that moment I was in phase one of a development called Old Greenridge Ranch. A couple of much bigger companies wanted that location. The area was growing so fast that they couldn't build quickly enough to keep up with the demand without gobbling up some companies like mine, and keeping the crews on the job. So one of them made a preemptive offer that was more than I'd ever imagined I would get."

"What happened then?" asked Diehl.

"I bought a three-bedroom house in Santa Barbara, and put the rest of the money into investments. For ten years I've spent most of my days going places on foot or reading books from the public library. If I go out at night it's usually to concerts or lectures at the university, or maybe a movie. I have about four really good sport coats and five pairs of expensive walking shoes. I replace maybe one of them a year. It doesn't cost much to live that way, so the money stayed invested and I got a lot richer in ten years."

Diehl said, "You're lucky." He stared at his coffee cup. "Or maybe you're a genius." He looked up to watch Mallon as he said, "I know some guys who went into construction at about the same time you did. They worked really hard, and they seem to still have plenty of work. But they tell me they're not ready to retire even now."

"You're right. I was lucky," said Mallon. "It didn't feel like luck at the time. It felt like a disaster. But at the end of it, I had a lot of money."

Diehl sighed impatiently. "You've got to help me here. There is absolutely no question in anybody's mind now that people have made attempts to kill you. My question to you is just this: have you told us every reason you can imagine for them to do that? Something left over from the construction business, maybe?"

"I've told the police here and in Santa Barbara everything I know," Mallon said. "I think it has to do with the death of Catherine Broward, and the murder of her boyfriend before that, not with me, or a business I sold years ago."

Diehl looked at him for a few seconds, his eyes still sad and tired and red. Then he placed both hands on the table and pushed himself to his feet as though it were a difficult exercise. "Then you may as well go. We'll be looking into everything you've told us. If we learn anything about the two bodies we have, we'll let you know. Meanwhile, try to take precautions so this doesn't happen again."

"You're saying that you won't do anything to protect me."

"The only way I can protect you is by breaking this case." He held his empty hands out from his sides. "That's all I have." Then he turned and went out the door.

||||||||||||||||||||||||||||||||||||||||||||||||||||||||||||||

CHAPTER 27

It was morning when Mallon was allowed to leave the station. He took a taxi to the airport, rented a car, and checked into a hotel on Century Boulevard. He sat on the big bed, took out the telephone book, looked up the nonemergency numbers of the police department, and began calling various divisions. After his third call, he found that Angela Berwell was assigned to homicide in Hollywood. He wrote the number on the small pad by the phone, then dialed it.

When he heard the call connect, a female voice said, "Hollywood." He shoved the sheet with the number into his pocket.

"I'd like to speak with Detective Berwell, please."

After half a minute, Mallon heard, "Homicide, Berwell."

He said, "Detective Berwell, this is Robert Mallon. Do you remember me? Lydia Marks and I met with you a few weeks ago."

"Yes, Mr. Mallon. Of course I remember. I've been trying to get in touch with you for days, since Lydia was killed. Are you all right?"

Her voice seemed so sympathetic, so calm and sane. Every other police officer he'd talked to since the beginning had seemed to suspect him of hiding something, or think he was crazy. "I'm not hurt or anything," he said, "but I seem to have become the next target."

"I heard about what happened at the hotel just a little while ago when I came on duty." Her voice became quieter. "Listen, Lydia's death and what's happened to you aren't part of my caseload—didn't even happen in my precinct—but I'd like to talk to you. I'll bet you've had your fill of police stations, so why don't you meet me somewhere?"

"I'd like to." He knew the relief must be audible in his voice. "Where and when?"

"Meet me on the corner of Wilshire and Fairfax at noon. We can walk and talk, maybe go somewhere quiet for lunch."

"Great," he said. "I'll be there."

By the time he had showered and dressed it was nearly eleven. He had no idea how long it would take him to drive to Wilshire and Fairfax. Sometimes the San Diego Freeway was so slow that it might be an hour or more. He went downstairs to his rental car and drove.

As he merged into the northbound side of the freeway, he tried to sort out what was happening. It was possible that Detective Berwell would tell him something that would indicate his predicament was about to improve, but he doubted it. He hoped that talking with her would at least provide him with an advocate on the Los Angeles police force. Even if she was only willing to help him because she wanted to find Mark Romano's killer, it didn't matter.

The traffic was moving smoothly, and it took him less than a half hour to reach the corner where he had agreed to meet Detective Berwell. Since he was so early, he drove up and down a few of the streets near the intersection of Wilshire and Fairfax, killing time and looking for the best place to park. Finally, he drove along Sixth Street behind the L.A. County Museum of Art, intending to find a space in the parking lot up the street and walk toward Fairfax. But on Sixth, just before he reached Curson, he found a space and took it. As he was about to get out of the car he looked up South Curson. It led into Park La Brea, a large apartment complex. Inside the entrance, he saw something that puzzled him. In the circle at the end of South Curson were two plain vans, one blue and the other white, stopped at the curb with their motors running. Each had a driver sitting behind the wheel and two other men loitering nearby. A few feet ahead of them was a car with another driver waiting behind the wheel and a person beside him.

Mallon decided not to get out of his car yet. He sat and waited. It seemed an odd gathering to him. Neither van had any markings to indicate that it was from a delivery company or a repair service. Maybe he was being overly jumpy, but who were these men, and what were they waiting for? Almost certainly there was some dull, benign explanation, but what was it?

After another minute, the passenger door of the car parked ahead of the vans opened, and a woman got out. Mallon recognized the blond hair at once. It was Angela Berwell. She stepped away from the car and he could see that she was wearing a navy blue pantsuit. As she moved toward the white van, she was talking. One of the men leaning on the van approached her, and the other went to the back door of the van and climbed inside. Mallon waited, and the man who had gone inside came out again and stood in front of Angela Berwell.

Mallon guessed that on her way to meet him, she and her partner must have detected some violation, and this man was going to show her some permit, or maybe just his license and registration. But he didn't show her anything. Instead, she opened her coat, held the lapel away from her body, and the man reached up to fiddle with something inside it. While he did, one of the two men near the blue van got into it.

The man with Detective Berwell said something to her, she talked for a few seconds, and then both of them turned to look at the man beside the blue van. He waved an arm and nodded. As Mallon watched, the man who had been sitting behind the wheel of the sedan got out and joined them for a moment, then returned to his car. The rest of the men got into the two vans, and all three vehicles drove around the circle and back down South Curson to Wilshire Boulevard. Then they turned right toward Fairfax. Angela Berwell stood and watched them make the turn, then began to walk alone down Sixth Street in the general direction of the corner where she had agreed to meet him. As she went, Mallon could see that she was talking to an invisible listener. She was wearing a wire.

Mallon sat motionless, trying to get over the shock and disappointment. She wasn't interested in helping him. She was meeting him to try to get him to say something incriminating on a surveillance tape. He supposed they must be considering prosecuting him for running over the two men in the parking garage. Maybe they had even begun to suspect him of killing Catherine, or killing Lydia. Once he became a suspect, there was probably no limit to the crimes they could link to him. Diane Fleming had been right: it had not been smart to keep bringing himself to their attention, offering his help and asking for theirs.

Time was passing. What should he do now? He could not go to a meeting with Angela Berwell knowing that she was planning to trap him into saying something she could use against him, but how could he refuse? He got out of the car, walked across the grass of the park toward the back of the county art museum. There were pay telephones to the left, just across the path from the entrance to the Page Museum, where the finds from the La Brea Tar Pits were displayed. He hurried to the nearest of the telephones, put in two quarters, took out the sheet of paper where he had written the number of the Hollywood station, and dialed.

A male voice answered, "Hollywood Division."

Mallon said, "I'd like to leave a message for Detective Angela Berwell in Homicide, please."

"I'll connect you with her voice mail."

After Mallon had heard her recorded voice say, "Please leave a message," he said, "This is Robert Mallon. I'm afraid I won't be able to meet you today after all. I hope it's not too late, and you check your messages in time. Anyway, I'm sorry."

He hung up the telephone, hurried back to his car, and drove. He hated not being able to get Angela Berwell's help, and the knowledge that she had turned on him made him afraid. He made his way to the San Diego Freeway and returned to his hotel. When he was in his room again, he dialed his own telephone number.

The telephone rang four times, there was a click, and his answering machine came on. "If you would like to leave a message—"

Mallon pressed the keys for his three-digit code. If the police in Santa Barbara suspected him too, they would hear him calling in to check his messages, but certainly they would have played them already. The machine said, "One. New. Message."

"Robert?" The voice was high, tense, and worried. "It's Diane. I've been trying to get in touch with you for days. Where are you? If you're there, pick up." There was a pause. "I guess you're not. Call me as soon as you get in."

Mallon hung up the telephone. He looked at his watch. It was after twelve, but he dialed Diane's office.

There were two rings, an unfamiliar clicking, then another ring. Sylvia said, "Law office. May I help you?"

Mallon said, "Hello, Sylvia. This is Robert Mallon. I'm returning Diane's call."

Sylvia's voice seemed uncomfortable. "She's not in the office right now, Mr. Mallon. But she asked that you leave a number so she can call you back."

Mallon said, "I'm in L.A.," then read the number to her off the label on the telephone.

"I'll have her call as soon as I can. She's due back from the courthouse any minute."

"Okay," said Mallon. He hung up and sat on the bed for a moment, staring at the wall. He had heard a sound while she had been writing down his number. She had heard it, and had immediately started talking again, with that business about the courthouse. She had been trying to distract him, in case he had heard it too. The sound had been the whistle of a train.

Diane's office was on De la Guerra. The nearest train tracks were south of Haley, near the ocean. The whistle he'd heard had been too loud, too close. She had not been in the office. She had not exactly said that she was in the building on De la Guerra Street. She had said, "Law office," which was the way all lawyers' phones were answered, for some reason. He decided it was foolish to make up excuses. She had lied to him. She had said Diane was on her way back from the courthouse. With call forwarding, either of them could be anywhere.

The telephone beside him rang. He took a breath. "Hello," he said, keeping his voice even and calm. His own demeanor seemed to be the only part of the universe that he was able to control, and all he could do with it was to hide his uneasiness, anger, and confusion.

"Robert?" It was Diane's voice, as he had expected. At one time he used to love to listen to it, the carefully modulated tones like music. He had never minded that the voice was an artifice. It had made him feel flattered, the way seeing a woman dress up to meet him did.

"Hello, Diane," he said. "You left a message on my machine to call." His own voice—the tone of unconcern—sounded insane to him. He had been attacked twice over the past two days by people he'd never seen before, and he was concealing it.

"Robert," she said, her voice tightening to a breathless whisper. "I'm so glad I finally reached you. I think we're both in terrible danger. I'm not calling from my office. I'm afraid to go near the place. The calls get forwarded to Sylvia, and she calls me so I can return them."

Mallon was disconcerted. Over the past two days, he had slowly come to the belief that Diane had been lying to him. He let his suspicion come into his voice. "You heard about the power of attorney?"

"What power of attorney? Robert, I'm not calling you about some stupid papers that need to be signed. I think somebody is planning to kill us."

"Listen to me," he said. "Did you know I revoked your signature power for my accounts?"

She drew in a breath, as though to raise her voice and insist that he pay attention to what she had been trying to tell him, but then the silence grew longer. The pause sounded as though she had sensed that he believed what he had said was extremely important, and now she was trying to fathom what had been happening to him. "Why would you do that?"

"Because the people at Wells Fargo called to ask me why I wanted to liquidate the whole account there—why I wasn't satisfied."

"I don't get it. Why are you doing it?"

"I'm not. They said they had received a transfer order with your signature on it."

"Mine? Oh, my God," she whispered. "Who are these people? How did they know about any account, let alone know that my name would do them any good?"

"That's what I want to know," said Mallon. It was not exactly the way he had wanted to put it. He had wanted to accuse her, to tell her she was lying. She seemed so guilty, but now he was beginning to wonder whether he was just being jumpy, suspicious of everybody. She seemed to read his thoughts.

"I don't know," she said. "Maybe I'm just so scared that I'm suspecting everybody, but I was the one who did most of the talking to the police in Santa Barbara and Los Angeles. Maybe I was too clear about our business relationship. It wouldn't be hard to find out the names of the banks you deal with. A credit check would turn up that much."

"Are you trying to tell me that you think one of the cops is involved?" he asked. He tried unsuccessfully to keep the skepticism out of his voice.

"I can't trust my own thoughts right now," she said. "I don't know who anybody is. There were people watching my office. There was a woman who took my picture when I parked my car at La Cumbre Plaza, and then again near the courthouse. That night there were two men following me when I tried to drive home. I did everything I knew to lose them, but they stayed right behind me. A couple of times they came so close I thought they were going to try to push me off the road. Instead of going home, I stopped at a neighbor's house and rang the bell. When he came to the door they drove off."

Mallon squeezed his eyes shut. The woman with the camera was certainly real. "What do you think we should do?"

"I think we've already done it," she answered. "We've both got to stay out of sight as long as we can, at least until we can find out what's really going on, and who we can trust to help us." She hesitated for a moment. "Have any of the police officers told you that you have to stay in the area?"

"No."

"Then don't."

"What do you mean?"

"I mean I don't know who is doing this. I thought it was something to do with Lydia Marks. But if somebody is trying to use my name to get at your money, then maybe Lydia was just killed to get her out of the way of that. Maybe it's . . . I don't know. Robert, you have to get out of there, away from southern California."

"What about you?"

"Oh, I'm going, believe me. I've been hiding in a hotel for days. The only thing that's been holding me here was that I couldn't disappear until I'd talked to you." She paused. "Robert, as your attorney, I can tell you that if nobody told you that you can't leave, then you can. And as your friend, I would tell you not to pay attention if they had. It's time to leave. And don't take a plane. If somebody who's getting information from the police is involved, they might be able to get your destination. Get in your car and drive somewhere. Just tell me where you're going, so I can meet you. We'll go to authorities we know can't be involved, because they're out of state."

"All I've got is a rental car. Two men shot up my car last night, trying to kill me."

She took a breath, and he could hear a tremor in her throat as she let it out. "You can't use a rental car. It's even easier to trace than a plane ticket. We'll go together. I'll drive you. I bought a new car."

"New car?"

"After those men followed me, I asked myself whether it was worth the money to trade my old one in and buy a new one. Believe me, it feels as though it is. I went to a lot of trouble to get a car that nobody will recognize. I don't want to go where you are. I'm afraid if somebody followed you there, they'll see it. We'll meet somewhere. I'll drive past. If somebody is following me, you'll see them, and know enough to get out fast. If I come past again and you're gone, I'll know I have a problem."

"Where do we meet?"

"I don't know . . . yes, I do. Do you remember about a year ago, I told you about a place where I was thinking about investing in some real estate?"

"Well, yes, I do," said Mallon. "I think I can get there. When?"

"After dark. Say, ten o'clock. Is that all right?"

"Yes."

"Well," she said, "we haven't said aloud where it was, and we haven't said what my car looks like or where I'll be coming from. We haven't said where we'll be going after that. I guess it's the best we can do."

"I guess so," said Mallon. "Good luck to us." He heard her hang up, so he did too. He sat for a time, going over the conversation in his mind. She had said something that would explain each of the suspicious facts: she had disappeared abruptly because she too had seen the woman with the camera, and then gotten stalked. She had claimed she had not known about the attempt to take the money from the private banking account at Wells Fargo. Of course, it could have been a lie, but suddenly he had realized that this was extremely unlikely. If she had wanted to get his money, or just deny him the use of it so he would be easier to kill, she should have been able to think of a better way than signing her own name to a withdrawal order. In a way, it seemed to him a sign of his emotional distress that he could have suspected her at all.

The most persuasive indication to him that she was innocent was her plan to drive him out of the area. She was the one who had been most cautious about setting up procedures that he could use to protect himself from ambush. He tried to think of a way to know for certain, but there was only one: he would have to show up to meet her.

CHAPTER 28

||||||||||||||||||||||||||||||||||||||||||||||||||||||||||||

Mallon sat in the bushes on the edge of somebody's front lawn. He felt a faint movement of air, and it gave him hope. It was a hot night, but something was going on far out at sea, and the breath of it was just reaching shore. He had chosen this spot because the interior of the house behind him was dark, and it had the look of a place that was locked up except on weekends. The alarm company signs that said ARMED PATROL and ARMED RESPONSE seemed to be placed more aggressively than usual, and the sturdy doors and shuttered windows were permanently lit by small outdoor floods.

He stared through the shrubbery at the house three lots to the north. He remembered the day only about a year ago when he had allowed Diane to drive him here to look at it. He had been reluctant at first: the reason for the trip had been that she wanted Mallon, a former contractor, to appraise the building. He had protested that he had never built anything within two hundred miles of Malibu. He had no knowledge of the current codes and regulations in Los Angeles County, he had not worked in almost ten years, and he had not kept up with any of the technological changes that were common in high-end houses, and so could not tell her whether the fixtures he found wired into the place were godsends or crap. But she had sighed. "Robert. You made millions building houses. I know you've kept your license current because I just called the state and they told me."

"For nostalgia."

"So take a brief stroll down memory lane with me to look at my wiring and plumbing." She had smiled. "I'll buy you a spectacular dinner in L.A. for your trouble."

"Why do you want me to do it? You'll have to hire an L.A. contractor to check it just to satisfy the bank anyway."

"I know. Come on, Robert. If you get a dog, I'll housebreak it for you."

"I don't want a dog."

"I'll bring you your next financial statement wearing high heels and a pearl necklace."

"Really?"

"Well, yes. Other things too, of course. But I really want you to do this for me." She had frowned. "I need a good investment that includes a tax write-off. This would be a beauty, but only if there aren't any nasty surprises. You've invested in coastal property lots of times since you retired. Won't you please do me this favor? You're the only one I know who's qualified and can't possibly be interested in making money from it. I need somebody I can trust."

That had done it. He had come down here with her, and spent three hours on that house. He had climbed onto the roof, checked the crawl space just below it. He had checked the plumbing, and randomly tested a few circuits for her. Finally, he had gone under the house. What he had found was a foundation that had begun shifting because it had not been anchored properly to the rock beneath the sand. A sewer pipe was already stressed, and might break within the next year. She could have paid the million and a half the realtors were asking and come here one day to see that the huge windows on the beach side had popped, and that she couldn't open the front door anymore.

They had driven home to Santa Barbara speaking in quiet, thoughtful tones. When he had gotten out of the car, she had thanked him warmly, but sadly. "Your friendship was all that saved me. I'll never forget it." Then she had brightened. "I'll never forget the realtor who tried to sell me that place, either. Can you imagine pulling that on a lawyer?"

He had grinned. "Actually, I can." He had added, "Not you, of course."

As Mallon remembered that night, he felt reassured. It was the ordinariness of it, the mundane, comfortable history of his relationship with Diane that made him feel his confidence growing. He had known her for eight years. Could she have been planning to do him harm all this time, and never done it? That made no sense. Diane would show up, and she would do exactly as she had promised. They could trust each other.

He heard the sound of an unseen car off to his left. He had been here for an hour, and this was only the second one to come along this narrow lane. In a moment he would see the shine of the headlights while the car was still far off, throwing faint light on the pavement where it curved. Next the light would brighten, throwing shadows and making the trees in front of the house across the street stand out from the undifferentiated grayness. Then the car would come around the bend, and for a second, illuminate this part of the street before it moved past. He lay flat in the brush and waited. If it was Diane, he would have to let her go by the first time without signaling her—just spot her in her unfamiliar new car, watch to be sure she was not followed, and await her second appearance.

Mallon kept his eyes to the left on the house at the bend. The car noise grew louder, closer. In the still air he could hear the tires tossing up bits of gravel, but the house across the street did not light up. Diane's car must be moving up the street without its headlights. He detected a change in the engine's pitch. It was stopped, idling. Why would she do that? Was she being followed? Could she be stopping to deceive some pursuer into making a premature move to reveal himself? He considered the possibility that the driver could be somebody other than Diane, and decided it was best to stay where he was and wait.

Mallon kept his body down behind the front hedge, but watched the road. He was staring at the bend so hard, expecting a change, that he was not startled when a man appeared there, walking along the shoulder on Mallon's side. The man stepped into a pool of dim light from a flood at the peak of a garage and Mallon studied him. He was tall and lean, wearing a sport coat and wool trousers in a drab color, with a pair of shoes that had no shine and had thick rubber soles. The man passed out of the glow, and kept coming.

Mallon felt a chill on the back of his neck, the sensation that hairs were beginning to stand up. The man must have walked past Diane stopped in the darkened car in the middle of the street. Neither of them had spoken, or Mallon certainly would have heard it. What if Diane had not come, and the car had belonged to this man?

Diane might have come by here already, not seen Mallon, and made a mess of looking for him. This man could be someone who had followed her. Mallon heard the car engine stop. That meant the driver was still in it: there were at least two people within a couple of hundred feet of Mallon. It also meant that Diane was not here: she would not have turned off her engine.

Mallon kept watching. This guy probably was a solitary resident out for a walk on a summer night. As he had the idea, it felt false to him. This man seemed wrong, somehow. Mallon tried to analyze the impression, to neutralize it, to argue himself out of it, but it was not working. The man was walking along with a kind of stiffness, his head held high but his arms and legs not quite moving naturally. It was as though he were just pretending to be loose and relaxed. And his clothes gave Mallon a strange feeling. The sport coat and the pants seemed too formal for the beach, and the night was uncomfortably warm. Mallon was wearing a sport coat because it was the darkest piece of clothing he had brought with him. He was using it to conceal himself. Why was this other man wearing one?

The man kept walking along the shoulder of the road, striding purposefully toward the house where Mallon was supposed to meet Diane. Mallon was a longtime daily walker who lived in a city full of walkers, and he was expert in the ways people looked when they walked on trails or the shoulders of roads. This one was strangely different. His body showed tension. He seemed to be straining to get to the house quickly.

The man did not change his pace, but he suddenly turned his head to look at the nearby houses, and then to glance over his shoulder. His head faced forward again, and his right hand reached inside his sport coat. The hand did not emerge. It simply stayed there as he walked. The man passed another driveway while Mallon waited for his hand to reappear. The next house had two pillars at the edge of the driveway topped by small electric lanterns. As the man passed the house where Mallon was hiding, Mallon was only thirty feet away, and he could see the man's face. Everything became clear and sharp, so he could study the man's expression. The head was up and slightly forward, the brow was set in concentration, but the eyes were wide, eager, excited.

As soon as the man's right arm shifted, Mallon was sure. When the man's right arm came up, Mallon could see the pistol he had known was there. The man walked on toward the deserted house where Mallon was supposed to meet Diane. Mallon watched from his hiding place across the street and three lots away, while the man walked around the house. As soon as the man had stepped out of sight, Mallon used the opportunity to retreat to the deep shadows at the side of the house where he had been hiding. He pried up a heavy piece of flagstone from the walkway where he stood, and watched as the man reappeared on the other side of the house down the street, then widened his search, the gun still in his hand as he prowled around the shrubbery in the garden. At last the man had satisfied himself that Mallon was not hiding there. He walked along the street a few feet, then crossed back to Mallon's side and started to return the way he had come.

Mallon held his breath, waiting. His hands clutched the heavy flagstone he had found. As the man drew nearer, Mallon suspected that something had gone wrong. The man was still walking, but slightly slower. His head was still held straight, but eyes had shifted to the left, searching. Mallon raised the heavy stone over his head with both hands. Suddenly the man spun, the gun in his hand. He jumped over the hedge where Mallon had been hiding and aimed the gun at the spot on the ground where Mallon had been.

Mallon hurled the big stone. As soon as it left his hands, he dashed after it. The man's head spun, but his eyes seemed to see only Mallon's body, not the flying stone. He raised the pistol just as the broad flagstone hit his torso just below his chest. The pistol went off, spitting a flash of sparks. There was a heavy huff of air leaving his lungs, he buckled and staggered backward into the hedge, and then Mallon was on him. Mallon's momentum propelled them both through the hedge into the street, with Mallon on top. He wrenched the pistol from the man's grip and turned it toward the man, just as the man's other arm jabbed hard at Mallon's throat.

Mallon fired twice quickly, the two rounds pounding into the man's chest like punches. His jab lost its power, and both of his arms went limp and fell lifeless to the pavement, spread wide from his body.

Part of Mallon's mind was suddenly, oddly, detached from his body's terror and agitation. He knew exactly what was about to happen, and knew what he must do to avoid it. He stood up. Then, without hesitation, he spun and ran across the road to the other side and hurdled a privet hedge, looking for the best place to take cover. He heard the sound of the car coming to life again. The headlights brightened the house to his left. In a moment they would be sweeping around the corner and onto him. He threw himself down behind the hedge and pressed his face into the grass.

The car came up and stopped with a short skid beside the body of the man Mallon had shot. The man in the driver's seat opened his door, and the dome light went on. He appeared to be in his late thirties, tall and lean like the first man. He popped out and shut the door to put out the light, produced a pistol, and bent his legs to lean on the hood of the car and take two-handed aim at the house above the fallen man. He made no attempt to kneel down and determine whether the man could be saved. He just gave a harsh, loud whisper: "Markham! You alive?" There was no response, no movement.

The man stared over his car at the houses on that side of the street, at the shrubbery and trees along that side, even up at the roofs, but never behind him. Mallon had a persistent ringing in his ears, and the sight of the man seemed distant and absurd. The man was devoting all of his attention to the dark hiding places on the side of the street where he had found his fallen companion. He had simply assumed that Mallon would have shot him and run up that lawn for the cover that was closest. The man would not even consider the chance that Mallon had run across the street, and was behind him. Mallon began to feel hope.

Mallon lay on the ground behind the hedge, carefully aiming the dead man's pistol through the space between two woody stems just above the grass. After thirty or forty very long seconds, the man stuck his gun into his coat, bent low, and began to drag his companion's body toward the door behind the driver's seat. He stayed low, apparently confident that Mallon was hiding on the far side of the car. When he had pulled the body to a spot just behind the door, he went lower, and swung the door open. The dome lamp threw a sudden bath of light onto the deserted street, and the man's face suddenly changed. Still bent low, he slammed the door and snatched the gun out of his jacket, and Mallon knew he'd been seen.

The man raised the pistol, and he and Mallon both fired. Mallon was aware of two shots tearing through the foliage above and around him, but after a moment, the man fell forward onto his face.

The two men now lay on the pavement. Mallon had seen the places where they had been hit, and the detached, calm part of his mind assured him that they were dead, but he stepped over the hedge and across the street to look down at them and confirm it. He put the pistol into his jacket pocket. He picked up the second man's pistol and put it into his other jacket pocket. Their weight stretched the material and pulled his jacket down on his shoulders.

He reached for the handle of the car door, but as he did, he realized he could hear another engine. He could see lights beginning to glow on the trees in front of the house at the bend again. This car was coming fast. He would not have time to run across the street to his hedge. He considered getting into the dead men's car, then considered hiding behind it. He saw that the pattern of blood on the pavement near the men's bodies was beginning to light up already. It was time to lie down.

CHAPTER 29

||||||||||||||||||||||||||||||||||||||||||||||||||

Mallon had to lie on his belly to hide the gun in his hand and to be able to get up quickly, but he felt keenly the hardness of the asphalt. The two men on either side of him lay in perfect, open-eyed repose, like two whitefish in a delicatessen's display case. He tried to imitate their stillness as the approaching car's headlights brightened, swept across the house at the bend, and then settled on them.

The glare intensified rapidly, until he could see red through his eyelids, and then the car stopped. He heard a door open and slam, waited for another that never came, but heard the sharp, small clop of a woman's shoes coming around the car. They stopped.

"Oh, Jesus." It was just above a whisper, but it was Diane's voice. "Oh, Jesus."

Mallon pushed off the pavement and got to his feet, and she gave a little cry. She was only a silhouette in front of the headlights, but he could make out that she was wearing tight, dark pants of some kind and a blouse. As he stepped toward her, she at first recoiled, then seemed to reel a little, as though she felt faint. "It's me," he said. "I'm not dead. Get in and drive us out of here."

She seemed to see that this was undeniably what she needed to do.

She trotted the three steps back to the car, got in, and immediately threw it into gear to drive off. Mallon was only halfway in when the car shot forward, but he pulled his leg inside and let the acceleration shut the door. She glanced at him, wide-eyed, for a second, then stared ahead at the dark road.

"What happened?" she asked, her voice going up the scale as she spoke. "Who are those men on the ground? What happened to them?"

Mallon stared at her, watching her face while the outdoor lights of houses passed across it, then left it in darkness, only the glow from the instrument panel giving her a yellowish pallor. "I killed them," he said.

"Killed them?" she repeated. "How?"

"I was going to say that it wasn't my fault, but of course it was. It took some effort. I heard their engine, so I knew they were coming. They guessed where I would be hiding, but I knew what their guess would be."

"What do you mean?"

"I could see that they were here to kill me, so I had to stop them."

Diane looked at him in disbelief, her eyes wide, then squinted ahead at the road for a moment. Her eyes shot back to his face again and again, as though each time she expected some change to have occurred, but each time was shocked to see that it had not. "You just decided they were all here to harm you? You just guessed that and shot them?"

He leaned close to her, and stared at the clock on the dashboard. "Ten-oh-five. I guess you were nearly on time. It was a good plan, but it didn't work out well at all," he said wearily. "No, I guess it did."

Diane was sitting stiffly, both hands on the wheel, but Mallon could see that her right eye was trying to keep him in sight. Mallon noticed that he was still holding a gun in his hand. He considered for a moment, then slipped it back into his jacket pocket.

He sat back in the seat, and he could see a change in her posture. She straightened so noticeably that it looked as though she were growing. "I'm not sure that this was a good idea," she said. "We'll have to make a convincing argument that we had a compelling reason to leave the scene."

"What for?"

"The trial," she said with a hint of impatience, as though it were self-evident. "When somebody dies of gunshot wounds, there will be a trial. I'm fairly sure we can get you off—either self-defense or, at worst, manslaughter—but you'll have to be very helpful and very forthcoming. We'll need to prove they were after you. Did you ever see either of them before?"

He answered all her questions. He marveled at the effect. As she talked, he could see her getting stronger and more confident that she had the right strategy. She was trying to make him weak and indecisive and, ultimately, passive, so that she would be in control. He felt a growing warmth in his chest and a tightness in his throat, but he did not let the feeling ignite into rage.

He said, "I'm really exhausted, Diane. In the past couple of days, people have tried to kill me on the beach, at a hotel, and now here. I think all we can do at the moment is get ourselves to a place where we'll be safe for a while."

"That's exactly what I'm doing."

"Good. Turn right up here at Malibu Canyon, and we can go through the hills to the freeway, and then east, out of state, as we had planned."

"That's not a good idea anymore, Robert," she said. "I can't let you do it."

"Why not?"

"Because if you kill some people—in self-defense or not—then fleeing the state has a bad effect on police, district attorneys, judges, juries. In a capital case, it could be a fatal mistake."

He studied her face for a moment. Her confidence was as high as he had ever seen it. "Then what *is* a good idea?"

"I think we should find a place close by, then try to get in touch with people who can help us. We should get some real protection for you while I try to make a deal with the police."

"All right," he said. "Drive up the coast as far as Ventura. I know a good place."

It was a house beside the ocean just north of Ventura, and he knew it because he had once owned it. He had bought it shortly after he had come to Santa Barbara, with the notion that he would remodel it and resell it. But before he had gotten around to drawing any plans, he had received an unsolicited offer and sold it for a profit to a couple from Los Angeles. He had driven by not long ago and seen that the house had been sold again. Then, a couple of weeks ago, he had read in the *Santa Barbara News-Press* that a Ventura investment partnership was planning to tear it and several others down to build enormous beach palaces for people who had the ante and wanted to be part of the final California land rush.

He did not need to direct her there, only to wait awhile and say, "It's up ahead on the left," then say, "Here's the one. Pull into the driveway."

The house was dark and the garage had a padlock on it, but the windows had not been boarded and there was no contractor's chain-link fence to interfere. He had known from experience that announcing a plan was one thing, but getting the building permits and the approvals from the Coastal Commission for a big project on the oceanfront was another. It often took years.

Diane said irritably, "What is this place?"

Mallon did not answer. He was out of the car and walking around to the side of the house to look in the kitchen window. The sound of the waves coming in on the beach was steady and regular, just loud enough to make her unsure whether he had answered her or not. He could see the small green numbers on the oven control panel, which meant the power was on. He looked through the doorway at the front entry, then at the back of the house, but there were no lights on the alarm keypads.

He remembered that the back door had been small and solid with heavy dead bolts, and the windows had been big, with double panes for strength. As he stepped around the back, he could see that some remodeling had been done since he had last seen the house. The back entrance was now through a pair of French doors with a simple bolt that turned by hand. He approved of the concrete patio that had been added and, even more, the low reinforced-concrete wall with an ir-regular row of boulders in front of it to break up any big waves that might come all the way up here in an extremely high tide.

He looked around the patio for a few seconds, but found that the owners had not left anything he could use, so he kept walking to the place where he remembered the gas meter was. There he found a wrench that was designed for turning off the gas in an emergency. He took it to the French door and swung it once into the small pane of glass nearest to the bolt. He reached in and opened the door, stepped inside, then crossed the living room to the front door, undid the bolt, opened it, and beckoned to Diane.

She was still sitting in the driver's seat looking uncomfortable. She shook her head and stayed there. Mallon left the front door open and walked to her side of the car. "Come on in," he said. "We'll be safe and comfortable here until we can get things straightened out."

She glared at him. "What are you talking about? You just broke a window to get in. I heard you."

He shrugged. "The house belongs to a friend of mine. He won't mind. I sold it to him." She stared straight ahead, the same resentful expression on her face. "Diane, get out of the damned car." He pulled her door open and waited.

She was looking up at him now, and he could see she was still re-luctant, but she slowly and deliberately swung her legs out, leaned forward, and stood up. She had her arms wrapped around herself with her purse dangling from one hand and her keys in the other as she walked to the front door and into the house.

She turned on the switch by the door so the overhead light went on, stepped to the center of the living room, and looked around her. There were a few movers' cardboard boxes collapsed on one side of the expanse of wall-to-wall carpet, and a few partial rolls of packing tape beside them. "There's no furniture. Is your friend Japanese?"

"He's not living here, he's putting the house up for sale again. That's why I know he wouldn't care about the glass."

She set her purse on the floor, tossed her keys into it, and looked around. "If you owned the place once, you must remember where the bathrooms are. Which way?" She watched Mallon point, then walked to the door, pushed it open, switched on the light, and closed the door.

Mallon immediately knelt to reach into her purse. He found her cell phone, but his hand had brushed a second object that interested him. He reached inside again, grasped it, and brought it out.

The gun was surprisingly small. It barely filled his hand. He slipped the gun and the telephone into the two inner pockets of his jacket, stood, and looked around him, trying to think clearly. He heard the toilet flush. He switched off the overhead light, stepped silently into the dining area, opened the back door, went outside, and watched through the windows.

She came out and looked around her. "Robert?" She stepped toward the kitchen and then to the hallway and looked around some more, then quickly snatched up her purse and slipped into the bathroom again. After a few seconds, she emerged and set her purse exactly where it had been. She stepped back and looked at it, adjusted its tilt a bit, and sat down a few feet from it, her back against the wall.

Mallon returned and shut the door, then went to the pile of movers' boxes and tape. He used his pocketknife to cut a square of cardboard off one of the boxes and then taped it over the broken glass.

"Robert," said Diane. "Why are we here?"

He turned and looked at her in the dim light from the bathroom. "I'm not entirely certain," he answered. "We need to talk a bit before either of us does anything."

"All right." She folded her arms and waited. "So?"

He took a deep breath and released it slowly. He had been dreading this, but he reflected that it had already begun: he had taken her gun and her phone, and she knew it. "How did those two men know that you and I were going to meet at that house in Malibu?"

She looked shocked. "Are you sure?" she asked. "What makes you think they knew it?"

"They arrived after I did. They might not have known I was already there, but they certainly knew I would be. I think that's why one guy came ahead alone. They wanted to see whether I had arrived."

She eyed him skeptically. "How could they possibly have known?"

"How could they possibly have gone to a particular block on a narrow, dark street in Malibu to find me if they didn't?"

In the light from the bathroom doorway, he could see her eyes. She had been rigid and tense, but now she was beginning to be frightened. "You're scaring me. Do you think they tapped our phone call? That they heard what we were planning, and then came to wait for us?"

He shook his head slowly, never taking his eyes off hers. "We never said aloud where we were going to meet, remember? You said it was the place we once looked at together."

"Did they follow you?"

"No chance," he said. "I took a taxi to the edge of Malibu. I went down to the beach for a time. Then I went back up on the road and walked there that way after it was dark."

"Then maybe they followed me," she said. "Oh, Robert, I'm sorry. I never saw them."

"You got there after they did."

She said, "This time, yes. But I drove down there earlier. I didn't want to sit around in a hotel waiting and then run into traffic and be late, so I left early. I drove through once as soon as I got to Malibu, just to be sure I remembered which house it was. Then I went to a movie."

"Why didn't they follow you to the movie, and stick with you? It's a great place to meet someone."

Diane shook her head, her body rocking impatiently. "How do I know? I don't even know if they did follow me. They didn't find me, did they? They found you."

All the time while Diane was talking he watched her. He could actually see her in the act of thinking: grasping at alternative explanations, but rejecting this one as too transparently foolish, that one as incriminating. "No matter what they saw," Mallon pointed out, "they couldn't have known that the time for them to show up was ten."

She shrugged. "Then they did tap the phone call."

"No," said Mallon. "They didn't. You told them."

"No." Diane began to move on the carpet, pushing herself slowly to get farther away from him. "No, I didn't. I would never do that. I don't even know who they are, and I'm your friend. I work for you. We've known each other for eight or nine years. Why would I want to help somebody kill you?"

Some instinct or memory or warning came into Diane's mind, and she stopped moving away. She seemed to have difficulty preparing herself. "There's no reason at all. We can't let ourselves get paranoid and turn on each other," she said, and she began to move a bit closer.

Mallon could see what she was thinking, as though it were printed on her forehead. She knew he was armed. She did not want to be ten or twelve feet away from him, close enough for him to be sure of hitting her if he fired, too far away for her to do anything to stop him. She was smiling with a sincere, concerned look in her eyes as she moved closer. Without any shade of change in her expression, and without a change in the direction of her movement, she sprang.

Mallon's reaction was a simple reflex, a lunge to the left to avoid her. She managed to land a single, hard blow that missed his throat but stung his chest near the shoulder. Her other hand was already at his jacket pocket, groping for the gun. Mallon swatted her arm down and held her wrist. He used it to spin her around, then pushed to get her to the floor face downward. He straddled her as she struggled, then clamped his left hand around the back of her neck to hold her there.

He leaned to the right to grasp the roll of packing tape he had left on the floor after he'd covered the broken window, and she used that moment to twist and push down with her legs to try to roll him off. He managed to snatch the tape, then flop his weight onto her back to keep her down.

In spite of his size and weight, she never stopped struggling to overcome him, and from the first few seconds he had been aware that she was better at this than she should be. She used every chance to keep him from gaining control. Every time he tried to shift his position, she would feel the direction of his motion and push off to try to accelerate it and free herself. They fought in silence in the near darkness, their breaths now coming in heavy, hard gasps.

At last, she had worn herself out trying to lift him. He was able to clamp both her wrists behind her, and wrapped five turns of the tape around them to hold them.

"What?" she gasped. "Why . . . what do you . . . want?"

He leaned close, so his lips were right behind her ear. "I promise I won't hurt you. I want you to tell me the truth."

||||||||||||||||||||||||||||||||||||||||||||||||||||||||||||||||||||||

CHAPTER 30

Mallon had used parts of three rolls of packing tape to bind Diane's wrists and ankles, then to connect the ankles and wrists.

He knelt beside her on the empty living room floor, and she recoiled from him. He said, "Diane, I'm not going to harm you. But you've got to tell me why they're trying to kill me." He stared into her eyes, and he could tell she had been listening to him and studying him. Her eyes were a bit calmer.

She took two or three deep breaths. "You didn't have to do this to me. I wasn't trying to hurt you. I just panicked because you took away my phone. I thought it was so I couldn't call for help, that you were planning to hurt me."

"And your gun," he said. "I found that too."

Her brows tilted in hurt. "Don't you think that's the best evidence you have that I only wanted to help? I never did anything with it."

"Why did you come to meet me with a gun?"

"Because we're in danger. I own it because I'm a female attorney who lives alone. I bought it when I was just starting out in general practice in Los Angeles, and lived in a neighborhood that seemed scary to a girl from a small town. That was a long time ago, so I hardly ever thought about the gun until now. After those men followed me home from work this week, I threw a few things into a suitcase, put the gun into my bag, and took off. At the time, I was very glad I owned it." She sighed, and looked as though she might cry. "Now I'm sorry."

Mallon said, "Diane, if you'll tell me the truth, I'll let you go. Why are you involved with these people?"

"Involved?" Her eyes looked scared again. "I'm not involved. I was only trying to help you, and now they're after both of us."

"They're not after both of us. They're after me, and you're helping them. Why are they so interested in killing me? What is it you think Lydia and I found out? Who are these people?"

She looked at him as though he were speaking a language she did not understand. "I don't know any more than you do. Robert, you know me. I'm an honest person. I don't consort with any criminals. I've never even represented any. I went into a general civil firm right out of law school and, when I had some experience, moved to Santa Barbara to open an office with a specialty I liked. You're one of my best clients. I have no reason to harm you."

Mallon said quietly, "Stop it. I'm giving you a chance to tell me the truth. Don't you understand what that's worth?"

"I am telling you the truth." She stared at him for a few moments, motionless, and then the tears came. "I am. I am," she said softly, and turned her face to the floor.

There was no doubt that she was lying. He stood up. The beach house was like the others in the row: it faced the sea. It had no lower-level windows on the street side, but presented to the world a plain front and a plain, closed garage door. Mallon had little reason to be afraid to leave a light on, but he decided to be careful. He switched the light off and took a step.

"Good-bye, Diane." He walked toward the front door.

"Wait!"

He stopped.

"Please!" she begged. "You're going to leave me like this? The house is closed up, and so are all the others along here. There's nobody to find me. I'll die."

"Most likely," he said. "I guess if I die, you will too." He opened the door to step out.

"Wait!" she yelled. "I'll tell you."

He closed the door, turned on the light, walked back, and sat beside her again. "I'll listen to it. All I ask is that it be true."

"It will be," she said. "If you go without knowing more than you do, they'll kill you."

"Why?" he said. "Why? I've asked you that over and over."

Her face assumed a hard, empty look. "No reason." She gazed into his eyes, and her expression became a grim amusement. "Does that surprise you?" She didn't give him time to answer. "It's true. The people involved in this—all the ones you've seen, anyway—were doing it because it gives them a thrill." She watched him for a reaction. "It's the sport of kings, the real one, you know. If you happen to be the sort of wealthy person who has gone to all the famous cities and to all the remote resorts that aren't famous because just knowing the name of them is enough to make you cool, and you've worked your way through all of the other big-ticket extreme sports, then this is *the* option."

"The big-ticket extreme sports?"

"You know. Having a helicopter drop you on some unreachable mountain nobody has skied before, buying a big sailboat to take across an ocean, setting speed records with racing cars. I guess people like that used to go shoot animals in Africa, but that's lost its aura. Those two that came for you tonight—Markham and Coleman—that's what they were in it for: fun."

"How in the world did you ever get involved with people like that?"

"Through my practice. I'm a servant of rich people: all kinds of rich people. If you manage money, you can't have too many requirements other than that the money belong to them. This business is too competitive for that."

"You got into this mess for thrills?"

She shook her head and closed her eyes. Tears seeped from the corners. Then she opened them again. "Not everybody gets a thrill. I got into it because I was afraid."

"Afraid of what?"

"Just before I came to Santa Barbara, when I was still in civil litigation in L.A., I defended a client named Carl Hayward. He wasn't a very nice man, and I didn't much like him, but that isn't supposed to enter into legal representation. He was being sued. He had bought a restaurant about three years before. As I understood it, what happened was this: he hired an old male chef and one male kitchen helper, but everybody else who worked for him was a young girl. It was a crummy neighborhood, but it was a well-known old restaurant that was a favorite spot for people to go after plays or concerts: lobsters, big steaks, lots of liquor. It stayed open twenty-four hours a day, so he needed three shifts, but most of the business was between ten at night and six in the morning. Because it was that kind of place, he made the customers pay premium prices. Every night at about three A.M. he would come in and count the money. That was the time when things would begin to slow down. He put the cash in a bag, made out a deposit slip, and sent out one of the young girls who was getting off her shift to take it to the bank to drop in the night-deposit slot on the way home. One night, there was somebody waiting. The girl was a sixteen-year-old, who wasn't supposed to be working at that hour or in a place that served liquor. She got killed."

"This was a civil suit?"

She nodded. "The girl was a runaway from New Mexico. Her parents were drug cases who hadn't even bothered to look for her when she left. But she had a brother. His name was Billy. He was five years older. He had been in jail when she left home, but she'd kept writing to him. He was still in jail when she got killed. When he got out, he got a good lawyer on a pro bono basis. Carl Hayward got me. Everybody expected us to settle. Hayward had clearly not checked anybody, least of all Tara, for age, or asked to see identification. She looked, if anything, younger than sixteen, and Hayward made no secret of the fact that he always had one of the girls carry the money because he didn't want to get robbed. Three or four of them would get off at once, and it might be a different one that had the money each time. But he knew that he was putting them in danger, because at least once before, men had stopped the wrong girl and ended up with nothing but a purse full of tips. I let them go to court, and I won."

"How?"

"A combination of things. I had a feeling about the jury. They weren't all old ladies with pearls, but I could tell they were conservative. The brother's record might be enough for some of them. I used it. I portrayed him as a creep who was happy to use his own young sister's death to ruin an honest businessman and get rich. I said he was a vulture. I used the letters she sent him in prison, and said that if it was a dangerous situation, he knew it. I said he was like a pimp, who had encouraged her to work a dangerous, illegal job so she would send him money, and then tried to cash in, to sell her even after she had died."

"Go on," he said.

She frowned. "I was young, and I wanted so badly to win. I thought it was my job to use everything I could find or invent to get my client off. The opposing lawyer was Reynolds Phelan. You probably don't know who that is, but every lawyer in the state does. He was president of the bar association when I was in law school. When the case was over, he waited for me outside the building. I actually thought he was going to congratulate me. He said that what I had done was disgusting. I'll remember that forever." She lapsed into silence.

"I'm waiting," he prompted.

She sighed. "That was my first indication that things were going wrong. I started to get other indications right after the trial. Billy was not going to forget either. He had been in for manslaughter. Billy was very tough. In jail he got meaner and smarter. He started threatening me right after the trial. He had been in jail with men who were experts at intimidating people. They had taught him to do it without getting caught. There were calls late at night, always from pay phones. I would leave home for the office in the morning, and there would be a scary man across the street, staring at me with a smirk. The same when I left work for home. But it was never Billy. Not once. And each one was replaced by another after a couple of times. I told the cops. But the cops can't charge somebody under the stalking law if he's standing across the street once or twice. I told friends, I told colleagues, but nobody could help. Finally I was at a party."

"A party?"

"Yes. It had gone on and on, and I started to hate being alone. I started working more, going out a lot more, just being with people so I wasn't alone. A woman I met at a party told me that a mutual friend had told her about my problem and she had a suggestion."

"What was it?"

"Her boyfriend had talked her into going to this self-defense camp, kind of for laughs, really. They had gone together, and she was hooked. It had changed her life. She had been afraid all the time, and now she wasn't. I had noticed her earlier in the evening and wondered about her, and I think it was because of that. She always had a serene look on her face, but she carried herself with a kind of swagger. She walked straight up to people she had never met and was comfortable talking with them—very easy, very friendly, just as she was with me. I knew she was telling the truth. I let her write down the name and phone number on a slip of paper for me. Overnight I thought about it, and called the next day."

"Was the camp what she said it was?"

"It was. I learned to use a gun. I don't mean just how to aim it and hit something consistently. I mean how to care for it, how to carry it concealed, how and when to take it out and fire it, how to move during a firefight. None of that stuff is obvious, and some of it is even counterintuitive intentionally, so your opponent can't anticipate it. I went to classes in hand-to-hand combat. I know it doesn't look as though I learned much—"

"Yes, it does," he interjected.

"Well, I did. I'm pretty rusty now, and I couldn't do what I was supposed to, which was to surprise the opponent. It also works best if you really want to hurt the other person, or at least don't care if you do. I care about you."

"Go on." There was a warning in his voice.

"I went for a month-long course. It was a rule that you had to go for a whole month the first time, and take an all-around basic self-defense course. After that, you could go for two-week intensive courses, even one-week brush-up sessions. The month was terribly expensive for me, but it seemed worth it. I was out of sight for all that time, safe from Billy. I knew nothing to begin with, so every hour I was there made a terrific difference. When the month was over, I had made a lot of progress. I found I didn't want to leave. I asked if I could take a two-week advanced course. That was even more extreme. It was urban combat: shotguns, things you could do with a car, even some booby traps. When that was nearly done, I went to one of the instructors and tried to sign up for another two weeks. She talked to me for a while, said she could tell that I was scared to go home, where I would be alone again. It wasn't that, exactly."

"What was it?"

"It wasn't that I had become fearful of being alone. I had convinced myself that what I was going home to was a fight to the death against Billy—it was that specific—and I wasn't ready. Do you see? I was easily good enough to not be afraid of living a normal life. I wasn't good enough yet to go head-to-head against a man who wanted me dead, a convict who had killed somebody before. I told the instructor. A day later, she brought me in to speak with Michael Parish."

"The one I met? The owner of the camp?"

"He's more than that. Owning something is just money. It's his, in a different way. The place is him. It's a reflection of his ideas. All the people who work there look up to him and some of them seem to imitate him—his expressions, his mannerisms. He asked me to talk about what had been bothering me, to tell him everything. So I told him. I started to talk in brief, general terms, but the other instructor, whose name was Mary, kept prompting me. And I spilled all of it. He listened patiently and asked me all the right questions—the ones that convinced me that he cared about me, and was really hearing what I said—and I told him more. Finally, he said, 'You seem convinced that at some point, you're going to have to kill him.' I said no, of course not. Then I said, 'I hadn't actually been thinking about it that way. I had only been learning to defend myself just in case. Shouldn't everyone?' All the time, he was watching me, not judging me or smiling or looking skeptical or anything, just waiting. And after a while, I said, 'Well, yes. I suppose I really do think that at some point he is going to either try to get me himself or have one of his prison friends do it. What I've been doing here for the past six weeks is get myself ready to survive it. Now that I know more about what that means, I guess I would have to say yes, I have been preparing myself to kill him.' "

"And what did he say?"

"We had been in the main lodge, sitting on those hard, straight-backed wooden chairs like they have in some bars. That's how he talks to you: sitting almost knee to knee in that empty room with nothing to look at but his eyes. What he did was kind of lean forward with his hands on his thighs and stand up. It brought his face close to mine, and in that second, he said, 'Then let's get it done.' It was so quick, so quiet that I said, 'What? I didn't quite catch that.' Then he called in Debbie, my martial arts instructor, and he said, "Tell Debbie everything about this man Billy—everything you know. If you need to go to your office to consult some file about him or something, bring her with you. Then come back. After we've got the information, it will take another week to prepare. Then we'll take you back so you can kill him.' "

"Did you do it? Did it happen?"

She ignored the question, but he could tell that she was only delaying the answer. "The week was partly so they could follow him, watch him, figure out how and where to kill him. But it also gave them time to give me a few special lessons. They call going out to kill somebody a hunt. There's a tracker to find and stalk the target, a scout to choose and secure the place, and a professional hunter to be with you and kill the target if you lose your nerve or make a mistake. I had to learn to work with them. And they wanted me to get used to what it looks like when anything the size of a man dies. They took me deer hunting out in the fields above the camp. The idea was to get me to shoot something that was alive, and see all the blood and suffering, and then I wouldn't get all nervous later. He tries to get you to like the killing, so you'll be good at it—have a dead aim. That's what he calls it. We didn't find a deer. After a couple of days of searching, we still didn't find one. It had been a wet spring, and I guess there was plenty of food for them farther into the backcountry, so that's where they were. I was relieved."

"Did you kill Billy?"

Her voice went soft, almost a whisper. "Yes. I did." She took a breath, and said, "Parish and Mary drove me to L.A. I was surprised to see where they had found him. It was a bowling alley. He worked there late at night, waxing the lanes after closing time. The place had a lighted sign that said MOONLIGHT BOWLING, MIDNIGHT TO 2 A.M. After that, it closed, and Billy went to work. It was really pretty easy. Debbie had been at Moonlight Bowling with some other people who worked for Parish. She went into the ladies' room at one-thirty or so, and hid in a stall. Everybody else left, but she stayed until the place was all locked up, then came out, went to the door, and propped it open a crack. It was a set of glass doors, so we saw Billy when we arrived. He was waxing an alley with a polishing machine. He was looking up toward the pins and walking backward, so he wouldn't leave footprints. He didn't even see or hear us come in. The scout was the first in the door, and that was Mary. She held it open for me. The last was the pro hunter, and this time that was Parish. The two of them waited in that sunken area around the scoring table, and I stood up on the foul line. I waited until he was only about eight feet away. I could have shot him in the back of the head, but Parish and Mary and Debbie were there, so I did it the way they had taught me. First and second shots go into the torso where the heart and lungs are, and the third, after he's down and incapacitated, can go to the head. You never leave until he's positively dead. When he was, we walked back out of the bowling alley and got into the car to drive home. I didn't feel bad about it until a couple of months later, after I had gotten over the fear and thought about it objectively. I had done something horrible to him, and because I had, I felt I had to kill him."

"But that's why you're here," said Mallon. "To do the same thing to me."

"I know," she moaned. "It's the same thing again. Only I couldn't help it, don't you see? Parish would kill me if I didn't. This is my fault. You're my fault. I didn't imagine that the woman who committed suicide had anything to do with the self-defense school. How could I? They didn't have her real name then. So I encouraged you to get through your obsession, even wrote up a contract so you could hire Lydia Marks to help you. I put everyone else in danger—Parish, Mary, Debbie, the other instructors, the special customers Parish teaches to kill people—so how could I refuse to help them solve the problem? They would kill me. How could they let me refuse and live?"

"Good question," said Mallon. "I guess they couldn't." He stood. "I'm sorry for you, and sorry for me. I've got to go now."

"You're not going to leave me?" she asked. "I told you the truth. You've got to let me go. You promised."

"I promised," Mallon said. "But I can't let you go until this is over."

She was appalled, desperate. "But without me, you won't get through this. You don't know enough. You're not good enough. They'll kill you. Now that they've tried, there's no way they can ever stop hunting you. They'll keep trying until it's done. I could tell you things, recognize people you would never suspect were after you. I can get you away from it. That's the only way. If you leave me and go out there alone, I'll just die here, waiting for you to get back."

"Maybe." He stepped out the door and locked it behind him. He could hear her shouting, but just barely. Out here, the sound of the ocean was much louder, and even tonight's gentle breeze made it hard to hear anything.

———————————————||||||||||||||||||||||||||||||||||||||||||||||||||||||||||||———————————————

CHAPTER 31

Mallon drove beside the ocean, heading back toward Santa Barbara. There was no question that the people Diane called the hunters and trackers and scouts would be trying to figure out where he and Diane had gotten to. Probably they had expected to hear from her by now. If they found the bodies he had left on that quiet road in Malibu, they would probably assume she was dead.

He was aware that he was going to have to do something quickly, or he was going to die. Diane had been right: there appeared to be a plentiful supply of people from that self-defense camp who had either been eager to join the hunt for him or been induced to join it to protect secrets. If their secrets were like Diane's, they had little choice but to try to prevent him from drawing attention to the camp. He thought about the police.

Detective Berwell had been trying to trap him into saying something incriminating. The Santa Barbara police seemed to Mallon to have been more receptive to his theories, or anyway more sympathetic, than the Los Angeles police. At least Detective Fowler had seemed to be. Maybe with what Mallon knew now, Fowler would be able to do something. Mallon writhed in the seat to reach his wallet, found Fowler's business card, picked up Diane's telephone, and turned it on. Instantly the silence was shattered by the annoying musical ring. The little screen showed him which button to press to answer, but he did not press it. Instead, he turned off the phone for a few seconds, then turned it on again and quickly dialed Fowler's number.

A male voice answered. "Police department."

"Hello," said Mallon. "My name is Robert Mallon. I need to reach Lieutenant Fowler right away. It's an emergency."

The cop's voice was beginning to change from sleepy to irritated when he spoke. "I'm sorry, but Lieutenant Fowler works during the day. It's now after one A.M. He'll be here in about six hours, and I'm sure he'll call you back. But if this really is an emergency, then somebody else can certainly help. Can you explain what the problem is?"

"You don't know my name—Robert Mallon?" asked Mallon, incredulous. "I'm the man that somebody tried to kill on Cabrillo Beach."

"Of course I know who you are," said the cop. "It would be hard not to. If you're in trouble again, tell me about it. Where are you?"

"I'm in a car, using a cell phone."

"Are you in danger?"

"Yes, I am. They've tried twice more in Los Angeles."

"Is someone after you now?"

"They're searching for me," he said. "They haven't given up. But I can't describe them yet, because I won't know the next set until I see them come for me."

"Mr. Mallon. Tell me exactly where you are."

Mallon had a panicky feeling. He instinctively evaded the demand. "I'm on a cell phone. I can't hear you very well."

"Are you still armed? Do you have a gun?"

Mallon hesitated. He had never said he was armed. He said loudly, "I guess my battery's gone. If you can still hear me, I'll call you again from a regular phone later, when Lieutenant Fowler is in." He pressed the power button to end the call. If the cop knew about the gun, he knew about Malibu. It had not sounded as though the cop had wanted to help. It sounded as though he wanted to get Mallon into custody.

Mallon was in trouble. He was driving the stolen car of a woman he had kidnapped. He was carrying three loaded guns—also stolen—and undoubtedly had powder residue on his hands from killing the men who had owned two of them. If he went to a police station anywhere, he was going into a cell. He would be in the newspapers, and the hunters would know exactly where he was. Even if the police released him on bail, the killers would be waiting for him. He had killed people. He had done it to stay alive, but at the moment he could hardly look less innocent. Tonight, he realized, the police were as dangerous to him as the hunters.

The term made him think about the people who were trying to kill him. The ones he had seen were spoiled rich people who were paying for the privilege of killing him for a thrill. But the others—Parish and his friends—were professionals who had made killing into a business. As he thought about them, he told himself it was because he was trying to decide what he would do about them, but he was not really considering anymore. He knew. He had to stop them from killing anyone else, and tonight was probably his last chance. He had to do it tonight.

He was calm, able to look at his own predicament from a distance. The facts that had been making him feel hopeless had not changed, but once he had gotten beyond hope, he could see other aspects of them. He was driving a stolen car, but it was Diane's. It was a car the enemy probably knew. If they saw it coming, they would sense no threat.

Mallon drove on, watching the sights along the freeway to detect signs that the exit for Route 33 was coming. What he had wasn't a plan. It was a reflex, a fighter's simple physical movement to block an attacker by striking first, a lunge to rock him backward before he could straighten an arm into Mallon's face. He was going to drive away from the ocean, northward past Ojai, and up into the hills to that camp. If there was any evidence to prove what these people had done, that was where it would be.

Mallon watched the rearview mirror for headlights, but he saw none after he had coasted off the freeway onto the exit ramp. He kept looking, because on a weeknight after one A.M., any other car on this stretch of road might be one of the hunters. There were no headlights coming toward him either, but the emptiness of the road ahead was little comfort.

The road meandered a bit as it came away from the coast above Ventura, and every time a new stretch presented itself to his sight he strained his eyes to see anything that might indicate someone was watching for him. He envisioned a car just off the highway, maybe parked on a narrow dirt road as though it belonged there, or shielded from view by bushes. If he had been running something like this camp, he would have defended it. After a time, he decided that he had not been thinking clearly. Ojai was still ahead. It was a good-sized town with plenty of traffic most hours of the day. If there was a sentinel somewhere, he would be on a smaller road somewhere north of the town.

Mallon came through Ojai at one-twenty A.M. He drove past the long, low row of stores along the main street, and reached the block with the overhanging roof and the tan fake adobe arches and pillars, still watching for a sign that anybody was awake and paying attention to him. The sight of the place brought back an old memory. During the brief period after the divorce, when he had discovered he was wealthier than he had imagined, he had considered Ojai as a place to live. He had driven along this street and liked the architecture. He had spent a day thinking about acquiring a block of businesses farther up the street and rebuilding them in the same Spanish-revival style, but his enthusiasm had faded with the sun. He'd had a quiet dinner in his hotel and admitted to himself that he could not go through with the project. It had seemed to him that going into another business was so unnecessary that it amounted to an absurdity, an indefensible vanity, like French aristocrats pretending to be shepherds and shepherdesses while real peasants starved.

Tonight those times seemed to Mallon to be distant, almost unimaginable, his concerns outgrown like the concerns of a child. Suddenly, he decided that he knew something more about Catherine Broward. He had never thought clearly about what happened when a person took the life of another human being. Now he knew, and he was beginning to understand why Catherine had been so determined to drown herself. Seeing what could be done to another person, the harm that needed to be done to a human body to kill it, was a minor revelation. The bigger revelation was that once a person had done that to someone, he was changed too.

Catherine must have felt different afterward. The knowledge, the memory of killing her boyfriend, had made her feel tarnished and diminished. She had wanted the feeling to end, but it didn't end. That was why she had been so determined: she believed that if she lived another day or a decade, there would be no improvement. Mallon knew that he too had changed, but his change had been different, and it felt like a clarification of his vision. He did not feel regret, or mourn the loss of the men he had killed, or search for a way that he could have avoided it so he could accuse himself of not having tried hard enough. He hated them. He was relieved that they were dead, and that he was not. The reward of victory was being alive.

Mallon was already through Ojai, and the road to the north was narrower and darker. There were no cars now but his. He endured a long period when nothing looked familiar to him. The trees seemed thicker and taller than he remembered, the dark hills lay in new patterns. He wondered how he could have gotten onto the wrong road. But then he saw a configuration of rocks that he had seen when he'd come here with Lydia—just a flash in the headlights, but undeniably the same—and then the turnoff to the right that led eastward into the hills. He drove from there unerringly to the spot where the high chain-link fence around the self-defense camp began. He resisted the temptation to turn his headlights off. If anyone inside the camp was looking, a pair of headlights moving past on the road would probably cause no alarm, but a driver trying to keep his car from being seen would be worrisome. He kept going at a slow, constant speed, and continued far past the gate before he turned off the lights and let the car quietly roll to a stop on the layer of pine needles at the shoulder of the road.

He got out, walked to the fence, stared through it, and listened. He could just see the back of the long, low building where he and Lydia had gone to talk with Michael Parish. Diane had called it "the main lodge." There were lights on, and now and then he saw something beyond the window shades that looked like movement. He was disappointed. He had felt confident that he would be able to find some piece of evidence in that building that connected Parish and his self-defense camp with at least one of the attacks on him. It had seemed likely that the staff would have retired to their quarters at this hour, leaving the building unoccupied.

He remembered the square blacktopped parking lot across the driveway from the building on the front side. He could see only part of it from here, but he could make out four or five cars, parked close to one another. Then he recognized one of them. It was the black Lexus that had blocked his way in the hotel parking garage, the one driven by the young man with the reddish hair. He could see no human shapes, hear no sound but the breeze in the upper boughs of the pine trees beyond the fence.

Mallon carefully arranged his weapons. He put the two identical Beretta Model 92 pistols he'd taken from the two men on the road into the side pockets of his jacket, where he could reach one easily with either hand but they did not restrain his movement. He considered taking Diane's small pistol with him, but he admitted to himself that the two Berettas probably held more rounds than he would live to use. He hid hers under the passenger seat, then walked off to search for a place to climb the fence.

Mallon strode along the road for about three hundred yards, looking up along the top of the fence at the coiled razor wire, and down at the fence posts. He had worked construction sites where somebody had deemed it necessary that the usual chain-link fence be wired like that. Whenever it had been strung, he had insisted that the fence rental company handle it, instead of his crew. The wire was treacherous stuff that had a way of springing around whenever it was cut, and taking a gash out of anyone nearby.

The wire along this fence was strung in a way that compressed it tightly, more like the wire around a prison than a construction site. The chain-link mesh was pulled taut, so there were no spots along the bottom where a man could get a bit of slack and slip under, and the posts were set in concrete.

But Mallon knew something about this kind of fence that Parish probably didn't know. Installing them was heavy, dull work that pinched fingers and dug gouges in flesh. It was work that the installation companies hired young, inexperienced laborers to do. A straw boss could go through, pound wooden stakes into the ground where he wanted posts, and then go away for a few hours while his crew dug postholes, mixed cement in small batches, and set posts. A day or two later, the crew could come through again, unrolling chain-link mesh along the line and connecting it to the posts. The work was hard and heavy. Mallon had no doubt that the posts near the front gate and the buildings were set in very deep, wide holes with plenty of cement. He could see that in the stretch he was walking now along the road, they were still pretty good. But the farther the fence got from the front gate, where the bosses and the customers were, the worse the work would be.

He reached the spot where the fence turned away from the road into the woods, and kept walking. When he was three hundred feet from the road, he knelt beside one of the posts and tested his theory. This one had been set in a hole that was only nine inches wide, which left room for only about three inches of cement around the three-inch post. He had been right. They'd had to dig through tree roots. They'd had to carry the bags of cement and buckets of water way out here through the brush to mix by hand. There didn't even seem to be a decent path that could accommodate a wheelbarrow. As the day had worn on, and they'd gone deeper into the forest, where the bosses didn't come very often, the laborers had used less cement, and less care.

Mallon walked along another hundred feet until he came to a post that looked a bit off plumb. He examined the base, and decided this was the one. He began to rock it back and forth, harder and harder, until he had it at a forty-five-degree angle. The shallow clump of concrete at the base extended only an inch or so from the pole. He went to his back on the bed of pine needles, lifted the chain-link mesh with both hands, and wriggled under, pushing with his feet. When he was on the other side, he pushed the post upright, stomped some of the loose earth around the concrete, and tried to memorize the way it looked so that he could find it again. He could tell that it was unlikely he would be able to pick it out in a hurry at night. The fence was a line of identical posts surrounded by nearly identical pine trees. He stepped to one of the trees, picked a broken bough off the ground that had already turned brown, then wove it in and out of the links.

He stepped back to be sure he could recognize it, then turned and moved off into the fenced-in land. He was still surrounded by trees, but he could tell that, somewhere off to his left, the land rose gradually to a ridge. He headed in that direction because he guessed that might offer him the safest way of observing the complex of buildings. The lights from the area near the gate and the driveway would not reach up there.

When Mallon had climbed for ten or fifteen minutes up the wooded slope, he came out into a field that led onto the ridge. He made out in the moonlight that it was only the first of at least three rows of foothills that stretched into the backcountry toward a high mountain range, without any glow of electric lights, or any lighter-colored gashes for roads. Just below the ridge where he stood were a couple of buildings. One was the size of a two-car garage, and the other was cabin-sized, both in the same plain style of rustic architecture as the buildings he had seen on his visit with Lydia.

He turned around to look down toward the buildings near the gate. There the slope was clear of trees and brush, like a field of clover and alfalfa. He could make out the main lodge, and now he could see all of the parking lot across the driveway. He counted six cars. He tried to decide what that meant. One would belong to Michael Parish, the man he and Lydia had spoken to. Diane had mentioned two women instructors and a man, which meant three more cars. That left only the Lexus the red-haired man had driven, and one other.

There was a second big building, this one with a high roof, like a barn. It had only high windows and skylights, but it was dark, so Mallon could not tell what was inside. He guessed it must be the gym that he'd heard Parish mention on his first visit, the place where they offered instruction in hand-to-hand fighting. Scattered around on the outskirts were six low buildings that he identified as barracks. Each had three doors on each side, so probably they were each divided into six private rooms with separate entrances. There was no sure way for him to tell how many of them were occupied, but from the six cars, he had to assume that at least two barracks were being used.

It was a difficult place for an intruder, he decided. The front gate, the parking lot, and the area around the main offices were bathed in light, even at this hour. The driveway, which he could now see deserved to be called a road, was lighted at intervals all the way to the big building he had identified as a gym. The living quarters were around the complex on the outer fringes, where it was darker and quieter. Any or all of them might be occupied by people who would hear a person walking by outside. The site did not offer any obvious places for someone like Mallon to enter and be sure of going unnoticed.

Mallon turned and looked away from the camp. Before he went down there, he would need to get a closer look at the buildings separated from the main complex. He had to be sure they weren't occupied before he turned his back on them.

Mallon kept to the shadowy places where groves of trees had been spared. He made his way to the more distant of the two buildings first. It was a cabin. He moved cautiously along the wall, examining it as carefully as he could. The siding consisted of rough slats nailed vertically to the frame of two-by-fours at top and bottom to cover plywood sheets, then painted a light olive to blend into the landscape.

Mallon moved cautiously to the window on a narrow end of the building and looked inside. In the moonlight that shone through the windows he could see one room with three sets of empty bunk beds, a table, and six chairs. There was a bathroom, which was open. He could see three kerosene lanterns: one in the center of the table, and two hanging from wrought-iron supports high on the walls. The cabin looked primitive. Maybe it was an extra place to accommodate guests who wanted the illusion of roughing it, or maybe its purpose was isolation. It didn't matter. There was nobody here now.

Mallon took off his jacket and pressed it against a windowpane near the latch to muffle the sound while he broke the glass with the butt of one of his pistols. Then he raised the window and climbed inside. He collected a lantern and a box of matches from the table, and went outside.

The walk to the second building was at least two hundred yards. Beside it was a wooden tower that he had mistaken for a big tree from a distance in the dark. It was on a ridge overlooking a dry riverbed that had been outfitted as a firing range. There were barrows of earth bulldozed up some distance away, where he could just make out a row of posts with white squares that were probably targets on them, and at one side, a wind sock. He knew what that was for. When he had been a boy shooting on the family farm, he had put one up himself, because the targets were far enough away so that on some days it had been necessary to adjust for the wind.

He stepped up to the garage-like building and examined it. The walls were painted the same color as the others, but now he could see that they were made of cinder blocks. He had a suspicion, a hope that he was right about what this building might be. He quickly walked around the building, looking for windows. The fact that there were none raised his hopes higher. When he reached the door and touched it, he was almost sure: the door was steel. This was the logical place to store the things they needed for the range: paper targets, the machinery for the pop-up combat targets, bench rests, spotting scopes. But maybe, just maybe, there would be other things inside that he could use.

Mallon examined the door closely. It opened inward so the hinges were not accessible, and there were three dead bolts set about a foot apart, so the door would be impossible for one man to batter in. The only way he could imagine opening it was with a cutting torch or a concrete saw. The cinder-block-and-mortar walls were impervious to anything he could do without tools.

He looked up and judged the distance between the spotting tower and the building. It was about eight feet, but the tower was a bit higher than the building's roof. He climbed the ladder to the tower platform and looked again. It seemed a bit farther than it had from the ground, but he reminded himself that he had made his judgment before fear had added a few feet. He climbed up to the rail, bending to stay under the roof of the tower, and held on to one of its supports. He took a breath, and jumped.

He hit the roof of the building about halfway up, then dug hard with his toes and scrambled with his hands to keep from sliding off. After a moment he was able to stop himself, then lie on his belly with his toes holding him there. He took out his pocketknife.

Amateurs who wanted to make a building secure often overlooked a single design problem, and he was lying on it now. A composition shingle roof was designed to keep out the rain, not intruders. He used his knife to help him pry up short roofing nails so he could pull shingles from the roof. He went at it patiently, tugging off shingles and leaving the tarpaper beneath until he could feel the long line where two sheets of plywood met. He stripped the tarpaper off to expose the nails.

He dug into the wood around each of the nail heads with a cutting blade, just deep enough to get a purchase with the bottle-opener blade, then pry the nail up a bit. He went to his knees, put both hands under the sheet, and lifted. There was a creak, and the sheet of plywood came up. It acted as a lever to bend and partially extract the nails on the other edge, so he didn't need to remove them. He held the sheet up like an open door and looked down into the building. It was too dark to see anything in the windowless space below.

Mallon took out the box of matches he had taken from the other building, struck one, and lowered it into the space as far as his arm would reach. The bare concrete floor was about twelve feet below him. He was fairly confident that he could drop straight down and not hurt himself, but even more certain that he would not be able to get back out. The match burned close to his fingers. He turned its head upward so that it would not burn him, then in a few seconds had to let it drop. Just before it went out, he saw the distinctive color of fresh pine board.

He lit a second match and stared at the spot to be sure he had not imagined it. He dropped that match too, lowered himself into the hole in the roof until he was hanging by both hands from the lowest edge, then let go. He fell longer than he had expected to, but managed to land on his toes, bend his knees, and fall sideways to break the impact.

Mallon collected himself, stood, and lit a third match. There was another lantern on the shelf in front of him, so he lifted the chimney, lit it, and blew out his match. He raised the lantern and looked around him. First he studied the inner side of the door: the dead bolts required a key.

Shelves along the near wall held the things he had expected to see: paper targets of various sizes with black bull's-eyes, a pile of cutouts in human shape that had been shot through many times and patched and painted, more glue and patches, a few spotting scopes and binoculars in leather cases, a bore-sighting kit, a whole shelf of cleaning kits with rods, rags, solvent, and gun oil. He moved closer to the shelf that held the binoculars. There was one set that seemed to have a single eyepiece, but not like a spotting scope. He took it off the hook where it hung, and removed the leather case. It was a night-vision scope. He turned it on and looked through the eyepiece, but it didn't work, so he opened the battery compartment and saw that the batteries had been removed. After a short search of the shelves, he found some batteries, inserted them, and tried the scope again. The eyepiece shone with a bright green glow. He hung the scope around his neck and held the lantern up toward the opposite wall.

In the light he saw a wooden rack that held five bolt-action hunting rifles. He came closer. They looked like the Remington Model 70 rifles he and his father had used at home when he'd been a boy, but these had polymer stocks and three-to-nine-power scopes attached. When he examined the receiver of the nearest one, it said MODEL 710. They must be what the shooting instructors used to teach the clients marksmanship. He looked to his right along a long, narrow workbench. There were two boxes of .30-06 ammunition. He nodded to himself as he looked around him at his discoveries. The room was an arsenal, a workshop, a storehouse. But it contained nothing that would convict anybody of anything.

He thought about the people behind the lighted windows in the building on the other side of the hill. They had corrupted and destroyed Catherine and Diane. They had murdered Lydia. They had trained killers, then sent them after Mallon too. They were staying up late tonight, undoubtedly discussing other ways of isolating Robert Mallon far from here and killing him cleverly and entertainingly. After they finished with Mallon, they would train other killers to go after other victims. He could not let them do that. He had to keep looking.

━━

CHAPTER 32

As soon as Mallon found the tool box, he set to work. Getting a way out of this building was his first task. He sorted through the pile of lumber, selected the few pieces he needed, and laid them out on the floor. He did not want to risk doing any hammering, so he used a hand drill and some screws to attach eight short pieces to one board and construct a crude ladder that was long enough to reach from the floor to the hole in the roof. He leaned it there to keep it out of his way, then examined the row of rifles.

There was a chain that had been run through the trigger guards to the metal rack and attached with a padlock, but the padlock was too small to present much resistance. He set a big screwdriver at the end of the loop, hit it once with the hammer, and popped it open. Mallon took two of the rifles out of the rack, then poured the boxes of bullets into his trouser pockets. He took the last three rifles from the gun rack, removed each of the bolts, hid them on a shelf behind some paint cans, extinguished his lantern, and carried it with his two rifles up onto the roof. He pulled his ladder up after him, ran it down the outside of the building, and climbed down to the grass with his finds.

When he reached the ground he dragged the ladder off into the nearest wooded area and hid it in the brush. Then he kept going, climbing the low hill that overlooked the camp. He kept at the edge of the trees, where he would be difficult to see, and moved along the ridge until he had found a spot behind some bushes where he could stare directly down the long driveway, see the front entrance to the main lodge, the gym, and the sides of the six barracks.

He released the box magazine from each of his rifles, loaded it with four rounds, and pushed it back in. Next he tested his night scope by turning away from the lighted buildings and scanning the woods. The world glowed eerily bright and greenish, and he could see clearly defined shapes of trees and bushes. He turned it off and left it around his neck.

He checked his watch. It was two-thirty A.M. He had only about three hours of darkness left, and there was a great deal to do. He took one of his rifles and his lantern, and stepped quietly down to the row of barracks. He leaned close to the first window, cupped his hands beside his eyes, and looked in. It was a small bedroom.

There was a sudden, loud pop and the glass beside his head shattered, spraying a shower of shards inward onto the polished wooden floor of the room. Mallon dropped to the ground, snatched up his rifle, and stared into the dark brush on the hillside above him. Somebody had shot at him. Either they had heard him coming down here to the barracks or they had seen him as soon as he had driven up the road, and had followed him. He strained his eyes to distinguish shapes in the dark brush, then remembered the night-vision scope. It was hanging from his neck, but he had not had the presence of mind to use it. He held it to his eye, and gazed up the hill at the brush. He could clearly see a man, crouching in a clump of bushes about a hundred and fifty feet away. As Mallon watched, the man raised his pistol to take a leisurely aim.

Mallon rested his left elbow on the ground, quickly cycled the bolt to bring a round into the chamber, and stared through the rifle's telescopic sight. The feel of the rifle was familiar—the weight, the shape of the stock. The only part that he had not felt before was the grainy texture of the polymer stock. He moved the rifle slightly, unable to find the man's shape again in the narrow field of the sight. Then the man fired, the round kicked up dirt beside Mallon, and he flinched involuntarily. But the muzzle flash had been bright, placed directly in the center of Mallon's sight. Mallon fired, enduring the long-forgotten kick of the recoil on his right shoulder and cheek. He lowered the rifle and raised the night-vision scope to his eye. In the bright green, he could see that the man had collapsed backward, but his torso was held upright by the branches of the bush he had hidden in. He recognized the face now. It was the young man with red hair from the hotel in Los Angeles. Mallon could see dark blood flowing from a big wound in his chest. The man was dead.

Mallon scrambled to his feet and ran toward the cover of the woods, then turned down the slope, away from the living quarters. He ran down the hill to the side of the gym and stood with his back to the wall. He used his night scope to study the six cabins, waiting for someone to emerge from a door. But after a few minutes, he still had seen nobody coming after him. Now and then he would lean outward from the side of the big building to see if there was any movement visible in the main lodge. When he could not detect any, he would return his attention to the cabins.

There was little to them but a two-by-four frame, half-inch plywood nailed on, and a layer of rough-cut vertical slats on the outside to serve as siding to keep the weather out. The one he'd broken into to steal the lantern and matches had been finished on the inside by having cheap wallboard tacked in to hide the studs, but the sheets had been left with their joints showing, not even taped and painted to make them look like plaster. He wasn't even sure whoever had built them had bothered to insulate them. No wonder someone inside had heard him prowling around.

Mallon kept moving his gaze from one to another, but seeing nobody come out, then turning around to look at the main lodge, where the shades still covered the windows. Maybe he could get down there, past the lighted area, and reach his car. But then he saw the shade of a window at the near end of the main lodge pushed aside, and half of a face—one eye, part of a nose and mouth—appeared, then vanished. There were quick dark shadows behind the window shade a moment later: the man was resting a rifle on the windowsill, searching for a target. Mallon aimed his rifle so he could see through the telescopic sight, and held himself still. The shade came up quickly, and Mallon could see two heads, figures in dark clothes, leaning toward the window to see what was happening. Behind them there was more movement.

Mallon tried to interpret what he saw. After a moment, he knew. They were scurrying around arming themselves, preparing to slip out into the dark to come for Mallon. The one with the rifle was going to cover them, wait for Mallon to shoot, and then fire at his muzzle flash. Mallon had to try to keep them inside, where they couldn't get to him. He steadied his aim, took two deep breaths to clear his lungs of the carbon dioxide that would make his hands shake, and squeezed the trigger.

The bang of the rifle's report tore the air; the recoil made the stock brush his cheek, kicked his shoulder, and raised the barrel. He lost his aim for a moment, but he brought the barrel down and cycled the bolt to chamber another round.

The window was empty again, but he believed he had hit the man. The others, he decided, must be cowering somewhere out of sight. Tonight, ducking down below or beside the window was not going to be an effective tactic. Mallon was aware that if the construction of the main lodge was anything like what he had seen in the cabins, the wall would not even slow a rifle bullet appreciably. His second shot had brought back to him the familiar feel, sound, and smell of a rifle, and he was more comfortable as he aimed to the right of the window frame and a foot above the floor, and fired again. He had no idea whether the shot hit flesh, but he knew there were still no heads up.

He fired his fourth shot, then removed the box magazine and

pushed bullets from his pocket into it. He kept watching the doors and the row of windows along the side. The people inside should be trying to scatter into the darkness, he thought. They should be trying to spot his muzzle flash, so they could aim at it and kill him. He clicked the magazine back into the rifle, then used his night scope to scan the ground near the lodge and the woods beyond it. There were still no human beings visible, but he knew they must be watching for his muzzle flashes to find him, so it was time to move. He raised the rifle again and fired a round through the wall high on the left side, trying to place it near the front door to keep them in.

He ran as hard as he could into the woods to make his way up the slope of the hill without being in the open, where he might be seen in the moonlight. He reached the trees, then stopped to reload and fired another round through the back of the building, turned, and continued uphill, just inside the line of trees. It was difficult to run up the hill as quickly as he wanted to, and after another two hundred yards his chest was heaving, and there was a burning sensation in his lungs. He knelt down, fired two more shots at the building, and ran again.

Mallon reached the crest of the hill, flopped down on the grass behind the bush where he had left his second rifle and his lantern, and raised his night-vision scope to his eye. There was no human figure outside the main lodge. Mallon looked at the window. He was much farther away now, but his higher vantage let him see the legs of the first man he had shot, still lying on the floor.

Mallon concluded that he must be dead. He tried to decode what he was feeling about it. For a second, he was almost fooled into imagining that what he felt must be remorse. Then he realized that it was something else: simple distaste for killing. He felt angry that he had needed to do this, that his life had come to this. He cycled the bolt of his second rifle, switched the safety off so he could lift it quickly and fire, then took the magazine out of his first rifle and began to reload it.

||||||||||||||||||||||||||||||||||||||||||||||||||||||||||||||||||

CHAPTER 33

Spangler lay on the hardwood floor of the lodge, his eyes and mouth open in a pantomime of amazement. The blood now pooled from above his shoulders to his ankles, still spreading like a cape. After the third or fourth shot had screamed through the wall, somebody had turned the light off, but Emily could still see him. She sat on the floor, her back to the front wall and her shoulder edged against the couch so the bullets weren't likely to plow the length of it and reach her. She was shaking, and when she turned her head she could feel bits of broken glass falling from her hair.

Emily could not stop looking over at Spangler. From here she could stare past him out the window, but then her eyes would flick downward, because something about the darkness or her terror had made her think she had seen him move. He had not moved. She had been on a lot of hunts now, and she should have known right away that Paul was dead, without anyone telling her. The first bullet had taken him.

At the sound of the first couple of shots, people had jumped. A few had even drawn guns. After a few moments, Paul Spangler had crawled to the window and looked out. Parish had handed Spangler a rifle and said, "Paul, see if you can spot him. Everyone else, get ready to go outside."

At first, she had thought she'd heard the snap of the shade rolling up and hitting the window. It had been the sound of the single bullet popping the glass. Then there had been the distant *pow* of the shot. In the sudden silence, Emily had turned and looked at Spangler. The bullet had hit him in the chest. The blood that leaked out on the floor was bright red, like paint. It was coming out so fast. Couldn't somebody stop it? How could they leave him lying alone on his back like that? She pointed, and called to Debbie, to Parish, to Mary, "Help him! He's been shot!"

Mary was crawling along the wall toward the other end of the building, but she stopped and frowned in Emily's direction. "He's dead, honey. Don't you see that?" Then she moved on.

A moment later, the shots had begun again, and she'd realized that Mary had taken cover because she must have known they were coming. When the next one simply popped through the wall, Emily at first thought she must be misinterpreting the sight and sound—that something else was happening. But somebody was out there with a rifle, and these flimsy wooden walls stopped nothing.

Tonight was partly her fault. She knew this debacle had been caused by her self-indulgence and lack of discipline on the day she had gone out with David Altberg to kill Mallon. She should have fought him for Altberg's gun, and killed him on the spot. Even if she had not done that, she should have insisted on killing Mallon that night. She stared at Spangler's ruined body and began to be angry at Parish. How could he have been so wrong? There was absolutely no excuse for picking a target and arranging a hunt and then having the target start shooting the staff. It was ridiculous. She had begun to compose what she was going to say to Parish.

Two more rounds had pounded through the wooden wall. She knew that one hit the couch she was hiding behind, because she felt the vibration where her right arm touched it. This building was no protection: it was a sham, a picture of what safety was supposed to look like. Parish was responsible for that, too.

She looked around for him. Then the shots started again. Each time she heard the bullet punch through the wooden wall and slam into the floor, or hit a metal fixture and ricochet crazily into another wall, she jumped, and remained stiff and trembling. She knew reacting was ridiculous: before her nerves could make her muscles contract, before her brain even received the message that there was a shot, the bullet had already burrowed into something, and the danger was over.

She saw Parish walk past poor Paul Spangler without even looking at him. Next he crouched facing the wall, craning his neck, moving his head one way or another. He was trying to see through a bullet hole in the wall. After a moment he gave up and slowly moved to place his right eye in the lower left corner of the window where Paul had been shot. Two more rounds punctured the wall to Parish's right. He turned and stayed low as he moved away, but there was the beginning of a smile on his lips. He stopped at the far end of the room and sat down on one of the hard chairs.

"I've picked out the location," Parish announced. Emily looked around to see the reaction of the others, but the only one she could see was Mary. "He's up on the hill about halfway, at the edge of the trees. I finally saw the flashes when he fired the last two rounds."

" 'He'? You mean this is only one person?" Mary asked. "I thought it was the police or something."

Parish shook his head. "No, this is just Mr. Mallon." He looked at Mary and Emily, his expression now confident. "This should hardly be shocking to you. That is not a deer out there. It's a man. He thinks, he learns, and he fights. Now we're past deciding whether or not to hunt him. He knows where we are, and who we are, and how to get to us. We have to kill him, or we'll be destroyed too. Do you both understand what I've said?"

Emily could see Mary's eye turn to watch her in the dim light, but neither woman spoke.

"Good," said Parish. "Now we've got to go after him. As I said, the muzzle flashes came from halfway up the first hill, at the edge of the woods. The way to get him is to use our superior numbers and fire-power. Arm yourselves immediately with every weapon you have, and all the ammunition you can carry. If you have dark clothing you're not wearing, put it on. You have two minutes."

Emily hesitated for a moment, then judged that obeying Michael was better than crouching behind the couch. It was the way out, into the darkness and the woods. She had carried a large purse that was like a backpack, and she had a Glock nine-millimeter pistol inside. She crawled to the table where she had left it, took out her pistol, and put it on the floor beside her while she slipped on the black sweater she had brought from her cabin, then picked it up again. She felt so much better with the gun in her hand that she stood up.

Parish said, "I have here some containers of camouflage makeup. Don't try to make a pattern. That's for daytime. Smear some on your face, neck, the backs of your hands—anything that's exposed. Any amount is better than none, and the more the better."

When Mary handed the flat can to her, Emily took a gob of it on her fingertips. As she rubbed it on her forehead, cheeks, and neck, she whispered, "Paul is dead. Where did Debbie and Ron go?"

Mary shrugged, but said nothing.

"Time's up," said Parish. "I'm going outside. The first thing I will do is cut the power to the whole ranch. That will be your signal to leave here. You know where he is, so try to stay out of his line of fire, and move quickly. He will fire his weapon. When he does, we'll use the flash to locate him and return his fire: all three of us at once. When you have fired, advance to the next protected spot and wait for your next chance. When he fires again, do the same, and move closer. Keep it up until he's dead. Do I need to repeat anything?"

There was no answer, so he said, "It will work if you keep your heads. See you later." Then he slipped out the front door.

Emily looked down at her watch and began to time Michael's progress. It had been thirty seconds, then a minute, two minutes. She looked away and tried to see the expression on Mary's face, and once again had the same feeling she'd had many times in her life. She was alone and apart, the only one who didn't really believe, the only one who had doubts and subversive thoughts. She could not see Mary's face, but she could read her posture. She was waiting eagerly for his signal, tense with the worry not that he might be wrong but that she might disappoint him. She might not move fast enough, or be smart enough, or something.

The lights went out, Mary swung the door open and disappeared, but Emily hung back. Maybe if they were out there stalking Mallon, then the safest place to be was right here. There was the sudden crack of a rifle, some wood chips in the air, and Emily hurried out into the night.

||||||||||||||||||||||||||||||||||||||||||||||||||||||

CHAPTER 34

The white lights that ran along the driveway from the gate to the gym went out, but Mallon raised the night-vision scope to his eye and saw the back door swing open. He fired shots at the people coming out, but they came out fast, ran hard, and spread out into the shadows.

Almost at once there was ragged gunfire, three muzzle flashes from different directions. Chips of bark from the trees above and behind him rained down, and he heard bullets thudding into the grass on the hill ahead of him. Mallon ducked down, his rifle empty. He left the rifle on the ground under the bush, took up the loaded one, crawled down the back of the slope a few feet, and slipped into the woods.

The next phase was going to be more dangerous, but he had known from the beginning that it would come. He had shot two people, and judging from what he had seen during the brief time while the window had been lit, he believed that left five who were alive and unhurt. It was a simple puzzle: anyone he met in the woods was an enemy. Anyone else meeting someone in the woods had four chances that it was one of his friends, and only one chance that it was Mallon.

He kept moving down the hill toward the buildings until he found a spot where several twisted old California oaks with trunks the size of a man's waist had clumped together, two of them with forked trunks. On his first trip through, he had noticed this spot because it was such good cover. He sat down with his back to a tree to wait for the hunters.

The night was quiet, the leaves on the trees hanging still and dead in the windless air. Mallon remained perfectly still, his rifle across his lap, and listened. He knew that anyone else in the woods would be walking, climbing toward the spot where he had last been seen. Mallon would stay here, looking like part of a tree, or like a shadow.

It was a long time before the first footsteps reached his ears. The soft carpet of pine needles in the evergreen grove had made their movements silent, but now, as they came nearer to Mallon, their feet crushed dried oak leaves and their pant legs whipped through the low weeds and wild plants that grew in the wider spaces between the oaks.

▓▓▓▓▓

Emily looked to her right to be sure that she was in line with Mary, and far enough away from her. Mallon was not turning out to be what everyone had expected him to be, and Emily was beginning to think he was likely to put a bullet between somebody else's eyes. As they had walked up the first few yards at the bottom of the hill, Emily had begun to listen for the shot. The best that could happen was that they would get Mallon to fire at one of them too early and miss, and the flash in the dark would reveal him. Staying far apart and moving was really the only tactic they could use in this situation of pistols against a sniper rifle. During the few seconds after he fired, Mary and Emily would pour about twenty rounds into Mallon's hiding place from both sides.

As Emily climbed in the dark woods, she found herself revisiting a thought she'd been having for about a week. It had started the night when she had served as the scout for Markham and Coleman. She had begun to suspect that it was time for her to move on. No, that was not true. She had begun to suspect that a long time ago. Watching those two perform had made her admit to herself that it was getting to be urgent. The disaster on the beach with David Altberg had made the impression stronger, but since then she had been so busy, so tied up with the problem of covering and cleaning up the mess, that she'd had no time to think.

She had gotten no sleep the night after the Altberg debacle. Two days later, she'd had to begin following Mallon to Los Angeles. He had kept her awake most of the night with his antics. She had been on the telephone for all those hours with two sets of amateurs, telling Kira and the boys where to wait for Mallon and holding Markham and Coleman back. She'd had no time when she was alone, awake, and rested to consider what she had been doing and make a decision about the future.

That had always been her main problem, she admitted. She was too passive, too reluctant to make her own decisions. Ten years ago, at the age of nineteen, she had gone all the way out to Arizona just because her boyfriend, Danny, had asked her to. Then, even though she had been terribly unhappy about Phoenix and about him, she had not thought of another plan and carried it out. She had simply stayed there until Mary had come along and brought her to the hotel to meet Michael.

She had been contented enough with her life after that, but somehow ten years had gone by. In one more, she would be thirty, and she still had no real direction in her life. She was better off than she had ever been before. She had improved physically from the constant exercise she'd gotten, and she had banked a lot of money. She could go somewhere and start over again. She looked up the hill at the cabin where she, Mary, and Debbie had kept their belongings. The one beside it was Spangler's. That, she conceded, was probably what had really set her to thinking tonight. She didn't want to die like that. She had to find something new. But what would it be, and where did she want to go?

It was really a question of getting herself to say good-bye to Michael. It was going to be difficult after all these years of trying to please him. He would know that the reason was that she had lost faith in him. It would not matter what she said; he would know.

┼┼┼┼┼

Mallon very slowly raised the night-vision scope to his eye and turned it on: there were two luminous human shapes with glowing eyes, both carrying pistols. They walked slowly, about a hundred feet apart, at least two hundred feet from where he sat. He let the scope hang from his neck and very slowly raised the rifle to his shoulder. He judged that the one on the right was the greatest threat because the brush on that side was thickest and afforded the best cover. He aimed the rifle using the crook of the double-trunked tree in front of him as a rest, and fired.

He stared ahead as he cycled the bolt, trying to keep his eye on where the other one had gone, losing sight of the shape in the dark. A second later, someone fired. The shots were wide and high, but he saw the flashes. He aimed at the spot just as that one ran for a new hiding place. He raised his aim to the person's chest, tried to lead him, and fired, then cycled the bolt again. He knew he had missed.

The person had disappeared, and the air was silent again. Mallon raised his night-vision scope to his eye again. The bright green glow showed him the bushes, the black sky, the trunks of trees, but no human shape. Mallon knew that he was in danger. He had shot this guy's companion, then fired from the same spot, then lost sight of him. It was time to move. He dropped to the ground and crawled to the right into a big patch of low bushes that looked as though it had grown up after a tall tree had fallen. He burrowed into the bushes until he reached a stump, and that confirmed his guess. It was two and a half feet wide a yard above the roots, and the top was flat, cut with a saw.

Mallon sat behind it, rested his rifle on the top, and listened. He had counted five shapes in the window of the lodge before the lights had gone off. If his count was accurate, there were still four out there. He used his night scope again, slowly turning first to the left, then to the right until he had studied the woods on all sides. It was possible that the second man had simply turned and dashed down the hill toward the main lodge.

There were more footsteps. Mallon could tell that they were coming from behind him. There were three, four, five crunches, and then the person stopped to listen. Mallon gripped his rifle and waited, using the sounds to judge the man's position. As soon as he heard the next crunch he threw himself back, rolled to his belly at the side of the stump, saw the shape and fired into it, rolled back and cycled the bolt. He could see the body was horizontal, but he could not tell more than that, so he rose to one knee and fired at it again, then trotted to get past it.

Mallon reached the spot and stopped involuntarily to stare down at the body. It was—had been—a woman. She had been tall and thin, her red hair in a ponytail and covered by a baseball cap. With the dark grease she had smeared across her face, he could not tell what she looked like, but she seemed young. He looked up and forced himself to move on.

He stopped at the edge of the woods and peered up the hill at the spot where he had hidden to fire at the main lodge. None of the hunters seemed to have reached it yet. He raised the night scope again and scanned the hillside. There was no sign of hunters in the open, so he moved up a few yards to try for a better view. As he climbed the hill, he remained inside the edge of the forest. Every ten or fifteen steps, he would stop beside a tree where his silhouette would not stand out, and spend ten seconds listening and studying the landscape with the night-vision scope. Near the top of the hill he moved deep into the woods and continued slowly. This time, when he raised the scope to his eye, it was dark.

He had drained the batteries. He closed his eyes in a pained wince. The scope had been an enormous advantage, the difference between seeing at night, like a cat, and being night-blind, like a bird. The loss was a huge one that made him frightened and sad at the same time. He lifted the strap from around his neck and placed the scope on the ground, made a mental note of where it was, then moved on cautiously. Mallon began to get used to moving without the night scope, but he could not get it out of his mind. His must have been the only one at the camp. If it had not been, then someone else would have seen him and killed him by now.

Suddenly, he knew something. Somebody else would have begun thinking about the night-vision scope by now. They would have thought of it at the very beginning, when Mallon had shot the man behind the barracks, and the hunters had looked out the window of the lodge at the dark woods and weedy hills, and seen nothing. There would be somebody in that group who had, at that moment, decided to make his way over the first hill and across the narrow valley to the dry streambed where the firing range was. It would have to be a person who had keys to the steel door of the cinder-block building, because without them there was not much chance of retrieving the night scope. The person who could do that was somebody Mallon needed to kill if he wanted to survive.

Mallon no longer tried to skirt the edge of the open ground. Now he moved deep into the woods, where he could move quickly with less fear of meeting hunters. In a few minutes, Mallon was descending the far side of the hill. He could see, ahead and off to his right, the observation tower and, beside it, the low, square cinder-block building he had broken into. From here he could not see the steel door, because it faced the observation tower and the firing range. If people had reached the building, they weren't making enough noise to carry this far.

Mallon watched and waited. He knew that a man's sense of time became terribly inaccurate when he was crouching in the dark, waiting anxiously for something to happen. But it had now been a very long time since he had seen his last hunter.

Now and then he took a deep breath and let it out to calm himself, but he tried to remain still. He heard a sound. He listened for a few seconds, but it did not come again. He was almost certain it had come from the direction of the observation tower. Mallon watched as one of the shadows under the roof of the observation tower moved. He lifted his rifle, rested his elbow on his bent knee to steady it, stared through the telescopic sight, and watched the shadow resolve itself into a person. Somebody had climbed the tower to see if he could make out where Mallon was.

Mallon very slowly and quietly cycled the bolt of the rifle once more, placed the crosshairs on the person, held them there, and squeezed the trigger. There was a click. He released the magazine, and the lightness of it in his hand told him it was empty. He groped in his pockets for any loose bullets that he had not loaded, but he found none. He looked up at the tower again. The person was climbing down the ladder.

Mallon gently placed the rifle in the weeds, took the pistol from his right jacket pocket, and crawled through the brush toward the building. He crawled until he could tell that the man was on the other side, where the door was. Then he stood and walked quietly to the nearest wall of the structure. He was careful not to touch the wall, because any small sound would carry to the inside. If the hunter was already in, he might hear it. Very slowly, Mallon came around to the side of the building, listening as much for any sounds he might make as for the hunter. He heard the key slip into the first lock. He heard it turn and the dead bolt snap back, then heard the second one. There was a pause, and Mallon was not sure whether he had made a noise—maybe just his breathing would be enough—or if the third lock wasn't the same. He waited, then heard the lock snap back. There was a rustling, and a clank as the person turned the handle. The door hinge creaked.

Mallon stepped around the building toward the doorway and saw the man standing in the threshold. The man raised the hand that held a pistol and turned toward Mallon just as Mallon fired.

Mallon knelt beside the body. He hoped the man had a flashlight so he could use it to search the building for more rifle ammunition. Maybe his night scope had not been the only one after all. If not, there could be more batteries in boxes on the shelves that he had missed. He held his pistol under his left arm and dug into his trouser pocket for the box of matches. He found it, struck a match against the box, and a sharp pain hit his hand so hard that he released it into the air. A second blow exploded into the side of his head.

He was on the floor already when he saw his match fall toward the cement surface a few feet away, the flame at the head just a streak of blue, the small aura of light it threw below it growing wider and brighter. It hit, bounced once, and kept burning a yard from his face. He only recognized that what had hit the side of his head had been a kick when he saw what was coming at him from the darkness beyond the small, dying flame.

It was a young woman, her hair cut as short as a man's. She was wearing a pair of gray sweatpants, black shoes that were not sneakers but thin-soled like racing shoes, and a black pullover with a tank top over it, as though she had been in the middle of a workout of some kind. The expression on her face was emotionless, her eyes not on his face but trained on his hands and feet in intense concentration. He realized that he had lost the gun. He tried to roll out of her reach, but the next kick caught the back of his leg above the knee, and he felt pain shoot through it up to his back, and down to his heel.

Behind him, he heard her say, "My name is Debbie. I want it to be the last thing you hear: Debbie."

He kept his body still until he got his left hand into his jacket pocket and around the second Beretta pistol. He heard her shoe squeak as she shifted it slightly on the concrete, and he knew that he had to ignore the pain and act now. He abruptly rolled toward her and fired through the fabric of his pocket.

Debbie looked at him with a terrible surprise, then began to fall as the match burned out.

—||||||||||||||||||||||||||||||||||||||||||||||||||||||||||||||||||||||||||||||||||—

CHAPTER 35

Michael Parish had been observing and evaluating over the past three days, and he had decided he would need to make a great many changes in the program. As it was, each of his students knew how to fire weapons with some accuracy, and each knew how to engage in limited hand-to-hand combat with an opponent of his own physical size, age, and sex. But none of them had developed into hunters.

When they appeared to have the advantage, they instantly became overconfident and foolhardy. When they were at a disadvantage, they seemed to become listless and dispirited and muddled, unable to think clearly or act decisively. They waited for a leader to emerge and tell them what to do, then needed to have him keep them at it. They had not yet learned to translate their fear into a need to act, or to remain calmly determined when a target wasn't hit with the first shot and became dangerous.

Parish walked slowly through the woods, his AK-47 assault rifle in his left hand, following the sounds of the shots. Parish was unhappy. Everything seemed to be going badly. Spangler was dead. Kira Tolliver had quit in the middle of the hunt and gone home, and he knew that she would not be back to hunt again, now that Tim was dead. They had both been only in their early twenties, and both had been wealthy in exactly the right way—with plenty of money in trust funds and no professions—and very much fascinated with the hunt. The loss of those two depressed him. Certainly he should drop the idea of sending groups of clients out after targets. He had known that for days. But the loss of Tim and Kira made him wonder whether it might not be better to scrap any hunt that involved more than one client. In fact, it was clear that he had not taken seriously enough the mistakes made by his students in the killing of Lydia Marks. The performance of Markham and Coleman should have been warning enough.

For years, the traditional hunt with a tracker, a scout, and one client who would shoot under the direction of a professional hunter had been perfectly practical. Virtually the only way that it could fail was if the client paid to hunt a target who was under close surveillance by some police organization. Even then, it would have to be a police group that was spectacularly good at staying hidden but was present in large numbers. Such a situation was always theoretically possible: clients paid to hunt people they hated, and sometimes people who prompted hatred also raised the interest of the police. So far, it had never happened. The targets had been a harmless and somewhat unremarkable parade of faithless lovers, business rivals, bullying bosses. Some of the grudges had been so old that the target had no idea he still had an enemy, so stale that even Parish's people had difficulty tracing the target to a current address. That had made the hunts even safer. He would return to his core business. Trying to train real killers, turning amateurs into experts who had the taste for it and the nerve, was simply too difficult.

He was on his way to the most recent set of shots, because they seemed to him to have come from the precise direction he had been hoping for. Parish was accustomed to the sound of shots reaching his ears from the firing range.

Debbie had volunteered to make her way around Mallon to the

range to get into the blockhouse, pick up a night-vision scope and a good rifle, and then end this. Parish had been prepared to do it himself, but he had been pleased to hear her suggest it. He took it as evidence that he had at least been right about his staff. They were not incompetent, and they were not paralyzed simply because there had been casualties.

He had agreed to let her go for several reasons, all of them practical. He wanted her to have the credit, the glory of being the hero, because he understood that loyalty came from such things: not what he did for her, but what she had invested in his goodwill. He also knew that although Debbie had a rapport with some of the campers—particularly certain women—the other staff members were less likely to be impressed. She wasn't apt to strike them as the ideal leader to obey while Parish sneaked up into the backcountry.

He had said to her, "I know you can do this, but I've got to be sure that absolutely nothing can go wrong. I need someone to watch your back while you handle this. Take Ron with you."

She had looked distressed for half a second, but the way he had said it had been the right way. She had understood that once she had a night scope and a rifle, she would be nearly invincible. But nearly was not good enough. There was still one strategy that could ruin everything. If Mallon could stay out of her sight and motionless until she passed him, he might be able to kill her before she found him. Debbie had understood this, and she had understood why the only possible companion was Ron Dolan, the other martial arts instructor. She had nodded and said, "Okay, Michael," and waited while Dolan had prepared.

Now, if Parish read the sounds right, Debbie and Ron had probably succeeded. He had not heard the distinctive crack of Mallon's rifle, but he had heard the pops of a couple of pistol rounds, first one, then a delay, then the other. That, very likely, had been the pistol Debbie had brought out there with her being fired into Mallon, and then someone—Ron, probably—firing the coup de grâce into Mallon's head to be sure he was dead. Those were the two kinds of people Debbie and Ron were, and it was another reason why he had insisted on their going together. He felt an upwelling of affection for them. They were like a pair of dogs that he had chosen from different litters and raised. He knew exactly what each of them could do, and he knew that they would do it.

As Parish passed the crest of the first hill and looked down at the range, he admitted to himself that he had mishandled Robert Mallon: he should not have considered him sport. There had been old students begging Parish for a second or third hunt, and he had decided this would get them all off his mind at once. He should have used his staff as trackers and scouts to lure Lydia Marks and Mallon somewhere together, and gotten rid of both of them himself. Then he would have been free of worry once more, and been able to arrange safe hunts for a few carefully selected amateurs in his own time, maintaining the orderly schedule of new self-defense classes and keeping his staff rested and happy and well paid. He had learned that much from this experience.

There was still one other thing that nagged at him, and that was the stubborn refusal of the human mind to be fully revealed and understood. He had made a terrible mistake with Catherine Broward. He had asked Catherine all of the right questions, made her tell him all the details of the relationship with her boyfriend from the first day. Parish had made her describe the period when she had been in love with Mark Romano and waited in their apartment each day for him to come home and ask her to marry him. Talking about that period had, strangely, seemed to make her more uncomfortable than the final phase, the one that had taught her what her boyfriend had really been like. The end she had narrated in a bored monotone, as though she were talking about someone else.

After hearing her talk for hours, Parish had been satisfied. Now he knew that he should not have been. He should have known that something was wrong, because she had talked with such feeling about

DEAD AIM ||| 361

the good times, and none at all about the bad. She had not felt the right kind of anger or hatred. She had fooled him.

Catherine had gone through with the hunt very smoothly and efficiently. She had politely thanked Parish for the training and for making it possible for her to kill her boyfriend. Then she had gone away. He had sometimes thought about her. He had even considered that she might be one of the young self-defense students who would come back soon, asking for more advanced training, or for a specialized apprenticeship with one of the instructors, all the while hungering for the next hunt.

Parish felt a dull jab in his right palm and realized his fingernails had been digging into the skin. He rubbed the open hand against his thigh. He had been wrong about Catherine Broward, wrong about Markham and Coleman, wrong about Tim Hillis and Kira Tolliver. They had all been weak. Parish had also misjudged Diane Fleming. Diane was another disappointment. Since Mallon was here and she was not, she too must have done something stupid.

Parish's course intersected with the dry arroyo he had converted to a combat firing range. He moved down the bank into the channel, where he would be difficult to see, and cautiously made his way toward the blockhouse. As he approached the building, he could see that the door was open, and there was a man's body lying on the ground outside it. Parish smiled: they had gotten him in two shots.

He stepped closer to the body and bent down to look. It was Dolan. He straightened instantly, raising his eyes to scan the hillside and the woods beyond as he stepped backward to get into the deep shadows under the eaves, and place his back against the cinder blocks.

"Who's there?" It was a scared voice, the voice of a woman who was in pain. It was Debbie's voice.

"It's Michael," he called softly. He took another look around him, then slipped inside. He reached into his pocket and took out the small Mag-lite he carried. When he turned the crown to switch it on, he kept the beam wide and dim, but what he saw was confusing. He moved the beam around the room, saw a big opening in the roof, and then saw a jumble of things on the floor: tools, wood, rifles. He kept moving it, and then found Debbie. She was sitting on the floor with her legs extended and her back leaning against the wall, her left hand clutching her belly. She seemed to have no gun, but there was one lying only a dozen feet away on the open floor.

"Michael?" she said weakly. "Thank God you came out here. I'm hurt."

"Where is he?"

"After he got Dolan I disarmed him, but he had another gun."

"It's going to be okay," Parish crooned softly. "Where is he now? Which way did he go?"

"I . . . I don't know," said Debbie. "Out there somewhere."

Parish blew out a breath to keep the anger out of his voice, then said in gentle reproof, "You should have paid attention."

Her voice was plaintive, almost a little girl's in this darkness. "I'm hurt bad, Michael. He shot me in the belly. I'm bleeding a lot. I've got to get to a doctor."

"The sooner I find him, the sooner I can get you out of here. Think. What did you see that will help me? What guns did he have? Just a pistol?"

"Yes."

"When he stepped out the door, did he turn right or left?"

Her voice became quieter, calmer. "He's gone. He ran away. You could bring the Land Rover up here. I could be in a hospital in a half hour."

"I can't risk him shooting you again," said Parish. "You know a car door is no protection against a rifle bullet. Just relax your muscles, keep your heart rate low, and rest. I'll be back for you as soon as I've cleared the way." He patted her cheek gently, then stood.

"You've got to take me now," she sobbed. "I can't hold out."

He said in an urgent whisper, "Keep your voice down, Debbie.

He'll hear you and know I'm here with you. Just sit tight." He stepped toward the doorway.

"Michael!" This time it was a wail, a high-pitched shout that made him bob his head from one side of the doorway to the other to see if it had attracted Mallon. He could detect no sign of movement.

He stepped backward into the darkness again, leaned his heavy rifle against the wall beside the doorway, and instead took out his pistol. He twisted the crown of his flashlight to turn it on again, this time into a thin, bright beam that illuminated Debbie's feet. In the dimmer glow around the small bright circle he could see that her pretty face was squeezed into a rubbery parody of its flawless structure, the big eyes narrowed to slits, the upper lip puckered, and the lower one protruding. He raised the flashlight's bright beam up to shine on her face. As he had expected, she turned her head to the side to avoid the glare, and he fired the shot into her temple.

Parish had known in advance what he was going to do next, and now he executed the plan quickly. He turned off the flashlight as he moved toward the door, snatched up his rifle, and sprinted straight for the top of the hill. He wanted to get there and take a firing position in time to see Mallon break cover to move toward the origin of the shot. He reached the top, just inside the edge of the woods, knelt, raised the rifle to his shoulder, and waited for something in the landscape to move.

He heard the sound of a footstep behind him, and that told him he had guessed wrong. He turned to bring the rifle around to fire at his opponent. But too soon there came the familiar, loud pop of gunpowder that Parish had learned to love, and he died on his belly and looking up at the dark shadow-shape of a man.

‖‖—

CHAPTER 36

I t was bright. There was an instant when Diane believed it was only another variation on the dream. It always had a stern, angry figure who had found out what she had done. Sometimes it was her mother, who had always been so sweet, with a voice like velvet and hands as soft and soothing as warm water, but who in the dream came back knowing of Diane's guilt and ready to punish her. Most often it was a male figure, a nightmare version of a judge. This time it was Robert Mallon.

The impression lasted only a fraction of a second, until she tried to roll over and cover her eyes to go back to sleep, and felt the cramped, sore feeling that made her eyes open. Her face had been pressed against the floor, her left shoulder, hip, and knee all hurt, and her neck was stiff. She considered trying to roll to her stomach, but the feeling was returning to her arms in needle stings, and it reminded her that they were taped behind her. She was afraid that if she were on her stomach, she would have a difficult time getting up again. Slowly, painfully, she extended her taped ankles and pushed her heels on the floor, raised her head, and rocked to sit up. She could not do it.

She was in the living room, and she saw that the sun was already bright and hot outside, but the front of the house faced roughly northeast, and the sun would not reach the tall windows that looked out on the ocean until afternoon.

When she saw Mallon, she gasped. He seemed not to have heard her. He kept staring out at the ocean, motionless. He still had the same clothes on, but now they were rumpled and dirty, and his face looked bruised and swollen on the right side.

She said, "It would have been kinder to shoot me while I was asleep." She shook her head in despair. "It serves no purpose to make me feel sadness and fear like this."

He turned toward her. His eyes were tired, not angry. He contemplated her for a moment. "I'm not going to kill you. If that's what you want, you'll have to do it yourself."

"Then why did you come back?"

"I'm going to do what I said, which was to let you go."

She began to cry. At first it was great silent sobs that kept her from catching her breath to talk.

He knelt on the floor. He took out his pocketknife, cut the tape on her wrists so her hands were free, then the tape on her ankles. She got to her knees, very slowly and tentatively, then reached to the wall and steadied herself to stand. She said apologetically, "I have to go to the bathroom." He nodded, and she walked there unsteadily.

She came back a few minutes later. She stood in the center of the empty living room tugging at her hair and muttering to nobody, "I look so awful." She heard her own voice and said, "Who cares, right?"

He walked toward the front door, and she followed. She turned her head to look around at the empty house. She was surprised to see that it was pretty in daylight, completely different from the place where she had been locked at night. Then the door closed on it.

She followed him to her car, and said quietly, "You'd better drive as far as you can before you stop. Parish won't stop looking."

Mallon stared at her for a few seconds. Then he said, "He's stopped."

"I don't understand." She looked confused, not allowing even a possibility that what he had said could be literally true.

"Parish is dead. A lot of the others are too—the hunters."

After a long pause, she said, "What are you going to tell the police?"

"The truth."

"About me?"

"Not you. I gave my word that I'd let you go. If they find out Parish had your name in his records or something, that's your problem."

She was silent for a moment, thinking. Then she nodded. "Thank you."

He opened the passenger door. "Get in."

She sat in the passenger seat and waited while he went around the car, got in, and started the engine. When he pulled out of the driveway and turned toward the north, she said, "But what are you going to do afterward? Just go back to live in Santa Barbara and pretend that nothing happened?"

He shook his head. "No. I'm going away." He looked up the road as though he were trying to read something figured on the pavement ahead. "Maybe I'll try to build something."

After that, he seemed to forget she was beside him. As he gathered speed, he kept turning his head to the left to watch a long line of brown pelicans gliding low over the rolling Pacific swells.

Tanya stood in front of the full-length mirror on the bedroom wall and brushed her hair. She watched the other girl, in another room, wearing the same new blue skirt and tank top, using her left hand instead of her right to brush the long blond hair to a shine. Tanya had always secretly relished the existence of the other pretty girl who lived in the other room beyond the glass, like a fish in an aquarium. She loved the whole idea of a second girl who lived a second life.

In Wheatfield when she was little she had sometimes turned her mother's dresser so the mirror would be directly across from the full-length one on the closet door. She could make a whole long line of other girls, then kick her legs and look like the Rockettes, the nearest ones as big as she was, and the others smaller and smaller as their line stretched off into infinity.

She had dressed up in her mother's clothes sometimes, so she could change the girl in the mirror. She would be someone who had a good life, someone who was loved and cared for, someone who was beautiful and had everything she wanted.

She could invent things that the girl in the mirror could say, and practice them, whispering so the girl in the mirror would not be overheard. She would assume faces that were distant and just a little disapproving, and know that seeing them would make people frantic, trying to find ways to please her. She tried expressions designed to reward too, opening her eyes and mouth wide in a grateful smile that admitted no possibility of darker thoughts, nothing held back or hidden. Sometimes when she did that she would add a laugh at the end—not a small, forced sound, but a delighted laugh that made her eyes glisten and her white teeth show to their best advantage.

The alarm system's cool male electronic voice announced, "Kitchen . . . door": Dennis was finally home. This was it. Tanya stopped brushing her hair, slipped the brush into her purse, felt for the other handle and gripped it once, then released it.

She could hear Dennis's hard leather soles on the slate floor of the kitchen. There was no sound of his dropping his briefcase on the kitchen floor, so he had set it down gently: he had brought his laptop home again. He was planning to spend the evening working. "Tanya?" He was in the living room now.

She put her purse on the floor beside the dresser. "Up here."

She spent the next fifteen seconds considering him—turning him around and around in her mind and evaluating him. Women always said men had a hard outer shell but were soft and sweet and vulnerable inside, but she had found the opposite. They had a layer outside that was yielding and squeezable, but when you squeezed you began to feel the hardness beneath, like bone. She had squeezed him a lot in a short time, and she was already beginning to reach the hardness. He was getting ready to say no to her, to deny her things. Maybe he would even criticize her when the bills came and he could see everything added up. It was time.

Dennis's heavy shoes thumped on the carpeted stairway, coming closer. She already saw each step of the stairway in her mind, even though she had only been with Dennis Poole for a month, and all but a week of that had been spent in hotels. As he climbed step by step, she began to enumerate his unpleasant qualities. She didn't like his laugh. It was a quick staccato that made his voice go one octave higher, like a jackass's bray. A few times she had gotten up from her chaise next to him and gone into the hotel pool to cool her sun-warmed skin, come up from underwater, and seen him looking at other women in their bathing suits. He tipped waiters exactly fifteen percent and never a penny more, and was proud of it because it showed he could do the arithmetic in his head. He was not a sincerely appreciative lover. He pretended to care and be solicitous of her, but there was a practical quality about it. His concern was to please her, but it wasn't the right kind of concern. He wasn't a man unable to stop himself because he was enthralled. He was merely thinking about whether he was pleasing her enough to keep her.

Dennis had reached the top of the stairs. As she turned to look at him, her detachment was complete. He was a forty-two-year-old man with a soft belly and thinning hair who spent his days selling computer equipment to other men like himself. He was nothing. She smiled beautifully, stepped into his embrace, and kissed him slowly, languorously. "Hello, cowboy," she whispered.

He laughed as she had expected. "I could get used to coming home like this and finding you waiting for me." He looked more serious. "You know, I'm glad you were here for another reason. I think we need to talk about some things."

"Sure. We can talk, but first, don't you want to get comfortable? I should think you'd be tired after sitting in that office all day." She knew that tone of voice. Anyone could tell he was getting ready to be cheap with her, to start complaining about money. She pulled back and said, "I'll bet you're sick of wearing that suit. Why don't you get out of it, relax, and soak in the tub?" She looked down at his tie as she loosened it, not into his eyes. "Maybe I'll join you."

"Good idea." He took his suit coat off and his tie, while Tanya went into the bathroom and turned on the water. The oversized Jacuzzi tub had jets that bubbled, so she turned them on too.

Dennis Poole was naked now, and he put his arms around her. She tolerated his embrace for a few seconds, then wriggled away and whispered seductively, "Wait."

She went back out to the bedroom and walked to the dresser, where she had left her purse. She waited until she heard him turn off the water faucet, so the only sound was the steady burble of the jets. She quietly walked into the bathroom.

He was lying in the tub with his head cushioned by a folded towel, looking self-absorbed and distant as the bubbles massaged his skin. Tanya reached into her purse, took out the pistol, held it about a foot from his head, and squeezed. The report was a bright, sharp bang that echoed against the tile walls and made her ears ring. She turned away from the sight of his corpse, the red blood draining into the bath, and stopped being Tanya Starling.

2

Hugo Poole's rubber-soled shoes made almost no sound as he walked along the sidewalk outside the CBS Studio Center's iron railings, past the soundstages on his way up Radford Street from Ventura Boulevard. He never would have set up a night meeting in the Valley, so far from the old downtown movie theater he used for an office, but he had often found that it was worth making small concessions just to learn what the other side wanted to do. There was no single precaution that would always work, and the least effective was never taking a risk. As soon as caution turned predictable, it became the biggest risk of all.

Still, he wished he could stay right here. He liked being near a television studio, because these complexes were usually on the itineraries of the people who heard voices telling them that God wanted them to punish a few actors. That ensured that there would always be plenty of jumpy security guards. He would have preferred to meet Steve Rao right here outside the gate, under the tall security lights.

Hugo Poole walked on beside the railing, now moving into the dimly lighted eucalyptus-lined blocks beside the big parking structure, and then he stopped at Valleyheart Street. He crossed the street to the city's chain-link fence and looked through it to the place where the concrete bed of the Tujunga Wash met the concrete bed of the Los Angeles River. On this hot midsummer night, the only water was the runoff from automatic lawn sprinklers, a steady trickle confined to a foot-deep groove a man could step across that ran down the center of each bed. In the rainy season this place became the confluence of two turbulent brown floods crashing together at thirty miles an hour and rushing south toward the Pacific.

Hugo Poole looked to his left, up the scenic walkway above the river toward the iron gate at Laurel Canyon that was designed to look like a big toad. At this hour nobody wanted to go for a walk above a concrete riverbed. He waited for the minute hand of his watch to reach the hour. Then he took out the key he had received in the mail. He unlocked the padlock on the gate above the wash, and slipped inside. Steve Rao's people had knocked off the city padlock and put on their own, then sent him the key to open it. Hugo Poole took a moment to close the gate. He reached into his pocket, took out his own lock, and placed it on the gate. He stuck Rao's key into Rao's lock, tossed them both down the hill into the bushes, and walked on.

He descended the sloping gravel driveway that the city had cut so its maintenance people could come down once a year to remove the tangle of dried brush and shopping carts from the concrete waterway before the rains. He reached the bottom, took a few steps onto the pavement of the river, and stopped to look around him. He could hear the distant whisper of cars flashing along the Ventura Freeway a few blocks away, and a constant dribble of water dripping out of a storm drain and running down the wall a few feet from him.

Hugo Poole's eyes adjusted to the darkness and picked out four silhouettes in the deeper shadow across the wash. They floated toward him, and Poole tried to pick out Steve Rao's short, strutting body, but couldn't.

The one who separated from the others was too tall to be Steve Rao. "What are you doing here?" the voice said. It was young, with a trace of Spanglish inflection.

It was the wrong question. Somebody Steve Rao had sent would know why Hugo was here.

Hugo Poole said, "I'm not here to hurt you. That's all you need to know about me."

The heads of the four shapes turned to one another in quiet consultation, and Hugo Poole prepared himself, waiting for them to spread out. There was a sudden, sharp blow to his skull that made a red flare explode in his vision and knocked his head to the side. He spun to see the two new shapes just as they threw their shoulders into him. His head snapped back and his spine was strained as they dug in and brought him down on the concrete.

They seemed to have expected him to give up, but he began to bring his knees into play as he grappled with them. They tried to hold him down on the pavement, but Hugo Poole fought silently and patiently, first separating them, then twisting his torso to jab a heavy elbow into a face. He heard a crack, a howl of pain, and felt his oppo-

nent fall away. He rolled to the other side to clutch the second as-
sailant, and delivered a palm strike that bounced the back of the man's
head off the pavement. The man lay still.

Hugo Poole was up on his feet again, sidestepping away from the
two motionless bodies. The other four had made it only halfway across
the riverbed toward him, and now they stopped with the shallow
trench full of water separating them from Hugo Poole.

Poole put his head down and charged at the one who had spoken
earlier. The young man hesitated, then looked at his companions, who
showed no inclination to help him. They backed away, not from Hugo
Poole but from their companion, as though if they could dissociate
themselves from his fate, they would not share it. As Hugo Poole leapt
the trench, the young man spun on his heel and ran about a hundred
feet before he turned to see if he was safe.

The other three interpreted his flight as permission to run too.
They dashed to the far wall where the shadows were deepest, and then
moved off into the darkness down the riverbed. Hugo Poole turned to
see that the two who had been on the ground were rapidly recovering.
One was helping the other to his feet, and then they hobbled off together up the inclined driveway toward the street.

Hugo Poole stood in the dim concrete riverbed and caught his
breath. The right knee of his pants had a small tear in it; the elbow of
his suit coat felt damp, so he looked at that too. It had a dark splash of
blood on it from the first man's nose. He sighed: this was turning into
an irritating evening, and it was still early.

Then Hugo Poole saw a new light. It began as a vague impression
in his mind that there must be clouds moving away from the moon.
Then the light brightened and the impression changed. The light was
coming from somewhere down the channel. The wall opposite him
began to glow, and then the light separated into two smaller, more focused circles.

A set of headlights appeared around an elbow bend in the channel
and came toward him. He was aware that it might be a police patrol
car, or the animal control people checking on the coyotes that used the
concrete riverbeds to travel across the city at night. Either way, it
would be best to stay still. It was especially important not to move if it
was Steve Rao.

Hugo Poole stood and watched as the ghostly vehicle drew nearer,
its headlights brightening until it pulled up beside him and stopped.

Now that the headlights were shining past him, he saw that it was a black Hummer with tinted windows. Someone in the passenger seat used a powerful flashlight to sweep the walls of the channel and the bushes and hiding places up above at street level.

The flashlight went out, the passenger door opened, and a large man with wavy dark hair got out. He wore a lightweight black sport coat and pants of a color that looked gray in the near darkness. The driver got out, and Hugo Poole could see that he was wearing a sport coat too. Almost certainly the coats were intended to hide the bulges of firearms. The driver stood with his back against the door of the Hummer and kept guard while the other man approached Hugo Poole.

The man said, "Sir, are you Mr. Poole?"

"Yes."

"Can you put your arms out from your sides for me, please?"

Hugo Poole complied, and stood with his feet apart so his legs could be checked next. He waited, staring into the distance as the man patted him down expertly, then stepped back. "Thank you very much, sir."

Hugo Poole said, "You're an off-duty cop, aren't you?"

He didn't deny it. "I'm a friend of Steve's."

Hugo nodded and watched the driver open the back door of the Hummer. Steve Rao was perched on the edge of the high seat when the door opened. He was wearing black jeans and a black T-shirt with a dark windbreaker, as though he were out to commit a burglary. His shoes were half light and half dark, like bowling shoes. He slid to the end of the Hummer's back seat and then jumped down, smiling.

He looked proud of himself, his eyes and teeth reflecting the distant light from above. "Hugo, my man. Thanks for coming. I hope it wasn't too inconvenient."

"You saw?"

Steve Rao looked very serious. "I didn't have anything to do with them, I swear to God."

"I didn't think you did," said Hugo Poole.

"It's terrible," said Steve Rao. "This isn't even gang territory. The city really has to do something."

"I'll write a letter to the *Times*."

Steve Rao's grin returned. "You're still pretty mean, though, aren't you? You can handle yourself against these young kids even now."

Hugo Poole did not smile.

Steve Rao gestured toward the two men beside his black Hummer. "These two guys are my solution to that foolishness. You won't see me rolling around on dirty cement beating the shit out of no gang of kids. I learned that much."

"I'll be honest with you, Steve. This night is beginning to wear on my patience. Why did you want to meet me in a place like this?"

"It's safe and secure."

"It's safe and secure up there on the corner of Ventura and Laurel Canyon, and you can get a cup of coffee in Du Par's," said Hugo. "What is it you want?"

Steve Rao began to walk. Hugo followed for about two hundred feet, and stopped. Steve Rao noticed, so he stopped too, and spoke. "I've been around for a while now. You know that?"

"I've noticed you for about five years," said Hugo Poole.

"I haven't been lying around all that time."

"I've noticed that too."

"I've been busy. I've been talking to people, making deals, making friends."

"No flies on you," said Hugo Poole.

"It's worked out. I've gotten big." It was a strange thing for a man Hugo Poole judged was about five feet five to say. "It's time to make a deal with you too." He glared at Hugo Poole. "I've put it off for longer than I should have."

"I'm listening."

"I want ten thousand a month from you."

"In exchange for what?"

"For being able to do whatever you want. For not having to worry. You can go on forever, just like you have been, and nobody will bother you."

"Nobody bothers me now."

Steve Rao stopped and pointed back at the Hummer, where the two off-duty cops were sitting. "See those guys?"

Hugo Poole gave his second sigh of the evening. "Steve, how old are you?"

"Twenty-four."

"When you're a young guy, just starting out, you have to consider the possibility that the people who were here before you were born aren't all dumb."

"What do you mean?"

"You should look around and say, 'What are people already doing that works? What are people not doing, even though it's an obvious thing to do? And why aren't they?'"

Steve Rao glared at him again, then resumed walking. "A lot of people are doing this. People have sold protection for a hundred years."

"Street gangs. They shake down a few Korean grocery stores, a couple of small liquor stores. They ask for just enough so the payoff is cheaper than buying a new front window. The game lasts a few months, until all the gang boys are in jail for something else or dead. Grown-ups don't do this in L.A. And they don't use off-duty cops for bodyguards."

"Why are you saying this shit?" Steve was quickly beginning to feel the heat around his neck cooking into anger. "It's all shit! Half the rock stars in town have hired cops with them wherever they go."

"I'm telling you this because I want to do you a big favor," said Hugo Poole. "That works great for musicians. Cops have to carry guns off-duty, so nobody has to make any guesses."

"That's right," said Steve Rao. "So don't even think about trying to get out of this. I might as well be made out of steel. Anybody opens up anywhere near me, my cops will drill his ass for him. They got my back. Nobody can do anything to me."

"That's probably true," said Hugo Poole. "But what can you do to anybody else?"

"Anything," said Steve Rao, but he sounded uncertain.

Hugo Poole said, "Off-duty cops will keep people from killing you if they can, just like they do for rock stars. But they won't let even the biggest rock stars grease somebody else."

"We have an understanding."

"They understand you better than you understand them."

"They're mine. I bought them."

"You're paying cops money to stay a few feet from you. They can see you make deals, they can hear what you say. When they've seen and heard enough, they're going to arrest you and all of the people who do business with you."

"You're full of shit."

"Steve, these guys know the system. They know that if they get in trouble, you won't be able to do them any good. The only people who can help them are other cops." He paused. "You aren't going to collect any money from anybody, Steve, because you can't hurt anybody in front of two cops. You just put yourself out of business."

"Hugo, I always heard you were supposed to be the smartest man in L.A. But this is pitiful," said Steve Rao. He took a small semiautomatic pistol from his jacket. He didn't point it at Hugo, just shifted it to his belt. "I want your ten grand tomorrow by five, and then once a month. Be on time."

"Ask me how I knew they were cops."

"All right. How did you know?"

"They're wearing microphones," said Hugo Poole. "See you, Steve." Hugo Poole walked down the concrete riverbed, away from Steve Rao.

"You don't walk away from me," said Steve Rao. "You wait until I walk away from you." His voice sounded strained and thin, as though his throat were dry.

Hugo Poole walked on, his pace the same smart stride he always used on the street that kept his head up and his eyes on the world in front of him and let him scan the sights beside him. He had decided that it would be best not to return to the street by the same path he had used to come down here, so he walked on for what he judged to be an extra two blocks before he came to the next ramp built for the flood maintenance people. At the top of the path he had to climb an eight-foot chain-link fence, something he hated to do, but since his suit was beyond repair, he supposed he could hardly ruin it twice.

He swung himself over, dropped to the ground, then walked back up to Radford. Just as he was coming out of the dimly lighted, quiet street toward Ventura Boulevard, he heard the distant pops of four shots in rapid succession, then seven more. They seemed to echo from the direction of the river. As he walked along, he considered the eleven shots. Eleven was a bad number for Steve Rao. The magazines for pistols like Steve Rao's held no more than ten in a single stack.

PHOTO: JO PERRY

THOMAS PERRY is the author of many critically acclaimed novels, including the Edgar Award–winning *The Butcher's Boy* and its sequel, *Sleeping Dog;* the five-volume Jane Whitefield series (*Vanishing Act* was chosen as one of the 100 Favorite Mysteries of the Century by the Independent Mystery Booksellers Association); the *New York Times* Notable Book *Metzger's Dog;* and the national bestsellers *Death Benefits* and *Pursuit*. His latest novel is *Nightlife*. Perry lives in Southern California with his wife and two daughters.

ABOUT THE TYPE

This book was set in Bembo, a typeface based on an old-style Roman face that was used for Cardinal Bembo's tract *De Aetna* in 1495. Bembo was cut by Francisco Griffo in the early sixteenth century. The Lanston Monotype Company of Philadelphia brought the well-proportioned letterforms of Bembo to the United States in the 1930s.

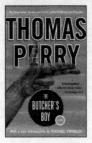
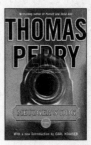
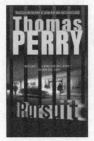